STREAMLINE

Jennifer Lane

Jennifer Lane
xx

Just Keep Swimming!

OMNIFIC PUBLISHING

DALLAS

Omnific Publishing
P.O. Box 793871, Dallas, TX 75379
www.omnificpublishing.com

First Omnific eBook edition, March 2012
First Omnific trade paperback edition, March 2012

The characters and events in this book are fictitious.
Any similarity to real persons, living or dead,
is coincidental and not intended by the author.

Library of Congress Cataloguing-in-Publication Data

Lane, Jennifer.
Streamline / Jennifer Lane — 1st ed.
ISBN 978-1-936305-02-5
1. Young Love — Fiction. 2. Child Abuse — Fiction.
3. Swimming — Fiction. 4. Naval Academy — Fiction.
I. Title

10 9 8 7 6 5 4 3 2 1

Cover Design by Micha Stone and Amy Brokaw
Interior Book Design by Coreen Montagna

Printed in the United States of America

I dedicate this novel to two special groups:

*All the quirky, intelligent, talented, driven, and fun people
I've met through the sport of swimming*

*The U.S. Navy for looking so sexy in uniform
as they keep America safe*

1. Bruises

Leo Scott tossed his backpack into his locker and swore under his breath. Being late to practice was unacceptable. He hurriedly undressed, exposing his light-brown skin to the dim light of the empty locker room.

His teammates had strewn their books and clothing everywhere. But even running late, Leo stacked and hung his belongings neatly in the locker. His father had trained him well.

Chewing on his goggle-strap and adjusting the tie on his black drag suit, Leo jogged onto the outdoor pool deck. The churning sound of thirty-five teenagers pulling and kicking through chlorinated water greeted him as he came around the corner. The sunlight bounced off the undulating waves with a shimmering glare, and Leo squinted as he scanned the deck for his coach, Matt.

Even with his competitive swimming days behind him, Matt Young still exhibited the chiseled, powerfully built physique of a sprinter. Leo liked to think he was one of Matt's favorites, but Coach didn't look too happy about his team captain's late arrival.

Leo avoided eye contact as he stood before his coach.

"Thirty minutes, Leo. They've already done twelve hundred meters." Forty years of Florida sun had weathered Matt's face and fried his messy blond hair.

"Yes, sir."

"I keep telling you there's no need to call me sir."

"There is if your father's Commander James Scott." Leo met the coach's stare. "I apologize for being late...I had detention."

Matt's eyebrows shot up. "Detention?" He shook his head. "Your dad asked me to tell him about things like this. I'll need to call him."

Leo's eyes widened. "Please, you don't need to do that. I'll stay after to make it up. I-I'll do the whole practice butterfly. I'll —"

Matt frowned. "Leo, if your dad finds out I kept this quiet, he'll yank you off this team. We need you at state. Besides, won't Mr. Morrison tell your dad?"

Leo mentally recounted his recent conversation with the assistant principal, where he'd promised to write a three-page paper on the importance of respecting teachers as long as the administrator kept the detention quiet. "Mr. Morrison agreed not to tell my father," he said.

Matt chuckled. "How'd you swing that? You work the old Scott charm on him?"

Leo's blue eyes clouded with resentment. Many times he'd heard about the *Scott charm*, and he wanted nothing to do with it.

Leo noticed his girlfriend, Audrey Rose, glancing at him from the pool as she swam. Her arms extended in front of her grasping a kickboard, and her legs swung out in perfect breaststroke whip kicks behind her as she led the lane, her goggles perched on her forehead over her swim cap.

When Leo didn't answer, Matt said, "They're in the middle of a kick set. One-fifty moderate followed by fifty sprint, four times through. Get going."

"Yes, sir." Leo grabbed his equipment bag and plopped it at the end of the fastest lane. He pulled his goggles over his buzzed black hair and waited for an opening to enter the pool.

A compactly built distance swimmer approached the wall. "'Bout time you got here," he hissed as he swung his kickboard around to make his turn. Before he was out of earshot, he added just loud enough for Leo to hear: "Lazy ass."

Taking that comment as yet another sign of Eric Alexander's jealousy, Leo grabbed a red kickboard and jumped into the iciness as soon as Eric's feet were out of his way. He prayed the cool water would wash away his worry. This would be a long evening, but he couldn't think about it now. His focus needed to be here, not on his messy family life.

Six thousand meters later, the swimmers slogged through the last laps of a tough pull set. About to end their second practice of the day, they were exhausted. All told, they'd logged close to seven miles in the pool. The sun now made its descent to the horizon, bringing with it the chilly November air of northern Florida.

"Okay," Matt said. "We've got about a thousand meters to go."

A collective groan emanated from the lanes.

"But…" Matt grinned mischievously. "I *will* give you a chance to escape this last set. Time for a get-out swim."

Excited chatter replaced the groans. Matt would choose a swimmer, and if the swimmer beat the time he determined, the whole team could get out early.

"Today's honoree is Leo Scott."

Leo looked up, his mind foggy. He ran his hands over his face and could feel oval indents from his goggles around his eyes. *I do not need this pressure.* He clenched his jaw. *Stop being a baby. Deal with it, Scott.*

Matt threw down the challenge: "One hundred free under fifty-six seconds."

Leo's eyes bulged. The team hadn't done much speed work — this was the endurance, build-up stage of the season — and the time Matt wanted was only four seconds off his best in a long course pool. With a drag suit, unshaved body, and serious case of exhaustion, the time would be difficult to make.

"C'mon, Scotty boy," Eric urged. He was suddenly Leo's best friend now that a strong performance would benefit them all.

"You can do it, Leo," Audrey whispered from the next lane.

He turned to her and nodded as he adjusted his goggles and set himself ready on the wall. Leo felt confidence envelop him, and his focus narrowed to the now-calm water ahead. His teammates huddled near the lane lines to give him a clear path.

He was the best swimmer on the team, a senior captain. This was *his* team, and he wouldn't let them down.

Clicking his stopwatch, Matt called, "Ready, hup!"

Leo pushed off, elbows squeezing ears in a tight streamline. His legs burst into whitewater behind him, propelling him like a motorboat. His fingers extended at the top of the stroke, and his high elbows sculled the water beneath his body. Nothing extraneous, no wasted energy. Everything with purpose. The 100 freestyle was his specialty.

He swam down the length of the fifty-meter pool and quickly flip-turned to begin making his way back. He could hear the faint cheers of his teammates build as he approached. Fighting fatigue, he drove to the wall.

When he lifted his head above the water, all he could hear were his sharp rasps for air. His teammates were silent as they waited to hear whether their tortuous practice was complete.

Matt cleared his throat. "It was fifty-seven five."

The swimmers' faces fell, and Leo winced as he surveyed his team. He lowered his head. He'd felt tired in the water, but he *always* rose to the challenge. Shame overtook him. *Failure.* He heard his father's cold voice in his head—a constant companion. *Scotts never fail.*

Matt shook his head and seemed to make an executive decision. "Y'all look like crap tonight, and we've already done eleven K, so I'll let you go anyway."

Suddenly an infusion of energy washed over the pool deck. Teammates laughed and pushed each other as they skipped to the locker rooms.

Leo's breathing gradually slowed, but he remained in the pool, dumbfounded and all alone. He wasn't accustomed to disappointment, particularly in swimming.

"It happens, Leo. It's early yet—don't worry." Matt's tone was gentle.

Leo pressed his hands on the concrete deck and pulled himself out of the pool in one graceful motion, water cascading down his sinewy muscles. "Did you call my father?"

Matt nodded, and Leo closed his eyes, trying to quell the dread rising within him. "I might miss practice for a few days then."

"If you're grounded I'm sure your dad will let me know."

Leo trudged to the showers. It wasn't about being grounded. It was about giving the bruises time to heal.

2. Big Fat Worries

Audrey grinned as she entered the locker room. Could it *be* any louder? Close to twenty high school girls crowded in the small shower area, talking and laughing. Combined with the pounding streams of water hitting the tile floor, the sound was deafening.

After chugging out miles for over two hours in the pool, gossip now came spilling out when the swimmers finally had the chance to catch up. Audrey recognized the bouncy, back-and-forth voices of her relay mates drifting out of the shower room steam.

"Thank *God* Matt let us out!" one said. "My arms are, like, so dead."

The other giggled. "Maybe he *finally* got a girlfriend. He hasn't been such a tool lately."

As Audrey went to her locker to retrieve some shampoo, she noticed her close friend and the last member of her relay team seated on the bench. Unlike her animated teammates, Elaine Ferris just stared into space.

"Laney?" Audrey asked.

When Elaine turned to see Audrey's concerned gaze, she quickly whipped around to dig around in her backpack.

"I'm fine, Aud. Don't worry about it."

The tall, strong backstroker typically exuded confidence, but she wasn't herself right now. Elaine stood and pulled pants over her solid, muscular legs.

"Hey, you're the only other senior on the team. Of course I worry about you," Audrey said. "Wanna talk about it?"

Elaine sighed and grabbed her shirt, her words muffled as the cotton came over her head. "Matt wanted me to get my body composition tested. He's probably wondering how I can swim fast being so fat."

Audrey frowned. "You're *not* fat, Laney! You're, like, super muscular."

"You're wrong. I did this underwater weighing thingy, and I have twenty-three percent body fat." Elaine's hazel eyes grew big, filling with tears. "I'm like one quarter fat! Disgusting fat!"

Audrey stepped closer. "Do you know the average body fat for women?"

Elaine sniffed. "No...Fifteen percent or something like that?"

"It's more like twenty or thirty percent. You're totally normal—not fat! Besides, we have a lot of hard training to go before state."

Elaine said nothing.

"You're a total badass," Audrey added. "Much faster than those skinny wenches on the Tallahassee team."

A grin threatened to emerge from Elaine.

"I wouldn't want any other backstroker on our relay. You always get the lead for me, right?"

Elaine finally unleashed a feisty smile. "Damn straight."

Audrey pointed at her chest. "And at least *your* boobs aren't concave."

Audrey knew that would earn her a snicker. They'd been friends and teammates since they were eight.

Elaine scooped up her bag. "Your boobies are lovely—at least Leo thinks so. Thanks, babe. See ya tomorrow."

After Audrey finished showering and getting dressed, she exited the locker room to find Leo slouched against the wall. He looked absolutely miserable, his lean face drawn with worry. His eyes bore into her as she approached.

As she held his gaze, Audrey remembered what she had to do this evening and began to frown as well.

"What's wrong?" they asked each other simultaneously. Audrey smiled. They were scary mind twins.

"You first," Leo invited.

"Oh, I just remembered I promised my mom I'd go visit my dad tonight." Audrey tried to sound cavalier.

Leo's eyes filled with sympathy. "I know you miss him."

She swallowed, wanting to redirect the conversation. "What ended up happening with the note?" During third-period AP chemistry, she'd handed Leo a note making fun of their teacher's thick New England accent: *The maaaaassssss of the gaaaaaaasss in the flaaaaaaask equals twenty-seven mL…*

Leo's snicker while reading it had drawn Mrs. Boyd to their desks to confiscate the note. Audrey had held her breath as the teacher read the mocking words.

"Who wrote this?"

Before Audrey had a chance to respond, Leo jumped in. "I did, ma'am."

Mrs. Boyd cut short Audrey's protest and glared at Leo. "Mr. Scott, take this note to Mr. Morrison's office immediately."

He'd nodded and gathered his belongings into his backpack, shooting Audrey a reassuring glance as he'd left.

"I got detention," Leo now reported. "I managed to convince Mr. Morrison not to call my dad, but Matt did anyway."

Audrey's eyebrows furrowed. "Now you'll be in major trouble. Why'd you take the blame? I wrote that note! Nobody cares if *I* get detention."

Leo sighed. "It was stupid. I'm sorry."

"Great, so now we both have to deal with our dads tonight, and you might be grounded forever."

Leo reached for Audrey and pulled her close. She blinked up at her boyfriend of two years and leaned closer. When he responded with a warm kiss, excitement ran down her spine. She *loved* their post-practice kisses. With the beta-endorphins flowing from all the exercise, her rush from kissing Leo reached an even higher peak.

Reluctantly they pulled away, and Leo squared his shoulders. "I can't be late—I'm in enough trouble already. Be careful visiting your dad."

She nodded, and they turned to go their separate ways. As she turned back to make sure he was okay, Audrey saw him pop a pill before swigging from his Gatorade bottle.

"Leo?" she called. "What'd you just take?"

His eyes widened but then quickly regained their typical coolness. "Uh, just an ibuprofen. My shoulder's been bothering me. Gotta run." Leo bolted and didn't look back.

Audrey turned, but didn't move, a crease across her forehead. He'd never complained about his shoulder before.

3. PT

The pink stucco house was eerily quiet when Leo entered the front door.

Six years ago the Scotts had lived in more luxurious surroundings, but his mother's burgeoning medical expenses had forced them to scale back to their current two-bedroom home. Leo and his older brother, Jason, had to share a bedroom, which had only added tension to their already strained relationship.

Ironically, now that Leo had his own space, he wished Jason still shared his room.

Despite a history of cruel teasing and physical domination, Jason had always protected his younger brother when it came to their father. That protection had not been appreciated by Commander Scott, and the resulting conflict had yet to be resolved. The Scotts had not seen Jason in four years.

Leo took a deep breath, steeling himself as he entered his father's study, but it was empty. He then followed the sound of his mother's voice to the kitchen.

"This detention's the first time he's gotten in trouble his entire high school career," she pleaded.

His father's voice was icy. "Other than his suspension, you mean?"

When Leo entered the kitchen, his parents' conversation halted.

Naval Commander James Scott stood stiffly by the sink, his khaki uniform complementing his ebony skin and neatly cropped black hair. James was an excellent physical specimen: six-two with a muscular, V-shaped body. His strong shoulders tapered down to a lean waist and solid, sculpted legs. His handsome face lent him a smooth charm, which he worked on nearly everyone he met.

Leo looked directly into his father's stormy hazel gaze. Leo read his father's eyes like a weather report. A cool gray indicated smooth seas and sunny skies. When the gray morphed into violet, there was a hurricane brewing—time to abandon ship. It was no coincidence that "violet" was one letter away from "violent" when it came to his father's eyes. Leo realized he hardly ever saw them shine warm brown anymore, like they had when he and Jason were younger.

As he watched, his father's eyes darkened. He felt a catch in his throat. "Good evening, Dad."

His father remained silent and frowned, seemingly at the frayed hem of Leo's jeans.

Leo turned to his mother. Her alabaster skin hadn't seen the sun in quite some time, but she remained beautiful, with long blond hair and arresting blue eyes. Leo always tried to keep his focus on her face instead of looking at the ugly braces on her legs. Mary Scott leaned on her canes to stir a saucepan of jambalaya on the stove.

Leo gave her a perfunctory kiss on the cheek.

"How was practice, sweetie?"

"Not so good, Mom." Leo looked down.

His father cleared his throat. "Your mother said dinner's almost ready. Go put your bag in your room and wash up."

"Yes, sir." Leo quickly left the tension of the kitchen behind him, but returned all too soon.

Dinner was a nightmare as usual. His mother attempted to initiate several conversations, but each died quickly and silence descended. Leo's stomach was in knots, and he ate very little, though he should've been starving. Matt was constantly on his case to build more muscle. He wouldn't be pleased to see him playing with his food.

As his parents finished their meal, Leo noticed a familiar glazed look in his mother's eyes and watched her retreat into a calm, sedated state. She'd taken one of her pain meds before dinner.

Feeling the heat of his father's stare, Leo looked up from his mostly full plate.

"Meet me in the car in five, wearing running clothes," his father ordered.

His mother jumped as Leo's chair scraped the floor.

As Leo ran into his room, his mind raced. So the punishment would be physical training, which had to be better than getting hit. The beatings had escalated over the past six years, and Leo shuddered, recalling how his father had responded to his school suspension two months ago.

He changed quickly and scuttled down the stairs to join his father in the car.

As they stood together on the Pensacola High School track ten minutes later, Leo realized they were all alone in the encroaching darkness.

"What was the detention for, Leo?"

He'd been waiting for this question since the moment he'd stepped inside his front door. Leo instinctively stood at attention, his eyes straight ahead and his shoulders back. "Mrs. Boyd caught me with a disrespectful note in class, sir."

"It better not be you who wrote it."

"No, sir."

"Who wrote it, then?"

His father now stood right next to him, speaking quietly in his ear. Leo paused. When he'd mentioned Audrey's involvement in his suspension two months ago, his father had exploded. But the punishment would surely increase if his father caught him in a lie now.

"Audrey, sir."

Leo felt his father's hot breath on the side of his face. "Give me fifty."

He dropped to the spongy track and silently counted his push-ups. His strong arms pumped up and down fluidly as he focused on making a perfectly straight line from his head to his feet.

As he passed the first thirty, his mind wandered back to the pushup contest his father had refereed when he'd been twelve and Jason seventeen. Leo had surprised everyone by pumping out over one-hundred pushups to Jason's seventy-five. Jason, a basketball player, was strong, but his upper-body strength was no match for a swimmer's.

Their father had mocked Jason mercilessly for losing to a boy five years his junior. As his father screamed, Leo had silently prayed his mouthy brother would keep his trap shut for once.

But instead Jason had yelled, "Get outta my face, you pompous Navy prick!"

Their father had immediately punched Jason in the gut. Leo had felt the sting of each blow as if he were the one getting hit. Jason had missed a week of school after that particular thrashing.

By the third set of fifty pushups, Leo could feel each one of the ten thousand meters he'd swum that day, and his arms began to shake. He completed fifteen more pushups, but his pace slowed and form wobbled. It was clear he was about to collapse.

His father finally ordered him to rise. "One mile warm-up," he added, falling into step beside Leo. The two loped around the track four times. A casual observer might have thought it sweet that father and son were jogging together, but Leo knew what was coming.

After the warm-up, his father fixed a measured stare on him. "You're doing mile repeats, starting at six-thirty and decreasing the interval by fifteen seconds each time."

Leo closed his eyes. At least at that blazing pace, the torture wouldn't last long. He started the first mile with a strong kick. He'd have to hustle to make the interval. He finished the first mile in 6:15, and had barely stopped when his father sent him off on the next.

Between gasps, Leo wondered how long he could run before collapsing or vomiting. *What a fun game.* When the punishment was a beating, the game was how long Leo could last before crying.

Two months ago he'd refused to cry, despite his father's crushing blows. He wondered if his lack of tears was why his father had chosen PT instead tonight.

Leo got two seconds' rest after the second mile before beginning the third, and he felt bile in the back of his throat as he rounded the second turn. He convulsed and leaned over the inner rim of the track to vomit onto the grass. His body writhed in the agony of being pushed to the absolute limit.

After heaving for several minutes, Leo stumbled back toward his father, dizzy and disoriented.

His father appeared satisfied. "No more disrespecting your teachers."

He managed a feeble "Yes, sir" as they made their way to the car.

Leo continued to pant through the ride home, his clothes stuck to his body with sweat. "Am I grounded?" he finally asked.

His father's mouth curled in disgust. "Getting grounded is for losers."

Leo stared out at the passing palm trees. Apparently a real man had to be barfing or beaten. He wasn't so thrilled about becoming a man.

4. Anchor

Audrey sat in her car, attempting to psych up enough to enter the cement building fronted by a row of bushes and barbed-wire fence. Visiting hours would be over soon, but she felt glued to the vinyl seat.

An old CD—a remnant from Audrey's childhood—played on her car stereo. "Gracie" was a sweet song from a father to his daughter, and Audrey's father had often substituted her name, singing "Audrey girl" instead of "Gracie girl." The rolling piano and singer's earnest voice made Audrey pause every time.

She finally kicked open the car door and scurried to the entrance before she could turn back. She tucked a strand of damp auburn hair behind her ear as she passed by the building's stark sign: *Naval Air Station Pensacola, Military Prison.*

Inside she approached a baby-faced Military Police officer, who couldn't have been much older than she was. His eyes traveled over her as he registered her as a visitor. Audrey wore her slim jeans low on her hips, her lean midriff peeking out below her white ruffled shirt. Feeling the MP's dirty eyes on her made her shiver. Typically she'd give the guy a direct, defiant stare until he looked away, but the prison threw her. She averted her eyes until the MP led her into the visiting room.

Drumming her fingers on the counter, Audrey stared at the empty chair behind the Plexiglas window. *Three months.* Her father had only been a prisoner for three months, yet so much had changed. And this was only the beginning of his sentence.

Another MP escorted former Lt. Commander Dennis Rose into the visiting room. Audrey smiled wanly, taking in her father's navy prison jumpsuit. He looked tired and hopeless. They'd shaved his brown hair — probably some regulation in the brig — which made him seem younger and more vulnerable. He appeared to have shrunk since the court martial.

Awkwardly picking up the phone with handcuffed wrists, her father waited until Audrey followed suit across the glass. "You look beautiful, honey."

"How, um, how's it's going, Dad?"

"It's fine."

She blinked nervously. He didn't *sound* fine. "Any word on the transfer?"

"Leavenworth's still over capacity." He gave her a tight smile. "Commander Scott visited me today. He's been the only officer standing by me through all of this." He paused. "How's the college search going?"

"Good."

Audrey brightened. She couldn't wait for college — her chance to leave the shame of being Denny Rose's daughter behind. All over Pensacola she caught piteous glances and heard the whispers. *That girl's father is a murderer.*

"I have recruiting trips lined up at Northwestern and Florida State," she said. "The FSU coach thinks he can offer me a full ride." *And you know I need one*, she added silently.

"What about the Naval Academy?" her dad asked.

Audrey's brown eyes narrowed. "I can't believe you'd even suggest that. I want *nothing* to do with the military."

Her dad's gaze shifted to the MP monitoring their conversation in a side booth.

Audrey ignored him. "They completely shafted you, Dad — sentencing you to life in prison without a shred of evidence. I want nothing to do with them."

"Calm down. Wishing things were different won't make them so. I must've killed him, Audrey...I—I just can't recall the how or why." His voice rose as he squeezed the phone. "I wish I could remember that night!"

Feeling tears bubble up, Audrey looked away. "I know you're not a murderer. You didn't kill Lt. Commander Walsh."

"Well, a jury of my peers says I did."

When she looked back at him she caught a glimpse of pain in his eyes. Then his features settled into stone. "I...I don't want you coming here anymore. I want you to forget about me. You have a bright future. Go live your life, Audrey."

Her lips parted, and she stared at him dumbly.

"I'm an anchor," he said. "I just bring you and your mom down. I—I can't be there for you. Your graduation...college swim meets... your wedding..." He swallowed. "Don't waste your time on me."

Tears now slid down Audrey's cheeks.

"Just forget about me. Do you understand?"

Shaking her head, she stared at her father through a veil of tears. "No, sir. I *won't* forget about you!"

Audrey slammed the phone back into the cradle and ran out of the room, her palm pressed to her mouth.

5. Get a Room

Leo lightly pressed the car horn, cringing when a loud honk resonated through the still darkness of pre-dawn. Audrey emerged from her house, toting her swim bag, and a grin spread across her face as she identified his rusty car.

Sliding into the passenger seat, she gave him a quizzical look. "I thought Laney was picking me up."

Leo put the car in reverse. "I called her last night and told her I'd get you. I hope I didn't wake your mom."

Audrey shook her head. "She's in Birmingham."

He frowned. Mrs. Rose had to start travel nursing to pay the bills, and she often left Audrey alone for weeks at a time.

Yawning, Audrey snuggled up to him. "I'm so happy you're not grounded. What happened with your dad?"

Leo smiled. Draping his arm around her shoulders, he shook off his morning sleepiness. "Just a little PT. No big deal. But I was up till midnight writing that stupid paper for Mr. Morrison."

He guided the car through the empty streets toward the high school. "How'd it go with *your* dad?"

Audrey took a while to respond. "I'd rather not talk about it."

"That good, huh?" Leo always felt a stab of hurt when Audrey shut him out, but to be fair, she knew very little about what really went on in his family. It was too embarrassing for anyone to know he was afraid of his father.

"It's just—we get so little time together…I don't want to bring you down by talking about my dad."

Leo squeezed her shoulder and kissed the crown of her head, keeping his eyes on the road. "You could never bring me down. Just seeing you brightens my day, every time."

After a moment she choked out, "He told me never to visit him again. He told me to forget about him."

"Shh." Leo tried to comfort her. "I hope you told him he was an idiot. Nobody can just forget their father." He wished that wasn't true.

As they pulled into the parking lot, Audrey sniffed. "I told him he was wrong, yeah."

Leo shut off the car and faced his girlfriend, enveloping her in an embrace. Their bodies pressed against each other, and Leo was definitely awake now.

"We can ditch practice if you want—go somewhere and talk about it."

"Then you'd really be in trouble." She sighed loudly. "C'mon, we don't want to be late."

They jogged into the weight room. Tuesday morning meant strength training. Their weekly schedule included practices before school four days a week and after school five days a week. It was grueling, but all the best swimmers trained twice a day.

Leo heard Audrey giggle as Alex Bradbury waltzed into the weight room behind them. The six-two junior had wavy black hair that stuck out in all directions. He wore a thick, white terrycloth robe over his T-shirt and shorts, along with striped Ralph Lauren socks and Adidas flip flops. Much to Leo's amusement, Alex was notorious for bringing his own sheets when the team stayed at a hotel for out-of-town swim meets. The kid was quite a lovable snob.

"Laney!" Alex called in his breathy voice, joining her at the lat pull-down station. Elaine and Alex were lifting partners, as were Leo and Audrey, and the foursome often hung out when Leo's father actually allowed him to leave the house.

Matt looked grumpy, likely tired from his late night at the restaurant—his *other* job. "Okay, people. Get to your stations!"

Choosing to get the lunges over with first, Leo and Audrey collected their weights and stood on a mat before the mirrored wall.

Matt adjusted the stereo, and European techno music blasted out before he quickly ejected the CD.

"Maaaaatt," Alex protested. "I brought that CD to pump us up!"

Matt shook his head. "That techno crap couldn't even pump up Michael Phelps," he snarled. Glancing at Leo, Matt asked, "*You* don't like it, do you?"

Leo held out his hands noncommittally. Matt rifled through the disks scattered on top of the stereo. The folksy strains of the Grateful Dead filled the room as Matt started them on the circuit.

"Now *that's* weightlifting music," he muttered.

Seven stations into the circuit, Leo and Audrey did squats while Alex and Elaine worked their chests at the bench press station. Leo felt sweat slide down his legs as he lowered his body, clutching the weighted bar across the back of his neck.

"Good form, Leo," Matt called from across the room.

While Audrey took some plates off the bar before her turn, Leo watched Elaine and Alex adding twenty-five pound plates to their bar. When Elaine flattened herself on the bench, Leo wrinkled his forehead. "Wait a minute. Does Elaine lift *more* than you, Alex?"

Assuming the spotting position behind the bar, Alex gave him a wounded look. "Shut up, Leo! Look at Laney's biceps! I could *never* lift as much as her!"

Chuckling, Audrey heaved the squat bar up to her chest and then over her head, resting it on her neck and shoulders as she lowered into a squat. Her lean muscles strained against the burden.

"Audrey, keep your back straight," Matt instructed. When she continued to struggle, he added, "Leo, help her with her form, will you?"

Leo nodded and came up behind Audrey, wrapping his hands around her hips to steady her. She seemed to shiver. Leo smiled and leaned in closer. "I think your form's absolutely perfect, Rose," he whispered.

He guided her through a couple more repetitions before he noticed Matt standing next to them, scowling.

"Get a room, you two."

"Yes, sir." Leo stifled a grin, and Audrey blushed. Matt returned to the other side of the room, and Leo again whispered in Audrey's ear.

Five minutes later Leo watched Audrey approach Matt, gingerly holding her arm. "Um, Matt, I think I did something to my elbow on the triceps machine. Okay if I go get some ice?"

Matt scowled. "Okay. Tell me how it's feeling this afternoon."

Audrey skipped out of the room.

After waiting a beat, Leo approached Matt. "May I go to the restroom, sir?"

Matt nodded and waved Leo off, turning his attention back to yelling at two sophomores for pausing too long between sit-ups.

Once Leo cleared the door, he sprinted to the men's locker room, where Audrey waited for him with hungry eyes. He grabbed her and drew her body flush. Their sweat intermingled as they attacked each other with urgent kisses.

Weightlifting had been amazing foreplay, and now their hands were all over each other, sliding over slippery, sweaty skin. Audrey exhaled as Leo knelt and lifted her shirt to ply her abdomen with hot kisses, his tongue licking drips of sweat. She skated her hands through his hair, massaging his head and clutching his skull. Shivers of excitement crawled up his spine.

After several minutes of mixing hormones, sweat, and skin, Leo heard a man clear his throat and broke their embrace. As he scrambled to standing, his throat tightened with fear. Audrey tugged down her shirt and smoothed the fabric of her shorts, her face blushing crimson.

"What are you *doing*?" Matt shuddered. "Check that—I have a good idea what you're doing. Why are my two team captains skipping valuable practice time to get it *on*?"

Leo took a deep breath. "We're just doing what you told us, sir."

Matt squinted in confusion.

"You told us to get a room." Leo held his breath.

Slowly the corners of Matt's mouth turned up. He shook his head slowly. "Freaking hormonal teenagers. Get your butts back to the weight room."

Leo grabbed Audrey's hand, and they scampered back to practice as Matt muttered behind them.

"*Teenagers.*"

6. Christmas Ornaments, Hood Ornaments

M ary Scott scrounged through the box of Christmas ornaments and sighed. *December fifteenth—the year has gone quickly.*

At least Leo had finally sent his application for nomination to the U.S. Naval Academy to Senator Frees. James seemed pleased his son had completed this first step, though it was nearly impossible to make James happy these days.

It had been so fun to decorate the house for Christmas back when they'd lived in Maryland. Each year Mary and the three "boys" had slogged through the snow to pick out a grand evergreen at a tree farm. Now in Florida, the eighty-two-degree temperature hardly put her in a festive mood, and these boxed reminders of a happier past filled her with sorrow.

Inhaling suddenly, Mary pulled out a framed photo of the family from twelve years ago and ran her hand across it.

She and James stood proudly in their crisp, black dress uniforms, flanked by ten-year-old Jason and five-year-old Leo. James had one arm around Mary and the other resting possessively on Jason's shoulders, while Mary's sweet Leo was close by her side. All were smiling and carefree in their annual holiday photo.

Mary felt a catch in her throat as she thought about how they'd all changed since then.

She'd met James in Annapolis, where she'd been a young engineering instructor at the Naval Academy. A plebe with incredible hazel eyes had shined in her class—when he'd actually made it to class. Midshipman James Scott had a penchant for fistfights, which often led to marching punishments that cut into his study time. He'd come to her office for tutoring to catch up, and Mary had developed a soft spot for the troubled student.

At first guarded, James had gradually grown to trust Mary. Eventually he disclosed that his parents had died when was eleven, and he'd fought his way through foster homes since then. Somehow James had reined in his aggression enough to graduate, and when he returned to the Academy as an aeronautics instructor, he sought out Mary to repay her kindness. They'd married within three months of his return, and she was soon pregnant with Jason.

For the most part, their relationship had been happy. Although her parents had been concerned about her interracial marriage, James had eventually won them over with his charisma and devotion. The couple's one ongoing disagreement involved James spanking the boys when they misbehaved. He insisted his sons needed structure and physical discipline to survive as men, and Mary tried to balance out the strict punishments with warmth and love, though she was certainly no pushover.

This family togetherness had all come to a crashing halt six years ago. Shuddering as she sat with the Christmas ornaments, Mary remembered the betrayal she'd felt that night. She'd sprinted away from James, fleeing to her car through blinding tears and driving off like a madwoman. She'd screamed when the headlights suddenly shone over her hood. She slammed on her brakes, but it was too late.

She recalled very little from the year following the accident. She'd been in a coma for days, and the rehabilitation for her shattered legs—the wheelchair, the leg braces, and canes, the permanent disability from the Navy—had paled compared to the devastation of the family. They'd never been the same.

Still holding the photograph, Mary struggled to stand, balancing precariously on her canes. Feeling a familiar throbbing pain in her legs, she reached to the end table for her bag and the bottle of Oxycontin inside. For some reason, she seemed to be running out more quickly than usual.

7. High and Wet

Finding himself alone in the locker room, Leo popped an Oxycontin and chased it down with some Gatorade.

This stuff was awesome.

At first he'd taken a pill for one specific purpose, but now he found all kinds of reasons he needed them. Butterflies fluttering in his stomach before a swim meet? Check. Sore muscles after a grueling practice? Check. Anticipating his father exploding with violence against him? Check. Needing to act respectfully toward his father despite being filled with rage? Check. Crushing sadness observing the shell of a woman his mother had become? Check.

The only thing Leo didn't like about the Oxy was stealing it from his mother. He was disgusted with himself every time he snuck into her bag or medicine cabinet. He was also terrorized by the thought his father might catch him in the act. And pretty soon his mother would figure out her pills were going missing, so Leo had to find another supply. He just had no clue about how to score drugs.

Leo jumped a little as Eric waltzed into the locker room, dripping wet, to rummage through his locker. He retrieved his asthma inhaler and took a couple puffs. "Yo, Scotty. You comin' out to warm-up or what? You're late."

"Thanks for being my personal freaking wristwatch."

Eric took a step back. "You've become an ass, Leo. I'm starting to regret voting for you as team captain." Huffing, he stomped out of the locker room, leaving Leo to stare after him.

Had he been an ass? He'd been feeling a little irritable lately, but the Oxy always seemed to calm him down. Leo grabbed his goggles and headed out to the pool.

The competition course was set up for twenty-five yards. Jumping into a crowded lane, Leo began his meet warm-up. Matt allowed the swimmers to choose their own warm-up, which Leo appreciated, and he followed the same routine for every meet: several easy lengths followed by stroke drills and sprints off the block. This time as he finished the last sprint, he tried not to notice how sluggish he felt.

Hugging the gutter, he watched Audrey towel herself off and put on sweats before climbing the bleachers to say hello to her mother. It was obvious where his girlfriend had gotten her reddish-brown hair and rich brown eyes. Mother and daughter squeezed each other in an extended hug.

When Mrs. Rose stifled a yawn, Leo remembered Audrey saying something about her mother coming home late last night from Alabama. Then Audrey laughed. *Mrs. Rose probably just botched some swimming terms,* Leo thought, a smile on his own face. Audrey's mother was clueless about the sport, in contrast to her over-involved father.

It was so beautiful to see his girl laugh. Her head tossed back, spilling auburn hair over her shoulders, and her lightly freckled face glowed with warmth. She hadn't laughed much since her father's conviction. And Leo certainly hadn't been making her laugh like he once could.

Leo hopped out of the pool as Audrey climbed back down the bleachers and huddled up the girls' team for a cheer. He smirked as he dried off while watching their stupid cheer, complete with choreography. He snuck a look over at the Tallahassee Tritons gathered across the deck. Leo hoped they wouldn't judge Pensacola based on the girls' cheer.

The guys wouldn't be caught dead doing anything that involved dancing — their cheers focused solely on amping up. As soon as the girls were finished, fifteen male swimmers congregated around Leo on the deck. He dug deep to generate some excitement. No matter how he felt, it was expected of him as team captain.

He yelled the first line in a raspy yet powerful voice, and the team chanted back, clapping to the beat:

Leo: I went down by the river!

Team: Oh yeah!

Leo: Took a little walk

Team: Oh yeah

Leo: Met up with a tiger

Team: Oh yeah

Leo: And we had a little talk

Team: Oh yeah...

The clapping and energy came to a crescendo, and the team was a frenzy of testosterone by the end of the cheer.

Buoyed by his teammates, Leo now felt like he might jump out of his skin. Why was it so hard to feel normal now? Shaking it off, he high-fived the closest teammate, but sobered when he saw his father standing in the bleachers, watching him sternly. Looking away, Leo trotted over to his swim bag and guzzled from his water bottle. He stood apart from the team and planned ahead for the 50 freestyle.

He watched Audrey, Elaine, Susan, and Kelly gather for the 200 medley relay. They were going after the school record, and Elaine looked particularly fierce as she lectured the two sophomores. When she finished, they lined up with five other teams, ready to start. Only the Tallahassee team offered any competition.

Alex came to stand next to Leo. "Go, Laney!" he cheered. "Go, my little hag!"

Elaine's face turned red as she jumped in the water for her back-stroke start. Leo snuck a look at his father, but he showed no sign of having heard the comment.

In a flash the race began, and Elaine's strong kick got Pensacola the lead as Audrey mounted the block for the breaststroke leg. She timed the relay exchange perfectly and dived into the water in a tight streamline. A quick underwater pullout and she popped up to the surface. Audrey's long stroke was better suited for the 100 or 200 breaststroke, but she was able to extend the lead slightly for Susan on the butterfly.

Susan maintained the lead, but the Tallahassee squad pulled closer on the anchor freestyle leg. Kelly somehow held them off and brought it all home. Elaine, Audrey, and Susan jumped up and down as they realized they'd beaten the school record by one tenth of a second. They practically dragged Kelly out of the pool for a group hug.

Audrey and her teammates met briefly with Matt to review the race, then she bounded over to Leo. "Did you see that? We broke the school record!"

Leo managed a non-genuine smile. "Way to go."

Audrey gave him a strange look, then turned and went to sit near Elaine and Alex.

Leo looked down. Great, now he'd hurt Audrey's feelings. He didn't even want to be at this meet. If only he could go home and sleep…Or maybe another Oxy would help.

When the 50 freestyle rolled around, Leo stood behind the blocks and tried to pump himself up. Usually he'd borrow a teammate's headphones and nod to the pounding beat while stretching and jumping around, but he didn't feel like going to the trouble today.

He felt like he was moving in slow motion as he mounted the starting block, and the race was over before he knew it. Lifting his goggles, Leo's eyes widened when he saw his time on the board: 22.0. He hadn't swum that slowly in a meet since his freshman year. Even worse, two Tallahassee swimmers had beat him.

Leo hung his head, pulled himself out of the pool, and zoomed straight to the locker room. He sat in silence for several minutes, trying to collect himself. *What had gone wrong?* He had no answers, but he felt a little calmer after a while, so he emerged and went to talk to Matt. As he crossed the deck, Leo noticed his father was gone. *Wonderful.* Apparently his swim sucked so bad his dad couldn't take watching the meet any more.

Matt studied him. "What's up with you?"

Leo felt a flash of panic zip through him. "What do you mean, sir?"

"You're dogging it at practice, then you stink up the pool with that fifty. I've never seen your turnover so slow, and my grandma could've gotten off the block faster than your start."

"I—I don't know. I felt like I was in a fog or something."

"Well, go cool down, and get yourself ready for your hundred."

"Yes, sir." Leo walked down to the part of the pool not used for the meet and tried to catch Audrey's attention. She wouldn't look at him.

"Join the club," he muttered as he slid into the cold water. *I'm disappointed in me too.*

8. Cartwheels though the Puddles

Winter in northern Florida was Denny Rose's favorite season, and he drank in the warm sun as he walked the perimeter of the courtyard.

At first the MPs had forced their listless inmate to walk during recreation time, but he'd now grown to enjoy the thirty-minute hustles. They seemed to lighten his mood.

He'd been thinking about Audrey's swim meet all day long, but his mind wandered as he walked. He recalled the summer Audrey had started swimming. Their neighbor's daughter, Elaine, had been on the officer's club swim team, and she'd convinced Audrey to give it a try.

Denny grinned, remembering how little he and JoAnne had known about the sport at that first meet. Audrey's saggy, bright blue swimsuit had been totally wrong for competition, but she'd still won all her events that evening.

Denny had overheard another father talking to his daughter about the final relay of the evening. The girl had been completely confident their team would win. When her father had asked why, she'd answered, "Because Audrey's on it."

Denny had swelled with pride and been hooked ever since. He'd kept track of the time and place of each of Audrey's races for her entire career.

That first meet, years ago, had been blanketed by angry storm clouds as it ended, and the skies poured down sheets of rain. Swimmers and their parents had raced through the parking lot, screaming with laughter and soaking wet. As Denny and JoAnne threw open their car doors to scramble inside, Denny cried, "Where's Audrey?"

JoAnne gasped. "I thought she was with you!" They frantically peered out the windshield and saw their daughter dancing toward them, wearing only her swimsuit and an enormous smile. Her hair cascaded over her shoulders as she threw her arms out wide, spinning in the teeming rain in front of her family's car.

Denny had stared in amazement at the carefree joy of his only child. She didn't need a pool to enjoy the water. She didn't need a pool to swim.

Feeling the cool breeze in the courtyard, his smile faded. He'd never watch his daughter swim again. Denny saw the MP signal the end of yard time, and he joined the other prisoners forming a line to head to the showers.

The majority of cons at the military prison were young enlisted men who'd earned short sentences for drunk and disorderly, insubordination, or theft. They kept their distance from the forty-three-year-old convicted murderer, but it didn't matter. Denny knew he'd eventually be transferred to Leavenworth.

As he scrubbed cheap shampoo into what remained of his buzzed hair, his stomach twisted. Audrey wouldn't have much time to visit him once he moved to federal prison in Kansas, and JoAnne barely made it to see him as it was. He fought the urge to cry. The streaming shower could hide his tears, but once he started sobbing, he might never stop. Instead he bit the inside of his cheek and willed his emotions back under control.

At the conclusion of the shower, the inmates folded their washcloths in neat squares and wiped down the shower room before dressing and standing at attention for inspection.

Next was dinner: congealed macaroni and cheese and cold green beans. His stomach was in no condition for food anyway. After he disposed of his tray, an MP informed Denny he had a visitor.

Denny exhaled with relief when he saw his wife standing on the other side of the glass. He barely got the phone up to his mouth before he blurted, "How'd Audrey swim?"

JoAnne smiled. "Her medley relay set the school record. She swam beautifully."

He beamed. "What was her split? Did she get under thirty?"

"I don't know."

"How about the overall relay time? What'd they go?"

JoAnne shrugged. "I'm not sure, honey. You know I don't follow times like you do."

Denny sighed. "Listen to me go on about the meet—I haven't even asked about you. How *are* you, Jo?"

"I'm good. Glad to be back in town." She paused.

"What is it?"

"I ran into Kate at the grocery store."

Denny stiffened. Kate was his ex-wife. They'd divorced twenty years ago.

"She feels awful about her testimony at the court martial."

"She did nothing wrong. She just told the truth." His hand clenched the prison phone. "I'm an alcoholic wife beater."

"You're neither of those things." JoAnne leaned forward, her brown eyes flaring. "You hit her once, then you got sober. You've been an excellent husband and father. You never drank again."

"Until the July fourth barbecue."

JoAnne shook her head. "Why, Denny? Why'd you take that first sip?"

"I ask myself that every day. If I hadn't been competing with Bill Walsh for that promotion, and if Commander Scott hadn't offered…" He shook his head. "Nope. This is on me. Nobody got me here but me. And now my family's paying for my mistakes."

"We'll get by. I'm making good money in Alabama."

"How's the job?"

JoAnne smiled and launched into a story about one of her crazy patients. As they caught up on the last three weeks, the couple eased into their old banter and even laughed once or twice. Denny almost forgot he was in prison for a moment. Almost.

9. An Eye for an Eye

Mr. Crawford droned on about the judicial branch of the US government, the branch enforcing the laws of the land, while Leo brainstormed ways to break those laws. He sat, absentmindedly tapping a pencil on his desk as he tried to figure out how to hook himself up with some Oxycontin.

It wasn't as simple as asking his druggie classmates how to score. Being the son of one of the most powerful men at the nearby naval base put Leo in the spotlight, and it would be too risky to approach someone he didn't trust. He knew a few of his teammates smoked pot on occasion, but Leo doubted they were into prescription drug abuse.

No, he needed a method more clandestine. Something untraceable. He wondered about online prescriptions from Mexico. His mind whirred, but the excitement evaporated when he realized he didn't have a credit card or a secure mailing address.

Then he remembered Jason's friend Tony. He and Jase had gotten into all kinds of trouble in high school, and if anyone knew how to score drugs, it would be him. Leo had heard Tony worked down at the docks, and he sensed it was time for a visit.

Leo had saved a little over a hundred dollars from the meager allowances his father doled out. Audrey sometimes complained about always walking on the beach for their dates. But the salty ocean air and pounding surf provided a romantic backdrop for their snuggles and kisses, and in the end she never seemed to mind that much.

Although they'd come very close, they hadn't had sex. Audrey wasn't quite ready, and Leo respected her caution. He was a bit cautious himself. He dreaded an unplanned pregnancy. His father had told him if he ever got a girl pregnant, he'd perform the abortion himself. And Leo wasn't entirely convinced he was joking. Most of the time they were both just exhausted from training, but when Leo was feeling friskier, he hoped she'd come around soon.

As Mr. Crawford reviewed the term length and requirements for Supreme Court justices, Leo thought about the previous evening. He'd come home after the swim meet, eaten a quiet dinner with his mom, and retired to his room for some homework.

A little while later his father had come home. He barged into Leo's bedroom and parked himself on the bed. Leo swiveled around in his desk chair.

"So," his father boomed. "What happened in that fifty free?"

"I don't know, Dad."

"How was your hundred?"

Leo reluctantly met his eyes, which thankfully retained their cool gray hue.

"Even worse. Forty-nine flat."

"Have you been staying up late, talking to Audrey?"

"No, sir."

"Have you been doing more yardage in practice than normal?"

"No, sir."

"Well, then, I'm back to my original question. What happened?"

Leo chose the stock answer for this situation and delivered it staring straight ahead. "No excuse, sir."

His father peered at him. "Why are you sweating?"

Surprised, Leo brushed his hand across his forehead. Why *was* he sweating? "Um, just nervous, I guess. I have a chemistry test tomorrow."

Narrowing his eyes, his father rose from the bed. "That coach better not over-train you. Maybe I'll speak with him."

When the door closed behind him, Leo exhaled and reached into his pocket to touch his one remaining pill. He had to figure out something fast.

Leo's attention returned to the classroom when he realized Mr. Crawford and his classmates were staring at him expectantly.

"Could you repeat the question, sir?"

"Mr. Scott, I asked you how long Supreme Court justices serve."

Leo cleared his throat. "As long as they'd like to, sir? They can only be removed through impeachment and conviction, or if they resign."

Mr. Crawford paused, then nodded before continuing the lecture.

Leo felt Audrey's curious eyes on him, and he gave her a reassuring smile. Good thing this class was easy. When he'd been suspended for a week in September, all the missed assignments and tests could've killed his GPA. But Mr. Crawford and the rest of his teachers had allowed him to make up the work based on his reputation as an excellent student.

Leo had felt on top of the world that first week of school. He was finally a senior and had less than one year left under his father's control. His father had insisted he apply to the Academy, but Leo had fought for permission to apply to other universities as well. His relationship with Audrey was going swimmingly, and he brimmed with excitement over the opportunity to win state in both the 50 and 100 free.

One small drawback was the year's locker assignments. Leo pulled books out and tried to ignore Billy Ryan, who had the locker next to his. A defensive back on the football team, Billy's sole communication with Leo up to that point had been grunts and menacing stares, but today he was suddenly chatty.

"So, Scott, what are you? Mulatto or something?"

Leo's face had burned, but he remained silent, stuffing books in his backpack.

"What's a sweet thing like Audrey Rose see in *you?*"

Leo fought for control. "Don't talk about her."

"I hear you two have an open relationship. Might have to hit that sometime."

Leo had tackled Billy with Muhammad Ali speed and unleashed furious punches. Blood streamed out of Billy's nose by the time Assistant Principal Morrison had grabbed Leo and hauled him to his feet.

Mr. Morrison led Leo to his office and immediately picked up the phone. He spoke to Commander Scott and asked him to come pick up his son since he'd been suspended.

Leo stared, mouth agape, as Mr. Morrison hung up the phone. "I'm suspended for a week? You didn't even ask me what happened."

"Leo, I don't care what he said to provoke you. I saw the whole thing, and you clearly threw the first punch. We have a district-wide mandate to suspend any student who starts a fight. I think Billy's bloody nose is punishment enough for him, don't you?"

Leo looked down. "Yes, sir."

Leo's stomach churned while Mr. Morrison completed some paperwork at his desk. Thirty minutes later his father strode in, looking official and powerful in his khaki uniform.

Both Leo and the assistant principal stood, and his father shook Mr. Morrison's hand. He didn't even look at Leo. "Wait outside while I talk to Mr. Morrison," he said.

"Yes, sir."

After a few minutes, his father stormed out. Leo could barely keep up with his brisk pace to the car, and they didn't exchange one word on the way home. He was utterly panicked about how his father would respond. His only glimpse of his eyes revealed violet, an unsettling sight.

When they walked in the front door, his father took hold of Leo's arm and shoved him into the study. His mother called down from her bedroom. "Is everything all right?"

"Go back to sleep, Mary!" Leo's father ordered. He shut the door and sidled up to his son. "I can't believe you embarrassed me like that. Having to pick you up at school for getting in a fight? Jason was no saint, but I *never* had to do that with him. Start talking, young man."

Leo felt strangled by fear. His father paced behind him, and he had no idea when or from where he'd pounce. "I screwed up, sir. I—I acted impulsively, and it was wrong."

"What'd that Ryan kid say to you?"

"I should've known better than to hit him, sir."

"Damn straight, you should know better. What'd he say?"

Leo hated how his father hissed in his ear. "He insulted Audrey, sir."

"This wasn't even about *our* family?"

"Yes, sir. I mean, no, sir—"

His father circled around, and Leo saw his eyes, flashing with fury, before he found himself doubled over from a slashing undercut to his abdomen.

The beating was swift and sharp. It left Leo dazed on the floor, bleeding from the lip and moaning. His head pounded with each beat of his heart. As he watched his father stalk away in disgust, Leo realized the irony of his dad teaching him not to be violent by beating the crap out of him.

The pain. He couldn't move, he couldn't sleep, and it hurt to breathe. That afternoon Leo had first taken Oxycontin.

10. CS

Leo arched his eyebrow, feeling Audrey's slender body beneath her thin coat as they hugged. "Is this really the only jacket you're bringing?"

They stood on the curb at the Pensacola Airport on a Friday evening. Audrey was about to depart for her second recruiting trip. This time to Northwestern University.

"It's the only coat I own," Audrey said. "Do you think it'll be cold?"

"Yes. CS took me to the Great Lakes Naval Base up there once, and it was bitter."

"Who's CS?"

Leo looked at her incredulously. "I've never told you the little nickname my brother and I came up with for Dad?"

Audrey shook her head.

Leo grinned. "It depends on who's listening. If my dad's within earshot, it stands for Commander Scott. Jason came up with it right after he moved up in rank. If my dad's nowhere around..." He scanned the departing flights area. "Then it stands for Cruel Son of a bitch."

Audrey smiled, but her eyes were sad.

"It was really cold in Chicago, and that was November, not January. Hold on a sec." Leo ducked into the back seat of his car and came out with a tattered Pensacola Panthers sweatshirt. "Why don't you take at least one more layer with you?"

Audrey smirked. "Thanks, Dad."

Leo realized her *father* should be the one to drop her off at the airport.

She pouted. "I wish you could go with me. It sucks it's the second weekend in a row we'll be apart."

"You know my father won't let me go on recruiting trips in season," Leo said softly, looking down. "Especially the way I've been swimming."

"Well, you're not missing much. I loved Florida State last weekend, but I'd rather catch up on sleep than travel again." She glanced at her watch. "I better get going."

She stepped closer, looking up at him. He gently leaned forward, and their lips met for a lingering kiss. Audrey clung to him for a final hug.

"You're trembling," she said.

Leo heard worry in her voice and immediately pulled away. "I am? That's weird. Maybe I'm cold or something."

Audrey placed a hand on his forearm. "Leo? Anything you want to tell me? You really haven't been yourself since, well, since our senior year began, I guess. Is everything okay?"

He held his breath. He wanted to tell her. He really did. "I'm fine. Six fifteen on Sunday night, right? I'll be here to pick you up."

Her frown lingered. As she walked toward the entrance he called, "Good luck with the Wildcats! I'm sure they'll love you up there."

On the flight north, Audrey tried to study for her upcoming calculus exam, but her mind kept wandering to Leo. She stroked his sweatshirt in her lap and brought it to her face. It smelled like him—a combination of chlorine, soap, and musk. His eyes had looked so sad when they kissed goodbye.

When had he begun acting so strangely? It seemed to start with that suspension from school—when Audrey hadn't seen him for an entire week. And now his declining swimming performance, the shouting matches with Matt…

Audrey sighed. She also wondered why Leo hated his father so much. CS sounded very strict, but lots of parents were strict. At least he still had his dad in his life.

A lot of thinking and only a little calculus later, Audrey found herself smiling at the Northwestern coach in the terminal at O'Hare Airport.

"Welcome, Audrey," he said.

"Good to meet you, sir."

He blanched. "We're pretty informal here. I forgot for a second you're from a military family."

Audrey looked down, embarrassed. Though she hadn't told any college coaches about her father's situation, she was sure most of them knew, and she dreaded the awkwardness. Their curious glances, their hesitation about whether to mention it, their sympathetic stares — Audrey hated all of it.

"So." She coerced a faint smile. "How long's the drive to campus?"

The next night Audrey reluctantly accompanied a swimmer to a fraternity party across the quad. She'd had to sign a contract not to use alcohol or other drugs as a Pensacola student-athlete, and she was nervous she'd be pressured at the party.

Once they entered the dimly lit mansion, Audrey followed her host over to a group of swimmers. She wished Leo was by her side.

"Audrey!" yelled a tall senior with black hair. "Let's get you some beer, girl!" She disappeared into the crowd. A few minutes later, she thrust a plastic cup into Audrey's hands. Audrey glanced at the swimmers. They were laughing about something, not really paying attention to her. She could probably dump the beer and nobody would be any wiser.

She'd been on edge all weekend, not knowing when somebody might ask about her dad and frustrated she couldn't communicate with Leo. CS didn't allow him to have a cell phone. Deciding to try a sip, she cringed from the bitter taste. But forcing down the rest of the beer helped her to loosen up a little.

After three more cups, she'd joined in the laughter. Why hadn't she done this before? This party was a blast, and the college swimmers were *so* nice. When a cute guy passed around a bottle of tequila, Audrey shrugged and took a big swig, barely noticing the burn in her throat.

She loved feeling so carefree — testing limits and not being so darn worried about everything. When an irresistible song coaxed the swimmers off the couch and on to the dance floor, Audrey joined them, throwing her head back and swaying her body to the pulsating beat.

A thousand miles south, Leo wasn't feeling so high. He sat on his bed, alone on a Saturday night, hugging his knees to his chest. Despite his previous declaration that being grounded was for losers, CS had kept Leo at home because of his meet performance.

Leo had tried to last all day without Oxy, which had left him shaking and nauseated by the afternoon, and he now felt lonely and desperate. He'd finally given in and popped a pill — his last one — a few seconds ago.

But Oxy didn't even make him feel good anymore. It had taken over his life. A tear slid down Leo's cheek, and he angrily wiped it away. He missed simpler times, he missed Jason, and most of all, he missed Audrey.

11. Betrayal

James stood in the doorway of his superior's office and adopted a deep, mysterious voice. "You called?"

Captain Russell Payson smiled as he rose from his desk. James immediately noticed the man's protruding belly — it strained the lower buttons of his uniform tunic. Had age or the stress of the job grayed the captain's hair?

"Have a seat, James."

"Thank you, sir."

"Coffee?"

"That'd be great."

Nanoseconds later a young woman entered carrying two steaming cups. James followed her every move, and she seemed more than a little uncomfortable as she stood at attention next to the captain's desk.

"Thank you, Petty Officer. That is all."

"Aye, sir." She completed a smart about face and exited.

James smiled. "I don't believe I've met Petty Officer…?"

"Richards. She just started, and she's been a pleasure to have in the office."

"I'm sure she *is* a pleasure, Captain. And she's lucky to have you as a mentor. It makes our jobs easier to be so visually stimulated."

Payson appeared taken aback, and James hoped his superior hadn't heard about his extracurricular dalliances. But he wasn't too worried. His work performance would no doubt wash away any questions the captain might have about him.

Payson finally spoke. "Well, Petty Officer Richards isn't quite as beautiful as Lt. Keaton, *your* former assistant."

James stopped breathing for a second, but recovered quickly. "Yes, sir, I hear Darnell's doing well as an instructor at the Academy."

"You know, James, I'm quite impressed by how you've managed to run your division so well despite losing key personnel. To have Denny Rose and Bill Walsh gone in one fell swoop? And then Darnell requesting immediate reassignment? Those are devastating blows."

"Although they're big losses, we have excellent people in Air Department V-Four, sir."

"And you're an excellent leader, James. Do you realize your division reached a ninety-nine percent safety rating in the last quarter? Your numbers keep up like that, and you'll be XO before we know it."

James basked in the praise.

"While I enjoy celebrating your success, Commander, your next assignment's the reason I asked you here. Air Department in Miramar needs some help, and I'm ordering you and Roland to provide it. You're leaving in three days."

James immediately thought of Leo's invitational swim meet, but the military wouldn't rearrange their needs to meet his. "Yes, sir."

Captain Payson rose, and James followed, then shook his hand.

"I'm sure you'll make us proud out there, James."

"Thank you, sir. Good day."

Once the door closed behind him, James muttered under his breath. He returned scads of salutes from inferiors passing him on the base, but barely registered their faces. He didn't like Roland Drake one bit and dreaded their trip together. The fact that he'd been promoted to Lt. Commander Drake immediately after Bill Walsh's murder wasn't lost on James. It seemed a little too convenient.

Back at his office, he sat down in front of his email and began putting out fires. Apparently the new flight deck supervision schedule left a gap in crew coverage. James shook his head. How did these idiots keep their jobs? He quickly created an alternate schedule and sent it along.

The phone rang, and James picked it up, his eyes still on the computer screen. "Commander Scott."

"James, I'm worried about Leo."

His eyes clouded with resentment. "Mary, I told you never to call me at work."

"Well, you completely ignore me at home, so you don't leave me much choice."

James sighed. Her endless complaints about him being aloof over the holidays only made him want to avoid her more. "Okay, why are you worried?"

She paused. "Leo's acting weird. He's tired all the time, and… grumpy. He seems really down."

"What do you want *me* to do about it? I'm kind of busy here, Mary."

"I don't know! I just want to talk about it — talk about our son."

He could hear an edge in her voice. "You're past due for your next Oxy dose, I see."

"Screw you, James."

When she hung up on him, he stared at the phone for a full ten seconds. Who the hell did she think she was?

After a few moments, his rage shifted into loss and regret. It hadn't always been like this. The accident had changed everything.

Immediately the image of Petty Officer Lisa Ramirez filled his mind, and he steeled himself against the stinging memories from six years before. Somewhere between two careers and two boys, his love life with Mary had lost its spark. James's charisma and engaging hazel eyes drew women to him like a magnet. He couldn't be blamed for that, could he?

One of those women had been his office assistant, Petty Officer Ramirez. Her dark Latina features stood in alluring contrast to Mary's fair skin, and James had begun manipulating Lisa into a sexual relationship from day one of her assignment to his unit. He hadn't yet become a seasoned pro at infidelity, however, and Mary had sensed betrayal.

After work one night, he'd whistled happily on his way to visit Lisa's apartment. But not long after he arrived, he looked up from Lisa's sofa to find Mary in the doorway, her silhouette framed by the sunlight streaming in the open doorway.

"Our marriage is *over!*" she'd screamed in a voice strangled by shock and hurt. Then she'd turned and sprinted away from the apartment.

"Mary!" James had slid on his uniform pants and turned to Ramirez. "You breathe a word of this to anyone and your career's *over*, got it?"

James didn't wait for her response and tore after his wife. But his frantic search of Pensacola streets failed to locate her.

Hours later, he pulled into his family's driveway and found eleven-year-old Leo immediately at his car.

"Mom's been in an accident!"

At the hospital, the awful waiting began. Finally a surgeon emerged, and James's knees almost buckled at his grave expression.

"Mrs. Scott has multiple leg fractures and lacerations, a lower back injury, and blunt head trauma," the surgeon explained. "She's in a coma, and…she may not make it. If you're a religious family, I suggest you start praying now."

James had collapsed into a waiting room chair, moaning softly. "Not again. Not again," he begged.

Another fatal car accident was his fault. His parents had been killed in a car crash on the way to his basketball game when he was eleven years old. Now Mary's blinding hurt from his betrayal had caused this accident, nothing else.

His younger son sobbed next to him in the hospital waiting room, and James had grabbed Leo in a fierce, suffocating hug. He vowed never to let Leo feel the pain he felt. He was determined to raise a good man — a man better than his father.

The soft bell of an incoming email drew his focus back to the computer screen. James tried to read the itinerary for his upcoming trip, but the details swam before his eyes. Leo *had* to succeed. He was the family's only hope.

12. The Best Kind of Ship

Five days after Audrey's return from Chicago, it was carbo-loading time: the night before the North Florida Invitational.

Leo, Audrey, Elaine, and Alex munched salad while awaiting their pasta, the main event, at The Olive Garden. The ravenous swimmers ignored their waitress's disapproving looks each time she brought a new basket of breadsticks. They were currently on their fourth.

Leo watched Alex brush breadcrumbs off his chest and laughed at his T-shirt: *I wish my lawn was emo so it could cut itself.*

"So, Mr. Cranky…" Elaine fixed a stare on Leo. "What puts you in such a good mood tonight?"

Leo grinned. "Cold-hearted Sadist left town for a week, and life is good."

Audrey tilted her head. "I thought you called your dad Cruel SOB?"

"Those terms are interchangeable." Leo winked. "It's all CS."

"When you said CS I always thought you meant Commander Scott," said Alex, suddenly piecing it together. "But I like these much better." He grinned. "I'll personally *really* miss Cocky Sucker's menacing stares at tomorrow's meet. Who can I thank for making him leave?"

"His CO ordered him to go to California or something. Who really cares?" Leo raised his ice water. "I'd like to propose a toast to the seniors."

They giggled and raised their glasses. When Leo noticed Audrey's stare, and he tried to stop the trembling in his hand. *Time for another pill.*

"Here's to our wives and girlfriends," Leo said with a laugh. "May they never meet!"

Snickers enveloped the table.

"Seriously, though, going into our last invite, I want to thank you guys for always being there. Four long years—I couldn't have made it without you. Friendship is the best kind of ship."

"Aw, that was so sweet!" Elaine said, smiling.

Leo put down his glass, turned to Audrey, and cupped her chin in his hand as he gave her a peck on the lips.

Alex groaned. "Get a room!"

Leo laughed, and Elaine was so amused she brought a forkful of lettuce to her mouth and missed, causing a salad cascade back onto her plate.

Alex appeared mortified. "You can't take my hag anywhere."

As the waitress scurried past their table, Alex's breathy voice rang out again. "Excuse me! Can we get more breadsticks?"

The waitress scowled.

"So, I think I'll get a tattoo!" Elaine suddenly burst out.

"Laney!" Alex bobbed up and down in his chair. "You have to let me design it for you."

"My dad would kill me if I got a tattoo," Leo mused.

"My dad too," Audrey said. "He hates tattoos."

An uncomfortable silence settled over the table at the mention of Denny Rose.

The waitress arrived with their entrees and seemed perplexed by the sudden decrease in volume.

Leo frowned as he watched Audrey stare at her steaming plate. She hadn't yet picked up her fork.

"But wouldn't tats give your dad street cred with the other cons?" Alex asked.

Leo's pasta-laden fork paused in midair as he waited for Audrey's reaction.

Her brown eyes looked startled, then a smile crept across her face. "*Street cred,* Alex? Where'd you hear that one—your extensive gangsta rap collection?"

Alex bristled. "I know some rap."

Elaine laughed. "Lady Gaga isn't a rapper!"

While Elaine and Alex argued the relative merits of the singer's costumes, Leo squeezed Audrey's hand. A few minutes later, Alex's imitation of Lady Gaga made Elaine spew chewed-up ravioli all over her plate. Audrey smiled at Leo, and he felt warmth spread through his chest. Friendship *was* the best kind of ship.

The next morning Mary had the house to herself. Some mothers would cherish a few moments alone, but for her it was nothing new, given James's busy work schedule and Leo's school and swimming demands. Truthfully, even when her boys were home she still felt lonely. James treated her with icy disregard, and now Leo avoided her too, holing himself up in his room.

At least the mood in the house had lightened since James left for California. When Leo had returned from his pasta dinner last night, Mary had capitalized on her husband's absence by trying to get to the bottom of his mood swings. He'd met her pointed questions with uncomfortable silences or a stock "I don't know, ma'am," which frustrated her to no end. She'd finally given up so he could sleep before his meet, and he was away in Tallahassee now, but she was still determined to discover what was going on.

Mary cranked up the radio and began to clean the kitchen. It took forever to complete household tasks now, but music helped the time go by faster. One break-up song after another played, underlining her bitter feelings for James.

Like so many things, it used to be different. She remembered her pride watching James teach seven-year-old Jason how to play basketball on their driveway. He could be a demanding and impatient teacher, but Jason was a quick learner who'd do anything to please his dad. Two-year-old Leo had toddled around the perimeter of the driveway, gleefully retrieving the basketball when it rolled his way. James had laughed when Mary finally offered Leo another toy so he'd relinquish the basketball.

A knock on the front door drew her back to the present, and startled her as well. "Just a minute!" she called, manipulating her canes toward the foyer.

Mary opened the door and inhaled sharply when she saw her son on the front porch.

He had flowers in his hand and a nervous smile. When Jason left he'd been just an eighteen-year-old boy—now he was a twenty-two-year-old man, his muscular frame filled out and his face wizened beyond his years.

"The prodigal son returns," she gasped.

Jason wrapped his arms around her. "Happy birthday, Mom."

Mary felt tears spring to her eyes as she melted into her older son's arms. "But my birthday's not for another five days," she protested.

His deep-blue eyes twinkled. "Well, consider these flowers a belated gift for the past three birthdays I've missed."

"I've missed your birthdays too, Jase." She managed a sad smile. "Please, come in."

Jason shut the door and followed her into the family room.

Before they sat, Mary asked, "Would you like something to drink? What can I get you?"

"Mom, please sit down. I'll get us some drinks."

As Jason rummaged in the fridge, Mary called, "There are some beers on the top shelf, if you want one."

He returned a few moments later and set two lemonades on the coffee table.

She sniffed. "I don't know you, Jason. I don't even know what you like these days. Do you drink beer?"

"C'mon, Mom. It's still morning." He sounded embarrassed.

"How long have you been in Florida?"

"Took the redeye from Seattle and arrived this morning. I came straight here after visiting Tony. That lazy bum was still sleeping! I had to rouse him out of bed."

"Well, it *is* Saturday. You must be tired."

"I got some sleep on the plane. It's okay. How's your rehab coming along? Any progress with your legs?"

Mary looked down at her twisted limbs. "I don't do physical therapy anymore. All I can do is take pain meds. This is as good as it gets."

Jason nodded. "So…what's this I hear about Dad's lieutenant commander getting murdered?"

"It happened last July," she said softly. "Denny murdered Bill."

"Denny?" Jason's jaw dropped. "Denny Rose?"

"Yes. He's serving a life sentence. The whole thing's so dreadful—especially since Leo's dating Audrey."

"Whoa. Did Dad have to talk to the police or anything?"

"Yes, Bill and Denny were both at our house for a July fourth barbecue the night Bill was murdered. Your father felt awful—he had to tell the police that Denny fell off the wagon that night. The police found him passed out in the woods behind Bill's home. They arrested him, then court martialed him."

Jason was silent for a few moments. "How's Leo doing?"

"Fine," Mary responded immediately. Then she frowned and shook her head. "No, he's *not* fine. Something's wrong, Jase. His swimming times are horrible, he's not doing well in school, and I feel like he's a stranger to me."

Jason nodded grimly, not looking the least bit surprised.

"But enough about us. What've you been doing the past four years?" Mary prodded gently.

Jason hesitated.

With an uncomfortable silence between them, Mary sighed. Why did the Scott men refuse to let her in? She hated chasing them.

"Mom, I want to tell you all about me. I do," Jason finally said. "But first we need to talk about Leo. He's in trouble."

13. Intervention

Leo clenched his teeth as he swam laps back in his team's home pool. He'd *so* been hoping to swim better in the meet earlier today, but he'd once again hit a wall of apathy and fatigue. He hadn't even looked at his times. He was so far behind his competitors—guys he formerly dusted in the sprint events—that there was no need to check the clock. The whole thing was hopeless. *He* was hopeless.

His coach had seemed infected by the same apathy, and he hadn't even bothered to yell at Leo following his horrendous swims. Instead, Matt focused on the swimmers having a good meet, which kept him busy. The Pensacola Panthers won the girls' meet and finished second in the boys' competition, and Leo tried not to let his sulking contaminate the exhilaration. He even managed to drum up a warm smile following Audrey's best time this season in her 200 individual medley.

But Matt had stopped ignoring Leo at the conclusion of the meet. "We've tried everything, Leo," he said, taking Leo aside. "I've given you more rest. I've analyzed your stroke. I've entered you in other events. But nothing's working, and you look miserable out there. I think you've lost your passion for swimming. Maybe it's time to quit."

Leo had flinched. "I can't quit, sir. I—I've been swimming all my life. Just give me another chance…I'll do better."

"The only thing I can think of to bring you out of this slump is to throw yourself into training," Matt finally said, shaking his head. "When we get back to Pensacola, I want you to do another workout—at least three thousand. Work these bad swims out of your system and try to reconnect with the water."

Leo hesitated. He had planned to go out with Audrey when they returned—this was a rare moment of freedom without his father. But he'd let Matt down countless times, and he needed to do what he asked.

Thus he found himself in the pool. His efficient stroke glided him through the water as he churned out endless laps. But the joy of propelling his body down the lane just wasn't there anymore. Maybe he *had* lost his passion. At the moment he felt only worry about having enough pills for the week. It had been easier to visit Tony with Callous Stalker out of town, but his money was dwindling fast.

Driving the familiar route home from school, Leo's mood was as dark as the night sky. He arrived home curious to find his house brightly lit. By this time of the evening his mom had typically retired to her bed with a book.

Waiting for him just inside the door was Jason, and Leo leaped into his brother's arms. He'd rehearsed in his mind what would happen if he saw Jason again, and he'd planned to curse him for leaving him alone to deal with their father. But now Leo felt only relief at seeing the one other person who understood what it meant to be the son of CS.

Appearing surprised by the hug, Jason stepped back. "God, you've gotten tall."

"And you've become buff." Leo said, taking in his bulky brother. "What're you doing here, Jase? Where've you been?"

"Seattle. But I came back when I heard CS was out of town."

"Isn't it awesome? Maybe they can send him off to war soon. Too bad this president's all into diplomacy instead of military solutions."

Jason shook his head. "You're too smart for your own good."

Leo brushed past him, headed to the family room.

"Hold on—" Jason began.

Leo stopped short when he saw his mother, coach, girlfriend, and an unfamiliar man sitting there, apparently waiting for him. Feeling a wave of confusion and fear, Leo swiveled around. But Jason stopped him in his tracks.

"It's okay. Just listen to what they have to say."

"No!" Leo struggled against his brother's hold. "Let me go!"

Jason held steadfast.

After repeatedly pushing against the wall of muscle formerly known as his brother, Leo's body eventually went limp. It was futile to resist. He slowly turned to face the group. He looked at Audrey, with her beautiful, frightened eyes. He suspected he knew the purpose of this gathering, and when the strange man stood and offered his hand, it confirmed his suspicions.

"You must be Leo," he said with a friendly smile. "I'm Marcus Shale, and I'm an interventionist. Your brother asked me to be here today."

The man was Black, like CS, but maybe taller and definitely heavier. Leo filled with fury as he looked at Jason, who stood watching with apparent apprehension.

"Leo, why don't you sit next to Audrey?" Jason said.

His brother guided him to the loveseat, then took a seat next to his mother and Matt on the sofa.

"Leo?" Mr. Shale asked gently.

"Yes, sir." Leo heard his voice crack, then felt Audrey's fingers snake into his. He clutched her hand but couldn't look her in the eye.

"I've met with your mom and brother today, and with your coach and girlfriend too when they arrived from the swim meet. These people here love you, son. They'll say what they have to say, and then you'll say what you have to say, and we're done. Okay?"

Do I have a choice? Leo sighed and nodded.

"Mary, how 'bout you go first?"

Leo's mother unfolded a piece of notepaper, and her tears started falling before she read one word. "Leo," she began. "I'm worried about your addiction to pain medication."

Crap. They knew.

Leo waited for fear to envelop him, but he felt strangely weightless and relieved. He didn't have to pretend anymore.

He sensed Audrey watching him, and he slowly met her eyes. "I'm sorry," he whispered.

She squeezed his hand.

His mother's lip trembled. "I'm the sorry one, Leo. The pills... it's all my fault. I'm so sorry I failed you."

Leo looked down, his heart thumping. How could she say this was her fault? *He* was the one who'd screwed up everything.

"Mary?" Mr. Shale said. "This isn't about assigning blame."

"I'm sorry." She flushed deeply. "We talked about this. This is about Leo, not me."

"Could you continue reading your letter?"

His mother cleared her throat. "Leo, I'm sad you've avoided me. You've been moody and unpredictable. I'm concerned your addiction's hurting you in school and swimming."

Her voice had grown stronger as she read, and she now looked up at Leo. "Will you go to treatment today?"

Fear jolted through him, which quickly morphed into suspicion. "What do you mean, *treatment?*"

"Your family would like you to go to a drug treatment center in town," Mr. Shale answered. "The center will probably recommend a few days of detox, then an intensive outpatient program, so you can continue going to school."

Leo felt panic swell in his gut. "What about swimming?"

"Your health's way more important than swimming, Leo," Matt said. "If we can work it out for you to keep swimming during treatment, we will. But you and I both know it's pointless if you continue to abuse pills."

Leo took all of this in. He typically wasn't asked, he was ordered, and it felt bizarre to have the decision in his hands.

Wrestling with competing impulses — fight or give in — Leo looked at the people who cared about him. His eyes lingered on his brother, who knew Leo like nobody else, even though they'd been apart for years.

"Will you go to treatment?" Jason asked.

Leo swallowed hard.

Audrey squeezed his hand again. Her voice was shaky. "Please. You haven't been yourself, Leo. I..." She looked down. "I miss my boyfriend."

Her wounded tone slayed him. Finally Leo looked at his mother. "Yes, ma'am, I'll go."

The group collectively exhaled, and Leo glanced around. "So that's it?"

Mr. Shale nodded. "Yep, that's it. You can go pack a bag, and I'll take you over to Still Waters Treatment Center right now. Do have any questions?"

"Wait. How'd you all find out?"

His mother glanced nervously at Jason.

"Tony," Jason said. "I called him to…ah, well, make amends, actually, and he let it slip you'd been visiting him."

Leo scowled. "So you suddenly show up here after four years, just to lord it over me how screwed up my life is?"

"Hey," Jason said. "I wanted to come for Mom's birthday, but I got here early because I knew something was up when I talked to Tony."

"What about *my* birthday?" Leo yelled. "What about my swim meets? You missed it all, Jase! You don't even know Audrey!"

"I'm sorry," Jason said. "I don't expect you or Mom to forgive me for being gone so long." His jaw clenched. "I didn't return because I'm an alcoholic. I was *homeless*. So no, I'm not 'lording it over' you. How'd you think I knew how to plan this intervention? It was because I've been through it too. I was lucky enough to have friends in Seattle intervene on my behalf. Marcus is a friend of a friend they set me up with here in town to help you."

Leo sat silently, unable to think of anything to say.

"I won't let you lose everything like I did, Leo. Without treatment, you're headed to a life of homelessness and misery, just like me."

As he sorted through the whirlwind of emotions, Leo felt his hands begin to tremble. Time for a pill. Suddenly another thought added to their tremor. "CS will kill me if he finds out about this."

Jason nodded. "Marcus and I already talked about that. We'll figure something out when Dad returns, okay? Don't let him stop you from getting better, Leo."

It was frightening to trust Jason, but Leo didn't have much choice. He gulped and turned toward the stairs.

Jason put out his arm, stopping him. "Before you start packing, give me the pills."

Leo paused. "That's not necessary."

"Yeah, it is. Hand them over."

The standoff seemed to last forever. Leo finally reached into his swim bag and pulled out a baggie. He practically threw it at his brother. "Are you satisfied now?"

"No. I want all of them."

Sighing dramatically, Leo reached into his jeans pocket and produced three more pills. Jason took them and tilted his head to the stairs. "I already confiscated some pills from your room, but I'll come with you now so you can show me all your hiding places."

"You're really an ass, you know that?" Leo said, starting up the stairs.

"Yep. But I'd rather be an ass to my living brother than a nice guy to my dead one."

14. One Day at a Time

This was more awful than the worst flu of his life. Leo had sweated through his sheets, vomited four times, coughed incessantly, and felt overwhelming fatigue despite not being able to sleep at all. And that was just the first night of detox. He really wondered if he was going to make it.

After a nurse checked Leo's vital signs, Mr. Shale stopped by. He sat in a chair near the bed.

"How's it going, Leo?"

Leo clutched his stomach while lying in the fetal position. He stopped moaning long enough to look up. "Fine, sir."

Mr. Shale burst out laughing. "Fine, huh? You certainly don't *look* fine, son. Let's face it, your body's going through complete hell, and you feel like crap."

"Yep, I pretty much feel like doggie doo-doo."

"That's better. This is serious stuff, Leo. The active ingredient in Oxycontin is oxycodone, which affects your body just like high-grade heroin."

"Heroin?" Leo's eyes widened, then he lurched to the other side of the bed and retched into the garbage can. He wiped his sleeve over his mouth and groaned. "Shoot me now. My stomach's killing me."

Mr. Shale rose, and even in his agony Leo flinched as the therapist's hand, holding a tissue, approached his face.

Hesitating, Mr. Shale studied him for several long seconds. Finally he handed the tissue to Leo, who used it to blow his nose. They didn't exchange a word.

"How long will this last?" Leo asked.

"Up to ten days, but Dr. Bright expects you to get through withdrawal more quickly since you're so fit. You haven't had any heart palpitations yet, which is a good sign—probably related to that strong swimmer's heart you've got there."

"This is far worse than any swim practice I've ever been through." Leo battled a spastic coughing fit. "It's even worse than the four-hundred-IM repeats we had to do the day Matt got mad at us for dogging it."

Mr. Shale smiled. "Okay, I have no idea what you just said, but it sounded really impressive."

"Sorry." Leo managed a weak smile and wondered if he'd ever be able to swim again. "So, you think I can get better?"

"I do, Leo. I don't know you very well, but from what I understand, you're intelligent, caring, hard-working, and tough. That should help you with recovery."

Leo blushed.

"But it won't easy," Mr. Shale added. "Are you willing to give recovery your best effort?"

"I'll try." He gave his sweetest smile. "You sure you don't have any pills you can give me? I won't tell anybody, I promise."

"Good try. I'm afraid it's short-term pain for long-term gain. Athletes know all about that, right?"

Leo nodded grimly. He felt another wave of nausea hit him, and he clutched his gut. Swiftly leaning over the edge of the bed, he dry-heaved, and tears welled up. He just wanted his mom to make it all better.

When the waves of nausea finally ended, Leo narrowed his eyes. "I'm gonna *kill* my brother."

It was surreal for Jason to walk the halls of Pensacola High School, which seemed to have shrunk during his absence. The confident twenty-two-year-old suddenly felt sixteen again: a great basketball player and average student turned rebel after his mother's accident, ticked off at the world.

With his mom in the hospital and his dad at work or at Leo's swim meets, Jason had often found himself alone. Unsupervised, lonely, and reeling from the family trauma, he'd turned to alcohol. His father had no idea how bad things had gotten until Jason showed up drunk one night after driving home. CS had gone ballistic, and when Jason mouthed off, his father had backhanded him, sending him reeling to the floor.

Jason hesitated outside Mr. Morrison's door. He and his mother had formed a plan for getting Leo treatment without alerting CS, but Jason needed the assistant principal to allow Leo to rearrange his study hall to make it happen. He hoped Mr. Morrison had forgiven him for all the crap he'd pulled in high school.

Ten minutes later, Jason emerged from the office, mission accomplished. But his back felt tense from carrying the haunting presence of CS on his shoulders wherever he went. He had to do a better job of protecting Leo from Crusty Slimeball.

"Jason Scott?" a voice called behind him as he headed down the hall to the exit. He turned and instantly recognized a young woman with long brown hair and blue eyes. What was *she* doing here?

"Cameron," he said, confused by her presence. But he couldn't stop his smile. "So you haven't graduated from this place yet?"

She laughed. "I'm a student teacher here—weird, isn't it? It's bizarre to teach at a school where I used to be a student. Are you back in town? I haven't seen you in forever."

Jason gazed at Cameron Walsh, flooded with flashes from their year of high school dating and filled with regret that their relationship had ended so abruptly. Suddenly he remembered what his mother had told him, and he searched for the right words. "Yeah, I'm back for a bit. Listen, Cammie—"

"It's Cameron now," she interrupted. "Or Cam. I don't go by Cammie anymore."

"Oh. Well, I just heard about…your dad. I'm so sorry."

Her face clouded. "Thank you." Her voice had changed. "I'm late. See you around." She scampered off, abandoning Jason in the hallway.

Jason shook his head at the turmoil all around him. He'd only been back in Florida two days, and he already wanted to leave. *I need a drink*, he thought. Then, he checked himself. What he really needed was to call his sponsor.

15. Tri-Care

U nsteadily walking the perimeter of the treatment center's courtyard, Leo slowly got his sea legs back. The comfort of Audrey's
visit—her warm body by his side—certainly helped.

He'd entered detox on Saturday night, and it was now Monday
evening. Once the vomiting had ceased and he was able to keep some
food down, he'd started feeling worlds better. Perhaps he could make
it through this. He still had some sweating and fatigue, but as the doctor predicted, his withdrawal hadn't been as severe as it was for most.

Leo's newest concern was group therapy the following afternoon.
He dreaded spilling his guts to strangers. But his mom and brother
would pick him up after the therapy session, and he couldn't wait
to get home.

Focusing on the present, and the presence of his girlfriend, Leo
broke the silence. "Thanks for bringing me notes from class today."

Audrey nodded. "No problem. We have a chem test on Wednesday.
Think you'll be ready for it?"

"Oh, probably not." Leo sighed. "School's the least of my worries right now."

"C'mon, who'll compete with me for class rank? We're still gunning to take over the valedictorian spot, remember?"

Leo put his arm around her as they continued their easy pace.
"I love your competitive fire, Audrey. You're an inspiration—to the

whole team, really." He squeezed her shoulder. "I'm glad at least one of us is having a good senior year."

"Leo, your year isn't over yet," Audrey said, her voice filled with that fire. "You're so freaking smart you'll probably ace the test without studying, and it's too early to count you out for swimming. The state meet in March is still more than a month away. Cut the pity party, already."

He stopped walking and looked at her. "What's that—tough love?"

"Yeah. I'm still mad at you for not telling me about the pills." She punched him lightly on the arm.

"Ouch!" He rubbed his triceps. "My muscles are really sore from withdrawal."

"Oh, sorry." She grimaced. "Has it been bad?"

"Let's put it this way, by Sunday I was offering Mr. Shale five thousand dollars for one pill. And I also told him the withdrawal was worse than a set of ten four-hundred IMs, which made no sense to him."

Audrey giggled. "Say no more! I remember that horrid practice. But Matt was in a good mood today—he let us out early."

"Drat, I always miss the short practices." Leo pouted before changing conversational course. "So how's your dad doing?"

"Not bad, actually. Things aren't so tense between us since he's realized I'm visiting him whether he likes it or not. Your dad helped pull some strings to get him some books and tapes, and now he's learning Spanish in his cell. He tried to say some things to me last time I was there, and I was laughing my butt off at all his mistakes."

Audrey and Leo were both in their fifth year of Spanish, and they enjoyed practicing their skills on each other, especially when they were making out. Spanish was simply a sexier language.

"*¿Qué dijo?*" Leo asked.

"I believe he was embarrassed, but he said, '*Estoy embarazado*!'"

"Freshman mistake, telling everyone he's pregnant." Leo grinned.

As the sun sank, the January air cooled, and the pair pulled closer together as they started another lap.

"Um, Leo? Why'd you start taking Oxycontin?"

He tensed. Others had asked him point-blank if his father physically abused him, and like a coward he'd denied it. He didn't understand why on earth he felt loyal to CS, but he just couldn't admit the abuse. He knew he deserved it.

As the silence extended between them, Audrey added, "Was it something I did?"

"No!" Leo said immediately. "You make me want to get better. I hated myself for getting hooked on pills, then I hated hiding it from you." His brows knitted. "I guess I'm glad you finally know, though you're probably embarrassed to be my girlfriend now."

She paused and turned to him. "I'm not embarrassed, and I'm not *embarazada* either."

"Thank God for that." He smiled.

"I'm *so proud* to be your girlfriend. The other girls are jealous I get to date such a hottie."

She leaned up for a kiss, and Leo felt butterflies in his stomach as her lips met his. She wore root beer-flavored lip gloss.

"You're smart and kind too," she added after a moment. "I couldn't find a better boyfriend."

Leo broke their second kiss by dashing into the bushes to vomit.

Audrey's voice came to him through the leaves. "I repel you that much, huh?"

Leo stood with a hangdog look, wiping his mouth with the back of his hand. He felt a little woozy. "Sorry you had to see that. I — I guess I'm not over the withdrawal yet. You're just exciting me too much out here."

She linked her arm in his. "Let's get you back in bed, Scott."

His eyebrows shot up. "I like the sound of that!"

The next afternoon, right after lunch, Leo looked around the meeting room at the seven other men in his therapy group, led by Mr. Shale. The closest to his age was AJ, a college football player who'd been in the program for three weeks. AJ was a tall wide receiver who'd smoked pot for years, until a positive drug test forced him into treatment.

"AJ, what part of 'You're not to use any substances while in treatment' did you not understand?" asked Mr. Shale.

"I'm here for pot, not booze!" he protested.

"It doesn't matter. Now we'll have to reset your sobriety date to today. If you have another positive test, for *any* substance, you could get kicked out of the program. How would your coaches react to that?"

"They'd probably yank my scholarship," AJ mumbled.

Leo listened to this exchange with interest. The coach at Florida State University had unofficially floated a potential half-scholarship his way. Audrey was pretty sure she'd attend FSU, and Leo liked the idea of joining her, especially if he didn't get into the Academy. But if he didn't get this addiction under control, he'd be facing the same troubles as AJ.

An older man in the group shared how alcohol caused him and his wife to lose their kids to foster care. Leo was horrified. As story after frightening story unfolded, Leo had listened silently for most of the three-hour session. Then Mr. Shale looked right at him.

"Leo? You don't *have* to talk today, but we do find the program more effective if you're engaged in the topic," he said. "What can you tell us about your addiction and relationships?"

Leo stared at him. He couldn't determine if his current sweating was related to withdrawal or nervousness.

"Some of the men have discussed how important people in their lives are also addicts. Is that true for you?" Mr. Shale prompted.

"I just found out my brother's an alcoholic," Leo said, feeling the group's stares. "But I don't really know him anymore. He's been gone for four years."

Leo then thought about the rage-aholic in his life who was intimately connected to his addiction, but he was not about to discuss his father.

Fortunately, the tidbit about Jason seemed to satisfy Mr. Shale. After the group, Leo sat outside the treatment center with his gym bag and an assignment to attend a Narcotics Anonymous meeting before the next group therapy session on Thursday. As Leo waited, he realized again how much time and effort treatment was going to require. He wished he could turn back time and never start taking those stupid pills.

"There you are." Mr. Shale emerged from the building behind Leo.

Leo instinctively stood, and Mr. Shale waved him to sit back down.

"I forgot to give you these." He handed Leo some slips of paper, sliding in next to him on the bench. "They're attendance forms to be signed by an NA member. Bring a signed form on Thursday."

"Yes, sir." He scanned the parking lot for Jason's rental car. "I'm waiting for my ride."

"You had a good first group session, Leo. What'd you think?"

"Um, I don't know, sir. They all seem worse off than me, and they're kind of old. I don't know if I can relate."

Mr. Shale smiled. "That's a fairly typical response to your first group, but you'll find you have more in common with them than you think."

Over Mr. Shale's shoulder, Leo watched a vehicle turn into the parking lot. Sheer terror pulsed through his body.

"What is it, Leo?" Mr. Shale asked.

Leo stiffened as tires screeched to a halt on the pavement in front of the bench. His father turned off the ignition and practically leaped from the car with a caged ferocity.

Leo jumped to his feet, his gym bag falling to the sidewalk.

Now standing just inches in front of Leo, his father whipped the sunglasses off his face and seethed, "What the *hell's* going on here?"

Mr. Shale stood as well.

"I — I'm here for drug treatment, sir."

"No kidding!" Hostility dripped from his father's voice. "I'm following orders in California, and I get a phone call from my insurance company informing me that my son's in detox. I tell them they must be out of their minds — *my* son's not in detox! Turns out Tri-Care knows my son better than I do!"

Leo absorbed the shouted words as if they were physical blows. *Jason! Where's Jason?* He'd promised CS wouldn't find out.

"Mr. Scott." Mr. Shale held out his hand.

CS eyed him and ignored his hand. "It's Commander Scott."

"Commander Scott, I'm Marcus Shale, a therapist here. I assure you Leo's getting the best treatment for his addiction. We're addressing all his needs—"

"His needs?" his father interrupted. "What do *you* know about my son's needs? He needs a kick in the butt, not this faggoty touchy-feely therapy you got going on here. I'll make sure he never takes another pill the rest of his life."

"Commander, your son needs drug testing and group counseling to recover."

"Leo, get in the car. Now," CS ordered.

"Yes, sir." Leo reached down to grab his bag.

"Leo, don't move," Mr. Shale countered.

Leo looked back and forth between his father and therapist, paralyzed.

Mr. Shale moved closer. "Leo, look at me. Does your father hit you? It's okay. You can tell me."

CS crossed his arms in front of him and looked smug.

Leo silently pleaded with the therapist, willing him to help. His frightened eyes begged Mr. Shale to realize his next words were untrue. "My dad's never hit me, sir."

His father pulled open the passenger door, and Leo swallowed and ducked into the car. His father slammed the door after him and stepped to Mr. Shale. "Stay away from my son," he said in a voice tinged with fury. "He won't be back."

16. The Deal

The only sound in the study was the ticking of the clock on his father's desk.

Leo had never noticed how loud it was, but he supposed his senses were heightened right now, since he had nothing to do but stand rigidly at attention.

His father sat on the edge of the oak desk, glaring at him. It appeared CS was trying to determine the best tactic for this interrogation as his fingers tapped the desk.

The waiting was almost worse than the beating Leo knew would come, and the pounding of his blood in his ears soon drowned out the clock.

His father stood and meandered to Leo's left. When he finally broke the silence, his silky voice was low and threatening. "You started using your mother's pain medication."

"Yes, sir."

"When?"

"September, sir."

"Last September, as in five months ago?"

"Yes, sir."

"Why?"

Because of you. "No excuse, sir."

"Did Audrey Rose put you up to this?"

"No, sir!" Leo was appalled. "She didn't know anything about this, sir."

"I leave for five days, and you royally screw up. You obviously need more structure in your life. There's no way you'll manage the freedom of a university. You're going to the Academy. That's all there is to it."

"No!" The disobedient word escaped before he thought twice. "It's *my* choice!"

His father narrowed his violet eyes and delivered a sharp blow to Leo's midsection.

Leo doubled over and cried out in pain. The waves of hurt coursing through his body were only intensified by the soreness lingering from withdrawal.

"What'd you say to me?" CS yelled.

Leo coughed violently and tried to stand at attention, panicked by the prospect of military rule for four years of school and five more years of duty. "That's nine years of my life, sir. You can't make me give you nine more years!"

"Well, I'm certainly not *paying* for my drug addict son to go to college." He smiled. "And you're not giving *me* those years in the Navy, you're giving them to yourself. They'll be the best nine years of your life. Let's try this again. Leo, you'll attend the Naval Academy."

Leo felt something dying inside. Any hope that he'd ever escape his father's dominion drained out like liquid onto the floor, and he stood in a puddle of despair. If it wasn't his father, it'd be some commanding officer forcing him to follow orders. It would never change.

The light in his eyes faded. "Yes, sir. I'm going to the Academy."

With a curt nod, his father moved on. "Your mother never complained to me about missing pills. Where'd you get them?"

Failure to answer earned Leo a stunning blow to his face, which disoriented him. He felt a warm stickiness below his bottom lip.

His father leaned in close. "Who gave you the pills, Leo?"

CS moved to unleash another punch, and Leo blurted, "Tony, sir! Jason's friend Tony."

"Unbelievable. Your brother's been gone for years, and he's *still* hurting this family."

"It wasn't Jase's fault, sir."

His father backhanded Leo's head, snapping his neck to the left and radiating pain down his body. Leo felt tears forming.

"I told you never to mention your brother's name again!"

Leo had no idea where Jason and his mother were, but he wished he could warn them. He couldn't imagine what CS would do if Jason confronted him.

"Your mother put you into that treatment center?"

"Yes, sir." Leo followed orders and didn't mention Jason. He clenched his jaw as a tear rolled down his cheek.

"Look at that." His father snorted with disgust. "That treatment's already weakened you. Crying like a baby. I'm going to have to toughen you up before Plebe Summer."

Great.

"What was Mary thinking, believing she could go behind my back like that?" he mused. "She and I will have a little talk."

"Don't hurt her," Leo warned.

"And what will you do about it?" His father swooped over, inches from Leo's face. "Do you want to hit me, Leo? C'mon, give it your best shot. Let's see what happens."

Leo's eyes widened. He wanted nothing more than to beat the smirk off his father's face, but he was terrified at what would happen if he tried. His hands curled into fists at his side, and he felt his heart pound.

His father shook his head. "Thought so. Despite my best efforts, I've managed to raise a crying little sissy." He stepped back. "Your little addiction to pills stops immediately, young man, and you don't need *therapy* to do it. That counselor — Shale is his name? He actually mentioned one useful idea: drug testing. I'm testing you every week until you leave for the Academy. If you pop one positive test, you won't like the consequences."

"Yes, sir." The floodgates had opened, and tears streamed down Leo's face.

"You're never to take another pill the rest of your life. Do you understand me?"

"Yes, sir," he choked out.

"Let's make sure you do."

Leo felt his father's hand on the back of his neck and the rush of air as his head slammed down to the desk. Leo heard his forehead crack on the oak surface and felt the familiar warm stickiness spread over his forehead just before all went black.

Slow, muted voices in the background pulled Leo toward hazy consciousness. The words were fuzzy and deep, each syllable stretched out. Was he underwater? He was peacefully floating in the depths of the pool, weightless. The muffled voices must be calling to him from the surface. But he was tired, so tired, and just wanted to keep sleeping.

The voices wouldn't stop, and when his eyes finally opened, he saw an angry copper bloodstain on the carpeted study floor, just inches from his face. Then he noticed the rubber casing at the bottom of one of his mother's walking canes. His eyes traveled up the cane to find her face, veiled by tears.

"Leo," she sobbed, leaning over to press a moistened paper towel against his forehead. "I'm so sorry."

Leo raised his hand to take the dressing and felt wetness. He wiped his cheeks and noticed the now-red towel. No wonder his mother was crying.

He tried to sit up, but shooting pain in his side halted his progress. He groaned as he returned his head to the carpet. At that moment he heard voices shouting in the other room. It was amazing how Jason's deep baritone now closely mimicked his father's smooth, commanding voice.

"Why'd you come back early?" his brother asked.

"Not that it's any of your business, but I asked my insurance company to contact me before authorizing treatment. Tri-Care screwed us over so badly with your mother's medical bills—I wanted to be on top of any denial they'd try to sneak past us. It's a good thing *somebody* alerted me to your little subterfuge while I was gone. How dare you, Jason?"

"How dare I try to help my brother?"

"How dare you come in here behind my back and think you know what's best for this family! You're twenty-two years old. What do you know? I'm surprised you're not in prison somewhere."

Jason exhaled. "I could say the same for you, child abuser."

Leo remembered when he was thirteen and Jason had called Child Protective Services. CS had warned his sons that if they said anything about their punishments they'd go into foster care, which would devastate their mother. Naturally Leo kept his mouth shut, and CS had skated out of any charges. But he'd never forgiven Jason for making the report and banished him from their home.

"Only one of us belongs in prison," his father sneered. "We had a deal."

"I know. As long as I never returned to Pensacola, you agreed not to report my thefts to the police."

Startled by that revelation, Leo tried to lift his head again.

"You being here violates the deal!" James yelled.

Leo felt his mother stir. "Things are about to get violent. Stay here, Leo."

He eyed his mother's bag left on the floor.

"What about the deal between father and son?" Jason yelled back. "You were supposed to take care of us, not destroy us! You've become a monster, Dad!"

"Get *out* of here!" CS hissed. "We're doing just fine without you!"

Leo heard a crash, followed by a sort of battle cry from his brother, and his mother screamed. She must have finally made it to the family room on her crutches.

After another crash, what must have been the ceramic lamp tinkled like glass as it broke. After a few moments, Leo heard his father's voice, seething with anger.

"Go back to the hole you crawled from, you got it?"

When there was no response, Leo knew CS had won. If his brother couldn't best their father, what hope was there for him? Leo had heard enough. Summoning every ounce of energy he had—and then some—he dragged himself out of the study without making a sound.

Leo had just made it to the trees behind his house when he heard his father's panicked shout. "Mary! Leo's gone!"

Somehow, Leo began to run.

Mary trembled as she sat on the sofa, wringing her hands. She hadn't taken a pain pill since morning because she wanted to be lucid when she and Jason picked up Leo. Now the skipped dose had caught up to her. Her doctor had told her she needed to "stay ahead of the pain," which was impossible in this family.

James stomped down the stairs, his phone calls to locate Leo evidently unsuccessful.

She was so tired of the vice grip his anger had on the family. "Do you remember the dreams we had for our sons?" she asked as he entered the room.

James looked up. "I know we hoped they'd go into the Navy, following in our footsteps. At least Leo will reach that goal."

"What do you mean? He hasn't made his college decision yet."

"I made it for him today. He's applied to the Academy, and I've heard he's been accepted."

"Don't you think that should be Leo's decision?"

"I think, Mary, that Leo lost that privilege the moment he started abusing drugs. He clearly isn't objective about what's best for him right now."

"How'd he react when you told him he was going to the Academy?"

"He didn't like it, but like a good sailor, he got on board."

"Our family isn't a military division, James! They're our sons, not sailors you can order like pieces of meat."

"I think they're doing just fine," James replied coldly.

"Fine? We have one son who's an alcoholic, homeless thief. Our other son needs treatment for drug addiction, and we have no idea where he is right now. You'd say they're doing *fine*? Would you say we're doing a good job parenting, James?"

He said nothing. It was rare for Commander Scott to be speechless.

"We've ruined Jason's life," Mary continued. "Leo's headed down that same path, and I won't let you destroy him too. I've made a decision. If you hurt Leo again, I'm leaving you."

"You can't do that."

"I can, and I will. I don't care if I have to go on welfare. I'm sick of you hurting our sons." Feeling her heart pound in the heat of James's glare, she added, "And I'll take Leo with me. You don't want to get in a custody battle with me."

He shook his head. "I can't believe our marriage has come to this. I won't make it easy for you to leave, and I won't let you take my son away from me."

"Why do you care about keeping me and Leo?" Mary said, shaking her head. "Clearly you hate us."

James recoiled. "*Hate* you? I love you both."

"You love us both," she said flatly. "You sure have an interesting way of showing it. I don't think you know *how* to love anymore."

Her husband stared at her, his emotions unreadable. His gray eyes morphed to violet, reflecting the daylight streaming through the windows.

Mary held her breath. James had never hit *her* in their twenty-three years of marriage, but she knew that potential must be within him. She abhorred when he looked at her with pity because of her crippled legs, but that same pity seemed to prevent him from lashing out physically.

Finally James stormed out of the room, slamming the front door behind him. She sighed as she heard his car start, the whirring noise fading as he backed out of the driveway.

17. A Skinny Dip in the Pool of Despair

I *should probably get on with it.*

The setting sun and cool night air left Leo shivering in his T-shirt. The blanket of trees and foliage in the woods didn't provide much protection from the ocean breeze, and the moist undergrowth had dampened the seat of his jeans. But other than the wind occasionally rustling the leaves, it *was* peacefully quiet.

Leo sat cross-legged in the forest a few blocks from his house, looking down at the bottle in his hands. He'd felt like he was on autopilot when he'd retrieved the pills from his mother's bag. He rolled the bottle back and forth from hand to hand, caressing it. It was nearly full, and the pills rattled as they shifted and tumbled inside.

From what he'd heard of the shouting match, he knew he should stop blaming Jason for being AWOL for four years. As always, the blame rested squarely with his father, who'd blackmailed Jason into staying away.

Leo wondered what Jason had stolen. Whatever it was, losing his family seemed like an unfair punishment. CS had made him pay dearly for that report to Child Protective Services.

Just as Cold Sadist had used secret information against his brother, Leo realized his father would use his drug addiction to control and manipulate him the rest of his life. If Leo tried to fight going to the

Academy, he imagined CS would tell other college coaches about the Oxy. If Leo didn't toe the line in the military, CS would tell his superiors about his drug history and ruin any chance at a successful career. His life was over.

Leo popped the cap off the bottle with his thumb and slowly poured its contents into his palm, mesmerized by the cascading shower of little white pills.

Oxycontin had been both his friend and his enemy. It soothed him when he was troubled. It didn't yell at him or hit him when he screwed up. But it had also distanced him from others, forcing him to keep secrets and leaving him out of control. And it made him feel sick when he couldn't get it.

Yes, both his friend and his enemy. And now it would end his life.

Trapped somewhere between numbness and despair, Leo barely registered his own sobs. As he stared at the mountain of pills in his sweaty palm, a tear fell from his eye and splashed onto one of his fingers. *Why does my father hate me so much?*

It had been different once.

Leo remembered hundreds of childhood car rides to and from swim practices and meets in his father's prized red BMW. His father used to ask endless questions about Leo's training and race strategy. And though he knew much more about basketball than swimming, he'd applied his engineering skills to studying the hydrodynamics of stroke technique, and he and Leo had spent hours discussing and experimenting with minute changes in hand pitch, body roll, or ankle movement. Leo swam faster than ever before, and his father had beamed with pride.

About the time Leo turned twelve, his father abruptly sold the BMW and replaced it with a junky Chevrolet. Leo asked about the change, and his father told him German cars sucked and everyone should buy American. Then he changed the subject. Still confused, Leo asked Jason about it one day.

"Why'd Dad get rid of the Beamer?"

"You really don't know?"

Leo shook his head. At seventeen, Jason seemed to know everything.

"We're broke now 'cause of Mom's medical bills. Dad had to choose between selling his car or forcing you to quit swimming. Your club's really expensive, you know. Anything for your *glorious* swim career," Jason added with a sneer.

Leo had been so grateful for his father's quiet sacrifice. But where had that man gone? The man who'd once had trouble controlling his anger had now arrived at a place where his anger controlled him. Seething hostility had worked into Cobra Snake like a slithering python, strangling any kindness or vulnerability.

Leo was tired of trying to charm the vicious snake to prevent it from striking. Its venom had seeped into his soul, infecting him with shame and hopelessness.

He cried harder now. What would his funeral be like? Would CS cry? Guilt gripped Leo when he visualized his mother sobbing, just as she'd done minutes ago, anguished that she couldn't protect him. His mom couldn't stop the physical pain his father rained down on him, and she couldn't heal his self-doubt and misery either.

Leo studied the pills in his hand, counting them in a silent chant. *Twenty-eight, twenty-nine, thirty*…a nice, even number. He'd almost be thirty by the time he could escape the Navy's clutches, and he'd heard life went downhill from there. He might as well end it now.

Then Leo thought of Audrey—her gorgeous brown eyes gazing at him, her telling him he was kind and smart and a "hottie"…her sweet, bubbly spirit infusing him with happiness…her fine mind and feisty zeal…her lean, sexy body…He remembered the first time he'd seen that exquisite body, before they'd even started dating.

Two years ago, when Leo was a sophomore, he'd finally grown taller and more muscular. His friends told him he'd drawn the attention of several girls, yet he was oblivious to their stares. Consumed by school, swimming, and trying to please his father, he hadn't even considered dating.

It had been a hot September evening, and the swim team had just finished a grueling round of running the stadium stairs. Leo then added an additional half-hour of stair climbing for himself, knowing his father would expect that extra effort. As he emerged from the showers and toweled off in the empty locker room, he heard giggles in the pool.

Once dressed, Leo went to investigate the sound. The pool gates were locked, but all the swimmers knew the security code for those occasional mornings when Matt overslept. Leo heard giggles again. He just had to find out what was so fun in there.

Quietly keying the code, Leo entered and stayed in the shadows of the pool deck as dusk encroached. Smack in the middle of the pool were Audrey Rose and Elaine Ferris, two sophomores on the girls team. They snorted with laughter as they attempted some synchronized swimming moves. Audrey's graceful arm flared over her head as she kept her body afloat with furious kicking.

Elaine applauded. "Brah-*vo*," she mocked.

When Audrey floated on her back and extended her lean leg in the air, Leo had gasped. Audrey was naked! Skinny dipping! He caught a glimpse of two perfect breasts: perky, curvy mounds he just had to caress. He suddenly saw the daughter of his father's subordinate in a whole new light.

Elaine started. "Who's there?"

Not wanting to be a creepy stalker, Leo had immediately stepped out of the shadows, his eyes alight with mischief. "I'm just enjoying the show, ladies."

Audrey's mouth dropped open. "Leo Scott!" She turned to Elaine, and they whispered. "Turn around, Leo!" Audrey ordered.

He gave a little mock salute and performed a sharp about face. He heard vigorous splashing as Audrey and Elaine swam to the other side of the pool, then a rush of water as they pulled themselves out.

"Don't peek!" Audrey shouted.

Leo put his hands in his pockets, rocking back and forth on his heels and reveling in every second of her embarrassment.

When he heard the patter of feet toward the women's locker room, Leo turned around. "Audrey?"

She halted, nervously tightening her towel around her chest. "What?"

Leo came as close as he dared, lest Audrey dart away like a gazelle from a hunter. He flashed a warm smile and watched her face flush. "I judged your routine, and I give you a nine."

It took her only a second to recover. "Only a nine?" She pouted. "What would I have to do to get a ten?"

"You need to get higher out of the water." Leo cleared his throat. "You know, so the judge can get a better view of your, ah, your, your beautiful smile."

"Is that right?" Audrey scanned the deck for Elaine, who'd walked over to the other side of the pool and now seemed busy organizing the kickboards and pull buoys. "Maybe you could show me sometime?"

Leo laughed. "I'd like that." They stared awkwardly for a moment, and Audrey shivered in the humid breeze. Fearing she was about to leave, Leo blurted, "Well, I gave you my number. How about you give me yours?"

Audrey narrowed her eyes and smiled. "The only way you get my number is if you change yours to a ten."

"Done." Leo nodded decisively. "You were absolutely perfect."

Even now he smiled as he remembered calling Audrey that very night, and many nights thereafter.

Looking out into the woods, Leo's smile vanished. Salty tears stung the cut on his lip, and he realized he'd been clutching the pills. He slowly relaxed his grip.

Audrey…he had to see Audrey. He couldn't kill himself without at least saying goodbye. Leo located the pill bottle and dumped them back in, listening to the clink as each pill found its home.

Then he rose, dusted leaves off his jeans, and trekked to Audrey's house.

18. Relapse

The amber liquid scorched his throat as he knocked back his third shot of scotch. It had been too long since he'd felt that burn light his insides on fire. Too long.

Navy Blue was Jason's old stomping ground, and the bar hadn't changed much in four years—other than the heightened security. He'd been surprised when the bouncer insisted on checking his ID at the door. As a teenager he'd come in no questions asked, even though they'd surely known he was Commander Scott's son.

Now it appeared nobody recognized him—not that the bar was particularly full in the middle of the afternoon. His black hair had grown out from its crew cut, and his well-defined biceps belied the lean, underdeveloped seventeen-year-old he'd been. Jason sat at the bar, ruing the disaster this day had become.

He and his mother had been full of optimism as they drove to Still Waters, buoyed by the reports of Leo's speedy detox. When he'd visited the day before, Jason had actually caught a glimpse of the little brother he remembered. But as they pulled up to the treatment center, they saw panic on Marcus's face. Before he'd even finished his first sentence, Jason and his mom were back in the car and peeling out of the lot in a mad dash home.

But they were too late.

Jason couldn't escape the image of Leo splayed out unconscious on the study carpet, blood oozing from a gash on his forehead. As his mother wept, Jason glared at his father, but instead of the smug satisfaction he expected, he saw a flash of regret, followed by surprise.

"What are *you* doing here?" CS had asked scornfully before brushing past Jason into the family room. Things had gone to hell after that.

His cell phone vibrated in his pocket, and Jason pulled it out to glance at the caller ID. *Crap.* His sponsor.

Jason knew he should answer and stop this relapse immediately, but didn't. His sponsor had drilled into his head that his extreme personality could get him into trouble. One drink didn't have to turn into twenty. Things weren't always black or white. But Jason didn't want to stop. He welcomed the contradictory sensation of stimulation and relaxation the alcohol offered like an old friend.

The door swung open, and Jason was startled to see Marcus sidle up to the bar. He sat on a stool a few seats down and nodded to the bartender, who raised his eyebrows before reaching for the bottle of vodka.

Glancing over, Marcus practically fell off his chair when he saw Jason staring at him. A look of silent understanding passed between them. They weren't supposed to be here. They were ashamed to be caught relapsing. They had failed to protect a certain teenage boy.

Jason acted swiftly. He placed some money on the bar and reached Marcus just as the bartender was about to fill the shot glass. "Don't do this, Marcus. Leo needs us. Let's not both mess up at once."

Marcus looked at Jason and turned to stare at the glass. "Some role model I am, huh?"

"I could say the same for myself," Jason scoffed. "C'mon, you can still be a role model today. I've already lost that chance."

After a moment Marcus stood, threw a ten on the bar, and walked out into the still-bright afternoon with Jason. There was an awkward silence as they leaned back on Marcus's car, hands stuffed in their pockets.

"It didn't go well at home, did it?" Marcus asked.

Unsure how much to disclose, Jason just sighed. "Nope."

"So your father abused you too, then?"

Jason looked away, feeling his chest tighten with an unexpected ache. "Listen, it won't help to make a report. Believe me, I've already tried."

"I'm mandated by law to make a report, Jason."

"Then you'll hurt my brother even more, because my dad will make him pay. Leo turns eighteen in four months—then he can get away from Crusty Stick-up-his-butt."

"Just like you've gotten away, hmm?"

"I live three thousand miles away, and I still can't escape that man," Jason said. "He haunts me. He just...he used to be different. My family used to be different. Now it's FUBAR."

Marcus chuckled. "Yeah, I know all about families putting the 'fun' in dysfunction. Do you, uh, do you need a place to stay tonight?"

"That'd be great, actually. Tomorrow I'll see if I can bump up my return flight to Seattle. I only make things worse by being here."

Marcus moved around to the driver's side door and unlocked the car.

"Okay if I call my sponsor?" Jason asked as he slid into the passenger seat.

Marcus nodded. "We'll hit a meeting on the way home."

"Time to face the music," Jason said. He tapped his fingers on the dashboard while holding the phone to his ear. What was taking his sponsor so long?

When he heard the familiar voice, Jason cleared his throat. "Walt, it's Jason."

"Jason Scott!" Walt boomed. "Calling me all the way from Florida? What's up?"

"Uh, my blood-alcohol level?"

"You don't sound drunk."

"Yeah, I think I had three shots. Good thing a friend walked in at just the right moment, and we got out of there." Jason gave Marcus a smile.

"Sounds like you're in a car. You're not driving, are you?"

"No, sir."

"Good. I want you to get to an AA meeting ASAP."

"We're on our way."

"I'm not happy, but I'm a little impressed," Walt said with a smile in his voice. "You're learning from past mistakes and getting back on track faster. So what was it this time?"

Jason paused. "The reunion didn't go so hot with my dad." Glancing over at Marcus in the driver's seat, Jason gave the edited version. "I shoved him, and we got into it. He, uh, he pretty much beat the crap out of me. Then he made the old threat of turning me in to the police if I stayed, so I left."

"Well, I can't say I'm surprised you relapsed."

Jason rolled his eyes. "Thanks so much for the support."

"Jason," Walt's voice rose with reproach. "What I *mean* is you can't stay clean till you come clean."

"Huh?"

"Until you turn yourself in for your crime."

There it was: surrender. He'd avoided that idea just like he'd shunned wearing a belt because holding one reminded him of his father.

"Jason, what step are you working right now?" Walt asked after a long silence.

"You know I'm on number nine, Walt. Making amends to people I've hurt."

"And which step were you working during your last relapse?"

Jason searched his memory. "Nine."

"And what step during the relapse before that?"

"Nine. What's your point?"

"My point is you're getting off track every time you try to make amends because you're missing the biggest one of them all. Who have you harmed the most with your alcoholism?"

"My brother and my mom," Jason said immediately. "My biggest failure is my inability to protect them from my dad."

"And what's preventing you from protecting them?"

Jason furrowed his brow. "The threat of jail time." An understanding dawned on him. "But if I'm in prison, I can't protect them from my dad any better than if I'm in Seattle."

"Jason, I can't imagine any court handing down a long jail sentence for petty thefts made when you were a minor, especially if you turn yourself in."

He took a deep breath. "I'll think about it."

"That's all I ask. Listen, I got another call."

"Thanks, Walt." Jason ended the call and stared out at the Florida landscape.

Marcus glanced over at Jason as he pulled into the church parking lot. "Looks like you've got a lot on your mind."

"Yeah." Jason picked at his fingernails. "I don't know how much you got, but basically I'm a criminal."

Marcus didn't say a word.

"I stole a bunch of cell phones from a warehouse when I was seventeen, and my dad caught me." Flashes of that beating overtook him—all he could see were livid violet eyes staring at him, hating him. That was the last time he'd ever even *thought* about stealing.

He heard Marcus speaking in the distance, and Jason forced his mind back to the present. "What?"

"I'm not too proud of my past either. But here we are."

Jason focused on the church. "Time to make a better present."

As they walked to the back entrance, Jason put his hand on Marcus's shoulder. It was a new experience for him to trust a tall Black man. He was grateful for the opportunity.

19. The Best Day of My Life

Audrey had the radio cranked up as she pulled into her driveway. The endorphins rushed through her body, and she always felt like singing following a tough practice. Her dad used to love listening to her. She collected her swim bag and backpack and, weighted down, she unfolded herself from her Hyundai.

Still crooning the song, Audrey paused to open the front door and noticed movement at the edge of her line of vision.

"Leo!" She held her hand to her chest and watched him approach from the side of her house.

Her bright smile faded as he got closer. His lip was swollen, and there was dried blood on his forehead. "What *happened?*"

Leo's eyes darted around the overgrown yard. "Can we go inside? I'll tell you there."

Audrey paused. Wasn't he supposed to be in treatment? "Okay. My mom's out of town again." She stuck the key in the lock, and Leo lifted her swim bag from her shoulder.

Once inside, they set down the bags and stared at each other. Something seemed different. He seemed tense, like he had so much to say but no idea how to say it. He was on the verge of something—she didn't know what.

"Can I hug you?" he asked tentatively.

She gave him a strange look. "Of course."

She buried her head in his chest. As soon as he scooped her into his arms, a dam released inside of him, and Audrey felt his body tremble as he sobbed.

"Oh, Leo." She squeezed him tighter. "What's wrong, honey?"

"I can't talk about it," he choked.

"It's okay."

After smoothing circles on his back, she attempted to meet his eyes, but he hung his head low and sniffed. She took his hand and led him down the hallway to the living room and the leather sofa, the only nice piece of furniture she and her mother had been able to keep.

Holding his hands in hers, Audrey sat quietly next to Leo as he cried. At one point she grabbed some tissues from the end table and handed them to him. He balled them up in his fist.

"My dad's back in town," he finally said.

It took a moment to register. "Uh-oh, you didn't want him knowing about the pills. Did he find out?"

He nodded, still looking down.

She suddenly understood. "Did your dad do that to your face?"

When Leo nodded again, Audrey felt sadness and rage envelop her. She didn't know what to say or do. Leo wouldn't look at her, but she sensed he was waiting for her response.

She clenched her teeth. "No wonder you call him Cruel SOB. I want to kill him."

Leo looked up, seeming startled. "It's my fault, Audrey. He wouldn't have exploded if I didn't get hooked on pills."

"Your fault? How is your dad beating the crap out of you *your* fault? You don't deserve that!"

The words came pouring out then, spoken through the tears that kept flowing. "CS yanked me out of treatment and said I couldn't go back," Leo confessed. "He's going to drug test me, and if I fail then I'm in huge trouble. Jason—he's been gone so long because my dad threatened to turn him into the police. I think CS beat up Jason too, and he's going to make him go away again. But the worst part is he's forcing me go to the Naval Academy. That's nine years we'll be apart! I won't get to go to FSU with you, I won't get to see you…" His voice cracked.

Seeing Leo so hurt and vulnerable disintegrated Audrey's resolve, and she began to cry too. She'd never loved Leo as much as she did in this moment. He'd hidden his emotions for so long, but he couldn't anymore. Just as he'd first come to know her when she was skinny dipping, she now saw him naked.

Her voice was gentle. "I always knew you'd go to the Academy."

"You did?" His eyes darted up.

She nodded. "You have this sick love of pain. Even if your dad didn't make you go, you'd end up there anyway."

He cried harder. "I wish I wasn't like that. I don't want to be apart from you."

"We'll make it. We'll survive." Although she knew how uncomfortable he was, his lowered defenses were the most potent aphrodisiac she'd ever experienced. To have him turn to her for help? Audrey felt intimately connected.

Slowly advancing, careful not to scare him, Audrey placed a soft kiss on the gash above his eyebrow, tasting his metallic blood on her lips. Drifting downward, her lips tenderly brushed a bruise near his cheekbone and tasted the saltiness of his tears. Her eyes met his, and she was overwhelmed by their closeness. "I want to take your pain away." She kissed the cut on his lower lip.

Leo slowly met her mouth, and he scooted down to lie back on the sofa as their kisses deepened. Their tongues played lightly with each other while Audrey took off her shirt, and tossed it to the floor. Leo stroked the length of her back, and she felt the arousal building inside her.

Straddling him, she stared down for several long seconds, knowing what might happen if they continued. Then Audrey lifted Leo's bloodstained T-shirt over his head. She admired his long, fluid swimmer's muscles. He wasn't bulky or beefy, simply lean and powerful. She brushed her fingers over a dark purple bruise below his ribcage and up his abdomen. He shivered.

Smiling as he watched her every move, Audrey reached behind and unclasped her bra, shyly showing Leo her breasts. He sat up to explore and caress her skin. Her heart pounding with excitement, Audrey reached down to unbutton his jeans and sensed they were about to enter uncharted waters.

Leo allowed her to help him out of his jeans, and he tugged off her pants, the removal of clothing adeptly performed between hot kisses. They held each other, skin-on-skin, Leo now wearing only his boxers and Audrey her lacy pink underwear.

"*¿Estás lista?*" Leo asked, gazing into her eyes.

"I'm ready."

"*¿Estás segura?*"

"*Sí,* I'm sure." She blinked rapidly, wondering if she should say it out loud for the first time. Boldness won over caution. "*Te amo,* Leo."

The tension in his face seemed to melt. "I love you too, Audrey."

Soon they lay naked together on the sofa, which didn't feel as strange as Audrey would've predicted. Perhaps so much time together in swimsuits lessened the awkwardness. Still, she felt nervous about what was to come.

Leo cleared his throat. "Uh, Audrey, I don't have any protection."

"Me neither, but let's not stop. I'm, um, I'm not very regular because of swimming, so we should be fine."

Leo hesitated. "We shouldn't do this."

"Probably not." She gave him a devilish grin and pressed her mouth against his. He eagerly returned her kiss, not seeming to care about his cuts and bruises. Their bodies melded together. Audrey felt him beneath her, and her excitement rose as well.

Audrey paused and lifted her head up.

"Have…have you changed your mind?" Leo asked.

She smiled. "No, but if you even *think* about throwing up right now, it's over between us."

Leo laughed and she giggled. It had been so long since he'd even smiled. It felt wonderful to share a laugh with him. She tried to relax as they fumbled together. He took it out like a sprinter, and brought it home like a distance swimmer.

Lying together, her cheek against his chest, Audrey hummed the song from the radio again while he rubbed slow circles on her back.

She listened to his steady heartbeat and the echo of his words in his chest as he spoke. "Today was horrible before I came over." He squeezed her tighter, holding her flush to his sweaty body. "You've made it the best day of my life, Audrey. Thank you."

All James could hear was the even sound of his breathing as he rounded the corner of the track. He ignored the high school track team as he left them in the dust. Running was the only way to soothe his anger and help him think. The conversation with his wife ran circles in his head as he ran circles on the track.

That she would dare threaten to leave him was unfathomable after all he had done for her. He could have easily left after the car accident, but nobly, he'd stayed. He'd stuck by Mary's side despite her crippling injuries and the crippling medical bills. He'd stuck it out, practically as a single parent to two rambunctious boys, with the older one constantly testing the limits. He'd stuck by her side even though they'd not made love since the accident. At first she'd said sex was too painful, then she'd had no desire.

Naturally he'd had to turn elsewhere. Her overall lack of gratitude was appalling.

Then there was his first son. For four years he'd blocked all thoughts of Jason, and the boy's surprise appearance had jolted him. Jason was more like James than either wanted to admit.

Despite what she'd become, had he not met Mary, James knew he'd be in prison or maybe even a homeless alcoholic himself. Jason hadn't encountered *his* Mary yet, and probably never would. James realized he was losing her—the woman who'd changed his life. But he'd fight to keep her.

James pushed himself harder as he began the fourth mile. It felt good for his lungs to burn and his legs to focus singularly on his pace. However, the sickening image of Leo's forehead wound kept flashing in his mind. His son unconscious and bloodied…he'd gone way too far.

But Leo *had* to succeed, and James's anger upon learning about the drug abuse had overtaken his senses. Leo was the one shining beacon for the family—the only sign James's life mattered at all. Sometimes the compliments he received about Leo's swimming and school performances were the only thing that kept him going. He'd given up on Mary and Jason long ago, but Leo could save the family.

As James accelerated his pace again for the fifth mile, he started planning Leo's glorious return to swimming. Now that the drug was out of his system, he might have a chance to come back for the state meet. James regretted that Leo's bruises would prevent him from returning to practice anytime soon, but maybe he could sneak in some laps at the community pool.

He'd just have to keep him focused — no distractions from school and sport. Up to this point James had mostly ignored Audrey, but the second Leo's grades slipped, he'd order an end to the relationship.

Suddenly James stopped on the track, hands on his knees and breathing heavily. He knew exactly where Leo had gone: Audrey's. James sprinted to his car. He had to retrieve his son and make his family whole again. It was his duty as a father.

20. Narcissus

Audrey peeled herself away from Leo, the leather making a scrunching noise as her weight shifted off the sofa. She bent down to retrieve the various clothing items strewn on the floor. Leo watched her intently. The only thing he wore was a look of bliss.

"You're gorgeous, Aud."

She blushed as she pulled up her pants. "Thank you." She threw boxer shorts in his direction. "Get dressed, and I'll make us something to eat. I'm starving!"

"Me too." He grinned. "That's the best workout I've had in days."

Audrey scooped up Leo's jeans from the floor. As she held them out, she heard a strange rattling noise. Curious, she reached into the pocket as Leo lunged for her.

He was too late.

"What are these doing here?" She held up the bottle of pills, the name Mary Scott clearly visible on the prescription label.

Leo looked down and cursed under his breath.

"Did you take any of these?"

"No."

She eyed him suspiciously—he looked quite guilty. "Then why do you have them?"

Leo continued to avoid her eyes. "I don't know. When I came to after CS smashed my head against his desk, I wasn't thinking straight. I guess I panicked. I'm not going to take them, Audrey… going through withdrawal *once* was awful enough."

"So you won't mind if I return them to your mother myself." She pocketed the pills.

He angrily grabbed his jeans and yanked them on. "Yeah, I do mind. Give them back to me now."

"No." She walked saucily into the kitchen.

"Audrey," he warned, buttoning his jeans and trying to follow at the same time. "Hand them over."

Feeling him behind her, Audrey ran, and he chased her through the house. At first he seemed dead serious about wanting the pills, and she felt almost scared, but then his mood changed. She was no match for his long sprinter legs, and wherever she went he ensnared her like his prey, then let her go with a goofy grin to catch her all over again.

Audrey screamed and giggled, trying to avoid his groping hands on her hips and pockets as they raced around the first level of the house. Finally Leo trapped her near the sofa and playfully pushed her down on the leather, lying on top of her in a flip flop of their previous position.

"Is that a bottle of pills in your pocket or are you just happy to see me?" he asked with a half smile, panting.

Audrey grinned, breathing heavily.

"Don't you trust me?" Leo's expression turned more solemn.

Her grin faded. "I trust you with a lot of things. I trust you to be faithful to me, for example." Stabbing his chest with her index finger, she added, "And now that we've slept together, you better not cheat on me. You won't be able to count the claw marks all across your back."

"Whoa!" His eyes danced. "That sounds like fun."

"*Men.*" She rolled her eyes, then placed her hands on his chest. "I don't want you to be tempted by these pills, Leo. I'm scared for you."

He held his body over hers, balancing his weight on his elbows, and leaned down to kiss her. "I don't deserve you. If it makes you feel better, you can give the pills back to my mom. Just don't let CS see you."

She nodded, and he pulled her to her feet. They ambled together into the kitchen and Leo pulled his T-shirt back over his head.

Audrey ran down several options for a quick meal, and they decided on spaghetti with meat sauce and a salad. As they cooked together, chatting amicably, she felt like a real adult, making dinner after a long day at work. She couldn't wait to have a house with him one day when he was in the Navy. She couldn't imagine spending her life with anyone else.

They scarfed down their food, and Audrey was again in awe of how much Leo ate. She wondered where he put it all, but such was the metabolism of a swimmer. He belched loudly, patting his stomach.

"Classy." She shook her head. "That was even louder than Elaine's monster burps at practice today."

"I *have* to get back in the pool. It's been what, three days? I can't remember ever being out of the water that long."

"So then go to practice with me tomorrow."

Leo shook his head, pointing to his swollen face. "Too many questions. I can't go back till these cuts and bruises fade."

"Hmm, that *is* a dilemma." She thought for a moment. "I have an idea." She explained quickly to Leo, who seemed impressed by her cleverness.

A phone call set their plan in motion. "The only downside is we just made that buffoon the happiest guy in the school," Leo said. Then he looked up and froze.

Audrey followed his gaze and gasped to find Leo's father standing in the kitchen doorway.

Leo scrambled out of his chair and stood beside the table, completely still. "Dad, I didn't know you were here."

CS's violet eyes bounced from Leo to Audrey. "The front door was unlocked, so I let myself in. You really should keep that door locked, Miss Rose."

"Y-Y-Yes, Commander Scott. My mom has to remind me to lock it all the time."

"And is your mother home?"

"No, sir. She's in New Orleans."

Her response seemed to placate him, and he turned his steely gaze to Leo, stepping closer. "We've been worried about you, Leo. You know you're not supposed to leave the house without my permission."

"Yes, sir."

Leo's father spoke so softly, yet with such menace. Audrey felt goose bumps prickle her spine. When CS moved even closer, Leo's hand gripped the edge of the table, as if to hold himself in place.

"There'll be consequences for breaking the rules."

"I'd expect nothing less, sir."

He was disgusting. How could he be so cruel? Leo already wore the bruises of their first confrontation. The words were out of her mouth before she could stop herself. "Don't hurt him, you, you jerk!"

Leo's eyes widened. "Shhh, Aud. Be quiet! Just go upstairs!"

"No." CS smiled smugly, approaching her. "I'd like to hear what she has to say."

Audrey felt her airway tighten as he neared. She could smell his sweaty running clothes.

"And where did *you* learn such excellent parenting advice, Miss Rose? It looks like your parents are nowhere to be seen."

Audrey had never been hit before, but she could easily read the impending violence. She braced herself.

Leo slammed into his father's side with a lightning-quick surprise attack, throwing CS to the floor.

Audrey screamed as Leo whaled punches on his father. Years of caged rage seemed to tumble out, and CS tried to defend himself, but the blows were too swift. After his punches drew blood, Leo slammed his elbow into his father's side, eliciting a weak groan.

Leo jumped up from the prone figure, only now seeming to realize what he'd done. He stared at his bloodied right hand.

His father didn't move, just blinked several times, and a tear leaked out of his eye. Leo still seemed stunned.

As CS slowly gathered himself up off of the floor, Leo stepped in front of Audrey. He didn't seem afraid anymore.

Brushing himself off, James lifted his hand to his face. He grabbed a paper towel and pressed it to his nose. "Time to go home, Leo. Your mother's worried sick."

"Yes, sir."

Leo turned and whispered to Audrey. "The pills."

"No!" She shook her head.

"Please. It's okay now," he said.

Finally she reached into her pocket and gave him the bottle.

Taking a deep breath, Leo handed them to his father. "I stole these from Mom, sir. Sorry. I didn't take any."

James accepted the bottle silently. "I'll be waiting in the car."

Once he left, Leo enveloped Audrey in a hug. She trembled.

"I don't want you going home with him."

Leo brushed his hand down her hair. "It's okay. He knows I'll hit him back now. Thank you for inspiring me to punch him."

Audrey looked up at him, her lip quivering. "I don't think I've helped things any."

Leo slid into the passenger seat of his father's Chevrolet, and CS started the car. "What did you two do before I got here?"

"Uh, um, nothing, sir. We...had dinner."

His father studied him. "I hope you used protection."

Leo glanced at his father, startled. He looked out the window as they backed out of the driveway.

CS seemed to relax. "You know, you could do a lot worse."

Again, Leo had no idea how to respond.

"All I want is for you to be the best swimmer and student in the school," his father said as they neared their home. "I just want to help you focus on your dreams."

Leo stared at his father, feeling a jumble of surprise, longing, anger, and mistrust. All he'd ever wanted was his father to be proud of him, but that seemed the most unachievable dream.

They pulled to a stop in the driveway.

"Uh, yes, sir," Leo finally managed. His heart pounded, and he had to get away from this enigma of a man.

He ran inside, swiftly ascended the stairs, and sank into his bed with relief. A couple of hours later Leo heard a soft knock. His mother poked her head inside the darkened room. "Are you asleep?"

"No, ma'am. Just thinking. You can come in if you want."

His mother maneuvered her way in and sat on the edge of his bed. She caressed the side of his face. "Are you hurt?"

"No, I'm fine."

"Your father's face looks almost as roughed up as yours."

"I'm sorry. I kind of lost it. I thought he was going to hurt Audrey."

She sighed. "He gave me back my pills, Leo. Why'd you take them?"

Leo looked away.

"I can get you into therapy," she said after a moment. "He doesn't need to know about it."

"Mom, I just had my first semi-normal conversation with Dad in years. Let's not press our luck. I'll be okay. You don't need to worry."

"I do worry. I love you."

"I love you too, Mom." After a moment, Leo asked, "What'd Jason do? Why's Dad threatening to turn him in?"

"He stole a bunch of cell phones and God knows what else when he was your age." She shook her head. "I wonder if Jason can talk to Mr. Morrison again about you missing school for the next few days."

"No need. I'm going back to school tomorrow."

"How? You look like you've been attacked by a pack of wolves."

"It was Audrey's idea. I'll tell everyone Billy Ryan kicked my butt. He finally got revenge for the smack-down I gave him in September."

His mother took this in, slowly smiling. "Audrey seems like quite a smart young lady."

"She is, Mom. She's the best thing that ever happened to me."

"Well, you're the best thing that ever happened to me. I'm so glad you're my son." She kissed him on the cheek. "Get some sleep."

"Yes, ma'am. Good night, Mom."

Leo rolled over, his face flushed with warmth as he relived his time with Audrey.

21. Step Number Nine

Jason woke with a start and tried to figure out what kind of hole he'd landed himself in this time. A dull ache throbbed in his brain.

He noticed a photograph on the end table and recognized a younger version of Marcus Shale with one arm draped over the shoulder of a woman who must be his mother. Marcus wore a bright blue graduation gown and a bright, hopeful smile. Jason wasn't sure he'd ever felt that sort of optimism.

The conversation with his sponsor still looped in his mind. After the AA meeting, Marcus had driven them back to his apartment in silence, and Jason was up half the night wrestling with the decision about how to make amends. He was tired of the merry-go-round of relapse and recovery. It was a misery-go-round.

Jason heard the groan of pipes as the water came on at the back of the apartment. Yawning, he shuffled over to the kitchen and rifled through the cabinets. By the time Marcus emerged from the shower, Jason had poured them both coffee and neatly folded his sheet and blanket.

"Coffee. Thank God." Marcus smiled as he accepted his cup and took some creamer from the fridge. "How'd you sleep?"

"Not great. I've got a hangover—doesn't seem right after only three drinks."

"You said it's been five months since your last relapse? You probably lost your tolerance."

Jason snorted. "Great, now I can't even enjoy my relapses."

"What's there to enjoy, Jason? A few seconds of relaxation followed by years of regret?" Marcus reached into the freezer and took out some cinnamon rolls, which he began to defrost in the microwave. He shook his head. "Listen to me, talking like I have all the answers when I came *this* close to relapsing myself last night." He turned to face Leo and leaned on the cabinet. "So, you called the airline to move up your flight?"

"Nope." Jason looked away. The image of Leo's bloodied face haunted him. "I think I'll stay in Pensacola for a while."

"I see. Won't be a vacation though, will it? Instead of palm trees and ocean, you'll have a view from behind bars."

"Something like that."

"How 'bout you talk to an attorney before you turn yourself in? I know a few who've defended my clients on DUI charges."

Jason shook his head. "Can't afford it. I used my last funds on the plane ticket and renting that car, and they probably won't hold my job for me at the restaurant."

"You've been working as a waiter?"

"Right now I'm only bussing tables." Jason chuckled. "I was making good money as a bouncer, but my sponsor practically disowned me when he found out. So now I work at a restaurant without a liquor license."

"I bet bouncing drunks out of a bar was way more satisfying than clearing tables," Marcus said.

"You can say that again. Speaking of bars, can you drive me to my car at Navy Blue?" Jason smirked. "Take me back to the bar before I go behind bars?"

"Hilarious." Marcus shook his head. "Don't you want some breakfast first?"

Jason eyed the gooey cinnamon rolls. "How 'bout some toast? I don't know how you eat that crap."

Marcus's laugh boomed. "Well, I don't smoke, so I need *some* kind of addiction to replace booze. Junk food's my main vice these days." He patted his generous belly. "Too bad I inherited my dad's slow metabolism."

Jason didn't respond. He hoped he hadn't inherited anything from *his* dad. He'd recovered by the time the toast popped up, and they chatted through breakfast. After Jason showered, Marcus dropped him off at his rental car in the bar's empty parking lot.

"You know where to find me if you or your brother need anything," said Marcus. "Don't be a stranger, Jason. And thanks for getting me out of here last night."

One more addict—one more caring person, Jason thought. *"I'm* the grateful one. Thanks for helping us."

Jason sat in the rental car, attempting to ignore his pounding heart as Marcus drove away. He had a vague notion of the closest police station, and he headed in that direction. He found it far too quickly. After a few tense minutes gripping the steering wheel, he forced himself to walk inside.

"I'm here to report a crime," he announced to the officer at the desk.

"Let me get you a report form," the man said, sounding bored.

"Uh, no — I mean…I'm the one who did the crime." Jason stumbled over his words. "I guess I'm here to confess."

This time the officer looked more interested. He motioned to another cop, who frisked Jason, then led him down the hallway. They stopped at an office where a tall, voluptuous blonde sat frowning at her laptop. "Detective Easton? This gentleman would like to turn himself in."

The detective stood, and Jason realized she was only a couple inches shy of his height. After dismissing the officer, she scrutinized Jason. "Are you for real?"

"Yes, ma'am?"

"If this is some sort of fraternity gag, I'll charge you with obstruction of justice, got it?"

Jason's eyes widened. He had a live one here. "I wish this was a gag, but it's not."

Still squinting at him, she gestured to the chair facing her desk and took a seat. "Okay, I'll open up a new file, Mister—?"

"Scott. Jason Scott."

The detective typed quickly, entering the information she gleaned from her rapid-fire questions. The interrogation had an easy rhythm, and Jason felt his father's presence lifting off his shoulders as he confessed the details of the theft. Maybe he would finally stay sober.

Then the detective asked who else was involved in stealing the cell phones.

"I can't say, ma'am. I'm trying to make amends to people I've hurt, not get anyone else in trouble."

Her tone softened. "You're working step number nine, huh?" Jason nodded. "I have a brother in the program. You remind me of him a bit, minus the part about taking responsibility for yourself. So who've you hurt?"

"My mom and brother."

She nodded, and after a few more questions, Detective Easton read him his rights and arrested him, informing him he'd be placed in a holding cell until he went before a judge. As if on cue, an officer came into the office and hauled Jason to his feet.

"You did the right thing, Mr. Scott," she said.

Their eyes met for a moment as the officer placed him in handcuffs. "Thank you, ma'am."

As they walked down the hall, Jason tried to convince himself the detective was correct. After a lifetime of wrongs, he hoped he was finally doing right.

22. Come Clean, Come Home

Leo stared at his reflection in the bathroom mirror, sweating and disoriented. His alarm had interrupted an intense dream of being chased by the police. He was glad Wednesday was the team's one morning off, but he already felt nervous about afternoon practice. Actually, he worried about the entire day ahead.

Splashing some cold water on his face, he leaned closer to examine the damage. The cut on his bottom lip looked better, but the gash on his forehead was a deep, angry red and crusted with dried blood. The bruise on his right cheek had bloomed into shades of purple and gold. Terrific. A loyal Pensacola Panther to the end, he now wore the school colors on his face.

Trudging down the stairs to breakfast, Leo reminded himself that his father had already left to catch an early military transport back to Miramar. He wondered how CS would explain his own colorful face.

A short time later, Leo walked into the high school feeling clear-headed and eager to make a fresh start. He made a beeline for the assistant principal's office and, taking a deep breath, he knocked and entered.

Mr. Morrison inhaled sharply when he looked up at Leo's face. "What happened to you?" He pointed to a chair.

"I got in a fight, sir. It happened off of school property, I promise."

"Who was it?" When Leo didn't answer, Mr. Morrison inquired, "Was it Billy Ryan?"

Leo gave his best poker face. "Let's just say the other guy looks a lot worse."

"And you're proud of that? Violence isn't the answer, son."

"Yes, sir."

"Your once-bright high school career's gone down the crapper, Leo. What's this I hear about you being in drug treatment?"

"Sorry, sir. I'll do better. At least the treatment center let me go early so I don't have to miss class."

Mr. Morrison appeared distracted by the thick stack of papers on his desk. "Good. First bell's about to ring so you better get going."

"Yes, sir." He stood to leave.

"Leo? Steer clear of your brother. He's a bad influence on you."

Leo bristled. "Jason's a good man, sir. Too bad you don't see it."

Rushing to chemistry, Leo barely made it to his seat before the bell rang. Mrs. Boyd gave him the arsenic eye as she distributed the tests. Leo panicked—he'd forgotten about today's exam.

Audrey reached over to pat his thigh before the teacher reached their row of desks.

"That's not helping with my concentration!" he whispered.

She smiled and removed her hand, turning to sit studiously in her seat. Leo took a deep breath and prepared himself for some creative guessing.

Leo felt sick after the test. He knew he'd bombed it. He gladly shoved his chemistry book into his locker. As he pulled out his government textbook, he noticed Billy Ryan had sidled up next to him.

"Scott," Billy growled. "Looks like Navy boy finally got what was coming to him."

Leo struggled for control. He should've expected Billy to gloat. Audrey *had* asked him to take credit for the beating. Having lived for years with a man who followed through on threats of violence, Leo knew Billy was all talk. Nothing had happened in the five months since their altercation.

"Leave me alone." Leo stared directly at him. Though they were both a little over six feet tall, Billy outweighed Leo by forty pounds.

"I think I need to multiply those bruises, Mr. Mathlete. I didn't get to experience the real thing." Billy squinted. "So who *does* get the credit for busting up that pretty little face?"

"Your dad punched me when he discovered your mom and me together in bed," Leo deadpanned.

Billy's black eyes narrowed. "You little punk," he snarled, stepping closer.

"You want a week's suspension, Billy?" Leo tilted his head to find Mr. Morrison in the hallway, watching them intently.

Billy patted Leo's shoulder with a beefy hand. "This ain't over."

"Whatever."

Leo gave Mr. Morrison a defiant glare and headed to his next class. He could come to enjoy this new bad-boy role. Instead of hiding at home, waiting for his bruises to heal while he was "grounded," sauntering around the high school with his busted face gave him instant credibility and coolness. How screwed up was that?

At lunchtime, Leo joined Audrey, Elaine, and Alex in the cafeteria, where they'd lucked into having the same lunch period for the second semester of their senior year.

Eyeing Leo's bruises, Elaine asked, "So, where'd Billy corner you?"

Leo exchanged an uncomfortable glance with Audrey. "I was actually coming out of Urgent Care as he was coming in—he was getting an x-ray or something. I heard he dropped a dumbbell on his foot in the weight room. Wrong place, wrong time, I guess."

"You had to go to the doctor to get tested for mono?" Alex asked. When Leo nodded, he clucked. "That sucks you got slapped around, Leopatra."

"Do. Not. Call. Me. That." Leo tried to hide a grin.

"Yeah, you really sound sympathetic, Alexis." Elaine smirked.

"Shut up, hag!" Alex stuck his tongue out at Elaine.

Audrey stuck to the cover story. "The good news is Leo doesn't have mono. He can return to practice today."

Alex rolled his eyes. "I bet you're excited he doesn't have the *kissing disease.* I don't care what your orientation is, just keep it to yourself, people, okay? I'm getting tired of you sticking your PDA in my face."

To spite Alex, Leo skated his hand through Audrey's hair and gently drew her close, touching his forehead to hers and planting a loud kiss on her lips. He tasted turkey sandwich on her mouth.

Alex pointed emphatically. "You see? That's exactly what I'm talking about. Stop flaunting your heterosexuality."

"Sorry, Alex." Audrey grinned. "We'll try not to make you lose your appetite."

A few hours later, Leo walked out onto the pool deck. It was unseasonably warm for late January, and he soaked in the sunshine as he tightened the string on his drag suit. The smell of chlorine relaxed him, and the clear blue water conveyed a shimmering peace. His coach's brusque approach interrupted his reverie.

"What happened to *you?*" Matt asked.

Leo hated lying. "Remember that fight I got into in September? Well, it was payback time."

"That Billy Ryan kid? That tool? You could totally take him, Leo."

"I guess I'm still off my game from the withdrawal."

Matt's tone softened. "How's treatment going?"

"Great!" Leo grinned. "Especially since it's over."

"*Over?* Treatment can't be over. It just started."

Leo shrugged. "Mr. Shale said I was doing fine. He didn't want me to miss so much school, so he told me I'm done."

Matt's eyebrows lifted. "Well…Good to have you back. You've got a lot of catching up to do."

"Yes, sir." Leo grabbed his mesh equipment bag and headed over to the fast lane. Audrey had already started her warm-up in the lane to the right.

"Hey, Eric." Leo reached down to shake his hand. "I forgot to tell you your five hundred kicked butt at the invitational on Saturday. Way to go, man."

Eric looked surprised, then pleased. "Thanks, Leo. I heard you were sick?"

"Yeah." Leo surveyed the lane ahead. "I was sick." *Sick in the mind, body, and soul.* "But I'm better now."

After gingerly pulling on his goggles to avoid the cuts on his face, Leo jumped in. At first the cold water stung the gash on his forehead, but then it washed over his wounds, cleansing him of the pain of the past twenty-four hours.

Leo popped to the surface and began taking sure, strong strokes. It felt good to be home.

23. Fathers

Audrey and her father sat on their respective sides of the visiting booth. "So, Dad, how's the pregnancy coming along?"

After a moment his puzzled look morphed into a smile. "Not so great. It's hard getting prenatal vitamins inside the joint." He looked down at his waistline. "Am I showing?"

Audrey giggled. "Not yet. Maybe in your second trimester."

"How's swimming, honey?"

"Good. We start taper in three weeks!"

Audrey couldn't wait to lighten workouts in preparation for the high school state meet. Though some swimmers got restless or even anxious during taper, Audrey entered the zone. Matt could rely on her to swim her best times when it really counted. Leo, on the other hand, was a crapshoot this year.

Her father smiled as he cradled the phone to his ear. "I know how much you love taper. Matt still hitting you with a lot of yardage?"

"Yeah, yesterday we did eight one-seventy-five IMs with long rest, trying to beat our goal time for the two hundred IM. My muscles were like jelly. I can't imagine college practices being much harder."

He brightened. "You decided on college?"

"Yep. Florida State. I'm getting a full ride, and I love it there."

Her father paused. "Why not Northwestern?"

"Because it's *freezing* there!"

"Okay, okay." He chuckled. "I just want to make sure the decision's best for *you*. You don't have to stay in Florida just because I'm here, at least for now."

She nodded.

"Will Leo go to FSU as well?"

Audrey's face fell. "He's going to the Academy. His father's making him."

"*Making* him? That's a nine-year commitment. I can't believe James would force him to go."

She hesitated. Leo's secret had weighed heavily on her for days. He'd be upset if she said anything, but she also knew there wasn't much her father could do from prison. "I think there's a lot you don't know about the commander, Dad."

Aware of the MP monitoring their conversation, Audrey tried to figure out a clandestine way to communicate. "Have you, um, studied the verb *golpear*?"

Her father shook his head.

She hit her right fist into her palm and then tapped her right fist against her jaw, and her father nodded. "*El padre de Leo...él lo golpea.*"

His eyes opened wide. "That can't be right, Audrey. I've known *su padre* for years, and he'd never do that."

Audrey shook her head. "*Es la verdad.* I saw it, Dad. He almost, he almost..." Her voice trailed off. She pointed at her chest and drew her fist close to her jaw. "*Casi me golpea a mí.*"

Her father's eyes narrowed, and Audrey quickly added, "But Leo stopped him."

His hand clenched into a fist on the counter in front of him. "You have to tell somebody! Child Protective Services, a teacher, a counselor—"

"I can't. Leo made me promise. He's thinks *su padre* won't do it again."

"That's what they all say." He slumped in his chair. "How'd this go on and I had no idea? Did it happen to Jason too?"

Audrey felt tears well up. "I think so. He, *su padre*, made Jason leave and promise to never come back."

Her father just stared.

"I shouldn't have told you," Audrey said. "But it's been killing me, and I didn't know who else to tell."

Her father cleared his throat. "I'm glad you told me, honey. I'm so sorry for you, and for Leo. Nobody should have to go through that. I hope he's right that *su padre* won't *golpear* him anymore." He forced a smile. "See? You taught me a new word."

Audrey nodded sadly, and they sat for a few moments. "I miss you, Dad."

He swallowed, blinking quickly. "I miss you so much, Audrey girl."

"It won't be the same at state without you."

"Well, I'll be there in spirit, honey. You'll do an awesome job as long as you keep working hard."

Audrey mustered a wan smile. "Yes, sir."

Lt. Commander Roland Drake waited in the Jeep for his CO.

Now thirty-nine, Roland had been part of Air Department V4 for less than two years, but it was by far the toughest assignment of his military career. He'd never served under a more demanding boss. Unfortunately that boss had just returned to Miramar after a mystery trip to Florida.

Commander Scott stepped off the plane and practically marched down the metal stairway onto the tarmac. Roland scrambled out of the vehicle to exchange a brisk salute. Scott was in his seat and ready to go before Roland could even get the door open. He fumbled for a moment, then began to maneuver the car through the base.

"How was your time in Florida, sir?"

"Excellent. How's the review of the maintenance quality issues?"

"Fine, sir," Roland lied, feeling the heat of his boss's eyes.

"Are we finished with the testing?"

"Not quite, sir. We had a holdup on the C-Forty Clippers. The air boss hasn't cleared them for flight."

"And how is that *our* problem, Mr. Drake?"

"I'm sure we'll get it figured out today, sir."

"Good. I want to get back home ASAP." The commander gazed off in the distance, seemingly at nothing.

"Are you okay, sir? It looks like you got in a fight."

Commander Scott glared at him, and Roland instantly regretted the question.

"Not that it's any of your business, but I was mugged last night."

"*Mugged?* Did they catch the guy?"

"I didn't file a report. I make my own justice."

Roland hesitated. "I'm sure the other guy looks much worse, sir."

Commander Scott nodded, his fury evident in his voice. "He won't be trying *that* again anytime soon."

They drove in silence to their assigned hangar and spent the next few hours consulting on safety measures. The EA-6B Prowler's electronic circuitry had problems, and it took most of the morning to run system diagnostics.

When they'd finished, Commander Scott left for lunch, and after a safe amount of time had passed, Roland moved in on a female lieutenant. He was just about to brush his fingers down her thigh when he found his CO screaming in his face.

"Did you think I wouldn't find out the C-Forty Clippers are already in the air?" he bellowed. "I was at lunch with Commander Branson, and I looked like a freaking idiot!"

Roland stood at attention alongside the lieutenant, his palms moist with sweat. "I thought Commander Branson deployed this morning, sir?"

"His deployment was delayed!" Commander Scott began to pace. "You thought you could pull a fast one just because the air boss would be gone? What's going on here?"

Roland's heart thumped. "I screwed up, sir. I haven't had time to study the C-Forty design blueprints yet. It's my fault the review's not complete."

"Why haven't you had time?"

"We were here till twenty-three-hundred last night, and you arrived at oh-eight-hundred this morning, sir."

"And what's occupied your time the past forty-five minutes? It appears you've chosen to flirt with your subordinate here instead of doing your duty, Mr. Drake."

Roland's face burned, furious at being chewed out in public. "No excuse, sir."

Commander Scott closed in once again, his voice soft, yet menacing. "You will *not* lie to me, Mr. Drake. Walsh and Rose were hardly adequate lieutenant commanders, but they knew damn well never to lie to me. This will go in your performance report, and you can kiss one week's salary goodbye."

Roland's face remained neutral, despite his nausea. "Yes, sir."

"Now, get outta my sight, and *do your job* so we can go home."

"Right away, sir." Roland did an about face and jogged into the hangar.

As he dashed to one of the offices, Roland's eyes tapered into slits. How dare the commander embarrass him like that? A superior hadn't dressed him down that way since the time Bill Walsh had caught him in a lie. Now Walsh was six feet under.

24. Bailing Out

Slouched on the bench in the shadows of the holding cell, his clothes now hopelessly wrinkled and his person in desperate need of a shower, Jason fought to hide his fear. A smattering of whistles and catcalls broke the silence, and he looked up to see Detective Easton approaching. She squelched the noise with a glare.

"Mr. Scott." She beckoned, and Jason couldn't conceal his relief as he stepped up to the bars. Her voice lowered. "You have a visitor. Place your hands through the slot so I can cuff them."

Confused, he complied.

As the detective led Jason down the hall, he noticed the T-shirt under her jacket. "Is that an R.E.M. shirt?" *And was that a blush?*

"Yes it is — from their Monster tour."

Jason chuckled. "My sponsor has that same shirt."

"Mr. Scott, I'm sorry you've been in that holding cell for two days. There's a backup on the docket, but they should get to your bail hearing this afternoon. We're also short-staffed with guards, so I offered to escort you to your visitor."

"And who might that be?"

"I believe it's your father."

Jason stopped short. "Why's *he* here?"

The detective shrugged.

"Do I have to see him?"

"You don't want to see your own father?"

Jason paused. He didn't know how to answer.

"Listen, you don't have to see him if you don't want to," she said. "But you might want to find out why he's here. Have you even met with an attorney yet?"

He shook his head.

"Maybe your father can help you get a good attorney, not some overworked, court-appointed one."

"That's not likely." Jason exhaled. "I don't really want to see him, but I don't want to go back to that cell either. Let's go."

As they neared the visiting room, Jason hesitated again. "Wait—what's the set-up? Any barriers?"

"There are tables in the room. No barrier."

Once they entered the visiting room, she unclasped his handcuffs. Jason immediately felt his father's harsh gaze emanating from across the room. Jason took a deep breath and willed himself to walk forward.

His father's crisp khaki uniform stood in stark contrast to Jason's crumpled, half-unbuttoned shirt and jeans. They stared at each other until Jason took a seat, and his father reluctantly followed suit.

"How'd you know I was here?" Jason asked.

"I have my sources. MPs and police officers like to talk."

Jason couldn't believe it, but as he watched, Cold Stone fidgeted a little on the bench.

"I—I can't believe you turned yourself in."

Was that a hint of admiration in his father's eyes? "My sponsor told me I should do it, and I agreed," Jason said. "I'm sick of you lording this over me. It actually felt good to confess."

"Well, I think it's the dumbest thing you've done yet." The typical hostility and impossibly high expectations returned. "You're dragging our family name through the mud."

"So it's okay if *you* turn me in, but not if *I* turn myself in? What kind of logic is that?"

His father did not respond. "Your mother tells me you're an alcoholic," he said instead.

Bitterness coated Jason's tongue. "Yes I am, Dad. I'm the family screw-up, just like you predicted."

"I don't know how both my sons became addicts. I don't know where things went wrong."

He looked off into space, and Jason was amazed yet again to hear self-doubt from his father's lips.

"At least Leo was clean on his last drug test," his father added.

"That means squat," Jason countered. "Leo will keep abusing pills until he gets treatment."

"He doesn't need treatment, and he doesn't need a *sponsor*. He has me to watch over him, to make sure he has a successful Navy career."

"What about when he goes to school? You can't watch him every second."

"His commanding officers will keep close tabs on him at the Academy."

"Leo's going to the Naval Academy? Is that what he wants?"

CS waved dismissively. "Who cares what he wants? It's what he needs."

So Calculating Swine had predetermined the next nine years of Leo's life. Jason hadn't had the grades to earn even a consideration at the Academy, which was definitely a blessing. His father had seen it as a betrayal.

"Why are you here, Dad?"

"I honestly don't know," his father said, after a long pause. "When I heard you turned yourself in, I was shocked. I guess I had to see it for myself."

"Well, freak show's over." Jason stood. He swallowed hard as his father also rose, and he straightened his spine to access every inch of his height. "When I get out of here, I'll do everything I can to make you stop hurting my brother."

His father gave a half-smile. "We'll see about that. And I'm not hurting Leo. I'm helping him, by the way."

Jason scoffed. "Whatever gets you through the night." Turning abruptly, he stalked off toward the waiting detective.

"That didn't look like a happy visit," Detective Easton said as they walked back to the holding cell.

"I need a drink," Jason said. He now actually welcomed the return to the holding cell. At least nobody was disappointed with him there.

25. Partners

The water rushed past his ears, obliterating all other noise.

Sensory deprivation was one of swimming's most appealing qualities for Leo. The worries of the day, the shouted voices around him, the disappointment of authority figures—all were far away once he submerged in the water and focused on swimming as fast as possible. He did a lot of thinking during practice, sometimes solving problems and sometimes making plans.

They were doing a set of ten one-hundreds, each on a faster interval, which made for a challenging aerobic workout. Eric led the fastest lane, and Leo went second.

He pushed off for his seventh one-hundred, his legs burning from exertion. *Long and smooth*, he told himself, taking the first length out relaxed. As he approached the wall, he whipped his body over in a swift flip turn and exploded off in a tight streamline. For the next three lengths, Leo focused on keeping a long stroke with a lively tempo and closed fast on Eric's feet. Both swimmers breathed hard at the wall and squinted at the pace clock. Leo only had little rest before he set off to repeat the process three more times.

Before number ten, Matt barked at him: "Make this one your best, Leo!"

Leo gritted his teeth as he pushed off for the last repeat. Lifting his head at the finish, he heard Matt holler "Fifty-two!" Leo grinned as he panted.

"Great set, guys." Matt nodded. "Fifty easy cool down."

In the lane next to Leo, Audrey still battled through her own set of ten one-hundreds, all breaststroke. Elaine led the lane doing backstroke.

Matt now hovered over their lane. "C'mon, Audrey, get these last two under one-eighteen."

As Leo finished an easy fifty backstroke, he heard Matt tell Audrey, "One-twenty-one. You can do better than that!"

"I'm *tired!*" she huffed before she pushed off on the last repeat.

Toward the end of practice, Matt surveyed the group. "Okay, I know you guys are itching for taper to start. Hang in there. For the last set we're doing partner pulls...*co-ed* partner pulls. Find your partner."

An excited buzz crossed the lanes as the swimmers paired up for the silly race. One swimmer would kick and the other pull, moving together as a unit. Leo submerged and crossed under the lane line to Audrey, grinning at his partner.

She smoothed her finger over the cut on his forehead. "It looks a lot better."

He glanced at Elaine and Alex in the next lane. "We're gonna win, Audrey." A competitive fire flared in his gut. "You think we'd be faster if you pulled or kicked?"

"Your upper body's stronger. You pull, and I'll kick."

Leo nodded.

"Fifty sprint partner pull," Matt said. "Let's have the puller float out in front and the kicker push off the wall on my signal."

There was more than a little splashing and giggling as the pairs got into position.

"Ready, hup!" Matt yelled.

Leo felt Audrey thrust off the wall behind him, and he pulled strong, quick strokes, striving to keep his legs still. It was an unnatural sensation, but so much fun.

Despite their best efforts, he could see Alex and Elaine nudge ahead in the adjacent lane. Somehow the awkward unit navigated a joint flip turn and headed back toward their coach. Leo touched the wall seconds after Alex, and he looked over with a smug grin.

"Leona, you're no match for me and my hag!"

Leo bared his teeth, breathing heavily. "Matt! We need a rematch."

"Anyone object to round two?" the coach asked. His eyebrows lifted when nobody complained. "Okay, we'll leave in one minute for a rematch."

Leo bobbed up and down. "This time I'll kick and you pull," he told Audrey. "We're gonna *win*."

Audrey smirked. "It's not that big a deal."

"How can you say that?" His jaw dropped. "Where's your Pensacola Panther pride?"

She laughed. "You're a dork." She got in position, and with twenty seconds to go, Leo tickled her feet. She shrieked.

Leo glared at Elaine in the next lane as she clutched Alex's ankles. "Bring it on, sistah."

She flashed an evil grin.

At the start, Leo's tired legs exploded, churning the water behind him and willing Audrey's body forward. They took a slight lead on the first length, and somehow they perfectly coordinated their joint flip turn. They sprinted back and managed to finish well ahead of the fag and his hag.

"Yesss!" Leo whooped, punching air. He grabbed Audrey in a hug and plunged her underwater with him. They exchanged goofy grins, staring at each other through their goggles.

He leaned forward and met her soft lips. Their first underwater kiss created bubbles that floated lazily to the surface. Audrey ran her fingers through his coarse hair, and they lingered until his lungs were bursting.

Surfacing and gasping for air, Leo waded to the wall. Matt beckoned, and Audrey came over too. "Hey, Leo, your brother just called. He wants you to pick him up at the airport."

"Jason's still in town?" Leo's brow furrowed. "Why does he need me to pick him up?"

"He mentioned something about returning a rental car."

"Huh. Thank you, sir." Turning away from Matt, Leo placed his hand on the small of Audrey's back. "I gotta run. Pick you up tomorrow at five fifteen?"

Audrey nodded, and Leo jogged into the locker room. *What did Jase need?*

Leo slowly cruised through passenger pick-up at Pensacola Regional Airport. Why was his brother still in town? He wasn't sure he wanted to see him.

After circling the airport twice, Leo finally found his brawny brother seated on a bench near curbside check-in. Jason wore the same wrinkled navy shirt and jeans he'd had on three days ago, and dark hollows smudged the skin beneath his eyes. He looked like someone who needed a friend, not someone who'd come to judge.

Time to man up and move forward, Leo told himself as he rolled down the window. He forced himself to smile. "Hey, big guy, got any Oxycontin you can sell me?"

Jason looked up and grinned as he sank into the passenger seat. "Watch out for those pills. I hear withdrawal's a bitch."

Easing the car back into the left lane, Leo wrinkled his nose. "Uh, I know Seattle's kind of earthy and granola, but they do believe in showers, right?"

"I'm surprised you can smell anything beyond the chlorine haze. This car stinks like a freaking swimming pool."

"Didn't have time to shower once I heard you needed a ride. I'll be in major trouble if I don't get home soon." Leo gave him a sideways glance. "So where to?"

"I'll take a wild guess that I'm unwelcome at the Scott home, so I'll see if I can stay at Marcus's for a while."

"Mr. Shale's?"

"Yeah. I know the way—he doesn't live all that far from Mom and Dad's. Here, take this exit." Jason gestured to the right.

"How do you know where he lives?"

Jason paused. "After Cruel Scumbag beat the crap out of me I hightailed it out of there and ran into Marcus. He's a really good guy. Where did *you* go that night, by the way? CS was ticked when you were gone."

"I went to Audrey's."

Jason nodded. "I meant to tell you earlier you got yourself a fine-looking girlfriend, Leo. Way to go."

Leo smiled. "Audrey's beautiful." He remembered the brush of her soft mouth on his for their submerged kiss. "On the inside too."

"Whoa, you got it bad." Jason laughed. "I hope she's going to the Academy too. You're so whipped you can't survive without her."

Leo's smile vanished. "She's going to FSU on a swimming scholarship." He stared at the road. "I can't believe I'm going to the Academy. Part of me always wanted to test myself there—you know, see if I could survive whatever they threw at me. But it'll suck to be away from Audrey."

"I'm sure you'll do great there, buddy." Jason squeezed his shoulder. "Pushup punishments will be like a breeze for you."

Leo blushed.

"Turn left here," Jason said. "What happened after you went to Audrey's? I was afraid of what CS would do when he found you… but I don't see any new bruises."

Leo sighed. "He barged in and told me there'd be 'consequences' for leaving the house without his permission. And then Audrey called him a jerk! It was so sweet. CS started threatening her, and I don't know what overtook me, but I attacked him."

Jason eyes grew big. "You did? What happened?"

"I got him good, Jase." A grin materialized.

"What, you weigh like a buck-sixty? How'd you pull that off?"

"I guess you started the job, and I finished it." Satisfaction warmed Leo's chest.

"I don't like this, Leo. He won't let this slide."

"Well, since he returned from Miramar it's been okay. As long as I keep giving him negative drug tests, he seems fine."

Jason scowled, clenching his fists. He continued giving curt directions to Marcus's apartment.

"Jason? How can you stay in Florida? Aren't you worried Dad will find out?"

"CS knows I'm staying," Jason said. "Before I returned the rental car, I was at the courthouse for my bail hearing, and Dad visited me there. I turned myself in."

Leo's eyes widened. "What? Why?"

Jason sighed. "The truth is I keep relapsing. I did it again after you got beat up. I felt awful I didn't protect you from CS."

"I don't need protection."

"You're *seventeen!* You might be all pleased with yourself for beating CS that one night, but he always wins. Don't you know that?" Jason's voice grew even louder. "He may end up killing you one day!"

Leo cowered.

Jason breathed out in a huff. "Sorry. I didn't mean to yell. I — I was trying to say I have to make amends to stop relapsing, and I can't make amends if I'm hiding from the law. My sentencing hearing's in March." They drove in silence for a while, then Jason pointed to the right. "There's Marcus's apartment building. Right here."

Leo pulled his beat-up car into the parking lot. "So you're, like, out on bail or something?"

"The judge didn't set bail because I turned myself in. And, the detective — she said the stolen cell phones mysteriously showed up after an anonymous tip." Jason turned to face his brother. "I think CS turned the phones in to the police. It had to be him, since he confiscated them from me. I'll never understand that man," he added.

Just then, a car pulled into the spot next to Jason, and the driver looked at them with surprise.

"C'mon," said Jason. All three got out of their cars, but Leo stayed at the driver's side door.

Jason asked, "Uh, Marcus, would it be okay if I stayed with you for a while? I, uh, I have nowhere else to go."

"Of course. You can stay as long as you need. What happened at the courthouse?"

"My sentencing hearing's March fourteenth. I'm charged with grand larceny, a third-degree felony."

"A felony?" Leo gasped.

Mr. Shale looked at Leo, who quickly tried to hide the scar on his forehead and bruise on his jaw. The counselor gave him a knowing look. "I knew I should've made a report."

"Don't!" Leo and Jason said at once.

"You're supposed to call right away," Jason added. "It's too late now."

"Please don't," Leo begged. "I hit my dad back this time, and he won't do it anymore. Please, it'll only make things worse, sir."

Jason nodded. "He's almost eighteen."

"Yeah." Leo glared. "If you make a report, I'll say I got into a fight at school. Mr. Morrison will back me up."

Mr. Shale expelled a long sigh. "We miss you at group, Leo."

"Yes, sir."

"Have you had cravings for the pain meds?"

"No, sir."

"That's bull, Leo."

Leo flinched and looked away. "I'm not going to use pills, Mr. Shale. I can't."

Mr. Shale sighed again. "If it gets bad, you call me." Leo nodded and took the offered business card. "My cell number's on there. Jason, you ready to go inside?"

"Let's do it."

"Wait, Jase!" Leo opened the car door and reached into the back seat. "Here's an extra shirt for you. It's all I have, but I can get you some more clothes if you want."

Jason took the shirt. "Thanks, bro. Don't tell CS where I'm staying. And give Mom a hug for me, will you?"

"When will I see you?"

"Once I figure out my next move, I'll find you." Jason's eyes locked on his, and Leo felt his worry mix with guarded optimism.

Maybe, just maybe, CS wouldn't always win.

26. Executive Officer of Cruelty

James beamed as he read the letter from Captain Payson. His department had achieved the highest safety and efficiency ratings for yet another quarter, and his CO was taking notice. James lingered on the praise: *excellent leadership, a demanding yet fair approach, deserving of greater responsibility.*

The only time he felt a modicum of peace were moments like these. Pursuit of perfection filled the rest of his days, and he was often enraged with himself and others for falling short.

Captain Payson's letter ended with a recommendation for promotion. James knew the report was making its way up the chain of command, so it was just a matter of time until the captain called to make it official. Good things were happening all around, and only two days remained until Leo's state swim meet.

With a start James realized it had been more than two months since he'd visited Denny Rose. How could he have let so much time pass? Failing to visit Denny meant failing as a leader. The glowing words he'd just read about himself suddenly disgusted him.

James jettisoned the letter and glanced at his watch. Visiting hours would end soon, so he rose quickly, snatching his cover from his desk. His long legs carried him across the base with purpose, and he returned a series of subordinates' salutes. James entered the prison and signed the visitor log, waiting only a few moments before a petty officer led him to the visiting booths.

MPs led a handcuffed Denny Rose to the other side of the glass, and James immediately noticed something different about his former second-in-command. Denny didn't bother to salute before sitting down in a huff.

James eyed him curiously, and both picked up the phones.

When Denny remained silent, James began the conversation. "You must be upset I haven't visited in a while. You know how things get in V-Four, Denny."

"That's not why I'm upset."

James realized he'd also dropped the *sir*. "Why are you upset, then?"

Denny paused. "It's not important. I—just don't visit me any more. It's not right."

"How can you say that?" James paled. "We're still friends, right?"

"No. Not anymore."

"What happened? What changed?" James stared at Denny's bald spot as he looked down, avoiding James's eyes. Then the likely reason for Denny's cold shoulder dawned on him, and his whole demeanor changed. "I see your daughter's been telling some tall tales."

Denny's head snapped up, eyes round.

"So I got a little physical with Leo." James shrugged. "What was I supposed to do? He was abusing prescription medication, and I was terrified for his health. The punishment was effective—he's been clean since then."

"That's not punishment! That's abuse."

James lowered his voice. "It is none of your business how I discipline my sons."

"So Jason got the same treatment?"

James didn't answer.

"It *is* my business when my daughter's involved. You stay away from her, James. And if I hear that anything else happens to Leo, I'll report this to Captain Payson."

"Don't mess with me, Denny, or you'll regret it. I can easily forbid Leo from seeing Audrey. I can make things much worse for you in here."

"Audrey and Leo are in *love*. You couldn't stand between them if you tried. I know they're young, but they're in love. As their fathers, we have to accept it and deal with it."

"I don't *have* to accept anything." James gripped the phone. "I make my own destiny."

Denny grimaced. "To think I used to *admire* you. What happened to your pride in your sons? Your great sense of humor?"

James felt his chest tighten.

"Get out of here," Denny hissed. "I never want to see you again."

Panic bloomed in James's heart, and his façade slipped. "Don't — don't say that, Denny. This'll blow over and everything will be fine again."

Denny gaped at him. "I have enough criminal friends right now." He gestured to the prison walls. "I don't need a child abuser in the mix. I don't care if you *are* the only officer who visits me in here — our friendship's over."

He returned the phone to its cradle and stood up. A guard approached instantly to lead him away.

James sat motionless after he left. How could Denny do that? He'd just lost his only friend. Blinking quickly, he shook it off. *His loss.*

27. Taper

Leo felt his muscles twitch as he visualized the last length of the one-hundred freestyle race.

Prone bodies littered the pool deck as Matt led the team through a visualization exercise in the warm March sunshine. Their last practice before departing for Ft. Lauderdale had included very little time in the water. Physically they'd trained all they could for the state meet, but mentally they still had work to be done. This was the time when mental toughness separated winners from losers.

Leo visualized sprinting to the wall. He imagined his lungs feeling ready to burst and his legs burning as adrenaline coursed through him. Lunging for the finish, Leo jammed into the touch pad at the end of his lane. As instructed, he shot up his hand when he felt himself finish.

His eyelids fluttered open, and he squinted in the brightness. A few teammates were still visualizing their races. He rubbed his eyes and stretched, his body all angles and elbows as he raised his arms to lengthen his triceps and laterals muscles.

Once most of the sleepy swimmers showed signs of life, Matt called, "Okay, let's get in. Two-hundred choice warm-up."

The coach winked as he passed. "Forty-four, Leo. Nice."

Leo grinned. Matt had clicked the stopwatch when Leo raised his hand. He'd just visualized swimming his goal time for the one-hundred free. He'd be *stoked* if he broke the forty-five-second barrier two days from now.

To his left, Leo noticed Audrey's eyes still closed. *She must really be getting into this visualization thing.* Leo leaned down and nudged her side.

Audrey woke with a start and looked momentarily confused.

He chuckled. "Did you fall asleep?"

"Yeah, I guess so." She yawned. "The last thing I remember was Matt telling me to feel warmth flow like liquid down my spine. Then I was out."

"Well, we're supposed to get in the water now, so you better wake up quick. Aren't you sleeping well?"

Audrey pursed her lips. "I've been really tired the past two weeks. You know how when you taper, sometimes you feel worse before you feel better? I think that's what's going on—my body finally catching up on rest or something."

Leo frowned. The team had been tapering for weeks. By now Audrey should've been feeling a burst of energy. Leo had been throwing open doors with vigor all week long. He helped Audrey to her feet and headed for his lane.

He chewed his goggle strap and laughed at Eric's scruffy face as he prepared to enter the water. They'd all soon be shaving their bodies to slice through the water with less resistance, and until then, Eric was sporting a thick Fu Manchu mustache.

The crisp water refreshed Leo as he jumped in to begin his eight lengths of warm-up. He felt high and light in the water—each stroke effortless yet powerful. Matt didn't have to yell because everyone knew this would be a brief, easy practice. And the pool was much less crowded as only about twenty swimmers had qualified for the state meet: an elite group who hoped to represent Pensacola High School proudly.

As he surfaced, Leo found Audrey hanging on the wall. She didn't look refreshed or powerful.

Matt put them through a series of stroke drills, then a pull set. Some completed the brief workout by swimming four easy lengths to cool down while the relay swimmers rehearsed their exchanges.

Leo joined Alex, Eric, and Jake behind the blocks to practice takeoffs for the four-hundred freestyle relay. As the fastest sprinter, Leo would swim the anchor leg. After the first three had practiced, Leo mounted the block, his myopic focus on Jake's approach. His hands dangled in front, almost guiding his teammate to him, then Leo swung his arms around and launched off the blocks in a tight pike. He entered the water with nary a splash.

"Team meeting in three minutes!" Matt announced.

"Matt?" Eric leaned on the block. "This practice's too short. I need more yardage."

Matt shook his head. "No you don't. I don't want you overworked like last year. We'll do some pace hundreds tomorrow when we get down to Ft. Lauderdale."

Eric scowled.

"Okay, here's your itinerary for the weekend." Matt distributed flyers to the gathered team. "Our flight leaves at ten thirty tomorrow morning. Make sure you're at the school by eight sharp so you can catch the bus to the airport. Once we arrive down south we'll grab a bite to eat, check in, and head over to the Hall of Fame Pool for practice. Room assignments are listed here."

Leo glanced down at the paper, relieved to discover he was rooming with Alex. Although Leo and Eric had been getting along better since January, his intensity sometimes distracted Leo and made him too nervous. Alex's goofy humor would keep Leo upbeat and loose. Leo knew his parents were also staying in the hotel. They'd made reservations long ago.

"Hey, roomie," Elaine giggled, grinning at Audrey, who had tucked herself under Leo's arm.

"*Hola, chica*," Audrey replied. "Get ready for some supersonic swimming."

Matt finished his instructions. "Drink plenty of water today and tomorrow, and scale back on portion sizes—we're doing less work, so you need fewer calories. Also, get some good sleep in the next two days. I want you resting as much as possible."

The team huddled. On the count of three came a collective shout: "Panthers!"

Leo grabbed his equipment and started toward the locker room with a happy glow, but he changed course when he saw Jason on the other side of the fence. He'd made it a habit to stop by practice when he could.

"Jase! Looks like both of us need showers again."

Jason smiled. "Yeah, it was a hot one in the warehouse today. Sure didn't miss this swampy weather when I lived in Washington, I tell ya. Gotta go soon and shower before I pick up Cameron."

Leo's eyebrows arched. "Wow, you guys are spending a lot of time together. It must be getting hot and heavy."

"Not as heavy as you and Audrey. Looked like you might go for it right there on the pool deck."

Leo felt his cheeks grow warm. "Well, she's sitting next to me in a *swimsuit*. This sport's like torture."

"Plus you're all energized from taper and everything." Jason winked.

"How is Cameron anyway?" Leo asked.

"Well, she's finally agreed to date me again, and I think she's pretty good. As good as you can be with a murdered dad."

Leo glanced behind him as Audrey disappeared into the locker room. "Must be tough with the murderer in prison just down the road."

Jason studied him for a moment. "Except Cam doesn't think Mr. Rose murdered her dad."

"Really?" Leo said, surprised. "Why not?"

Jason drew his hand down his mouth. "I shouldn't go into it. It's…it's not my story to tell. Anyway, I came by to wish you good luck on your meet. I know you'll do awesome."

Leo smiled, warmed by his brother's support. "I wish you could go."

"Yeah, well, I don't have money for a plane ticket, and there's no way I'm driving with Cold Spice and Mom." Jason met his eyes. "I've got an AA meeting tonight at ten. Why don't you sneak out and go with me?"

Leo immediately looked down. "I can't go…Matt just told us we need to rest, so I can't be out late."

"That's a new one." Jason shook his head. "At least you didn't use the old 'I have too much homework' or 'CS will kill me if he finds out' excuse again."

"C'mon, Jase. I don't want to think about this stuff now. I'm focusing only on swimming the next few days."

Jason shook his head. "You gotta stay vigilant. It can sneak up on you whenever you let your guard down."

"I've already got CS on my case every day about this. I don't need to hear it from you too."

"Okay, okay." Jason offered his palms in apology. "I'm sorry. I just worry about you. I want you out of that house, away from him."

"That makes two of us." Leo glanced at the digital readout on his brother's watch. "I better get home, and you shouldn't keep Cam waiting too long." He smirked. "Make sure you practice safe sex."

"TMI, bro." Then Jason seemed to think for a moment. "But where were you four years ago? You be safe too."

Leo watched Jason leave, wondering what the heck *that* comment meant.

28. Good Night and Good Luck

Her father leaned in closer, his eagerness apparent even through the prison phone's tinny distortion of his voice. "What was Marcie's time at districts?"

Audrey smiled. "Marcie went two-oh-five and I went two-oh-six in the two-hundred IM at districts. But she swims faster in season. I'm a better taper swimmer, so I should be able to beat her."

"Good. Remember to get after the backstroke, Audrey. No Sunday strolls."

She rolled her eyes. "I will, Dad."

He nodded solemnly, his eyes shining.

Sensing her father's impending melancholy, Audrey switched the topic. "*¿Caminas mucho?*"

It took a second for him to adjust to her shift to Spanish. "Uh, *sí*. I walk a lot."

"*Eso es bueno. Es bueno para la salud del bebé.*"

Her father gave her a quizzical look. "I didn't catch that."

"Oh, I was making a stupid joke about walking being good for the baby—remember? You need to work harder on your Spanish, Dad! That was pretty easy vocabulary."

"Yes, ma'am." He seemed to force a smile.

"Aren't you studying Spanish anymore?"

He averted his eyes. "They…they took the books away."

"Why?"

He sighed and seemed to struggle for words. "It's okay, Audrey girl. Please don't worry about it. How's your mother doing?"

Audrey pulled her cell phone from her purse. "I checked with the MP, and he said I could call Mom while I was here, so maybe we can all talk together this way."

"That's so thoughtful. Thank you."

"No big deal, Dad." She sat with a phone in each hand and grinned when her mother answered. "Hey, Mom. I'm here with Dad. We thought we'd call and say hi."

"Wonderful!" her mother said. "How's he doing? Oh, hey — make sure you get a good breakfast on Friday."

Audrey rolled her eyes a second time. "Mom, Dad just went over race strategy, and now you're giving me nutrition tips. I *have* a coach, you know."

"But you still need your parents," her mother insisted. "Listen, I feel awful about this, honey, but they're not giving me time off for your meet. I won't be able to make it."

Audrey swallowed. "That's okay, Mom. I know you'd be there if you could."

"*Sorry,*" her father mouthed, catching her eye.

Her blinks came rapid-fire as she tried not to look at him. "So, um, Mom, how do you like the new hospital?"

Getting herself back under control, Audrey acted as a relay between her parents until her mother had to say goodbye.

"I'll be thinking about you every minute this weekend, Audrey girl," her dad said. "Just do your best and have fun, okay?"

"Okay, Dad. I'll be thinking about you too."

Her father craned his neck toward the MP on his left. "Permission to stand, sir?" The MP nodded, and her father turned back to her. "Honey, I can't be at your meet, but I wanted to tell you good luck to you in my own way. They'll probably haul me out of here when I try this, so I'll tell you goodbye now too. I love you, Audrey girl."

She tilted her head, watching him rise.

He cleared his throat and burst into Audrey's favorite cheer. He punched his arms in the air, then straight ahead, then scooped down and gyrated his hips as he chanted:

Say can you dig it!
Our team's got soul, soul
Our team's got might, might
Our team's gonna win, win,
This meet tonight!

Giggles spilled out of her as she watched. Had he been rehearsing in his cell? Before he got through the first verse, the MP approached with a disgusted look and yanked him toward the exit.

"Audrey!" her father yelled, laughing despite being manhandled.

She could barely hear him through the glass.

"I love you, Audrey girl. Good luck!"

She watched him being carted away, a goofy grin on her face.

Leo swung open the front door and jumped when he almost stepped right into his father. "Dad!"

Chilly Sourpuss's face hardened. "You're five minutes late."

Leo bit his lip as he closed the door "I'm sorry, sir. Matt had a team meeting after practice to give us our itinerary for the state meet."

"Let me see it."

Leo handed him the paper and waited.

"Your mother and I arrive at nineteen-hundred tomorrow," he said after a moment.

"Yes, sir." Leo's chest loosened. He'd have almost an entire day free of CS.

"How was your practice tonight?"

"Fine, sir. I think our four-hundred free relay's going to be good this year."

"That Jake kid's inexperienced. He'd better not screw it up for all of you." His father stood up a bit taller. "I'm headed to the office to get some work done before I miss two days for your meet. I'll drug test you before I go."

"Yes, sir." Leo reached for the specimen cup that had appeared in his father's hand.

His father hovered outside the bathroom door as Leo provided the sample.

"Here you go, sir."

CS took the cup, and Leo braced for the usual list of questions.

"Any chance there'll be opiates in here?"

"No, sir."

"Because if you're going to pop positive, you'll be in a lot less trouble if you tell me now."

"Understood, sir. I haven't taken any pills."

His father gave a satisfied nod. "I'll probably see you tomorrow night before the meet, but I wanted to wish you good luck, Leo."

"Thank you, Dad." Leo searched his father's multihued eyes for any hint of feeling. He could draw no firm conclusion before CS turned to go.

His father's departure typically cued a deep exhale, and Leo felt tension drain from his shoulders once he stood alone. After a moment he loped down the stairs to the empty kitchen. *Mom must be at one of her classes.* He scrounged around the refrigerator until he located some leftover lasagna, which he piled onto a plate and slid into the microwave. Enjoying the peace of the empty house, Leo munched his dinner and watched TV.

Later that evening, as he packed his swim bag in his room, he was overcome by excess energy and emotion when one of his favorite songs came on. He cranked up the volume.

He gave a fantastic air band performance, lost in the lyrics, until he turned to find his mother standing in his bedroom doorway. Registering her frown, Leo clicked off the music immediately.

His mother's face was flushed, likely from the exertion of climbing the stairs.

"I didn't hear you come in, ma'am."

"No wonder—the walls were shaking," she said sternly.

"Sorry, Mom. I really like that song. I guess I got carried away."

"What do you like about the song?" she asked suddenly.

Leo's brow furrowed. His mother hadn't asked him a question like that since before the accident, and he wasn't quite sure how to approach her now that she was actually acting like his parent again. She'd changed a lot since January—replacing some of her Oxycontin doses with acupuncture, massage, and yoga, and updating her teaching certificate at the community college.

"Uh, I don't know...I guess the stripped down guitar riffs at the beginning...and the hollowness of the lead singer's voice. They make it really intense."

"Go on." She nodded.

He swallowed. "And...the lyrics...they're, like, so poetic. She says she's going under, but you just know she's fighting like crazy. She won't let them get the best of her."

His mother's lips trembled. "You're talking about...your relationship with your father?"

Leo looked away.

"I remember the reason I dragged myself up here," she said after a moment. "Well, besides the opportunity to learn such fascinating information about a song you like!" Her smile faded. "The kitchen's a disaster zone. I want you to put your dirty dishes in the dishwasher."

Leo hesitated. He'd become used to doing what he pleased in the rare moments when CS wasn't around. But he couldn't refuse her. "Yes, ma'am. I'll get those dishes right now. Do you need any help down the stairs?"

"That's all right, sweetheart. Just come down when you've finished your packing." As she turned to go, struggling a bit with her canes, she added, "Leo? Good luck at the meet. I'm behind you one hundred percent."

"Thanks, Mom." Leo felt butterflies dive-bomb his stomach. He was ready to swim fast. He knew it.

29. Shaving Party!

A vibration on the hotel bed jarred Audrey awake. She opened her eyes to find Elaine bouncing like an ADHD poster child. The energizing effects of taper had made her even more boisterous.

"Wake up, girl! Time to shave down."

Audrey groaned, rolled over, and stuffed a pillow over her head. But the pillow didn't stay there for long.

"If you wake up, Audrey, I'll help you shave those hard-to-reach spots."

She bolted upright and saw Leo and Alex grinning at her. Leo's lanky body slouched against the fake wood dresser, and he held a Styrofoam container.

Audrey finger-combed her hair as she climbed off the mattress and sniffed the food. "How was dinner?"

"Blech." Alex stuck his tongue out. "If I have to eat bland pasta one more time, I'll gag."

"Alexa, not everyone has your snobby culinary tastes," Leo said.

Audrey had stayed behind with a stomachache while the team went to dinner. Her abdominal pain had ended once she was able to throw up, but then dread had set in. Was she getting the flu right before her big meet? Audrey had simply decided she wouldn't let illness impede her swimming performance. And now she'd almost forgotten about getting sick. She was ravenous.

Closing in on Leo, Audrey reached for the container. "What'd you order for me?"

He pulled it from her reach. "You think this food's for *you*? It's for me, for when I get hungry later."

"Hand it over! I'm starved!"

Leo transferred the food from one hand to another behind his back as she lunged for it.

"Give it to me!" She lost her footing and careened into him.

He gave a low laugh as he held her in his arms, the food now safe on the dresser. "I should know better than to stand between a hungry swimmer and food."

"Darn straight." She leaned in for a kiss. "I think I'll have you for my appetizer."

"*Ugh.*" Alex winced. "I know when I'm not wanted. C'mon, Laney, let's go to my room."

"Okay, let me grab my razor."

While Elaine rifled around in her bag, Audrey scooped up the container and sat on the bed. Soon she was shoving forkfuls of pasta into her mouth.

"I'll be right back." Leo followed Alex and Elaine out the door.

When Leo returned, he held electric clippers. Audrey continued inhaling linguini carbonara as she watched Leo buzz a path through his tightly coiled black hair.

"Is Alex shaving his head this year?"

Leo chuckled. "No way. Alex says a shaved head looks stupid on him."

"It is all about fashion," Audrey said with a laugh.

After guzzling water, she flipped on some music videos on the way to the bathroom, where she set out towels, shaving cream, and her razor.

As she peeled off her clothes and stepped into an old training swimsuit, she heard Leo's voice. "Are you feeling better?"

"Yep, that nap was awesome."

She emerged from the bathroom to stare at Leo's newly shorn head. His face appeared almost gaunt, and his blue eyes popped with an even brighter intensity. He looked like a badass, which would come in handy trying to intimidate competitors behind the blocks. She smiled. "You said something about helping me shave?"

Leo's eyes floated down her body, and she hoped her melon-colored suit showed off her suntan. He took a step toward her and cocked one eyebrow. "Yeah, you're pretty hairy, so it'll probably take two of us to do the job."

Mouth open, she pushed him with mock distain, then moved her hands down to his waist and lifted his T-shirt over his head. It fell to the floor in a heap. Audrey sauntered into the bathroom, glancing behind her with beckoning look. She turned on the faucet in the tub while Leo stepped out of his cargo shorts and joined her, clad only in his boxers.

They sat on the edge of the tub, with the pounding water drowning out the sound of the television. "Let's shave our legs first," Audrey suggested.

Leo seemed entranced as she soaped her legs. He squeezed shaving cream onto his palm, and the calming scent of lavender filled the air.

"Gimme that beautiful leg." He placed Audrey's foot in his lap and smoothed the shaving cream over her leg. Audrey closed her eyes as Leo's fingers skated across her skin. She dipped her razor into the tub and slowly dragged it through the foam, leaving sleek smoothness in the sharp blade's wake.

"Yay, I get to be a girl again!" Audrey smiled as she rinsed her razor and went back to work. "It sucks not getting to shave all season long."

"The sacrifices of swimmers," Leo mused. "Finally my sweet hairball gets to shave her legs."

She whisked her hand through the water and splashed him. "Get going, baldy. *You're* the hairy one."

"Okay, okay." He lathered cream over his legs, extending them into the tub with his feet toward Audrey.

Audrey turned off the tap and hummed along with the music floating in from the television as she started on her arm. "Are you nervous?" she asked.

"Yeah, I'm pretty jacked. You?"

"I definitely feel butterflies. But I'm also kind of enjoying this—our last state meet. I want to go out with a bang."

"That's what *she* said."

She rolled her eyes. "I'm dating a ten-year-old." A few minutes later her legs were slick and slippery. "Leo? Will you, um, will you shave my back?"

He sighed dramatically. "I guess. If I have to. C'mere, little swimmer."

She slid down the edge of the tub and swiveled her back to him, shyly pulling down her swimsuit to her waist. There was hardly any hair on her back, but you could never be too careful, so swimmers shaved it *all*.

Audrey closed her eyes as Leo massaged shaving cream over her back. He slowly drew the razor over her skin, and she shivered despite the heat.

"You're so beautiful," he murmured.

She reveled in the glide of the blade across her skin, interspersed with light splashes of water. Her eyes were still closed when she heard him say, "Okay, I think I'm done here, but let's make sure your entire back's smooth."

Leo skimmed his hands across the small of her back, using gentle pressure as he massaged up to her neck and shoulders. Audrey moaned. The sound increased in volume as Leo planted wet kisses down her spine.

Turning to face him, she pressed her lips to his. Leo let the razor drop into the water, freeing his hands to embrace her in a fervent meeting of lips and tongues.

Suddenly there was a pounding on the door, and their kisses were replaced by looks of alarm. Audrey instinctively pulled up her suit straps. "Who could that be?"

"Leo? Are you in there?" came a deep voice.

Leo's eyes widened. "That's CS!"

Audrey scrambled out of the tub. "Hide in here. I'll get rid of him."

"No, Aud. Maybe he'll go away if you don't answer."

More pounding at the door soon squashed that hope. Audrey stepped out of the bathroom and tossed Leo his clothes. They exchanged looks of desperation as she closed him in.

Audrey trembled as she opened the door and looked up at Leo's father. She hardly ever saw him in civilian clothing. She followed his gaze as he scanned down her swimsuit and noticed haphazard patches of shaving cream on her arms.

CS cleared his throat. "Miss Rose, I'm trying to locate Leo."

Smiling sweetly, Audrey shrugged. "He's not here, sir. I've been shaving down and haven't seen him since he brought me some dinner."

"You didn't eat with the team?"

"I've been feeling a little sick."

He took a step back from her. "I stopped by Leo's room, but he wasn't there." His frown turned into a conspiratorial grin. "I think I interrupted something going on between Alex and Elaine. I didn't know they were dating."

Audrey suppressed a laugh. "That'd be news to me too."

"Well, if you see Leo, tell him to report to room three twelve."

"Yes, Commander." Audrey shut the door and leaned back against it. She realized she was shaking.

Now dressed, Leo stuck his head out of the bathroom. He crossed the room in an instant and swept her up. "You're an awesome girlfriend."

Feeling steadier and calmer in his arms, Audrey giggled. "Guess who CS thinks is dating?"

Leo pulled back and stared into her eyes. "Who?"

"Alex and Elaine."

"Oh, I'll make sure they never hear the end of *that*." Leo let go of Audrey to grab the ice bucket. "I'll tell CS I was getting ice…Mr. Cold-as-ice Shark will certainly understand that. I should get going. What room number did he say?"

"Three twelve."

"Drat, I really wanted to finish this shaving party…" His eyes twinkled. "But I better go." He leaned in for a lingering goodbye kiss, then held their foreheads together for a moment. "Sweet dreams, Audrey."

She smiled. "Sweet gold medal dreams, Leo."

He opened the door, peeked into the hallway, and was gone.

30. The State Meet, Day One

As soon as Leo jumped into the crowded warm-up lane, he grinned. He loved the feel of his shaved body. Last night he'd shivered as he slid into bed, the smoothness of his skin gliding under the covers. Now surrounded by cold water, every nerve ending in his skin tingled.

Popping to the surface, Leo took only a few strokes before he arrived at the opposite end of the pool. Swimmers littered the wall, draped over the gutter, and Leo squeezed in a flip turn.

The sun had decided to grace the Ft. Lauderdale International Hall of Fame Pool. The meet format for Friday and Saturday involved morning preliminary races, which would qualify swimmers for evening finals.

Almost finished with his warm-up, Leo waited in a line behind lane one to do a sprint off the blocks. Surveying the scene around him, he saw a familiar face. "Hey, Gary." Leo smiled, shaking the hand of his closest competitor from St. Petersburg.

"How you been, Leo?" Gary Gable's shoulder muscles rippled as he gripped Leo's hand. Gary was shorter and more compact, and his ebony skin stretched taut over his pectorals. Their minority status in a sea of white swimmers had helped forge a friendship between them.

"I hear you got a scholarship to UF," Leo said. "Congratulations."

"Thanks, man. And where are you headed?"

"To the Naval Academy. I hope I get time to train with the crazy schedule they have for plebes."

"That's so awesome. With all this Mideast stuff going on, I'm really impressed you'd do that. You're a better man than me."

"We'll see 'bout that. Who's gonna win the fifty this year?"

Gary grinned. "It'll be one of us touching out the other by mere hundredths."

"So it'll be just like last year's meet then," Leo said as his turn arrived. "Good luck, dude."

After his warm-up, Leo grabbed his towel, water bottle, and racing suit from his bag. He noticed Matt timing Audrey on some pace fifties as he headed for the locker room. They appeared to be having an intense discussion, and Matt had leaned down close to the water.

Leo's eyes took a moment to adjust to the cool semidarkness of the locker room. Ducking into an open stall, he stripped off his drag suit and stepped into his high-performance racing suit. Aware of its hefty price tag, he was careful with the technical material. If he ripped the suit before getting even one race in, Cheap Spender wouldn't be happy.

The meet began with the girls' 200 medley relay. Elaine, Audrey, Susan, and Kelly gathered behind the blocks, looking jittery yet optimistic about making the top eight. Sure enough, they gave a strong performance—an auspicious start for the team.

After her cool down, Audrey came to sit next to Leo, whose first race wouldn't begin until she'd completed both her morning swims.

"How was your split in the relay?" he asked.

"Okay—twenty-nine-two. I want to get under twenty-nine tonight."

"I thought you stayed underwater for your pullout a tad too long."

"Hmm...I'll practice some starts tonight and play around with it a little. How'd you feel in warm-up?"

"Pretty good." Leo smiled. He'd actually felt amazing but didn't want to jinx himself by saying it out loud.

"Well, I better go for my IM."

"What's your heat?"

"Heat three, lane four," she told him over her shoulder.

"Kick some butt!"

She looked back with an impish smile.

Leo watched her fidget as she approached the blocks. Where was her confidence? She'd won this event at last year's meet.

"Hey, Leo."

He looked up to see a blonde hovering over him. "Oh, uh, hi, Marcie."

Marcie Sayer was Audrey's nemesis in the 200 IM and 100 breast-stroke, and he hoped she wouldn't catch him talking to her. Audrey claimed Marcie hit on him at meets.

"You're lookin' good, Leo," Marcie said with half-closed eyelids. She licked her lips. Did she actually think she could seduce him?

He tried to think of a response. "What heat are you in?"

"I'm in heat...heat four." She leaned closer, the wet strands of her hair almost brushing his shoulder. "Right after Audrey's heat. Which one of us do you predict will win tonight?"

"Audrey, of course."

Marcie pulled back, emitting a slight hiss. "We'll see about that."

After she walked away, Leo snuck a look at Audrey and felt relieved to find her oblivious to the interaction. Audrey stretched behind the blocks, her graceful limbs like a ballerina's. A tense ballerina.

Leo watched her take the race out smooth and easy, but she seemed to fall off the pace. The other girls began to close the distance, and Audrey barely held them off to win the heat. Leo looked up to the clock and saw 2:03, a full three seconds off Audrey's best. He knew she'd be disappointed.

Audrey grasped the gutter for a few seconds, her back heaving. She dragged herself out then almost stumbled to the cool-down pool. Marcie's heat started, and exactly two minutes later it ended. Audrey wouldn't be happy to know her rival had bested her by three seconds in the prelims.

Ten minutes later Audrey sat back down next to him.

"What did Matt say?" Leo asked.

"He said I died on the breast and free. I *told* him I didn't feel right in warm-up!"

"It'll go better tonight. I gotta get ready for my fifty, okay?"

Audrey nodded. "I hope your swim goes better than mine, Leona."

He laughed and grabbed his goggles.

Despite her best hopes, Audrey stared at the clock, dumbstruck after her swim in the evening finals. Had she really just swum that slowly? Last year she'd won the 200 IM in two minutes. This year, her senior year, the year she was supposed to have the meet of her life, she swam a 2:04 and ended up in third place. Marcie had swum an incredible 1:58, setting the Florida state record, and a freshman from Sarasota had snuck in for second place with a 2:03. Not only had Audrey failed to defend her title, she hadn't even finished in second place, which lost valuable points for her team.

Instead of cooling down after her race, she stormed over to her coach.

Matt didn't meet her eyes. "Go cool down."

"Won't you even *tell* me what went wrong in that race?" She could hear the shrillness in her voice.

"We'll talk after you cool down." He turned to focus on the next heat.

"You didn't taper me right. My meet's ruined."

Matt turned back to her. "Listen to me. You have races tomorrow, so you need to work out the lactic acid. I know you're disappointed, but sometimes swimmers have bad races. It happens. And the good swimmers don't sit down and pout — they move on, and they cheer for their teammates. You're our team captain, Audrey. Please act like it."

He walked away, leaving her standing alone with her cheeks on fire. Her eyes welled up. She'd worked so hard! She'd tapered like she always did, yet she felt exhausted. Her entire senior year was a complete waste.

Just then Leo draped his arm around her and guided her away from the pool, into the evening shadows.

She sniffed. "Don't you have to get ready for your race?"

"I've got a few seconds. I'm so sorry you had a bad swim."

She continued to cry. "That's not the worst part. I just had a complete temper tantrum. I told Matt he *ruined* my taper." Tears flowed. "My dad would be so embarrassed right now."

"Shh." Leo scooped her into a hug. "Your dad's always proud of you, you know that. Just go cool down and apologize to Matt. He knows you didn't mean it."

She nodded.

"You're upset because you care so much about swimming. There's nothing wrong with that."

Audrey took a deep breath and gently pushed Leo away. "Thank you. Now go get ready for your fifty." She attempted a smile. "Be a madman out there. This is your race!"

Leo held her hand for a moment, searching her eyes, before reluctantly letting go.

Once Leo was in place behind the blocks, he checked the cooldown pool and was relieved to see Audrey slide into the water. He had no idea why she was having a bad meet. Elaine's speedy backstroke split had given the Pensacola girls' 200 medley relay a third-place finish earlier in the evening. Audrey had a decent breaststroke leg on the relay—nothing stellar but nothing awful. Yet her IM was clearly off.

Gary grinned at him from lane four, and Leo returned the smile from his position in lane five. Both Gary and Leo had swum their 50 free in 20.22 during the preliminary heats. It was a personal best for Leo.

Listening to his teammate's iPod, Leo jammed to a pounding beat and felt ready. Then he glanced up to the stands and saw his father glaring at him. CS probably wasn't too pleased with Leo hugging Audrey on the pool deck. At lunch his father had hinted that Leo shouldn't surround himself with "losers" whose slow swimming might be infectious. He'd been relieved that his father hadn't directly ordered him to stay away from Audrey, but that action might be forthcoming after her performance tonight.

He tried to put his father out of his mind, instead focusing on stretching his hamstrings. Matt had told him to concentrate on his breathing and repeat the word "bullet" to himself behind the blocks. Leo wanted to get off the blocks like a bullet fired from a gun. A perfect start and turn were essential.

He took deep, energizing breaths. *Bullet...bullet...bullet.* He shook out his limbs and jumped a few times.

The starter called them to the block, and the cheers gave way to deafening silence.

"Take your mark."

Leo crouched to grab the front of the block, his feet spread in a track-start position. When he heard the electronic beep he rocketed off the blocks but came to a halt underwater when the beeps sounded in a rapid-fire staccato, indicating a false start.

The field of eight popped the surface and nervously made their way back to the blocks. Whoever false started would be disqualified, and every swimmer prayed it wasn't him.

Leo pulled himself out and readjusted his goggles, resuming his deep breathing and repeating his trigger word. He stared ahead at the water, funneling all his energy and attention to one focal point.

The starter walked over to the referee to compare notes. Nodding, the starter headed toward the lanes. As he passed lane eight, seven, six, and began slowing down near lane five, Leo stopped breathing. He hadn't false started, had he?

When the starter passed his lane, Leo was flooded with relief, but his heart sank when the starter stopped in front of Gary. Gary grimly nodded and grabbed his towel. Leo's toughest competitor had just been disqualified.

As Gary passed, Leo grabbed his arm. "I'm so sorry."

"It happens." Gary's disappointment was obvious, but he was trying to be a good sport.

"Race won't be the same without you, man."

"Get it done, Leo," Gary said. "I'll be cheering for you."

The swimmers stepped back up to the blocks, with the block for lane four noticeably empty.

When the electronic beep sounded, Leo once again launched himself and sliced into the cool water. Instinct took over as he poured all of his effort into lightning fast arm-strokes and an explosive kick. He took only one breath, as he'd planned, and drove to the finish.

Leo looked up at the clock and pumped his fist in the air when he saw his time: 20.09, another personal best. He was state champion in the 50 free!

His teammates cheered riotously, and Leo found Audrey clapping with a look of sheer joy on her face. They shared a grin.

Forgetting for a moment about all of the misery of the past year, Leo lazily floated on his back, enjoying his accomplishment.

On the van ride back to the hotel, Leo still basked in a happy glow, now holding Audrey by his side. Matt answered his cell phone, then handed it to Leo.

He'd managed to avoid seeing his parents after the meet, but CS had still tracked him down. "This is Leo."

"How was your fifty, bro?"

"Jason!" Leo's eyes crinkled with a smile. "You called."

"Of course I called, idiot. So, how'd you do? Don't leave me hanging!"

"It was awesome, Jase. Twenty-oh-nine, my best time."

"Sweet! Did ya win?"

"Yup. It kind of sucked because Gary false started. Maybe if he was in the race we could've both broken twenty."

"Well, that's something to look forward to for college, I guess. Under twenty seconds? That's seriously fast, Leo."

"It would be *incredible* to swim that fast. How's everything at home?"

Jason paused. "Pretty good. I'm with Cam, and we're headed for some pizza. Hope day two goes even better. Wish I could be there, man."

"Thanks, Jase."

Audrey watched Leo beam as he handed Matt's cell phone back to him. This was his moment, and she was thrilled for him. He'd certainly earned it.

When they arrived at the hotel, Audrey sent Leo on ahead without her. While the other swimmers piled out of the van, she stayed and waited for her coach, who was gathering his clipboard and other belongings from the space between the front seats.

"Um, Matt, could I talk to you for a second?"

"Sure, what's up?" Matt sat with her in the front row of van seats.

She took a deep breath, trying to think of what her father would do — what Leo had encouraged her to do. "I'm sorry for yelling at you like that. I was being a crappy team captain."

"Apology accepted. I've seen a lot of swimmers bounce back from a bad first day, Audrey."

She said nothing, feeling tears just below the surface, threatening to erupt.

"I have a story for you." Matt skated his hand through his surfer-blond hair. "There was once a boy growing up in Louisville, Kentucky. His family was poor. He was jealous of all the other kids in the neighborhood riding their bikes, because his family couldn't afford to buy him one."

Audrey wondered what this had to do with swimming.

"When he was old enough, he got a job bagging groceries, and he saved his money until he had enough to buy his own bike. And what a bike he bought, I tell you — a beautiful red bicycle he proudly rode around the neighborhood. Unfortunately, one morning he woke up and discovered it had been stolen."

"Aw."

"When the boy grew up, he started boxing. He worked hard at developing his skills, and started winning every bout. Before he faced an opponent in the ring, he'd stare across at him and think, 'I bet that's the guy who stole my bike!' And Muhammad Ali became a pretty good boxer in his day."

Audrey's eyes widened. "Muhammad *Ali?* Is that a true story?"

"True story. Audrey, all you can do is give your best effort. Now go get some rest, and tomorrow I want you to go get your bike back!"

"Okay!" Audrey grinned and climbed out of the van.

Matt wrapped his arm around her shoulders as they walked into the hotel, and the pressure on her chest lightened a little. She only wished her father could be there.

31. The State Meet, Day Two

Spectators filled the stands to capacity for finals on Saturday night. Before the meet began, it was time to honor the senior swimmers on their last night of high school competition.

Leo and Audrey stood with Elaine, Alex, and Eric representing the senior class of the Pensacola High School Panthers. Their team surrounded them in a sea of purple and gold, congratulating them and handing them bouquets of flowers.

Leo smirked as Alex hugged Elaine. "Hey, I know you two are lovers, but keep it PG — there are kids in the stands."

Alex laughed. "Your dad's such a twit."

Leo led the way when the announcer called for the seniors to line up. "Can't wait for that free relay, dude," Eric said, falling into place behind him.

Leo nodded. "It's gonna rock." Leo had swum a strong 45.2 in the morning's 100 free preliminary, which seeded him first for the finals, with Gary close behind at 45.4. Eric had had a breakthrough performance in the 500 freestyle, and his 4:35 nosed him into eighth place. He'd made the finals for the first time.

After instructing the crowd to hold their applause until all the names had been read, the announcer eventually got to Pensacola's senior squad. "Eric Alexander...Alex Bradbury...Elaine Ferris... Audrey Rose...Leo Scott."

The five seniors stepped forward, hugging their flowers and surveying the crowd. As the announcer went on to the next school, Leo sensed Audrey's sadness about her parents' absence. He snuggled closer. "I'll be your family tonight," he whispered.

"It's hard to believe high school's almost over," Audrey said. "It's gone fast."

"For me, the first two years kind of dragged," Leo said. "I just wanted to go to college and get away from CS. But then I met you, and now I never want high school to end."

Audrey reached for Leo's hand. "That's one of the nicest things anyone's ever said to me."

His gaze swept down her body. "How'd we meet again? Oh, yeah, you were skinny dipping."

Audrey chuckled. "You'll never let me live that down."

"I *do* think we need a repeat performance before we graduate. Maybe you can finally earn a ten for your synchronized routine."

"Or maybe we can score another way," Audrey countered.

Leo's eyes lit up. "How am I supposed to focus on swimming when you say something like *that?*"

"Ladies and gentlemen, your seniors!" the announcer finished. Thunderous applause rang out in the gathering night.

A few events into the meet, Leo stood behind lane four, listening to Elaine's iPod. He imagined himself exploding off of the block, and his heart thumped by the time he opened his eyes. Smoothing his hands down his sleek black suit, Leo gulped deep breaths and pressed his goggles into his eyes. Next to him, Gary was in the middle of his own pre-race routine.

The starter called the heat up to the blocks. After a clean start, Leo broke out of his streamline a touch ahead of the field. Gary soon caught up during the straightaway, but Leo nudged ahead on the turn. The two swam neck and neck the first three laps. On the third turn, Leo edged in front of Gary once again only to lose his edge as both came barreling toward the wall in their last length.

It was difficult to know whose hand first reached electronic touch pad. Panting, Leo searched for the clock to find Gary in first place with 44.92 and himself in second with a 44.98.

Leo reached across the lane line to grasp Gary's hand. "We both broke forty-five!"

He was genuinely happy for Gary after his disqualification in the fifty. Swimming faster than ever before was really the name of the game, regardless of which place he finished.

Audrey's voice was hoarse from all the cheering. After her talk with Matt, she'd decided if she wasn't swimming fast, she'd at least do her best to help her teammates. Beaming with pride for her boyfriend, she watched him head to the cool-down pool while she gathered her cap and goggles to ready herself for the 100 breaststroke.

Audrey passed Marcie already in place behind lane four, looking carefree and relaxed. *Wench.* Audrey waggled her fingernails, painted gold with purple polka dots, at Marcie as she removed her team jacket and began stretching. This was her last race of the meet. Though she'd relinquished her title as state champion in the 200 IM, she was hell-bent on getting her bike back in her best race. Taking a deep breath, Audrey made one final adjustment to her cap as she stepped up on the block.

"Take your mark," the starter announced, and then they were off. All was quiet underwater as Audrey completed one pull and one kick, but she popped up high out of the water to piercing cheers. She could make out some teammates at the end of her lane, screaming at her to speed it up at the turn.

Audrey had no idea where she was in the field. Her quick stroke thrust her body forward with each glide, spearing the water. During the fourth length she felt her energy fading, but she willed her body forward, surviving on guts and anger to finish her race. She touched the wall and scrambled to see the clock.

Her time was 1:02.1 and her place was first. Audrey nearly fainted with relief. It wasn't her best time, but she'd defended her title, and after a horrible IM, she'd take it.

Marcie didn't even look at her, just quickly popped out of the pool and stormed away. As Audrey pulled herself out, she felt a stab of pain in her abdomen. The pain grew in intensity, and she barely made it to the locker room before she doubled over in agony. Feeling the return of nausea, Audrey shut herself in a bathroom stall, trying not to moan out loud. She wondered if her period was finally starting — but she'd never had cramps like this before.

As a moan escaped, she prayed for the pain to disappear. Eventually she turned to throw up in the toilet. She was shaky and unsteady, but she began to feel better once she vomited. Resting her head against the cool stall, she reviewed the last few days. Was it the flu? She didn't think so. Was it food poisoning? No, it couldn't be...the nausea wouldn't come and go, and none of her teammates were sick.

Audrey racked her brain to find what was making her sick and ruining her meet. She had so looked forward to going out with a bang her senior year, just like Leo. Suddenly she gasped and splayed out a hand on each side of the stall. She knew the source of her fatigue, nausea, and cramping. She knew the exact source of her pain.

Leo scanned the team area for Audrey. Where the heck was she? She'd won her race more than twenty minutes ago, and he still hadn't congratulated her. Now it was time for his relay.

"Laney!" he called. "Have you seen Audrey?"

"Nope. Maybe she's in the locker room?"

"Can you go check on her? She looked like she was in pain or something after her race."

"Sure. Good luck on your relay." Elaine turned toward the locker room, and Leo joined his teammates for the last event of the meet. Jake, the scrawny sophomore was listening to his headphones, staring off into space. Then he grinned and jumped up. "Yo, check it — I love this song!" He grooved to a beat only he could hear as the three older swimmers stared. "It's Weird Al!" he cried. "*Perform This Way.*"

Alex recoiled. "That's a parody of *Born This Way!* How dare he mock Gaga?" Alex lunged for Jake's mp3 player, but he swiftly eluded him. Alex chased the weaving and bobbing sophomore around the pool deck until an official yelled at them for running.

Eric grinned. "I'll miss this."

Leo smiled. "Me too." He beckoned them. "Let's huddle up." The four swimmers formed a circle and slung arms around shoulders. Leo made eye contact with each teammate, one at a time. "For three of us, it's our last race ever as Panthers, and I want to make it incredible. Let's lay it all on the line. Put it all out there, guys—everything you got."

"Alex, get us a good start," Eric added. "I'm a D-man, but I'll try to keep up with all you crazy sprinters."

Alex shook his head. "Distance swimmers are the crazy ones!"

Leo noticed Jake's wide eyes. "Jake, you'll be fine. Just pretend it's practice and do your best. If you can keep us close to St. Petersburg, I promise I'll do everything I can to win this race for us."

Jake gulped and nodded.

"No matter what happens," Leo said, "we've had an awesome meet. I'm proud to be your teammate." The four exchanged nods and broke their huddle. Excitement coursed through Leo as they headed as a unit to lane three.

"Audrey? Are you okay?"

She could see big feet with purple-and-gold toenails outside the stall. "Laney?"

"Open up."

After a few moments Audrey found the energy to open the door. She wiped her tears and leaned against the stall.

"Are you sick, *chica?*"

Audrey nodded and bit her lip. "I just threw up. I've been sick all weekend."

"Oh, you poor thing! I'm so sorry. Hey, Leo's relay's coming up. You feel okay to come out on deck and watch it?"

At the mention of his name, Audrey's eyes welled up again. "Go ahead. I'll come out if I can."

"You sure?" Elaine looked worried.

Audrey nodded, and her friend left, looking over her shoulder as she went.

Audrey once again locked the stall door, trying to find some sense of security as her world crashed down around her. She could hear cheers rising, and she knew the final heat of the relay approached.

Leo…Leo…how would he react to the news? She sobbed, clutching her lower abdomen with trembling hands. What would she do?

Leo completed the last of his springy jumps and stood completely still behind Jake as Alex mounted the blocks. Three teams in the heat had a good shot at winning the race, but Leo knew the main competition was the squad to their left: the St. Petersburg team, anchored by Gary.

Leo exhaled forcefully as the crowd quieted. Alex was the only one on the blocks wearing a swim cap—the rest had shaved their heads. Leo felt electricity in the air as the raucous cheers abruptly silenced. "Take your mark…"

Alex got out to a slight lead, and Jake and Leo yelled encouragement to Eric on the block as Alex approached the wall. Eric had a decent start, though he soon fell behind in the first fifty. His stellar endurance kicked in, and he made up some distance in the second fifty, closing in on the lead swimmers in lanes four and five. Alex joined Leo in shouting, "C'mon, Jake!" as the third swimmer mounted the blocks. Then Jake was off, thrashing through the water.

The Pensacola squad was within half a body length of the teams in lanes four and five, and Leo willed Jake to keep up. *Just stay within striking distance.* He stepped up on the block. Zoning in on the turbulent wake, Leo felt his skin tingle. Goose bumps prickled along his spine.

He couldn't freaking wait to get to that water. Leo felt more alive than ever, his peripheral vision blurring and the sight of Jake swimming toward him coming into sharp relief. Then all he heard was the pounding of his heart. This was his moment.

He rocketed off the block in a perfectly timed start, his limbs a powerhouse of smooth and efficient action. He had Gary in his sights in the first length and pulled even after the first turn. The thrill of connecting to the water and pushing himself as hard as possible consumed Leo. On the third turn, he pulled ahead of Gary and actually picked up speed on the fourth length, leaving the field behind.

As soon as Leo looked up after the finish, his three teammates raised their arms in victory, jumping up and down. The Pensacola Panthers had won a relay at state for the first time!

Leo hopped out to exchange hugs and high-fives with his teammates. They grabbed their sweats and found their coach to continue the celebration. Leo reveled in watching his normally cool and composed coach shake with excitement, sporting a look of shock. *We did that.* They'd pleased their coach so much he was dumbstruck.

As the lead-off swimmer, Alex already knew his split was 45.8, six tenths faster than his individual race. Matt looked up at Eric. "Forty-seven point oh, Eric. Not bad for a distance swimmer!" Glancing back at his clipboard, Matt looped his arm around Jake's neck and knuckled his hair. "Jake you were forty-five-nine! You might be faster than Leo by the time you're a senior."

Finally turning to Leo, Matt paused dramatically.

"What was my split?" Leo asked.

"That was one amazing swim, Leo. Forty-three-four."

Leo's eyes bulged. "I went forty-three?"

"Forty-three." Matt nodded.

Alex whooped and pounded Leo on the back while Eric shook Leo's hand.

"Not many college athletes swim that fast, Leo," Matt added.

Leo was in a daze. What an incredible meet. How he'd pulled that off after such a tumultuous year, he'd never know. What he *did* know was he needed to share his happiness with Audrey or it wouldn't mean much at all.

Scanning the deck, he caught a glimpse of long reddish hair across the pool. He jogged in her direction, slowing his pace as he drew near. She looked almost scared to see him, but he *must* have been reading her incorrectly.

"I went forty-three!" He wanted to grab her in a hug but sensed he should keep his distance.

"Wow. That was a beautiful race, Leo."

"And you pulled out the one hundred breast! How're you feeling?"

"I actually just threw up. I've been sick all weekend."

"What bad timing." His face fell.

"I know. So unlucky. Maybe it was the flu or food poisoning." Audrey glanced at something behind Leo. "Hi, Coach."

Brett Turner, the men's coach at Florida State University, waved at Audrey. "Hello! I hear from Nancy you're going to be a Seminole next year."

She smiled. "That's right. This is my boyfriend, Leo Scott."

"Ah, yes." Brett grinned, shaking Leo's hand. "This man needs no introduction after that relay performance. Great job, Leo."

"Thank you, sir."

"So, word on the street is you're going to the Naval Academy. Is that true?"

Leo looked down. "Yes, sir."

"Well, one of our international recruits didn't pass his English test. We have a fifty-percent scholarship still available at FSU. Think about it, Leo."

Leo swallowed, feeling his father's glare from somewhere in the stands above. "Thank you, sir, but I've made a commitment to the Navy. I can't back out now."

Brett frowned. "I was afraid you'd say that. Maybe we'll see you when you visit Audrey in Tallahassee?"

"If I have any time off from the Academy, I'm there," Leo promised.

Brett nodded and looked as if he might say something else, but then just walked away.

A tinge of green colored Audrey's face. "I-I-I think I'm going to be sick again," she got out before sprinting back to the locker room, leaving Leo standing by himself. She seemed so distant and preoccupied.

After his shower, Leo emerged to find Matt conversing with his parents.

"I'm so proud of you, son!" CS beamed, stepping up to meet him. As his father put his arms out, Leo felt himself flinch. Once he realized his father was hugging him, Leo could barely remember what to do — it'd been years since his father had tried that. Over his father's shoulder, Leo watched Matt's forehead crease. He tried to act more enthusiastic about the hug.

CS let him go. "We're going out to dinner to celebrate when we get home. You can invite anybody you want."

Leo squinted. "Anyone, sir?"

"Anyone."

"Audrey," Leo immediately replied. "Audrey, and...Jason." Leo held his breath, studying his father's gray eyes for any signs of change.

His father hesitated, a smile frozen on his face. "Fine."

Leo turned to his mother, whose blue eyes twinkled. They'd all go out to dinner together, just like a normal, ordinary family. But somehow he knew nothing would ever be normal or ordinary when it came to the Scotts.

32. Unborn Babies

The chocolate birthday cake looked delicious, but Jason's appetite was nonexistent, and it was clear Cameron and her mother didn't want any either.

Jason stared at the cake, feeling the cake stare back. He tapped his fingers on his thigh and worried he was crashing their Sunday afternoon gathering — even though Cam had explicitly invited him.

"He didn't even like chocolate," Cam said.

"He didn't?" Mrs. Walsh seemed distracted. "Yes, he did. He always bought chocolate for me on Valentine's Day."

"That's because *you* like chocolate, Mom."

Jason glanced back and forth, sensing tension. He felt like a major third wheel. He hadn't even really known Lt. Commander Walsh.

"Great. I got the wrong cake." Mrs. Walsh glared at Cam. "Why don't you get next year's cake then, since you seem to know him so well?"

Cam opened her mouth, but her face crumpled. Tears slid down her cheeks as Jason sat in pained silence.

"I'm sorry." Mrs. Walsh's tone softened as she patted Cam's arm. "This was a bad idea. Let's throw away this stupid cake. It's just…since it's his birthday, I thought we should do something to honor your father's memory. But this turned out all wrong."

Sniffing, Cam nodded. "There's no way I want to eat birthday cake right now. Especially without him…He should be here."

"He'd be forty-six today," Mrs. Walsh murmured.

Jason cleared his throat. "Seems like you both honor him, and you don't need a birthday cake to do that. He'd be proud of both of you. Cam, you got a teaching job—what he always wanted for you. And Mrs. Walsh, you've moved on too."

"Jason, I told you to call me Patti."

She'd finally stopped him from calling her "ma'am," but it would be even more difficult for him to call her by name. CS would be aghast. Cancerous Slimeball was all about showing respect. Never mind that Jason had zero respect for his father.

Sometimes Jason felt almost jealous that Cam didn't have to deal with her father anymore. Sometimes, on his lowest days, Jason wished his father was dead. But such thoughts were always followed by a tremendous wave of guilt.

He was simply amazed that Mrs. Walsh had welcomed him into her family, especially since he'd learned Cam was pregnant with his baby when he'd left town years ago. The fact that he was an alcoholic facing prison time didn't really sweeten the deal either.

Terrified of raising the baby alone and with no idea how to get in touch with him, Cam had decided she had no choice but an abortion—a decision that had shocked her parents when they'd discovered it after the fact. Cam had told Jason her parents had been fighting more the last year of her father's life, but otherwise they'd had a happy marriage.

Mrs. Walsh clearly missed her husband, and Jason wondered if her grief had skewed her judgment about the man she allowed her daughter to date. He and Cam had been together when Mr. Walsh was still alive, and it seemed like Mrs. Walsh needed to turn back the clock to those positive memories. She'd just dismissed the more troubling aspects of his previous time in Pensacola. Still, he was grateful—almost as grateful as he was for Cam's willingness, finally, to trust him again.

When Jason's cell phone vibrated, he saw it was his parents' home number and excused himself to the foyer. "Leo?"

"Hey, Jase."

"Hey, you're back from Ft. Lauderdale, huh?"

"Yep, our flight landed about an hour ago. Mom and Dad aren't home yet."

"Still stoked about your forty-three in the hundred?"

"Absolutely...I hope I can hold onto this feeling for a long time. But it's back to the water on Tuesday. The high school season's over — now on to nationals."

Jason exhaled. "You swimmers are *nuts*. You've been swimming nonstop since when? September? And now you keep going?"

"Well, we get a break in April after senior nationals." Leo's voice faltered. "I'm calling you to, um, ask you out to dinner on Monday night."

"Sure. That's the night before my sentencing hearing. I'm buying. Where do you want to go?"

"You don't have to pay, Jase. I, um, I..."

"What's going on?"

"It's dinner with Audrey, and Mom...and CS. He offered after I did so well at the meet."

"What?" Jason exploded. "I'm not spending my last night of freedom with Criminal Shithead, Leo."

"He told me I could invite whoever I wanted, and I wanted you. Please? For me?"

Jason sighed. Leo sounded so needy. "Where is this dinner?"

"Bonefish Grill on Twelfth Avenue."

"CS okay with me going?"

"Truthfully, he seemed kind of mad. But he didn't say no."

Jason sighed again, licking his lips. "Okay. But you owe me. You better visit me in prison, Leo."

"I seriously doubt you're going to prison, but if you do, I'll be there. Thanks for coming, bro. I'll call when I know what time dinner is."

They hung up, and Jason stared at the linoleum floor, shaking his head.

"What's wrong?" Cam asked when he returned.

"I have to go out to dinner tomorrow night with CS."

"Who's CS?" asked Mrs. Walsh.

Jason winced. "Uh, that's an abbreviation for my father. Commander Scott."

Cam chuckled. "That's not what it stands for."

Jason's eye's widened.

"Relax. Mom and I tell each other *everything*. Life's too short to keep secrets." She turned to her mother. "Jason and Leo call their father Cruel SOB."

Mrs. Walsh shook her head. "You boys sound exactly like Bill. Sometimes he'd be so frustrated with your father, Jason. I'd hear him rant for hours when he got home from work."

"Yeah." Jason nodded. "I feel sorry for his new second-in-command. What's his name? Ronald something?"

Mrs. Walsh seemed to bristle. "It's Roland Drake. I do not like that man. He seems so...slick...so smug, or something." She shuddered. "I'm glad I don't have to deal with the lot of them on the base anymore...Anyway, I'm going shopping. Will you be here later?"

"We should be," Cam said.

"If I miss you, good luck at your hearing, Jason. I'm pulling for you."

Once again he was awed by her kindness. "Thank you, Patti." They smiled at each other. "My attorney thinks it's looking okay for me."

Cam tilted her head. "Is he still scared of you?"

"Yeah." Jason grinned, flexing his sizeable biceps for the ladies. "I've got no idea why."

The women laughed.

Once her mother left, Jason reached out and stroked Cameron's hand. "This day's almost half over, Cam. You can get through it."

Her mouth formed a tight line.

He tried to distract her. "I'm kind of hungry. S'okay if I have a piece of cake?"

"Sure." She served him a big piece.

Digging in, he purred in a deep rumble. "Mmm." He took another forkful and held it out to Cam. "Will you eat a bite?"

She pursed her lips, considering for a moment. When she nodded, he lifted the fork to her mouth, accidentally smearing frosting near her lip. Oblivious to her chocolate moustache, Cam grinned at him.

Suppressing a laugh, Jason took another forkful, this time purposefully smudging frosting on her face.

"Hey!" She snatched a napkin to wipe her mouth.

This time he didn't bother with a fork and instead grabbed a gob of icing and lathered it on her cheek, eliciting a shriek. Ducking her head, she scooped some frosting and tried to plaster it on his moving target of a face.

It became an all-out food fight, and both screeched with laughter as they flung chocolate frosting everywhere.

Finally Jason took Cam in his arms and languorously kissed and licked the sweetness from her cheek, chin, lips. They ended up on the sofa, kissing and caressing.

"Thanks for getting me through this day," she whispered.

"March twelfth isn't only your dad's birthday. It's also the day we had our first food fight."

She beamed. "Our *first* food fight? Well, then, I can't freaking wait for our second."

Leo strolled the hallways of Pensacola High, trying to hide his disappointment at the lack of attention he received. He felt like a changed man after reigning victorious in one individual event and helping his relay win their first state title, but besides congratulations from a teacher or two, no one else seemed to care. They didn't even notice his shaved head.

At lunch, Leo studied Audrey while Alex and Elaine bickered over the sexual orientation of Tom Cruise. Alex was convinced he was gay, but Elaine said the rumors were simply to sell magazines. Audrey seemed far away.

"I don't think you two will figure out it out anytime soon," Leo finally interjected. "Why don't you just let the guy live his life?" Offering his hand to Audrey, he rose from the table. "Want to take a walk?"

Audrey hesitated a moment before she slung her purse over her shoulder and grasped his hand. She tossed her half-eaten sandwich in the garbage. He led her outside, and they meandered the school grounds. The clouds seemed to reflect Audrey's gloomy mood.

"I'm sorry you didn't have the meet you wanted," Leo said. "I'd be upset too."

"What?"

"I…uh…it's not right you had a bad meet, and I had a great meet. You worked so hard, and you didn't screw up like me. It should've been the other way around."

"Leo?"

He forged on. "I wanted to tell you I'm sorry. I'm sorry you had to intervene on my behalf at a crucial time in the season. I totally ruined it for you."

Leo looked down and Audrey let go of his hand. "No—"

"You'll be better off without me next year."

"Will you *shut up?*"

He turned to her with frightened eyes.

"My meet had nothing to do with you!" She chewed on her lip. "Well, it did, actually, but not in the way you're thinking."

"Audrey, don't be mad," Leo pleaded.

"Leo, I know you have to go the Academy, but I hate that we'll be apart. I could *never* be better off without you…you got that? Don't say anything like that again."

He'd jammed his hands into his pockets. "Sorry."

They resumed walking. "So you don't think the Oxycontin mess screwed up your swims," Leo said. "Then why've you been acting so weird since the meet?"

Now Audrey looked down. She stopped short and gazed at him. "There's a reason I didn't swim well."

Leo nodded. She turned to continue their walk. After a few moments, she spoke again. "There's a reason I didn't swim well."

"I got that part." He smiled to encourage her.

She kept walking in silence, seeming to grow increasingly frustrated. "Ughhh!" She threw her arms up.

Leo once again took her hand and led her to sit next to him on a bench, far from the other students who'd ventured outside.

"There's a reason I didn't swim well," she said a third time. She gripped the strap of her purse and stared at her hands. "Oh, okay... This is how I'll tell you." She groped in her purse and took out a pink box. She shoved it into his hands.

Pregnancy Test. It took a full ten seconds to realize why she'd given it to him. His stomach dropped to his feet.

"You're *pregnant?*" he whispered.

Audrey's slow nod made him feel sicker. Horror clouded his vision, and his breaths came quick and shallow. He'd managed to destroy his life once again in one fell swoop. But this time his life wasn't the only one ruined. He'd taken Audrey down with him. The ramifications of this huge mistake would grow and affect everything they knew — like a massive rock splashing into a pond, creating ever-expanding ripples of disruption on the once-smooth surface.

He quickly stood, stuffing the pregnancy test back into her purse and towering over her, clenching his fists at his sides. Then Leo drew his right arm back and sent his fist careening into the brick wall behind the bench. He barely heard the sound of knuckles hitting brick.

When he again drew back his fist, Audrey screamed, "No!"

She leaped up and grabbed his arm. He tried to shake her off, then snapped out of his trance when he saw her tears.

"Why are you crying?"

"I...I don't know," she sobbed.

His eyes flared. *"Why are you crying?"*

"Because you're scaring me!" She cowered.

He suddenly saw his behavior through her frightened eyes and grabbed the sides of his head, totally repulsed by himself.

"Oh, Audrey." He crumpled into her arms. "I'm so sorry." He felt her trembling, and he squeezed her tighter. "What are we going to do?"

She let out a strangled cry. "I don't know. I've known for sure just since last night, and I'm still in shock. I can only imagine how you feel, hearing about the baby right now." She untangled herself from him. "Let me look at your hand."

Leo pulled away and stared at the swelling and bruising already forming. Audrey carefully examined the damage. He felt nothing. No physical pain — that would come later. There was only emotional pain right now: self-loathing and terror.

He swallowed. "Does anybody else know about this?"

"No."

Her response calmed him a bit. Nobody else could know. They would have to make sure nobody found out...especially one certain commander. Leo had been consumed by avoiding his father to minimize the damage to his own well-being. Now he had to keep three lives safe from the venom of Cobra Snake.

"I won't go to dinner tonight with your family," Audrey said softly.

"No. I need you there." He had to pretend things were okay for at least one more night. "We'll figure this out. Together."

She choked down a sob and nodded.

33. Awkward, Party of Five

The hostess smiled at them. "Scott, party of five?"

Jason stood with the rest of his family, taking intentionally deep, even breaths. She should've announced, "Dysfunction, party of five," or maybe even, "Awkward, party of five." Jason swallowed a dark laugh and filed that away to share later with Leo.

He looked over at his brother, who'd barely spoken to him since arriving at the restaurant. Leo had his arm wrapped protectively around Audrey and a worried face. If Leo planned to ignore him the whole night, Jason wondered why he should even stay.

He'd expected things to be awkward with Callous Sadist. His father had avoided all eye contact and appeared uncomfortable standing with his *criminal* son. He'd wedged his hands into the pockets of his khaki uniform pants and jingled his change while they waited to be seated.

When they arrived at their round table, Jason quickly calculated the way to sit the farthest from his father, making the clockwise seating arrangement CS, Leo, Audrey, Jason, and his mother. Jason helped guide his mother into her chair and tucked her canes into the corner.

When his mother giggled at something his father whispered in her ear, Jason scowled. His parents seemed somehow closer since returning from the state meet, and he wondered what the heck was going on.

Everyone busied themselves with the menus for a few moments. Leo sipped his water and tilted his body toward Audrey, as if to shield her from CS. The waiter arrived with bread and prepared to take their orders, looking expectantly around the table. Leo reached to pick up the bread basket and the waiter asked, "What happened to your hand?"

Everyone stared at Leo's bruised right hand, which he quickly yanked away and hid under the table. "Um, it was an accident."

Curious Suspect gave Leo a strange look, then told the waiter he'd like the peppercorn-crusted salmon.

"Let me see it," his father ordered once the waiter had collected the other orders and left.

Leo reluctantly offered his hand.

"What kind of accident?"

"Not an accident, really, sir, um…I actually punched a wall at school."

Nearly silently, Audrey gasped.

"Why?"

"Billy Ryan was provoking me again, sir. I thought you'd rather me punch a wall than punch him."

"I don't care what *anyone* says to you, Leo. I don't want you punching anything or anybody. It shows a lack of self control."

"Yes, sir."

Jason watched this exchange with disgust. His father was the last person who should lecture on self control, and he was pretty sure CS wasn't getting the true story.

Suddenly their mother jumped into the conversation.

"Leo, I'd like to take a look at your hand when we get home—decide if we need to get an x-ray."

Leo shook his head. "That's not necessary." CS shot him a look of reproach, and Leo changed his tone. "Yes, ma'am."

A few moments of silence passed before their mother smiled warmly at Leo. "I didn't get a chance to tell you at the meet that I'm very proud of you."

"That was some meet," CS chimed in.

"I don't mean about your swims," his mother continued, with a sideways glance. "Though I'm pleased your hard work paid off."

Leo glanced at Audrey and looked down.

"What impressed me most was your sportsmanship," his mother said. "You showed a lot of class every time you competed with Gary."

"He's my friend, Mom."

"You're a better sport than me," said Audrey. "Sometimes I get so mad at Marcie I can't stand her."

"It's okay to be competitive, Audrey," CS said. "It's a dog-eat-dog world out there, and you have to claw your way to the top. It doesn't matter who you step on to make it. People always let you down, anyway."

Jason rolled his eyes. He couldn't disagree more. Coldhearted Stalin wouldn't last a second in AA. The addicts would rip into him for his arrogance.

When their food arrived, Jason watched Audrey look at her chicken and close her eyes. She appeared slightly green. He didn't realize he was pushing his food back and forth on the plate until his mother asked, "Don't you like your swordfish, Jason?"

"It's great, Mom. Just not that hungry, I guess."

"How're you feeling about your court date tomorrow?"

Jason snuck a glance at his father, who pretended not to listen. "Nervous."

Suddenly Audrey shot out of her chair and mumbled a quick "Excuse me" before disappearing into the restaurant.

Leo dropped his fork. "May I leave the table, sir?"

CS nodded curiously. Audrey's purse hung on the back of her chair, and as Leo passed by, it fell to the floor. When his neat-freak father rose to right the purse and tidy up Audrey's hasty departure, his mother asked, "Jason, what does your attorney think will happen?"

Jason began to answer but CS interrupted with his brusque call for the waiter. His father returned to his seat, and Jason could tell something had changed. Coming Storm's eyes churned like a roiling sea, and he barked, "Box up these dinners. We have to go home."

"Yes, sir," the waiter said.

His mother recoiled. "But why, James?"

"Dinner's over," he said.

By the time Leo and Audrey returned to the table, the meals were stacked in boxes.

"What's going on?" Leo asked.

"I've got work to do," CS growled.

"Everything all right?" their mother asked.

Leo nodded. "Yes, ma'am. Maybe we should go so Dad can get home?"

As they rose from the table, CS glared at Leo, but his brother was so focused on Audrey that he didn't notice. Jason didn't like this at all.

After the group walked outside, his mother turned to him. "I made a cake! Audrey's coming home with us to have some. Would you like to join us?"

"Sure, Mom. I'll follow you home."

Her face lit up. "Wonderful, honey. We'll see you there."

Jason avoided looking at his father and headed to his car, cursing under his breath. Something wasn't right, and he needed to figure out what—even if it meant spending more time with CS.

34. Violent, Party of Two

Audrey sat in the back seat next to Leo. His hand on her belly did nothing to quell the tension she felt as they drove in silence. Finally they pulled up in the Scotts' driveway.

As she got out of the car, Audrey decided she'd had enough of the Scotts for one evening. Leo appeared miserably tense and preoccupied, and Jason seemed even unhappier. Why had he even agreed to come for dessert? Mrs. Scott was sweet, but Audrey disliked how she constantly deferred to the commander, who hadn't been too bad during the meal but who now seemed furious about something.

The last thing Audrey wanted to do was force cake on her sensitive stomach under the intrusive watch of CS. "Mrs. Scott? I'm not feeling well so I think I'll walk home. Sorry to miss your cake."

When both Leo and Mrs. Scott pouted, Audrey regretted opening her mouth.

CS eyed her coolly. "Still not feeling well, hmm?" His deep, smooth voice had an edge to it. "Well, then, you shouldn't walk. Jason, drive Audrey home."

Jason was silent for a moment, but then agreed. "Yes, sir. C'mon Audrey, let's go."

"Will you come back, Jason?" Mrs. Scott asked.

"It's getting late, Mom. Sorry. Have a good night." Jason turned, and Audrey followed him to his car.

He drove a few blocks and stopped. "Sorry you had to suffer through that dinner from hell. I gotta get back there. Can you walk home from here?"

Audrey's eyes widened. "What's going on?"

"No time to explain. I wanted to get you somewhere safe, but now I need to get back."

"It's your dad, isn't it?" Her voice rose. "Is he going to hurt Leo?"

"Audrey, get out of the car!"

"No, I want to go with you!"

Jason reached across the seat and opened Audrey's door, not so gently shoving her out. "Go home!" He managed to push her clear of the car, and she watched helplessly as he executed a four-point turn in the road before speeding away. Through the back window, she could see him cradle his cell phone to his ear.

Audrey was now crying, and her mind swam with questions and fear as she stood, abandoned on a neighborhood street. Instead of beginning the two-mile trek to her house, she jogged in the direction Jason's car had gone. Her sundress and sandals slowed her progress, but she was determined to get back to Leo. She couldn't bear the thought of him getting hurt.

"Now there's just three of us," Leo's mother said wistfully as they went inside. "How 'bout we have cake later? I'm still full from dinner."

CS went silently to his study, shutting the door behind him. Leo's mother stared at the closed door. "I wonder what's bothering him." She turned to Leo. "You should get some homework done. I know you missed class for the meet."

Leo sighed. "Yes, ma'am." He headed up the stairs.

Leo sat at his desk, overtaken by irritability as he pulled out his chemistry notebook. Now that he'd fallen from the upper echelons of class rank, school wasn't as much fun. Mrs. Boyd had told him if he aced the last four tests of the year, he might be able to pull off an A-, but that simply wasn't good enough. He didn't have the heart to tell his father his grades had slipped.

Just then CS barged into his room, his eyes blazing. "Get up!" he hissed as he closed and locked the door behind him.

Leo scrambled out of his chair, consumed by fear.

His father whirled to face him. "When did you plan to tell me you just completely ruined your future?"

"What do you mean, sir?" Leo's eyes darted around the room.

"I poured *everything* into your school and sport," his father screamed. "I made sacrifices for you! And in one instant, you threw it all away."

When Leo still said nothing, his father leaned in with quiet menace. "Exactly how long have you known your whore of a girlfriend was pregnant?"

Leo's mouth dropped open. *He knew.* "Eight hours, sir."

"And how long has Audrey known?"

"Since yesterday." Leo felt his body tense in preparation for battle, his fingers balled into fists at his side.

"You stand at attention, damn it."

Despite the clench of his gut, Leo slouched defiantly, placing his hands in his pockets and keeping his eyes trained on his father. If he was going down, he'd go down swinging. "No, I won't."

CS lowered his head and came at him, his fist crashing into Leo's side. Leo recovered quickly enough to take a jab at his father's face, but as soon as his fist connected with his father's jaw, fireworks of pain erupted, the existing cuts and bruises throbbing at further injury.

In the moment Leo hesitated after that punch, CS backhanded his face. As Leo staggered to the side, CS caught him and threw his body face-first against the wall, yanking his right arm behind his back. Leo writhed in agony as his father squeezed his injured hand and twisted his wrist behind him.

"Don't you *dare* try to hit me again."

Leo tried to wiggle out of his father's hold, but he was too strong.

His bedroom doorknob jiggled. "James!" his mother cried. "Let me in!"

"Go away, Mary!"

Over the sound of her knocks and pleas, CS interrogated Leo. "So, are you two planning on having the baby?"

Leo squirmed as shooting pains traveled up his arm. He didn't see a way out of this. "I don't know, sir."

"I don't think the Academy has *family housing*. How will you or Audrey go to college? Did you think of that?"

"We haven't thought anything through yet."

"Well that's frickin' obvious!"

His mother's cries continued. "James! Don't hurt him!"

Then Leo heard his brother's voice outside the door. "Get out of the way, Mom."

There was a huge thump against the door, and the walls of the house shuddered, but somehow the lock held in place. Jason cursed.

"Don't move." CS let go of Leo's arm and moved to one end of the dresser. He grunted as he pushed it in front of the door.

Leo cradled his wrist. Now he was trapped. Sensing his only opportunity to attack, he jumped on his father's back just as CS got the dresser in place.

Jason's second rush again shook the house, but the dresser did its job. Leo held on tightly, trying to lock and squeeze his elbow around his father's throat as he clawed at his arm. CS propelled himself backward and slammed Leo into the wall. Somehow he held on.

CS again body slammed him, and this time Leo's right foot caught and tangled in the open closet door, twisting his ankle. Leo screamed and let go of his father's neck, crumpling to the floor in a heap.

The pounding on the door increased in volume. "Dad! Let us in!"

From his position on the floor, Leo looked up to see CS panting, pawing at his throat and sucking in air. "How dare you!"

Leo watched his father's shiny black shoes shuffle toward him, then felt an explosion of pain in his side.

Time stood still as Leo sprawled on the floor, absorbing repeated kicks. His right wrist and ankle pulsated with pain, but each blow to his side was a scorching burn of agony. All he could do was moan and pray the beating would end.

He thought his situation couldn't get any worse, but then CS unbuckled his belt and whipped it out of the belt loops. With wild eyes CS doubled the leather and raised it high before cracking it against Leo's legs. The stinging belt kept coming, and Leo was helpless to stop it.

On the other side of the door, Jason heard a rhythmic thumping. He didn't know what to make of the fact that Leo had stopped groaning. He looked at his mother's tear-stained cheeks, trying to think of something to say. He heard footsteps on the stairs and was shocked to see Audrey. "I told you to go home!"

"What's happening?" Audrey ignored Jason's glare. "Is Leo in there? Is he okay?" Audrey stepped back. "It's locked? Oh my God, is his father in there with him?"

As an answer, his mother stepped forward and embraced her. Jason felt sick. He needed to man up and save his brother, but he couldn't get in the room! When the doorbell rang, he sprinted downstairs.

"What's this about, Mr. Scott?" Detective Easton demanded when he opened the door. "An attempt to get out of your sentencing hearing tomorrow?"

"No, Detective. Thanks so much for coming. Please, come in. Please, hurry."

Detective Easton stepped inside.

"You have to help us. My father's beating the crap out of my brother, and I think he's really hurt."

"Where are they?"

"In my brother's room upstairs. My father's barricaded the door somehow."

She whipped out her cell phone and barked, "Get paramedics to eleven thirty-seven Ridgeway. And I need some backup here as well." She tilted her head toward the stairs. "Lead the way."

At the top of the stairs, Detective Easton asked, "What're their names?"

"My father's James and my brother's Leo. This is my mother, Mary, and Leo's girlfriend, Audrey."

She nodded at them and turned to Jason. "Any chance James or Leo has any weapons in there?"

"Don't think so. My father's hands are weapon enough. But I think he's been beating Leo with a belt too."

Audrey gasped.

"Anybody know what this violence is all about?" Detective Easton asked.

Jason shook his head. "No, ma'am."

Leo moaned from his fetal position on the floor. For once his face wasn't bloodied after a beat-down from his father, but the jagged pain in his side made it hard to breathe. His wrist and ankle continued to throb.

He could see CS sitting against the wall near his bed, mumbling something. Listening intently, Leo finally heard him. "He threw it all away."

"Mr. Scott?" A female voice rang out from the hallway. "This is Detective Amy Easton with the Pensacola Police Department. I order you to open this door, sir."

CS snapped out of his trance and moved to the door. "You can leave, Detective. We're doing fine here."

"Sir, you need to let me in now. Either you open the door or we're coming in by force. I understand your son might be hurt?"

CS glanced at Leo. "He might be hurt, yes."

Ya think?

"We need to get him some help, sir. Please open the door, and we'll get everything sorted out. I know you were simply disciplining your son."

Leo heard the dresser slide across the carpet, followed by the door opening.

"Commander, please step into the room."

CS slowly stepped back, and a tall, formidable woman followed him into the room. She looked over at Leo and her eyes narrowed.

Audrey barged in behind the detective and gasped. "Leo!" She rushed over to him, sobbing. He barely registered her hand caressing his face.

Jason stood over him with his fists jammed into his pockets, glaring at CS.

"You son of a bitch!" his mother yelled.

"An ambulance is on the way for your son," the detective said. "Are you hurt, sir?"

CS shook his head.

"Do you have any weapons on you, sir?"

He appeared indignant.

"I need you to place your hands on the wall, Commander Scott."

He backed away from her. "You can't arrest me! You leave now, and I won't file a report with the department regarding your illegal entry, detective."

Slowly and calmly Detective Easton reached into her holster and withdrew her weapon, pointing it at James.

It became dead quiet in the bedroom, and Leo couldn't take his eyes off the gun.

The detective's voice was firm and icy. "Put your hands on the wall, now."

CS seemed to weigh his options for a moment before turning to the wall and spreading his arms and legs.

Detective Easton frisked CS with her left hand while training the gun on him with her right. Then she holstered her weapon and yanked one arm then the other behind his back. She encircled his wrists with handcuffs as she read his Miranda rights.

Kneeling next to Leo, Audrey continued to sniffle. Suddenly she sat back with a cry and clutched her stomach, rocking back and forth.

His mother kneeled beside her. "What's wrong, Audrey?"

Audrey shook her head as her tears fell harder.

Blackness clouded Leo's vision, and he felt himself drift away.

35. The Mean Human Daddy

Mary watched Audrey's face contort in pain. "What's wrong?" she repeated. When Audrey didn't answer, she looked wildly around the room.

James stood with his hands cuffed behind his back. He shook his head, glaring at Audrey. "She's pregnant."

Mary gasped. "Oh, honey."

Audrey lowered her head.

Jason kneeled to grab Leo's hand, but he barely stirred.

"Jason, please wait downstairs for the police and EMTs," instructed Detective Easton as sirens filled the air.

"Yes, ma'am."

"Let's go, Commander." The detective led him toward the door.

As he went, he turned to look at his wife. "Mary, bail me out."

Kneeling between her unconscious son and his whimpering girlfriend, evidence of her husband's cruel handiwork, Mary's eyes widened. How had she once loved him? How had she once adored this arrogant, aggressive man?

She struggled to stand with her canes, trembling with rage. "Get him *out* of here!"

As the detective hauled him away, James pleaded over his shoulder, "I'm sorry, Mary! I didn't mean to hurt him!"

When he was gone, there was a sudden peacefulness, a whooshing away of all menace from the room. Mary looked down at her son's mangled right hand and kneeled again to hold it tenderly, finally having the opportunity to examine it. *Too late.* Just like James's apology moments ago…too little and too late. Leo's hand was cool and clammy, his skin abnormally pale. His right wrist was obviously swollen, and Leo whimpered when she turned his hand to inspect the bruising.

"Help is coming," she whispered, choking down a sob.

What kind of mother failed to protect her child? What kind of mother stood by helplessly while her sweet, innocent son faced such brutality?

She'd been ignoring the signs a long time, Mary realized with a jolt. Even her fondest memories of Leo's childhood were tainted. When he'd been only four, she'd taken advantage of a day off work to bring him to the Maryland Science Center.

She'd watched her younger son gleefully climb into the minivan, his blue eyes shining as he settled his little bottom into the car seat, clutching an action figure.

"We going on an adventure, Mom?" he asked.

"We are!" Mary smiled, reaching to buckle him in. "Just you and me, on an adventure to the science museum."

"Are we gonna see terror pens?"

Mary chuckled. "Yes, there'll be *terrapins* there. And we'll see all kinds of fish in the Follow the Blue Crab exhibit."

"Okay!" His head bobbed.

As they drove from Annapolis to Baltimore, Mary played an audio book of *Mrs. Frisby and the Rats of NIMH* in the cassette deck. Jason had simply loved that book when James had read it to him, and though it might have been a little advanced for a four-year-old, Mary couldn't wait to introduce Leo to the wonderful world of talking mice and rats, who banded together to battle a big, mean cat and big, mean humans.

"What's your favorite part so far?" she'd asked as they arrived at the museum.

Leo thought for a moment, his mouth pursed in a small "o". He kicked his feet up and down, bouncing in his car seat. "When the rats moved Mrs. Fwisby's house. It was scary!"

"What'd you think would happen if the humans discovered them?"

Leo gulped. "The mommy human would be nice, but the mean daddy human would hit their bottoms."

Mary had struggled to compose herself as she helped Leo unbuckle his car seat. She tried to sound cheerful. "Let's go see the big blue crab!"

He bit his lip. "Is it scary, Mommy?"

She took his hand. "I don't know, sweetie. If you're scared, take a deep breath and give me a hug, and you'll feel better."

He nodded and folded his little hand in hers. As they neared the entrance, he grinned. "Just you and me, on a 'venture!"

Tears filled Mary's eyes as she remembered just how cute he'd been, but he'd been troubled by his father's physical discipline even then. Her eyes drifted along the length of his now lanky, muscular body, curled up next to her. He was no longer a sweet little boy — he was becoming a man. Angry bruises peeked out from underneath his shirt. She heard a gasp next to her and turned to look at Audrey.

"I'm so sorry, Mrs. Scott." The girl stared at the carpet. "I'll clean it, I promise."

Mary could see a deep red stain, which matched an even larger coppery stain on Audrey's white sundress. Audrey shivered.

Mary let go of Leo's hand and reached for Audrey, rocking her slowly in her arms. She probably should've been angry about the pregnancy, but all she felt was sadness and loss, particularly since it already seemed to be over.

She remembered James's ridiculous comment once that if Leo ever impregnated a girl, he would abort the baby himself. In a way, James had made good on his promise. The wounded cry Audrey had made upon finding her boyfriend motionless and beaten rang in Mary's ears.

"The paramedics will be here any second. Hang on, Audrey."

Lights bounced off the lawn in a kaleidoscope of blues and reds as officers led CS to a cruiser. About to close the front door and follow the paramedics to Leo's room, Jason caught a glimpse of a neighbor peeking out her window, eyes round. *Great.*

When Jason got upstairs, the two paramedics were already examining Leo. One checked his vitals, and the other lifted his shirt, revealing deep purple bruises. "There could be some internal bleeding."

The other nodded. "Yep, he's got a low BP and a high pulse." He looked up at Jason's mother. "Who did this to him, ma'am?"

"His father," she said in a barely audible voice.

Another paramedic talked softly with Audrey and helped her to her feet. Jason inhaled sharply when he saw the blood on the carpet and her dress. He thought instantly of Cameron.

His mother looked up at him. "Jason, go with Audrey—I don't want her to be alone. Is that okay with you, Audrey?" When Audrey nodded, she added, "I'll call your mother when I get the chance."

Audrey closed her eyes. "Please don't tell her, Mrs. Scott."

"Your parents *will* find out about this pregnancy, you know," she said. "It'd probably be better if you told your mother yourself. Will you call her?"

Audrey's lip trembled. "I'll try."

"Good. Jason, make sure she calls JoAnne."

Jason nodded. He watched the paramedics secure Leo to a backboard for a moment before he followed Audrey down the stairs.

Just a few minutes later he climbed into one ambulance with Audrey as his mother waited for the paramedics to load Leo's stretcher into another. She struggled with the huge step up, and the paramedics pretty much loaded her in as well. The last time his mother had been in an ambulance had been her car accident. Jason prayed this trip to the hospital would end better.

36. Self Blame

"Okay to use a cell phone in here?" Jason asked the paramedic.

"Yeah, but make it quick."

Jason turned to the patient, who paled and gripped the stretcher as the ambulance bounced over the road. "You should call your mom, Audrey."

"How'd your dad figure out I was pregnant?" she asked.

He realized she was trying to distract him, but he wondered the same thing. "Dunno." A few moments later he added, "CS seemed fine at dinner till you left the table."

Audrey grimaced. "Yeah, I got sick. Morning sickness is a stupid name for it—I've been nauseated all day long at times. I can't believe I didn't realize I was pregnant."

"Well, it's not like you've been through this before...*have* you?"

"No!"

"Okay, okay." He chuckled, quiet for a moment before pointing his finger in the air. "I remember! Your purse got knocked to the floor. CS put it back on your chair, and that's when he started acting weird."

Audrey closed her eyes. "The pregnancy test! It was in my purse... He must've seen it." She turned away. "It's my fault he found out."

Jason studied her profile: smooth skin framed by wavy auburn hair, and a cute button nose scrunched with culpability. He knew exactly how she felt — he'd once again failed to keep Leo safe. Calling Detective Easton had been his last hope, and he prayed that this time Criminal Sadist would be forced to stop hurting Leo. It certainly had been satisfying to watch his father get arrested.

"Hey." Jason gently tilted Audrey's chin. "It's not your fault. CS would've found out eventually. He always finds out."

Audrey sighed. "We didn't even have a chance to figure out a plan. I just told Leo about the baby at lunch today."

Jason nodded, the pieces clicking together. "That's when he punched a wall."

"How'd you know?"

"That's what *I* wanted to do when…" His voice trailed off as he thought of Cam. "Never mind. You're stalling. Call your mom."

Audrey bit her lip. "She's got enough to worry about with my dad in prison. I don't want to disappoint her."

"I'm thinking your mom would be pretty mad if you went to the hospital without telling her." Audrey looked down, and he continued, "And though my mom doesn't hit us, she's a tough lady. Well, she used to be. She was a naval officer, and you want to do what she says."

Audrey reached for her purse and dug out her cell phone.

"Hi, Mom," she said just a few moments later. "It's an ambulance siren…I'm okay, Mom." She took a deep breath. "I'm pregnant…but I'm bleeding, and they're taking me to the hospital." She clutched the phone, listening to her mother. "I started bleeding about twenty minutes ago…It was a lot, Mom. I got blood all over the Scotts' carpet."

Audrey shot a guilty glance at Jason. Then she gripped her belly with the hand not holding the phone.

"Yes, Mom. Mrs. Scott told me to call you, and Leo's brother is with me right now."

Audrey looked up and asked the paramedic, "Where are you taking me?"

"The Naval Hospital."

She relayed that to her mother. "I was really hurting, Mom. Then it got better. Now I think…it's starting again." She groaned and curled her knees to her chest on the stretcher.

"Your phone call's over," said the paramedic, moving in to check her vitals.

Audrey got out a quick goodbye before hanging up and handing the phone to Jason, along with her purse.

"We're almost there now," said the paramedic. "Take some deep breaths and try to relax."

Jason could see panic in Audrey's eyes.

He took her hand, and she squeezed it tightly with each wave of cramping. He was determined not to let another Scott girlfriend deal with a pregnancy by herself.

A doctor and nurse hovered over Leo while Mary stood by, clutching her canes in the curtained-off ER station.

The nurse had removed Leo's shirt, exposing an array of angry bruises. The doctor now examined his torso, and anytime his palpations neared Leo's belly, the half-conscious patient flinched. Leo groaned when the doctor squirted gel on his skin for an ultrasound, and the sound was like sandpaper against Mary's eardrums.

Guiding Mary to the nurse's station, the nurse gave her a sympathetic look. "How 'bout you wait here, ma'am? Dr. Anderson will be out when he's done with his exam."

Mary could still hear the physician speaking to the nurse. "Class two hemorrhage…hmm…eighty-five isn't all that high…looks like some involvement of the spleen."

A few minutes later the physician emerged. "Mrs. Scott, I'm afraid your son has internal bleeding. As best we can tell, the source is a ruptured spleen."

Mary held her hand to her mouth.

"It *looks* like internal bleeding, but he's not as pale as we'd expect. His pulse should be higher too."

"He *is* pale, Doctor. His father's Black." She blinked rapidly. "And he's a competitive swimmer. His resting pulse was fifty-two at his last physical, I think."

"Good to know. We'll be taking him to the OR when they're ready for him. For now we're administering saline through his IV."

Mary bit her lip, and the nurse poked his head out from the drawn curtain. "The saline seems to have improved his mental status. Would you like to see your son before surgery?"

Nodding, Mary made her way to his bedside. Leo's eyes slowly fluttered open. He tried to focus. He attempted to sit up, but gasped at the effort.

"Stay down, Leo," she said. "You're at the Naval Hospital. You passed out in your bedroom, and they brought you here in an ambulance."

"Where's Audrey?"

Mary ignored his question. "You have a ruptured spleen, and they're taking you to surgery. You've been really out of it."

His eyes darted around the room. "Why isn't Audrey here?"

"Shh, Leo." She took some tissues and gently wiped his sweaty forehead. "Everything's going to be okay."

Two orderlies entered and began wheeling Leo's bed away. He craned his neck back to look at his mother, his eyes frantic.

"I'll see you soon." She smiled bravely until he was gone, then stumbled to the waiting room and crumpled into a chair.

A couple of hours later, Jason appeared and Mary woke with a start from her fitful sleep. He kneeled and gave his mother a much-needed bear hug.

Leaning into his strong body was so comforting. Thank goodness he'd returned to Pensacola. "How's Audrey?"

"They did a pelvic exam and an ultrasound." Jason looked down. "She lost the baby."

"Oh! And her mother isn't here. How awful."

"I, uh, had to hold her hand during the exam, and it was kind of embarrassing, Mom. Audrey had me call Elaine, but she's not here yet."

"And she called her mother?"

"Yes, ma'am. They decided to keep her overnight for observation because of all the blood loss. Where's Leo?"

"He's in surgery. They're removing his spleen." She looked away. "He kept asking me where Audrey was, and I didn't have the heart to tell him."

Jason rubbed his hands over his hair. "How'd this happen, Mom? Leo was supposed to be the good one, never getting in trouble."

"He *is* the good one. And you're the good one too, Jason."

He looked down, and she knew he didn't believe her. "It's just that *nobody's* ever good enough for your father. Even he himself isn't good enough."

"I wonder what's happening to him," Jason said softly.

Her face felt hot, and she clenched her teeth. "He's caused so much damage. Whatever they do to him will never be enough."

It had been a long night.

James rubbed his eyes, careful not to smudge his face with the ink on his fingertips. Being fingerprinted and photographed before being stuffed in this holding cell was to be expected, but he was fairly certain the full body-cavity search wasn't standard procedure. He bet that witchy detective had put them up to it.

Dozing men had littered the dingy holding cell as he entered, each attempting to get comfortable on the hard metal benches along the walls. The fetid stench of body odor hung over the space. Continuing his reconnaissance, James's eyes had landed on a huge white guy across the room, and he was startled to find the man glaring at him. James defiantly returned his stare. Eventually the man averted his gaze. James exhaled.

He could barely keep himself still and was filled with restless energy, craving a good run — the only thing that would quiet his racing mind. Since that wasn't an option, he'd dropped to the floor to pump out some pushups, but after just a couple he realized this position left him too vulnerable.

So he'd sat on a bench. And sat, and sat, eventually overwhelmed by the images and sounds filling his brain. Repeatedly he saw Mary's face contorted with rage as that detective hauled him out of Leo's bedroom in handcuffs. Over and over he heard Leo's whimpers, barely audible above the current of adrenaline rushing in his body. The vision of Leo's prone form, the fight finally knocked out of him. Jason's heated words: "You're a monster!" Leo's flinch when he'd hugged him at the state meet.

James stared at his shaking hands, the hands that had caused such damage to those he loved. He shoved them into the pockets of his pants, disgusted by the sight of them.

More haunting visions flickered in his mind. He saw Mary standing in the doorway of that petty officer's apartment, devastated by his betrayal. He'd never wanted to hurt her like that again, but he felt desperate when she'd refused him repeatedly after the accident. Forced to look elsewhere for comfort, he'd sampled lots of options, then found the perfect candidate. But she'd wanted nothing to do with him. If only she'd submitted, things would have been so much easier.

A wave of anger washed through him, and suddenly he remembered the days following his parents' death when he was eleven. His lone remaining adult relative, his father's sister, had refused to take him in because she was a single mother raising four children herself. James was still furious with his aunt for closing her door, and since then he'd had no contact with his cousins, one of whom was now in prison.

In the time it took a semi to slam into his parents' car on the highway, James's life had transformed from happiness to horror. A social worker had led him straight from the double funeral to a boys' home, where the other boys had eyed him greedily. He was fresh meat, and they were hungry.

He'd learned to use his fists to survive. By the time he was placed in a foster home three years later, he was full of rage and had multiple arrests for assault. His foster father was a naval lieutenant who literally whipped him into shape. And though James had hated each strike of the belt, the structure of his new home forced him to apply himself to school, where he found success in both academics and athletics.

His foster father's mantra had been "rise above," and James had done just that. He'd risen above his grief and criminal history to earn a scholarship to the Naval Academy. There he'd met Mary.

He surveyed the pathetic group in the holding cell once again. He was so different than them. He was a father determined to help his son succeed.

Six hours later Mary and Jason dozed in chairs next to Leo's bed in the hospital room.

"Mom?" Leo croaked.

Mary opened her eyes. "What is it, Leo?"

"Where's Audrey?"

Leo's question also woke Jason, who yawned and stretched his arms over his head. Mary cleared her throat, smiling sadly. "She's in another hospital room." His confusion was evident, and she continued, "Audrey had a miscarriage, honey."

His eyes welled with tears. "No…no. It's all my fault. And I wasn't there for her."

"I stayed with her, buddy," Jason said. "Audrey knows you would've been there if you could. But you were in surgery."

Mary studied her younger son, who seemed small and so tired against the bank of pillows behind him. "You and Audrey both need to get more rest. Then you can see her for yourself."

Leo continued to cry, but it wasn't long before the aftereffects of anesthesia and blood loss took over. Mary watched him finally give in. He'd be brimming with self blame again when he woke, she knew. They all seemed to blame themselves for what had happened. But assigning blame didn't make it any better. It only made the pain worse.

37. Mama Don't Preach

Audrey tossed a hostile glance at her mother. "It'd just kill Dad," she said. "Don't you know how awful it is for him in there? He'll blame himself for not protecting me, and that'll only make serving time worse!"

Her mother shook her head. "You can't keep this a secret, Audrey! That's just ridiculous."

Elaine yawned from the other side of the hospital bed and pulled a notebook from her backpack. "Guys, it's not even seven yet. Let's not wake up the entire hospital."

"Just give me some time," Audrey pleaded, ignoring her friend. "I'll tell Dad what happened when the time's right."

"The time's right now. When you get discharged, we're headed straight to the prison."

Audrey sniffed, feeling close to tears. Elaine sidled up and offered a piece of paper.

"What's this? A poem?"

"It's what you can tell your dad when you see him," Elaine said.

Audrey read the scrawled lines and couldn't help but smile. "Laney, these are they lyrics to 'Papa Don't Preach.'"

"Yep." Elaine grinned.

Audrey shook with laughter. "That'd be so funny if I said this to my dad!"

Elaine channeled Madonna, bursting into a slightly off-key version of the song's chorus. Audrey joined in, and when they held the last note extra long, they erupted into giggles. It felt wonderful to laugh.

"Most of the time you act older than your age, Audrey," her mother said. "But watching you switch from anger to sadness to hysterical laughter in the span of two minutes reminds me you're a teenager. The pregnancy hormones probably don't help either."

Audrey's smile faded. "Sorry I let you down, Mom."

"Oh, honey." Mrs. Rose sat on her bed and reached for her hand. "I'm so sorry I haven't been there for you. You've been all alone in this."

Audrey looked down.

Just then the nurse bustled in for Audrey's morning check. After she'd confirmed everything to be okay, she left behind a wheelchair. At least they let Elaine take the handles.

Her friend adopted a stuffy English accent, bowing as Audrey lowered herself into the chair. "Your chariot, madam."

Audrey reached behind her to smack Elaine, but before she knew it she was practically airborne. Elaine zoomed her out of the room and booked it down the hallway. They screeched to a halt to avoid collision with a nurse and somehow arrived at the elevator intact.

"Careful, Elaine!" Her mother came up behind them and pressed the down button.

"I can't believe they're making me use a wheelchair," Audrey grouched.

"And I can't believe you went a freaking one-oh-two in the breast when you were *preggers!*" Elaine shot back.

"Say it a little louder next time, Laney. A few patients down the hall didn't hear you."

"Remember, if Leo's asleep we're coming right back to your room," her mother said.

"I *know.*"

"I hope Leo's okay," Elaine said.

Audrey squeezed her eyes shut. "Me too."

As Elaine wheeled her into Leo's room, Audrey was dismayed to find his eyes still closed. He'd resumed the fetal position, the sheets scrunched around him in disarray. His right wrist and ankle were secured in beige compression wraps. Yet Leo's face looked almost angelic. She could see the faint outline of a scar on his forehead, which had become part of his features since the last beating by his father.

Jason stretched out on a chair, snoring softly. His arm hung over the armrest, and a small thread of drool drained down the side of his mouth.

Audrey's mother scooted around her and Elaine to hug Mrs. Scott where she sat by the window. Pointing to Leo, she whispered, "We'll go back to Audrey's room."

"You can stay," Mrs. Scott whispered back, grimacing.

"What's wrong?"

Mrs. Scott hesitated. "I forgot my pain medication at home. The past few hours have been a little rough, but I don't want to wake Jason."

Audrey's mom immediately held out her hand. "Give me your house keys. I'll go."

"Would you? Honestly, I think I left our front door unlocked. It's not something you think about when you're climbing into an ambulance with your son. Or when your husband's just been arrested for putting your son in that ambulance."

Audrey heard Elaine inhale sharply then looked down. She had no idea how they'd lived with the abuse for so long.

"Where's the medication?" her mother asked.

"It's in my bedroom—in the nightstand next to my bed. But, the drawer's locked. You *will* need a key for that." Digging in her purse for the key, Mrs. Scott glanced at Leo.

Once she had the key, Audrey's mother patted her on the arm. "I'll be right back. You girls should let Leo get some sleep. He's been through a lot."

Audrey nodded as her mother left.

The sound of the door clicking closed woke Jason with a start. He had a wild look in his eyes, but seemed to settle down once he recognized his surroundings.

"Oh, this damn chair," he groaned, massaging his neck. As he did so, his eyes landed on Audrey, then scanned up behind her.

Audrey gave him a nervous smile. "This is Elaine. She swims with Leo and me. This is Leo's brother, Jason, Laney."

"How're you feeling?" Jason asked.

"Okay. I'd feel better if Leo would wake up." All eyes turned to look at Leo, who twitched in his sleep.

"Maybe he's having a nightmare," Audrey said. "If somebody beat me up so bad I needed surgery, I don't think I'd ever sleep again." She turned back to Jason. "Were *you* just having a nightmare?"

He exhaled. "Yeah, it was stupid. I dreamed Cam accused me of killing her dad. One of those anxiety dreams, you know." Jason jumped. "Crap, what time is it?"

"It's seven-thirty," Mrs. Scott answered.

"Oh, man. I gotta get to the courthouse by nine, and my attorney will kill me if I look like this." He surveyed his wrinkled clothes, and Audrey noticed blood on his jean jacket—probably her blood.

Jason took Audrey's hand. "You'll get through this, tough swimmer chick."

"Thank you, Jason. Thanks for being there for me."

"Well, I'm a cheap substitute for my brother, but you're welcome. Leo's a lucky guy."

Jason rose, stretched, and gave his mother a peck on the cheek. She grasped his arm. "I'm proud of you, Jason."

He winced. "Tell Leo, uh, tell him I'm glad he didn't die. No, that's stupid. Tell him…"

"Tell me yourself," a voice rasped from the bed. Audrey turned to find Leo's eyes suddenly glittery and alert.

"Hey, buddy." Jason leaned down and gave his brother a careful hug. As Leo returned the embrace, he gave Audrey a sad look. She knew they had a lot to talk about.

"I have to get to the courthouse," Jason said. "But I'll be sending healing thoughts your way."

"Just stay away from my girlfriend," Leo warned with a smile. "I heard you say I'm a lucky guy…Don't be getting any ideas, Jase."

Jason grinned. "Yes, sir." Walking out he muttered to himself, "I mean, yes, your honor. Yes, your honor. I gotta get that right today."

Leo continued to stare at Audrey.

Mrs. Scott cleared her throat. "I'm sure the nurse will check on you soon, Leo. Until then, Elaine, how about we give these two some privacy?"

Elaine squeezed Audrey's shoulder then shot out the door.

Slowly rising from her chair, Mrs. Scott set her canes in place. She looked sternly at Leo. "If I leave you alone with Audrey, do I have to worry about you two making more babies?"

A deep crimson bloomed across his cheeks and slowly spread down his neck. Audrey could only imagine how red she was.

"No, ma'am."

"Good. We *will* discuss this, Leo."

He gave a somber nod.

"My mom's making me tell my dad," Audrey said, unable to keep quiet any longer.

Leo's eyes flashed with fear. "Wait, Mom…Where's Dad?"

Mrs. Scott pressed her lips together. "He was arrested last night."

Leo's eyes widened.

"Jason called a detective he knew. I assume your father's at the courthouse awaiting his bail hearing."

"Whoa." Leo turned to gaze out the window. "Everyone's gonna find out now."

"It'll be okay, Leo. Just focus on getting better." Mrs. Scott's voice sounded strangled, and Audrey knew she must be holding back tears.

Once Leo's mother left, Audrey stepped out of her wheelchair and crept toward the bed. "I'm so sorry."

"*You're* sorry? What're you sorry about? I'm the one who's sorry."

"It was my fault CS found out. He saw the pregnancy test in my purse when it fell off my chair at dinner."

"Ohhh."

She sniffed. "I'm responsible for you getting beaten so badly."

"No. It's not your fault my dad's a Coldhearted Satan. Come here." He grimaced as he scooted back on the bed, then thumped the sheet.

Audrey's eyes darted around the room. "Your mom could walk in, or a nurse."

"I don't care." He lowered his head. "I — I heard about the miscarriage. I'm so sorry you had to go through that alone."

Audrey felt a sob in her chest slowly make its way up her throat. She crawled into bed next to him, chest to chest. They'd never shared a bed before.

Once she was in his arms the tears began. "I was so scared." She cried as he ran his fingers through her hair. "When I saw you lying there, unconscious...I — I thought you might be...dead."

"You're not getting rid of me that easily." He squeezed her tighter. "*Te amo*, Audrey."

She cried harder. "*Me destruiría perderte.*"

"It'd destroy me to lose you too. No matter what happens, let's never lose each other, okay?" His smooth voice was resolute.

"Okay." She wiped tears from her cheeks and, despite her best efforts, drifted off to sleep.

38. Step Number Ten

Jason sucked air through his teeth as he passed a clock in the courthouse. He rounded the corner and found his attorney, Rob, pacing the hallway outside the courtroom.

"So you made it," a husky female voice called behind him.

Jason spun around to face Detective Easton. Noticing the royal blue T-shirt beneath her black suit jacket, he laughed. "Let me guess, another R.E.M. shirt, Detective?"

She grinned. "Of course. I have them on rotation." Her expression grew serious. "How are Leo and Audrey?"

"Both are in the hospital. Leo had his spleen removed, and Audrey had a miscarriage."

"I'm sorry, Mr. Scott." She clasped his shoulder.

Noting his attorney's confusion, Jason explained. "Detective Easton came to the rescue last night. I won't bore you with the long story, but if you hear James Scott needs a public defender, run as fast as you can."

Jason turned to the detective. "Speaking of him, do I need to worry about crossing paths in here?"

"He's in a holding cell right now."

"I hope you throw the book at him."

The detective looked away. "I'll do my best, but there may be some things out of our control…"

"What is it?" Jason asked. "What's going on?"

"Hey," Rob interrupted before the detective could speak. "It's our turn. Let's go."

Jason took a deep breath and followed his attorney into the courtroom, wondering why Detective Easton followed.

She smiled when he turned to look at her. "I wanted to be here for your sentencing — see this thing through."

The judge wasn't ready, so Jason had a moment to survey the scene. He noticed Cameron and Marcus, and his cheering party of two gave him a wave. Although he'd waited almost two months for his sentencing, the additional delay now seemed interminably long.

His leg wouldn't stop jiggling. The detective leaned in. "What happened to your mom?" she asked. "I mean, why does she use canes to get around?"

Jason looked down.

"You don't have to tell me if you don't want to."

"It's okay. She got in a really bad car accident a while back." He looked over at Detective Easton. "She almost died."

The detective simply nodded.

"The thing is, she was a great driver. I can't figure out how she crashed so bad. It's not like she has road rage like my dad or anything."

"The commander has road rage? I would've never guessed!"

Jason sighed. "My dad wasn't always such an asshat, you know."

"You don't have to explain."

"It's just that he didn't always hate us so much. Sure, he was hard to please from the get-go, but at least I felt like he cared. He told us we were Scotts, and that meant we were special." He shook his head. "Sometimes that man's ego is the size of a house." Reflecting a moment, he added, "And his heart's the size of a tic-tac."

The detective laughed. "Seems like he's gotten pretty far in life, though, being a commander and all."

"He's one charming SOB. He and my mom are both aeronautical engineers — I don't even know what that is. But his emotional IQ is the pits."

She tilted her head to the side. "How's *your* emotional IQ?"

"Alcoholics suck at dealing with their feelings. I've got a long way to go."

"Still on step number nine?"

"Actually, my sponsor said I'm ready for ten."

"What's that again?"

"Taking personal inventory, admitting when we're wrong." Jason scoffed. "Something my father would never do."

Just then an "All rise!" boomed over the courtroom. As they stood for the judge, the detective leaned in.

"Well, you're certainly *not* your father," she said. "You're admitting when you're wrong just by being here. Nice work. I'm pulling for you."

Jason smiled, feeling a mix of puzzlement and gratitude. He certainly didn't deserve her kindness. He was a thief and an alcoholic, the older brother who couldn't protect his sibling, the deadbeat who'd left behind a pregnant girlfriend. And now he was a felon. His shoulders tensed as he steeled himself for the sentencing.

After verifying Jason's daily attendance at AA and reading aloud a glowing letter about his character, the judge looked at him over the bench. "Mr. Scott, you entered a guilty plea to the charge of grand larceny, a felony of the third degree. You're hereby ordered to complete one hundred hours of community service, and you'll be on probation for one year. But first you'll spend three days in jail, although two have already been served. If you complete this sentence satisfactorily, I'll recommend this conviction be expunged from your record." He gave Jason a hard stare. "You will report back to me in one year's time, Mr. Scott. I expect to hear good news from you then. The bailiff will take you into custody now."

Jason couldn't speak. Only one day in jail? He could do that. No problem. And the community service and probation thing would be a piece of cake. He shook himself out of his daze as Cam and Marcus approached the defense table. Jason returned his girlfriend's encouraging smile.

"Marcus," Jason said. "Sorry I didn't make it home last night. Leo's in the Naval Hospital. Can you visit him there?"

Marcus's eyes darkened. "Your father's doing?"

Jason nodded, and Cam held her hand to her mouth.

"I'll go there now," Marcus promised.

The bailiff placed Jason in handcuffs as they finished their conversation. "Talk to the detective," Jason told them. "She'll tell you what happened last night." He then turned to Rob. "You didn't keep me out of jail, but one day's not bad."

Rob exhaled. "Call me when you get out, and we'll discuss the terms of your probation."

Jason absorbed one last reassuring glance from Cam before an officer led him away. He looked forward to jail, as it meant putting the thefts behind him at last. Perhaps after this, he'd actually stay sober.

That positive feeling instantly evaporated when he arrived at the holding cell. Standing in the middle of the room was a man in a khaki Navy uniform. His eyes flashed violet, and Jason's stomach dropped.

Jason felt his hands come free of the cuffs. "You got any other holding cells?"

"Nope." The bailiff halfway smiled. "A big guy like you is worried? You'll be fine in here."

The bailiff unlocked the door and waited for Jason to walk in. The clang of the cell door closing behind him, metal on metal, made him flinch.

Jason refused to meet his father's eyes as he hightailed it to a corner of the cell. But he didn't stay long after he noticed a beefy prisoner glaring at him. He was on his way to the other side when CS grabbed his arm.

"Fancy meeting you here." His father's eyes faded to a cool gray.

"Yeah, all we need is Leo getting arrested for drugs, and we'd have the Scott trifecta in here."

"Are you going to call the cops on Leo too, then?" His father sneered.

Jason held his breath. Of course CS knew he'd called Detective Easton. He'd seen her when he'd visited him here back in January.

"How *is* Leo?" his father asked, maintaining his firm grip on Jason's arm.

"You ruptured his spleen, Dad. He had to have surgery," Jason said.

CS opened his mouth and took a step back, releasing Jason's arm.

"The doctor told us Leo could've died. He had internal bleeding."

CS looked down and rubbed his hand over his closely cropped hair. Jason decided to go for full disclosure. "Audrey had a miscarriage too."

His father's eyes were pleading. "I-I didn't mean for this to happen. I was just so furious at Leo for throwing away his future…"

Jason felt a surprising flash of pity. He'd always feared CS, but now his flaws were glaringly apparent. Why had Jason let this pathetic man rule and ruin his life?

"Why can't you make it easy to hate you?" Jason roared, agonized by his own conflicted emotions.

CS looked bewildered. All got quiet as the other cons turned to watch.

Aware of their stares, Jason lowered his voice, but his tone was no less intense. "I just want to hate you, but you always throw a curveball. You almost killed Leo, then you act all sorry afterwards? You admit to being wrong? And what the *hell's* up with that letter you wrote to the judge? You never say that stuff to me in person!"

CS gaped at him. "You won't understand until you have children of your own — until you sacrifice yourself for them, do *anything* for them, only to have them treat you with hate and disrespect."

As Jason tried to make sense of that ridiculous response, the hulking man from the corner approached. "You two need to shut up. Some of us are trying to get some sleep in here."

Jason glared at the man. "Go to hell."

Sneering, the behemoth stepped closer. Already smelling body odor, Jason now caught a whiff of putrid breath as the man cursed at him.

Then the big man's eyes bulged as CS yanked his arm behind his back, adroitly restraining him. He groaned as CS twisted his wrist.

"Get *away* from my son," CS hissed. "When I let go, you'll return to that corner and there you'll stay. Do we have an understanding?"

Obviously in pain, the man nodded. CS relaxed his grip, and the con skulked away, cradling his wrist and not looking back.

At first Jason suppressed a laugh as he watched his father intimidate the big guy. But then all he could think about was Leo crumpled on the bedroom floor. He sighed. His father was a bastard, but at this moment it was working in his favor.

"See what you can learn in the Navy?" CS said proudly. "The hand-to-hand combat training is quite useful."

Yeah, Jason thought, *especially when you're beating the snot out of your sons.* He studied his father, whose mood had morphed from remorse to ebullience with the successful domination of the bully.

"You should think about signing up, Jason. The Navy could give you some structure."

"I think I'll pass."

"So what was your sentence?" CS demanded.

"One day in here, one hundred hours of community service, and one year of probation."

"Sounds fair."

"Commander!" a booming voice called. They turned to see two MPs standing next to a bailiff. "We're here to escort you to the base, sir."

"It's about time." CS drew himself to his full height and moved swiftly to the cell door.

Noting his father's relief, Jason realized what Detective Easton had been trying to tell him. The Navy would protect one of their own, and his father could easily go Scott-free once again.

"See you later," CS tossed over his shoulder.

Watching his father walk away sans handcuffs, with the MPs trailing him, Jason felt sick. Turning back to face the men in the cell, he saw the sizable prisoner in the corner smile. Jason exhaled slowly. This would be a long day.

39. Swimectomy

Smoothing his sheets, the young nurse stared at Leo's shaved head. "So are you a skinhead or something?"

He chuckled then groaned, feeling pain in his abdomen. "Don't make me laugh — it hurts the scar too much. My dad's Black. I don't think they let people like me in their little group. I shaved my head for a swim meet."

The nurse recorded his vitals. "Swimming, huh?" She eyed his body. "Your BP's still a bit low, but your pulse has come back down to a normal range. Either your cardiovascular system's in great shape, or you're still recovering from the internal bleeding."

"Well, I *think* I feel better." Leo studied his chest, picking at the bandage covering the upper left side of his abdomen. He tried not to look at the bruises lining his ribcage or the welts all over his skin. "But I don't really feel much of anything. Are you guys giving me something?"

The nurse smiled. "You've got a Percocet drip in your IV." She glanced at the door. "Your surgeon will be here soon for grand rounds, and I believe your mom had some questions for him. Do you know where she is?"

"Yeah, she's trying to find out what happened with my brother. He, uh…" Leo looked down. "He was in court this morning."

"Is he the one who beat you up?"

"No, ma'am."

Right after the nurse's departure, his mother walked in with Mr. Shale. She gasped when she saw Leo's torso. Mr. Shale had a better poker face, but he squeezed Leo's mom's shoulder before approaching the bed.

Feeling self-conscious, Leo covered himself with the sheet, moving his left hand to free the IV from the bedding.

"Thanks for visiting, Mr. Shale."

"I came as soon as Jason told me what happened. I was just telling your mom about your brother's sentence."

Leo raised his eyebrows, eager to hear.

"Good news." Mr. Shale smiled. "Only one day in jail, one year of probation, and some community service."

Leo nodded. "That *is* good news. Um, Mr. Shale, is Jase in jail with my father?"

Mr. Shale cocked his head to one side.

His mother maneuvered her way closer. "I didn't think about that." Her voice rose. "Do you think your father figured out Jason called the police?"

"No point in worrying about it because we don't know the facts." Mr. Shale shrugged. "Nothing we can do anyway. Jason knows how to take care of himself."

His mother turned her attention back to Leo. "Audrey's mother told me she's getting discharged soon. They'll stop by before they leave."

"Thanks, Mom." The nurse who'd woken him to take his vitals early this morning had sent Audrey back to her room. *So much for getting some rest in the hospital.* Since then the nurses had bothered him nonstop.

There was a bustle of activity outside the door, and a gray-haired man stuck in his head. "Knock, knock. We're making our rounds." He approached Leo's bed as Mr. Shale and his mother backed toward the wall. The space was soon crowded with five medical staff.

"How're you feeling, Leo?"

"Fine, sir."

"The nurses treating you okay?"

"Yes, sir." Leo anxiously eyed the group surrounding his bed.

"I have some residents and interns with me today, and we're here to review your progress. Dr. Patel, please do the honors."

The surgeon nodded at the resident next to him, who gave her report. "Leo Scott's a seventeen-year-old male admitted to the ER last night at twenty-one-fifteen, presenting with tachycardia, low BP, distended belly, paleness, decreased alertness, and sweating. Dr. Anderson was the attending, and the ultrasound revealed a probable ruptured spleen. Mr. Scott was taken to the OR where Dr. Lee performed a splenectomy."

Leo listened with fascination, feeling like the star of a medical TV show.

The older physician surveyed his group. "Who can tell me the suffix of the word splenectomy?"

A young blond student piped up, "It's from the Greek word, *ectomy*, meaning 'to remove.' It's the removal of his spleen."

"May I?" Dr. Lee grasped the corner of the sheet.

Leo hesitated then nodded.

The doctor pulled down the sheet, and Leo watched the medical students try to look impassive.

The surgeon pointed to the angriest bruises. "You can view the multiple traumas to Mr. Scott's upper abdominal quadrants. I elected not to do a laparoscopy because we were concerned about other organs being damaged and needed a good view of his internal cavity. Fortunately only the spleen was hemorrhaging.

"Dr. Kennedy." Dr. Lee nodded to a sandy-haired, freckled medical student. "What are potential long-term risks associated with splenectomy?"

"The patient now has increased vulnerability to infection," Dr. Kennedy responded, earning a satisfied nod from the surgeon.

"That's correct. Any questions for this patient?"

The blond student bit her lip. "How'd this happen to you?"

Leo looked at his mother, who nodded. "Well…my father was punishing me, and he kind of went overboard."

The student gasped. "Your *father* did this to you?"

Feeling his face on fire, Leo watched the student look at Mr. Shale, her eyes narrowed.

"Oh, no," his mother said. "This isn't Leo's father."

The student's ponytail bobbed.

His mother seemed to squirm, and Leo noticed her blush as well. "His father was arrested."

"We'll keep Leo for observation at least one more night," Dr. Lee told the group. "After that we'll send him home with some pain meds, and he'll be as good as new in about six weeks."

"Dr. Lee?"

All eyes turned toward Mr. Shale. "You should know Leo's struggled with addiction to pain medication — Oxycontin, to be specific."

Leo's lip trembled. *Just tell the whole world, why don't you?*

"I see," Dr. Lee said. "Thanks for making me aware of that. We'll adjust his medication as necessary." He aimed a stern look at his patient. "How long have you been clean?"

Leo refused to meet the surgeon's gaze and yanked the sheet back up to his neck. "Since January, sir."

"Keep up the good work." When an awkward silence filled the room, the surgeon said, "We'll move on and let you get some sleep."

"Wait a minute," Leo interrupted, feeling panicked. "Did you say six weeks? I need to go to swim practice tomorrow."

Dr. Lee turned back to the bed. "There'll be no swim practice tomorrow, Leo. You can't physically exert yourself for six weeks, and that includes swimming."

"You can't do that! I *have* to swim. I have to get ready for the Academy!"

"You just had major surgery. You need to allow your body to heal, son. The nurse will give you more instructions for your discharge, but now we need to move on." The surgeon swept out of the room with the flock of students hot on his heels.

"Splenectomy," Leo muttered, the medical student's words echoing in his head. *It's Greek, meaning to remove.*

Not only had CS's violence led to the removal of his spleen, it had removed swimming from his life for six whole weeks. Not just a splenectomy — a swimectomy. It was the punishment that kept on giving.

40. Stronger

The news had gone over like a thousand-pound anchor.

Mary sighed as she and Marcus left Leo's hospital room. "He sure didn't take that well."

"Give it some time." Marcus shook his head. "Obviously he's not thinking clearly. The way he yelled at Dr. Lee was kind of intense. I didn't realize swimming was so important to him."

Mary smiled sadly. "I think swimming's his refuge from his screwed-up family." Several seconds passed. "I knew it would happen. I knew it was just a matter of time before James really hurt him. I knew, but I didn't do anything about it." She looked into Marcus's kind eyes and felt the burn of tears. "I failed him."

He seemed to want to reach for her, but instead crossed his arms over his ample middle. "You're all caught up in the James vortex. Living with Jason for six weeks has shown me what a good man he is. He's actually taught me a thing or two. Leo tried so hard to get clean, and watching his father show up to yank him out of treatment…" Marcus sighed. "I understand your guilt, Mary. We *all* failed him."

He patted her forearm, providing a steadying presence. Mary didn't like anyone seeing her cry, but somehow it was easy to let it all out around Marcus.

"I don't know how you've kept it together these last few years," he said. "You've managed to raise two remarkable sons despite the constant threat from your husband. Most people would've folded like a tent after an accident like yours."

Mary sniffed. "I used to think no matter what happened, I had to keep the family together. Now I'm not so sure."

Marcus let her words sit between them for a few moments. "You're thinking of leaving James."

She met his eyes. "Yes. It's terrifying to consider."

"It's terrifying to consider *staying* with him too."

"That's true." Mary paused. "I told James I'd leave him if he hurt Leo again, and I have to follow through. There've been too many times when I haven't. But where will we live? How will I support Leo? And James threatened to fight me for custody, even though Leo has only a few months left in Florida."

"I think if you make a decision to care for yourself and your family, Mary, it'll somehow work out in the end. I don't know how, but I have faith."

He grasped her hand. Encouraged by his support, she took a deep breath, contemplating the decision ahead.

Audrey followed her mother out of the elevator.

Still feeling some mild cramping, she wished she could walk faster to get to Leo, but she did enjoy being free of the wheelchair.

They traveled down the hallway, but stopped when they saw Leo's mom and Mr. Shale huddled together near the door. When Mrs. Scott looked up and saw them, she swiped at her cheeks, letting go of Mr. Shale's hand and plastering a smile. "It must be time for Audrey's discharge!" she said in an overly cheerful voice.

Mr. Shale straightened.

"It's been a long night," Audrey's mother said.

Mrs. Scott nodded. "Yes, and I fear it'll be a long day too."

"Is he okay?" Audrey asked. "May I go in and see him?"

Mrs. Scott nodded. "He may be sleeping, but you're welcome to go in, Audrey."

Audrey stepped inside to find Leo turned away from her, his broad shoulders outlined by his pajama top, his long legs covered by the sheet. She sighed at this perfect body his father had brutalized. She was glad his wounds were covered for now.

"Leo, are you asleep?"

Though he hadn't stirred, she thought she heard a faint sniff.

"Leo?" she whispered.

He finally sighed and scooted up, moaning in pain.

She flinched.

"Hey." He'd managed to sit now, an elbow resting on one knee, but he continued to look down. "No, I wasn't asleep. Just thinking about stuff."

She lowered herself to the edge of his bed. "Why are you crying?"

"I wasn't crying...I was...just thinking." He sighed. "My surgeon told me I'm out of the water for six weeks."

"Six weeks?" Audrey recoiled. "But then you can't swim at nationals."

"I know. Matt's going to be mad."

"The doctor told me I'm out for a week, so he'll be mad at both of us."

"I can't even get out of this bed by myself," Leo muttered through clenched teeth. "What a joke I thought I could actually go to practice tomorrow."

"I'm sorry, Leo." Audrey reached for his hand.

He stroked her skin. "So, you got discharged, huh?"

"Yeah, my mom's taking me home."

Leo nodded.

Back in the hallway, Mary mulled over the possibilities for a future that would or wouldn't include James.

JoAnne shook her head. "That's a lot to consider, and you look so washed out. I don't think it's a good time to make such a decision."

She gestured to the hospital room. "After they kiss their goodbyes, I'm taking Audrey home. But then I'm returning for you, and you're coming home with me to rest."

"I need to stay with Leo."

"I'll stay with him…as long as you're there for Audrey." Her gaze fell to Mary's canes. "With his sprained ankle, Leo needs help moving around and, well, that's easier for me to provide."

Mary wrestled with the idea of leaving Leo. JoAnne cleared her throat. "Mary, there's something I'd like to ask you."

"Would you like me to leave?" Marcus asked.

"No, that's okay. I'd actually like your opinion on this too. I have to return to New Orleans in a couple of days. Their nursing shortage is so severe they could only give me a few days off. What I'm wondering is…would you and Leo consider moving into our house?"

Mary felt her eyes bug.

"I know it's a lot to ask, but obviously Audrey needs more supervision, and I just can't be there for her right now. The bills are killing me, even with travel nursing. And I don't want you living with James."

Mary thought for a moment. "Marcus and I were just discussing how I need to leave James, and a major stumbling block was figuring out where to live."

He nodded.

"I'm honored you'd ask me to help with Audrey. But if we do this, you realize Leo and Audrey would be under the same roof, right?"

"Believe me, I thought about that." JoAnne giggled. "We'll have to implement a 'hands to yourself' rule."

Mary chuckled. "One teenager's bad enough, but now they might double-team me."

"I've seen you lay down the law with Leo. I know you can handle it."

Mary sighed. "Okay, let's do it. I have to talk to Leo about all of this first, though."

"Yeah, I'm sure he'll *hate* living with Audrey." JoAnne rolled her eyes.

"That's not the part that worries me. It'll bowl him over when I tell him I'm leaving his father."

"I agree," Marcus said. "Even if James *has* torn the family apart, it'll be tough for Leo to lose that stability."

Mary started, causing all three to jump, when she noticed a man dressed in a tan Navy uniform coming toward them.

Mary stood a little taller as the man drew near. "Hello, Captain," she said, nodding to her former commanding officer. Captain Payson's short blond hair had grayed since she'd last seen him, lending him an increased air of authority.

"Mary," he said with a nod.

"Sir."

He seemed nervous as he turned to JoAnne. "Hello, Mrs. Rose."

She reached out to shake his hand. "Please call me JoAnne, sir. And this is Marcus...?" JoAnne gave him a questioning look.

"Marcus Shale." He pumped the captain's hand. "I'm, uh, a therapist."

"Cameron Walsh came and told me exactly what happened. I still can't believe it. Has this been going on for long?"

Mary's tears answered for her.

The captain grimaced. "I'm so sorry." He cocked his head toward the hospital room. "Is your son in there?"

"Yes, sir."

"Pensacola PD called, and I was having MPs bring James to my office when Cameron visited me. I thought about ordering a Family Advocacy Board investigation, but I..." He looked down. "I thought it was another fake allegation of abuse—some racist ploy to make James out as the angry Black man." He shot Marcus an uncomfortable look. "But, but...Leo had to have surgery?"

Mary nodded and watched his face sag with regret, a feeling she knew well. "Leo had to have his spleen removed," she said. "You can go see him if you want."

Leo and Audrey's conversation halted the moment Captain Payson entered the room. Leo froze for a second before nudging Audrey. "Stand up."

Audrey bolted upright. "Um, hi, Captain. Hello, sir."

He took a step closer. "You're Denny's daughter?"

"Yes, sir. Audrey Rose."

Leo blinked up at him. "I apologize for staying in bed, sir. But it's doctor's orders."

"Of course." The captain nodded. "Do you know who I am?"

"Yes, sir, Captain Payson. You're my dad's boss."

"That's right. Your father talks about you all the time, Leo."

Leo blushed.

"He tells me you're a real scholar-athlete. You won two state swimming titles, and you're in the top five of your class."

Leo shook his head. "No, sir, not anymore. Audrey still is though."

The captain nodded at her. "I have to decide what'll happen to your father," he said, returning his focus to Leo.

"Where is he, sir?" Leo felt a catch in his throat as he suddenly wondered if CS was near.

"He's in the brig for now, at the base."

Audrey paled.

"What is it?" Leo asked.

"My father…" Audrey began. "He's there too. I hope he doesn't try anything crazy when he sees him."

"But your dad doesn't know anything, and they'll probably keep them apart."

Audrey looked away.

"You didn't tell him, did you?"

"Leo —"

"Audrey!" He heard his voice shake. "I told you not to tell anyone!"

"I'm sorry. I just couldn't deal with it alone anymore. There's nothing he can do from inside prison…" Her eyes pleaded with him.

Leo clenched his fist and sighed. "The whole world knows about this now anyway. What's the difference?"

"I have to decide what's going to happen to your father," Captain Payson repeated. "Son, could I…could I see what he did to you?"

Leo's eyes closed. What possible good could come from parading his bruises and welts? To show how miserable he was at fighting back? To show how much he deserved punishment?

When he opened his eyes he saw Audrey chewing on a fingernail. Her voice was soft.

"You can't keep hiding it. He needs to see what kind of man your dad is. He needs to see what he did. Maybe then he can stop him from hurting you again."

Leo dropped his head. "Nobody can stop him from hurting me." He waited a few moments, then slowly lifted his shirt, wincing.

Captain Payson's voice was icy. "You said nobody can stop your father from hurting you," he said. "Well, *I* can stop him. I can, and I will. Your father tells me you're going to the Academy, and I can imagine you're not too impressed with the Navy right now. But the Navy needs men like you. And, well, you need men like me, to finally do something to protect you. I promise I'll do everything in my power to see that this abuse stops. Give me the chance to prove it to you, Leo."

In spite of himself, Leo did feel a shred of hope. Maybe *this* Navy man wouldn't let him down. "Yes, sir."

Audrey reached for his hand and gave it a squeeze.

41. Afterbirth

Denny Rose held his breath as MP Perrick smoothed his hand over the blanket tucked neatly around his mattress.

Inspection time. Denny stood at attention in his cell, hoping his contraband would go unnoticed. His navy blue jumpsuit was wrinkle-free and his bedding taut. The obsessive orderliness demanded by the prison was nothing new to Denny, a Navy lifer, but the daily doses of humiliation were something he hadn't encountered since his days as a seaman.

Perrick reached under the blanket and yanked it free. A photograph tumbled to the floor. From the corner of his eye Denny watched as the MP crunched his boot on the photo, marking his prized possession with a dirty footprint.

"Pick it up, Rose," Perrick sneered.

"Yes, sir." Denny bent down to retrieve it, but Perrick refused to move his foot, forcing him to twist and turn the photo to loosen it. Finally he snatched it free, ripping a corner in the process. He returned to attention and did his best to keep his fury hidden beneath an expressionless façade. As an officer, Denny would never have allowed an MP to get away with such degrading treatment of a subordinate. But things had changed. Now Denny was lowest on the food chain.

Jerking the photo from Denny's hand, Perrick barked, "This is against regulations. No personal items in your cell." The faded image of his daughter in her pink swimsuit with four medals across her chest undulated as the MP waved it in front of him.

Denny braced himself, unsure of the guard's next move.

"Drop and give me fifty."

Denny began his punishment immediately. He wasn't a young man anymore, and the nine months in prison had weakened him. As he struggled through the twentieth pushup, he heard Perrick bark to the other MP. "Get rid of this, Ollie. I'm taking the other cons to chow—I'm sick of waiting for this old man."

His arms shaking and his breath coming in quick gasps, Denny finally finished his last pushup and returned to attention.

The remaining MP handed him back the photo. "Will you please hide this better next time?"

Denny stuffed it underneath a cracked tile in the floor. "Sorry, sir…couldn't sleep so I looked at it last night. I still haven't heard how she swam at state."

"I'm sure she did great. C'mon, it's time for you to force down some of that crap they call dinner."

As they approached the cafeteria, the MP said, "So I hear you're no longer the highest ranking officer in here."

"What do you mean? Who's here?"

They entered the cafeteria, and Denny had his answer.

He bristled the moment he saw Commander Scott sitting off to the side, slowly eating his chicken and rice while another MP stood guard right behind him. James still wore his khaki uniform and looked out of place in the sea of navy blue jumpsuits.

"What is it?" the MP asked when Denny stopped moving.

The prisoner's eyes honed in on his former CO, weighing the odds of getting in a few good punches before being restrained. "The commander's a child abuser. He threatened my daughter. What's he doing here?"

"Supposedly he beat up his kid so bad he's in the hospital."

Denny inhaled sharply. His heart pounded.

Perhaps feeling their eyes on him, James looked up and met Denny's cold stare. He put down his fork.

"I have to talk to him, sir."

"That's not a good idea, Denny."

"I just need to find out if Audrey's hurt, Ollie. Please."

Hearing no response from the MP, Denny headed for James's table. The commander stood as he drew near. The guards hovered nearby. "So, you finally got caught," he said when he was close enough for James to hear. "This time you went too far. You put Leo in the hospital?"

James said nothing.

"You're still in uniform," Denny observed.

"I won't be here long," James said. "I don't belong here."

Denny took a step closer. "You're *exactly* where you belong."

"Denny," the MP warned. "You don't want to go to solitary over this."

"You don't know what I want!"

"You won't be able to see visitors if you're in the hole," Ollie reminded him.

"Just tell me if Audrey's okay," Denny demanded, glaring at James but keeping his hands at his sides.

James's eyes widened. "She'll be fine."

"She'll *be* fine? What does that mean? What did you do?" Denny eyed him suspiciously. What if James *was* leaving the brig shortly? This might be his only chance.

Sizing up the taller, fitter man, Denny scanned for the spot he'd hit first, hoping to unleash nine months of imprisoned emotion in one swift punch.

A radio squawked on the MPs belt: "Visitors for Prisoner Rose."

Ollie grasped Denny's arm. "Let's go."

He continued to glare at James.

Ollie stepped in front of Denny, blocking his view of James. "Hands forward, Rose. I'm transporting you to your visitors."

Denny sighed and drew his hands together at his waist.

Ollie snapped handcuffs in place. "About face." He guided the prisoner to visitation.

The moment Denny caught sight of Audrey, a wave of relief crashed over him. She was safe. But he knew he'd never seen her so miserable. She looked as unhappy as he felt.

He brought the phone to his ear, waiting for Audrey to mimic him. When she'd failed to visit him on Sunday, he'd suspected her meet hadn't gone as planned, and her reluctance now only confirmed his suspicions.

He watched JoAnne cajole Audrey but couldn't hear their words.

Audrey finally picked up the phone and lifted her head.

"It's okay if the meet didn't go so well, Audrey girl."

She exhaled. "Well, I won the one hundred breast again."

"What'd you go?"

"One-oh-two."

"That's right near your best. How was your IM?"

"Two-oh-five—I got third place." She studied his face.

Attempting to hide his disappointment, he then realized how unimportant swimming was in light of current events. "What am I thinking asking you about your meet?" he said. "First I should find out how Leo's doing. And are you okay?"

"You know what happened?"

"I just ran into James."

"Did he hurt you?"

Denny shook his head.

"Did you hurt *him?*"

"No. I wanted to, believe me. But you and Mom got here just in time…two minutes later and I might have been in the hole for some time, unable to see you. So thank you."

"Leo's father really hurt him, Dad. He had a splenectomy." She glanced at her mother, who nodded grimly. "We just left the hospital."

"I'm glad you visited him there."

She looked down. "Uh, Dad, I wasn't at the hospital only for Leo." She sniffed. "I had a miscarriage."

He felt his mouth fall open.

Audrey's face crumpled. "It was our first time, I promise," she sobbed. "I-I didn't think it would happen. It ruined my meet."

JoAnne wrapped her arms around Audrey.

Denny felt sick. He scooted forward on his chair. "James found out about the pregnancy..." he said softly, replaying his recent conversation with the commander.

Audrey gave a culpable nod. "When he found out, he beat Leo unconscious. I was so scared when I saw L-L-Leo lying there. And then, then it happened—I started bleeding and cramping."

Her tears reminded Denny of another girl crying about an unplanned pregnancy. Cameron Walsh. She'd come to him after a swim meet he'd officiated, begging for his help. He'd helped her the only way he could, and thankfully her parents had forgiven him.

Now looking through the glass at his daughter, Denny longed to help her too. But he couldn't. He wanted to wipe away her tears and squeeze her tight. But he couldn't. He wanted to shout barbarically and hurl a chair across the small visiting room. But he couldn't.

He could only watch the devastation caused by James Scott play out in front of him. He shook his head. By jettisoning Jason from the family and beating Leo unconscious, James had caused the deaths of both his grandchildren.

"Audrey." Denny was surprised at the steadiness of his voice. "Look at me."

She glanced up, trembling.

"I love you, Audrey girl."

Her head dipped back down, and she seemed to cry harder.

Denny tried to keep it together. "Now, please go wait outside while I speak to your mother."

"Yes, sir." Audrey walked out, her eyes barely leaving the floor.

JoAnne took the phone and they stared at each other wordlessly.

Denny spoke first. "I sure didn't see that one coming."

"She obviously needs more supervision. I wasn't there for her."

"This wasn't your fault, JoAnne. She's practically an adult, making adult decisions. Even if you weren't traveling, you couldn't be there all the time."

"Denny, I need to tell you something." JoAnne hesitated. "I have to go back to New Orleans soon. So, I, uh, asked Mary and Leo to move in to our home."

"You *what?*" Denny's fist clenched. "You just invited the boy who knocked up my daughter to *live* with her?"

"I didn't know what else to do!" JoAnne cried. "I'm leaving soon—"

"And by inviting his wife and son to live with Audrey, you bring the menace of James Scott into our home!" Denny grew even more incensed. "What were you thinking?"

"I'm sorry! You don't know what it's like to do this all by myself. I have absolutely no help!"

He closed his eyes. A tense silence hovered between them.

"I already asked Mary, and she agreed," JoAnne finally said. "There's no way I can rescind the offer now. And I won't send Leo back to that house, back to James. I just can't do it. You didn't see him, Denny. You didn't see how badly he was beaten."

"The only way I allow this is if Leo comes and talks to me. I have some things to say to him."

"Well, I'll ask Mary, but I can't imagine Leo would willingly come to see you."

"The *only way*. You make sure Leo's here. If he's man enough to father a child, he's man enough to talk to me."

A voice broke in on the line to inform them the visit was over.

"I'm so sorry, JoAnne," Denny rushed to say. "This is on me. I'm not there to protect you and Audrey."

Before the MP yanked the phone away, Denny whispered, "I'm an anchor."

42. Corollary

Jason grinned from the passenger seat. "Thanks for picking me up."

Cam smirked. "Oh, just another day in the life of dating Jason Scott...You know, attend his sentencing hearing, pick him up from jail, chauffeur him to an AA meeting..." Her eyes left the road for a moment to meet his.

Jason continued her list of duties: "Attend Al-Anon, drive him to the hospital to see his brother...I owe you big time." Warmth settled in his chest as he looked at her. "How was Al-Anon?"

"Good. I found out I wasn't the only one retrieving an alcoholic from the courthouse today."

"Ah, Brett's wife was at Al-Anon too? I figured she came to post bail after he saved my butt. CS riled up this big dude in the holding cell, then left me alone to deal with him. The cretin was about to pound me when Brett showed up. Then it became two against one again."

"And you like those odds." She smiled.

"Yep, the guy changed his mind." Jason smiled for a moment, then snapped back to the present. "Uh, Cam, can you drive any faster?" There'd been an image in Jason's head of Leo lying vulnerable in his hospital bed ever since he'd watched the MPs lead CS away from the holding cell.

"Leo will be okay, Jase."

"Don't underestimate my father."

"I know what CS is capable of. That's why I handled it."

"Cam?" Jason's voice rose with reproach. "What'd you do?"

"After the detective told me how badly Leo was hurt, I went to Captain Payson to make sure your dad wouldn't weasel out this time."

"Really? How'd he take it?"

"He was shocked. He said he'd make sure to protect Leo."

As Cam parked in the hospital garage, Jason shook his head. "That was freaking brilliant. Why didn't I think of that?"

"Because I'm smarter than you."

Jason laughed and stroked her hand, rubbing his thumb over her soft skin. "Now the Navy knows. They can't turn a blind eye to the abuse anymore."

"They better not."

"Now I *really* owe you." He grinned.

"Big time."

To express his gratitude, Jason delivered an urgent kiss.

"Wow," she mumbled, smoothing her fingers over the stubble on his jaw. "Not only a kiss, but free exfoliation too."

"Do you need anything before I leave, Leo?" Mrs. Rose asked, standing over Leo's hospital bed.

"I'm fine, ma'am."

"You sure? I'll be gone over an hour while I check on Audrey and bring your mother back."

"I'm sure, ma'am."

Mrs. Rose nodded faintly and left.

Leo sighed. He was so sick of being in bed, so sick of people staring at him with thinly veiled pity. He'd been a strong, untouchable athlete. Now he couldn't even go to the bathroom on his own.

Audrey. He missed Audrey.

She was the only one who truly *saw him* when she looked at him. Everyone else — the surgeon, the nurses, Captain Payson, his mother, even his brother — stared at his wounds while trying to hide their distress. They were distracted and repelled by the welts covering his body, and they couldn't see past them. Nobody saw an athlete, a scholar, a boy who tried to do the right thing — all they saw was an abuse victim. They saw the son of an abuser, nothing more. Leo wondered if he was forever marked.

Worst of all was the Navy social worker who'd taken photographs of his injuries — a stranger forcing light conversation as she recorded evidence. All privacy was out the window, and Leo felt the heat of a huge spotlight, highlighting his helplessness and humiliation.

"Leo?"

Looking up, he found Coach Matt in the doorway wearing jeans and a tie-dyed shirt that read *Gratefully Deadicated to Swimming.*

"You came to visit me."

"Of course. When you didn't show up to practice, I figured you were either getting a huge head after that meet you had and thinking you didn't need to practice anymore, or sneaking off somewhere with Audrey to get a room."

Leo smiled.

"I called your house to chew you out, but there was no answer. So I called the Roses'." Matt's smile faded. "And your mom told me you were here."

Leo turned away. "Did she tell you what happened?"

"Yeah, you had a splenectomy."

"A swimectomy, you mean," he mumbled.

"What was that?"

Leo set his jaw and stared straight ahead. "I can't swim for six weeks, sir."

"I heard that too." Matt paused. "So you'll miss nationals, our last meet together, and I won't get credit for coaching the first spleenless swimmer under twenty seconds in the fifty."

"Stop it." Leo refused to be cheered up.

"Some college coach will get all the credit. Story of my life." Matt heaved a dramatic sigh and dropped into a chair by the bed.

Leo stared at his hands, fiddling with the medical wrap on his sprained wrist.

"I should've known this was going on," Matt said after a few moments. "Why didn't you talk to me?"

Leo glanced up, worried about disappointing his coach, but he read nothing but concern in Matt's weathered face. He looked down again. "I don't know. I didn't want to think about my crappy life during swimming." He sighed. "I wanted to keep it separate…" He created a separate box on each thigh with his hands. "There's swimming, and then there's all the bad stuff." His hands collapsed together in his lap, his fingers intertwining. "But now they're all mixed together."

Matt squeezed Leo's shoulder. "We'll just have to untangle them again, okay?"

The coach reached into his knapsack and pulled out a paper bag. "Total contraband." He grinned, handing it to Leo. "I brought you a couple cheeseburgers since we all know how delicious hospital food is." He squeezed Leo's arm. "Maybe we can finally get some meat on those bones without you swimming away all your calories."

"Great, now I'll be out of shape *and* fat." Leo put the food aside, not feeling one bit hungry, then realized how rude he sounded. "I'm sorry. Thanks for being here. I'm just…tired or something."

Matt studied him. "I should get going, let you sleep. Visit practice when you can — it'd be good to see your face on deck."

"Yes, sir," Leo said, but he knew he didn't want to be anywhere near a pool if he couldn't be in it.

Jason and Cameron tiptoed into Leo's hospital room. Cam must have noticed Jason's immediate fixation on the untouched fast food by the bed, because she whispered, "I'll go get us some dinner. Be right back."

As the door closed behind her, Jason sank into the chair and watched his brother's chest rise and fall with even breaths. Leo looked so young and defenseless in his sleep. He was curled on his side with his hands up next to his pillow. His bandaged right wrist rested on his left arm, and the fingers of his left hand unfurled against the sheet. Jason was struck by his brother's lean grace, even when not in motion.

A nurse bustled through the door and gave him a perfunctory nod. She fiddled with Leo's IV, and he stirred.

"Evening, Mr. Scott," she chirped. "How're we feeling tonight?"

His only reply was an annoyed grunt, eyes still closed.

"Sounds like *we* are feeling grumpy," Jason supplied.

Leo's eyes popped open. He coughed. "Hey, Jase."

"How ya feelin', buddy?"

"Better."

"Well, that's good to hear," the nurse chimed in. "Because we're removing your IV."

Leo forced himself to sit up. "Wait a minute, isn't that where my pain med's coming from?"

"Yes. But you can take the medication orally for the next few days."

"When am I getting out of here?"

The nurse paused. "The doctor's ordered you to stay four more days."

"What? Why?"

She fidgeted. "Because of your addiction...issues, we can't send you home with pain medication. So we have to keep you here a little longer."

Leo shot Jason an accusatory glance. "This is Mr. Shale's fault. It's yours too."

As the nurse left, Jason took a deep breath, determined not to get defensive. "I'm sorry you have to stay here so long, Leo. This must be like your own prison sentence, stuck here in bed."

Jason watched the anger drain from his brother's face.

"Speaking of prison, you're out now?" Leo asked.

Jason nodded.

"Was it bad?"

"Guess who my cellie was."

Leo's eyes widened. "Criminal Slayer?"

"Yeah. We had a good ol' time together until the MP jerks came and got him. I thought he'd get off again, but Cam told me she talked to Captain Payson."

"Cam did that? Wow." Leo nodded approvingly. "The captain came and saw what Dad did to me. He said CS would be in the brig for a while."

"What's he like?" Jason asked.

"Captain Payson? I don't know…he actually seemed kind of nice. He looked really upset when he saw what had happened to me. He made all kinds of promises—it won't happen again, blah, blah, whatever."

"I know why you have doubts. Cobra Snake's slippery. But this is the first time his bosses have known. Have some faith, bro."

Jason stood and reached for Leo's arm, motioning for him to take hold. "C'mon, I'll help you to the bathroom."

"How'd you know I have to pee so bad? My eyeballs turning yellow?" Leo asked.

"Because you suck at asking for help."

With a slight grin, Leo swung his legs off the bed and leaned on Jason's shoulder. Leo hopped on his good foot as they made their way to the bathroom.

His mother knocked and entered the room on her canes at the same moment Leo began using Jason as a human crutch. They locked eyes and stood in awkward silence until the male Scott contingent decided to continue on.

Their mother sighed and collapsed into a chair.

When Jason had returned his brother to his bed, his mother said, "I'm glad you're both here. I have something to tell you."

Jason quickly found a seat and prepared himself for the worst.

"Leo, Mrs. Rose has asked you and me to stay in her house for a while. How'd that be for you?"

At first Leo appeared puzzled. "I'd be living in the same house as Audrey?" A smile played across his lips.

"Leo," his mother warned. "We'd be laying out ground rules, of course."

"Yes, ma'am." Leo nodded.

Jason chuckled. His mother would certainly have her hands full.

"So that's settled, then." She took a deep breath. "I've made a decision," she continued, looking at each of her sons in turn. "I'm leaving your father."

Silence enveloped the room. Then Jason finally found his voice and boomed, "It's about freaking time!" He grinned at her. "I'll help with whatever you need. You deserve better, Mom."

"Thank you, Jason. We all deserve better." She turned her attention back to Leo, who looked away.

"Are you getting a divorce?" he finally asked.

"Probably, yes. But right now I guess we're separating."

"So, what…will I be, like, living with Dad part time?"

"I sincerely hope not, Leo. I'll do everything I can to prevent that. But at this point I have no idea what will happen. I don't even know when you can leave the hospital."

Leo frowned. "The nurse told me I'm here for four more days."

"Maybe we'll know more about your father's situation by then." She blinked at Leo and seemed nervous. "Staying at Audrey's isn't entirely a done deal yet, either. As soon as you're discharged, Mr. Rose wants to speak with you."

Leo looked up with alarm. Then he closed his eyes and sighed. "This just keeps getting better."

43. Consequence

Petty Officer Richards seemed distracted by his stare as she typed at her computer.

James admired her shiny black hair, which was drawn neatly into a bun and showcased her high cheekbones. As he sat wedged between two MPs, waiting for Captain Payson, James wondered if she liked bad boys. Drinking in wafts of her perfume, he wished he smelled better. He'd been wearing the same uniform for more than two days.

After speaking on the phone for a moment, Petty Officer Richards stood. "You may go in now, sir."

James marched to the captain's door and entered the office to stand at attention two paces from his superior's desk. The MPs flanked him.

Captain Payson paused before returning James's salute. "MPs, leave us."

They exited, and the captain walked around to sit on the edge of his desk.

As the seconds ticked by, James realized his superior wasn't going to allow him to stand at ease anytime soon. No matter. He could withstand anything the captain threw at him. When he'd been a plebe at the Academy, one ticked-off midshipman had forced him to stand at attention for several hours. Such mistreatment only made him stronger. He'd just let the captain make his point, and then he'd get back to work.

"Commander, how long has this abuse been going on?"

"I don't know what you're referring to, sir. Could you be more specific?"

"Specifically, how many years have you been beating your sons, James?"

"I've been disciplining my sons all their lives, sir."

Captain Payson spun around and grabbed a photograph on his desk. He shoved it in James's face, forcing him to look at the patchwork of cuts and bruises on Leo's body. "That is *not* discipline!"

James swallowed, looking away.

"It sickened me to see your son recovering from major surgery because of you. This is the son you brag about constantly, James. There's nothing he could've done to deserve this."

"Sir, he's seventeen and got a girl pregnant!"

"I don't care what he did. You're not to lay one finger on him again. A Family Advocacy Board investigation's already begun, and you're suspended until it concludes. You can also kiss your promotion goodbye."

James flinched. "Captain, you've made your point. You've showed me who's boss. There's no need to suspend me or put my promotion on hold, sir."

"You're seriously deluded if you thought two days in jail would be the only consequence of your violence. During your suspension, you're to stay away from your family. If I or any member of the Board discovers you've made contact with them, I'm returning you to the brig."

James's entire body tensed. "You can't take my family away from me!"

"*You're* the one who lost your family."

Suffocating on anger, James struggled to breathe. He'd worked his whole life to support his family—he'd made countless sacrifices for them—and some pot-bellied captain would try to tell him what to do?

"I have a message for you from your wife, James," Captain Payson continued. "She'd tell you herself, but she's so disgusted she doesn't want to see you right now."

James stopped breathing.

"She's leaving you."

It took everything James had to keep his face neutral and remain standing upright. He should have known this was coming, but he'd stuffed that idea into the far recesses of his mind. If he lost Mary, he lost everything. He felt tears rising and could not will them away.

Captain Payson picked up his phone and began speaking. James could barely make out the words "Send in the lieutenant commander" above the rush of adrenaline in his ears.

Roland Drake entered the office and stood at attention to James's right.

"At ease, Lt. Commander Drake."

James wished he could wipe away his tears.

"Mr. Drake, Commander Scott's been suspended during the course of a Family Advocacy Board investigation. You're to assume his duties during this time period. Do you have any questions?"

"I'm sure I'll have many questions, sir. It'll be near *impossible* to fill the commander's able shoes."

James fought the urge to smack the smug off Roland's face.

"Good. We'll discuss the parameters of your new assignment after the MPs escort the commander home." Payson plucked a tissue from the box on his desk and handed it to James. "Clean yourself up, commander." Then he called the MPs back in and ordered them to drive Commander Scott home.

Through a fog of shock and loss, James somehow managed to salute, turn precisely in an about face, and exit the office. Numb to the core, he followed the MPs' orders as they proceeded directly to the parking lot.

Hopelessness surrounded him as he slouched in the Jeep. He stared straightahead with glazed eyes, considering ways to end it all. He longed for his parents and knew only one way to see them again.

44. Meeting a Murderer

Audrey leaned forward, her hands flying around as she recounted what had happened in chemistry lab. "I didn't know why my Bunsen burner kept going out. It was driving me crazy!"

Leo listened from his hospital bed, willing himself to seem interested.

"And then I came back from talking to Mrs. Boyd and totally caught Alex blowing out the flame. That little weasel! Without you as my lab partner, I don't have a clue what I'm doing. I'm lucky I didn't burn the whole school down. Anyway, I brought you the next homework."

Leo took the papers and shuffled them onto the untouched stack next to his bed. "Thanks."

"When do you get discharged?"

"Don't know. Not sure I want to."

Somewhere along the line, as the days in the hospital dragged by, Leo had stopped caring. Assisted trips to the toilet and shower, bland meals, occasional awkward chats with visitors who seemed much more interested in the discussion than he was — it had all bled together in an exhausting jumble.

He also dreaded what awaited him when he left the hospital.

Audrey studied him. "Don't worry about talking to my dad. Obviously the pregnancy upset him, but overall he's a really nice guy."

"A really nice guy?" Leo quirked his eyebrow. "Is that what you call a murderer?"

Her face fell, and he immediately regretted his words. They'd conveniently avoided any real discussion of her father's conviction in the nine months since his arrest. Leo didn't want his suspicions to slip out, and Audrey seemed more than happy to leave the subject alone.

Her voice trembled. "He's *not* a murderer."

He couldn't find the words to apologize. "How do you know, Audrey? How'd the court martial get it all wrong?"

"How can you date me—how can you *love* me, if you think I'm the daughter of a murderer?"

"After everything I've been through with CS, do you honestly think I'd judge someone by their father's actions?" he snapped.

Leo realized he was shouting. He hated arguing with Audrey, but his anger certainly felt more satisfying than the apathy consuming him. He managed to lower his voice. "I do love you, Audrey. But your dad's still a murderer."

Dr. Patel, his surgical resident, walked into the room and froze, sensing the tension. "I could come back another time?"

"Don't bother. I was just leaving." Audrey flipped her long hair over her shoulder as she reached down for her bag.

"Audrey, don't go."

She ignored him and disappeared.

He closed his eyes. Of course she'd left. He couldn't stand to be around himself these days, and he didn't imagine his company was any better for others.

Dr. Patel smiled. "It's finally time for you to go home."

"I can leave?" Leo's eyes lit up. As he sat up, he was pleased to find himself nearly pain free.

"Hold on, there." The physician held up her hand. "Before you go, I want to review instructions for cleaning your surgical scar. And you'll need someone to help with the wheelchair I've ordered."

"Wheelchair?" Leo narrowed his eyes. "I'm *walking* out of here, Doctor."

"And how do you plan to walk on your sprained ankle?"

"Okay, then give me some crutches, please, ma'am."

"Leo, your wrist sprain means you can't apply pressure to that joint. You can't use crutches. You'll have to use a wheelchair."

He slumped back on the bed, extending his legs and sinking his head into the pillow. He rubbed his forehead with his palm. "No way. I'm *not* going in a stupid wheelchair."

As if on cue, an orderly wheeled it in and parked it by the bed. "Thank you. We'll take it from here," Dr. Patel said.

She patted his leg. "It'll take some getting used to, but you'll need to use the wheelchair for probably about a week. You wouldn't want to push your wrist or ankle too fast or they might not heal correctly."

"This just sucks…ma'am."

"I bet." Dr. Patel nodded. "Here you are this stud athlete, and you can't even walk on your own. But it'll get better. I'm wondering, who's taking you home?"

He looked away. "Apparently not my girlfriend. Suppose I can call my brother."

"He can take you home?"

"Yes, ma'am." His eyes rolled up to the ceiling. *We'll just have to make a stop first, I guess.*

As Jason drove him to the brig, Leo's legs jiggled. He chewed his lip. He rubbed the stubble on his head. He picked at the bandage covering his right wrist.

"You nervous about seeing Audrey's dad?" Jason asked.

He halted his fidgeting. "No."

Jason nodded, but appeared to stifle a laugh.

When his brother stopped in the parking lot, Leo froze, staring at the prison. "Can't I just kind of, you know, hop in there without getting into the freaking wheelchair?"

Jason shrugged. "Fine by me, man. But you might want to play the wheelchair card."

"What?"

"Listen, Leo, you're pretending you're all fine with going in there, but we both know you're crappin' your pants. This is the father of the girl you knocked up. And the guy's a convicted murderer to boot. All I'm saying is you might want to stir up some pity by wheeling yourself on in there."

Leo rubbed his mouth. Maybe Jason was right — maybe this could work to his advantage. Visions of Audrey danced in his head. Not many people could say they'd done it in a wheelchair!

Oh. But Audrey wasn't even speaking to him at the moment, and the next person he'd be wowing with the wheelchair was her father. He'd be lucky to emerge with his equipment intact. Still, it had to be done.

"Let's do it."

Jason wheeled Leo into the visiting room.

Once Leo saw the glass barrier and an MP leading the handcuffed prisoner to his seat, he felt better. "You can go, Jase."

"Okay, man. Good luck." Jason patted his shoulder and hightailed it out of there.

Leo eyed Mr. Rose, who picked up the phone and gestured for Leo to do the same. Leo took a deep breath and put the phone to his ear.

Mr. Rose cleared his throat. "You're…you're in a wheelchair."

"Yes, sir."

"Why is that?"

"I sprained my wrist and ankle, so I'm not allowed to use crutches for another week."

Mr. Rose looked down. "Your father did that? He hurt your wrist and ankle?"

"Yes, sir," Leo mumbled. He closed his eyes for a moment as the struggle with his father, being pinned to the wall and fighting to stay conscious, washed over him.

"Thank you, ah, for coming to see me, Leo. I know this must not be easy, but Audrey's always told me good things about you. I know you try to do the right thing."

Leo said nothing and felt his face grow warm.

"You've been very brave to deal with the abuse all by yourself. Thank God now people know." Mr. Rose looked down again. "I'm sorry I didn't know. I should've protected you."

"You're apologizing to *me*? I'm the one who's sorry, sir. I'm, I'm sorry…for hurting Audrey."

Mr. Rose's shoulders slumped. "I can't be there for her, Leo." His voice cracked. "I can't protect my Audrey girl. I…" He gripped the phone with whitening knuckles.

Leo felt goose-bumps prickle his skin. He hoped Mr. Rose wouldn't cry.

"I need to trust you…to take care of Audrey. I need you to be there for my daughter…to never hurt her, no matter what. Can you do that for me, Leo?"

He winced. "I hurt her feelings today. I said something mean to her."

"We guys say stupid things all the time," Audrey's father replied, unfazed. "Just tell her you're sorry and mean it. She'll come around. I used to put my big size-twelve foot in my mouth all the time with Audrey's mother." He gave a sad smile. "Now we hardly get to talk to each other."

Leo's conscience prickled a little. What if the court martial *had* convicted the wrong man? Mr. Rose certainly didn't *seem* like a murderer…

"What I'm asking you, Leo, is if you'll love Audrey," her father said, his eyes locked with Leo's. "Will you put her needs ahead of your own?"

"Yes, sir. I will love her. I do love her."

"I know you do. Which brings me to our next topic: how you express your love." He fidgeted. "I'm sure your mom and Audrey's mom will be talking to you both about, uh, sex, but we need to discuss this man to man."

Leo wondered if his face might burst into flames, but Mr. Rose soldiered forward. "If Audrey hadn't miscarried, do you think you'd be ready to become a father?"

"No, sir."

"I agree with you, son. I know you both have big dreams about swimming and careers, and you and Audrey aren't ready to be parents. Therefore, I believe you aren't ready to have sex." He let his words hang between them for a moment. "I know that may seem harsh, but you've already demonstrated you can't handle this responsibility. I need to know that you'll restrain yourself while you live with my daughter, Leo. Please promise me you two will learn from this and act like the intelligent people you are."

Leo swallowed. Embarrassment overtook him as he realized he'd been visualizing his next sexual encounter with Audrey just moments before meeting with her father. He had so little time left before he had to leave for the Academy. But Mr. Rose's plea weighed on him.

Leo took in the prison surroundings: the gleaming metal of handcuffs, the stern stare of the MPs, the watchful gaze of the petty officer monitoring their conversation. It was a cold, hopeless place. How did Audrey's father survive here? He couldn't fathom denying him this request.

"I promise, sir."

Mr. Rose exhaled. "I thought for a moment there I'd have to threaten you with a chastity belt for Audrey."

Leo hadn't heard of that, and his confusion must have been evident.

"Look it up: chastity belt," Mr. Rose said. "I'm not above going medieval on your butts."

Mr. Rose smiled warmly at Leo, and he couldn't help but reciprocate. They were from different generations, with different histories and different futures, but their common bond was Audrey. They both loved her like crazy.

45. Lobsters Swim Backward

Matt sounded angry. "Audrey, hop out."

Shading her eyes with a cupped hand, Audrey looked up at her coach — a dark, muscular silhouette framed by the sun. Sighing, she pulled herself out and chewed on her goggle strap.

"You're swimming like a lobster today," Matt said.

"Okay?"

"Lobsters swim backward."

She shook her head. "I didn't think I'd be this slow. I've only been out a week."

Audrey had decided to keep the miscarriage secret. She told Matt she was having "girl problems" when she'd missed a week of practice.

"I don't know if nationals are in the cards for you this season," he said. "Missing your boyfriend at practice?"

Audrey's head snapped up. "No way!"

"Yikes. Trouble in paradise? He's not abusing pain pills again, is he?"

"I don't think so. This time he's being a jerk all on his own."

"Well, cut him a break. He's been through a lot."

What about me? Audrey wanted to yell. She'd been pregnant and lost a baby! Didn't that count? Sure, Matt didn't know the whole story, but everyone seemed a lot more concerned about Leo.

Audrey's anger lingered as she and Elaine dressed in the locker room after practice. "Wanna go out?" Audrey asked her friend. "I need a drink."

"It's a school night, Aud."

"So what? We're seniors."

Elaine considered the invitation. "Alex's parents *are* out of town." She hooked Audrey's elbow. "C'mon, let's catch Alexa before he goes home."

Jason wheeled Leo from the car to the Roses' house just as his mother opened the front door. "Welcome, boys. I've got you all set up on the sofa, Leo."

Jason rolled him down the hallway past the kitchen. Finally Leo sank into the leather sofa. This piece of furniture held good memories. Too bad he'd just promised Mr. Rose he wouldn't create any more.

His mother sat next to him, and Jason brought in two ice waters.

"Thanks, Jase," Leo said.

"So," his mother began, taking a sip. "How was your visit with Audrey's father?"

Leo sat up and looked straight at her. "Mom? What's a chastity belt?"

Mid-sip, his mother spewed water everywhere, and Jason burst out laughing.

"I'll go get some paper towels," he said.

Her blue eyes twinkled. "Is Denny going to make Audrey wear one?"

"He threatened to...what *is* it?"

"It's a device to prevent young girls from having sex, Leo. It's a metal belt that's locked to prevent, uh, access."

"Oh." He started snickering too.

Jason returned and mopped around the sofa, then stood nearby with his hands on his hips.

"Thank you, honey." His mother's smile faded as she turned back to Leo. "All jokes aside, did you come to an understanding about you and Audrey living together?"

"I think that's my cue to leave," Jason said. "I have a date with Cam."

"Jason, I want to get to know Cameron better," his mother said. "Why don't you bring her around more?"

"I wasn't going to subject her to Dad. But we might hang out here sometimes, as long as Dad keeps his distance." Jason turned to Leo. "I'll pick you up for school at seven tomorrow, okay?"

Dread tightened Leo's chest. "Okay. See you then."

When the front door shut, his mother returned to her questioning. "You and Denny talked about things?"

"Yes, ma'am. Uh, you don't — this is kind of embarrassing. Um, you don't have to worry about us. I promised Mr. Rose I'd be smart."

"Okay." She sighed. "I haven't been here for you...but you know you can talk to me, right? You don't have to deal with everything yourself."

"Yes, ma'am." Leo vowed silently never to burden his mother with his drama. She had enough to deal with. He smelled the faint scent of coconut and chlorine. "Where's Audrey?"

"This was her first day back at practice. She should be home soon."

"Good." Leo nodded. "I need to talk to her."

"So, why'd you miss a week of practice?" Eric shouted over the vibrating bass.

Audrey knocked back a swig of her vodka tonic.

"It's personal, Eric," Alex jumped in. "Give Audrey a break."

Eric shrugged. "I just didn't know if she had to take care of Leo or something."

Audrey looked down. News of Leo's surgery and his father's incarceration had spread quickly through Pensacola High, and she wondered how he'd handle the stares and whispers when he returned.

She remembered the first few miserable weeks at school after her father's conviction. She surely didn't envy Leo.

She thought about her poor father stuck in prison, and the revelation that Leo believed he belonged there hit her all over again. She felt sick and took another swig of her drink. It was a little less noxious with each sip.

Elaine shuffled playing cards then herded the group to the kitchen table. "C'mon guys, I'll teach you to play euchre. Alexis, you'll be my partner. We'll whip Audrey and Erica's butts." Elaine pointed to where each should sit.

"Jeez, you get bossy when you drink," Eric noted.

"Elaine thinks she's all that, but we'll be the champs, Eric," Audrey said. "*My* euchre partner's the only sober person here."

Eric blushed and glanced at his soda can.

"I mean, I'm really glad you're not drinking, Eric," Audrey said quickly. "*Somebody* needs to be responsible around here, and it's sure as heck not going to be me. I'm sick of being responsible."

Elaine began Euchre 101, and Audrey was immediately confused. "Wait, so the jack of spades isn't a spade sometimes? It's a heart?"

Elaine sighed. "No! When clubs are trump, the jack of spades becomes a club."

Still confused, the booming music distracted Audrey even more. "Oh, yeah!" she yelled as the beat called to her. She boogied around the kitchen, splashing some of her drink on the tiled floor.

Laughing, Elaine and Alex joined her on the kitchen dance floor while Eric watched from his chair, shaking his head.

When Alex mimicked the choreography from the music video, Audrey and Elaine shrieked with laughter. Setting her drink on the counter, Audrey backed up to Alex, shimmying her body against his while she shouted the lyrics. Alex grabbed her hips and guided her through some dance moves.

When the room started to spin, Audrey threw her head back, letting her long hair tumble onto Alex's chest. She felt free—free of her father rotting away in prison, free of her perfectionism in school and swimming, and free of grief over losing the little life inside her.

"Leo?" his mother called from near the counter. "I don't know how I'll get your dinner to you."

Leo gathered himself off the sofa, balancing on one leg. "S'okay, Mom. I'll hop on over." He took small hops and accepted the plate in his left hand. "This should be interesting." Taking even smaller hops back to the sofa, Leo considered it a small miracle he made it without spilling any food.

"I wish Audrey would come help us cripples," she said. "I wonder where she is. I thought she'd be back by now."

"Here, come eat with me." Leo made another bunny trip to the kitchen and back and set his mother's plate on the coffee table as well. They collapsed into their respective seats.

Leo began to eat, but also studied his mother. After starting to speak several times, he finally blurted, "How do you do it?"

"How do I do what?"

His face got hot. "How do you, um, deal with…this?" He gestured to her leg braces. "I—I don't mean to be disrespectful, ma'am."

"It's fine to ask me questions, Leo. You're not being disrespectful. And feel free to lose the 'ma'am' since you'll certainly use that enough at the Academy." She offered him a wan smile. "How do I deal with being scary old cane lady? Not very well, I'm afraid." After another moment she admitted, "I hate it."

Leo looked up.

"I was top-ranked in practically every physical fitness category in ROTC. I could do anything I wanted, and my body never let me down. My pregnancies with Jason and you were a breeze. And now my body's betrayed me." She met his eyes. "Probably how you feel too. Your strong body's not working so well right now. It sucks."

Leo nodded. It sure did.

"I hate the effect on my relationships too," she added. "I can't do what everyone else can, so I get left behind. I miss your swim meets, and I don't have friends anymore." There was a catch in her throat. "I feel all alone." Her lip trembled. "But the worst part…the worst part is I couldn't protect you boys from James. I failed you and Jason. I'm so sorry, Leo."

His mother cried, and Leo looked away, fighting his own tears. Her strength overwhelmed him. He was out for six weeks, and she was out for a lifetime. The car accident was her *life*ctomy.

She sniffed. "James became another person after my accident. He wasn't always like this, Leo. It's like something died in him that night. He had a role in what happened, but I didn't know the guilt would stay with him so long."

"What? What do you mean Dad had a role in your accident?"

Her eyes widened. "No, no...I said that wrong. What I meant is your father thinks he should've stopped me from driving that night."

Leo stared at her for a long time. Finally he lowered his gaze and tried to take a few bites. "You're not eating much," he said with his mouth full.

"Well, I'm not a swimmer."

"I'm not either."

"You'll always be a swimmer, Leo. It's in your blood."

His fork rattled to the plate as he leaned back on the sofa. "I'm not very hungry."

"I guess now's as good a time as any to tell you this." His mother swallowed. "I...I called Brett Turner when you were in the hospital."

"The Florida State coach?" Leo sat up, his listlessness suddenly gone.

"Yes. He gave the fifty-percent scholarship to another swimmer."

Leo sank back into the sofa.

"But if you choose FSU over the Academy, we'll make it work. I doubt I can get loans in my name at this point, but you can take out student loans, and I'll help you pay them back. You don't have to go to the Academy."

Leo's stomach tightened. "How will you help me pay back the loans, Mom?"

"I don't know. I'll think of something."

He sat for a few moments. "I'm sort of freaked out. I don't even know if I can make it through school tomorrow, much less think about college."

"Then take some time to think about it, Leo. You don't have to figure it out right now. Speaking of school, do you have homework?"

"So much I don't even know where to start." He closed his eyes.

"Well, what's your favorite class? You can start with that."

"I used to like calculus and chemistry, but now I'm so far behind I'm kind of lost. Maybe government? That's my easiest one anyway."

"Since when do you like the easy classes? You're always up for a challenge."

"I guess I'm tired of challenges…Mom? I'm not doing so great this semester. I'll…I'll be in big trouble when Dad finds out. I might get a B in a couple of classes."

"Then get a B, Leo," she responded immediately. "Get a C. Fail a class. I don't care."

He gaped at her.

"You pile way too much pressure on yourself, and your parents certainly don't need to add to it. So what if you get a B? I'll still love you, and your father will too, even though he's totally clueless about showing it."

"So you don't care if I'm not top five anymore?"

"I thought it was silly you got so wrapped up in class rank. It's about learning, not GPA. We'll just celebrate one top five in this house instead of two." His mother frowned. "And where *is* she? Audrey should definitely be home by now."

"Get back in the car, Audrey!"

Audrey felt Eric grope for her arm from the driver's seat. She ignored him and whooped, feeling the wind whipping her hair behind her.

Only when the breeze made her eyes water did she finally bring her head back inside. Her cheeks burned from the wind, and she giggled at her naughtiness. Audrey fumbled for the radio but Eric fought her off. "I have to concentrate!" He smacked her hand.

"Humph." She crossed her arms. "You're a total party pooper, Erica."

"And *you* are obnoxious, Audrey!"

When he pulled up in the Roses' driveway, the raucous evening faded to silence. Eric turned to her, his anger seeming to turn to affection as he gazed into her eyes.

Audrey had the bizarre sense he was about to kiss her. "You should realllly try this some time," she said. "Bein' drunk is the bessst."

Eric looked down. "I'm afraid if I started drinking, I'd never stop. I don't want to be like my dad...Aren't you worried?" Eric asked after a moment. "Isn't your dad an alcoholic too?"

Audrey felt her throat tighten. "I don't want to talk about him." She glanced at the brightly lit interior of her house. "Do you think I'm in trouble?"

"Why would you be in trouble? Isn't your mom out of town?"

"Yeah, but Leo's mom's staying in my houssse. Leo is too, whenever he gets out of the hospital."

Eric suddenly slouched in his seat, his eyes darting around. "I gotta get out of here. I'm not getting blamed for you being sloshed."

"Maybe I can stay at your house tonight?"

Eric shook his head. "No, you have to go inside. Mrs. Scott's probably having a freakout right now, wondering where you are." He reached across and opened her door, then shoved her out onto the driveway. Jason had heaved her out that way once too. What was with boys pushing her out of their cars?

As his tires screeched away, Audrey took a deep breath and shuffled toward the door. She just wanted to go to bed. Stepping inside, Audrey heard Mrs. Scott's voice.

"I think I hear her, Jase. Hold on. *Audrey?*"

"Yesss, I'm here."

"Thank God. You can call off the search, Jason. She's home."

Audrey wanted to shield her eyes from the sunny yellow kitchen. Mrs. Scott hung up the phone to glare at her. "Where've you been?"

"I was at Alex's." She looked over and froze when she discovered Leo on the sofa. Rather than angry, she felt merely curious. Her head tilted to the side. "They discharged you?"

"Audrey!"

Mrs. Scott's urgent tone drew her attention.

"It's almost eleven! I expected you home at six."

"Whaz the big deal? I come home whenever I want when my mom's outta town."

Mrs. Scott's eyes narrowed. "Are you drunk?"

"No." Audrey began to retreat.

"Stay right there, young lady."

Audrey heard Leo gasp and fought the urge to turn and run upstairs.

"What's the *big deal?*" Mrs. Scott hollered. "The big deal's that you're underage, and you're drunk! Plus, you didn't call, and I've been worried sick! I was about to file a missing person's report with the police."

"The police?" Her voice shook. "I'm s-s-s-sorry." Her nose burned. "I juss had a little vodka. I did-ent think about calling."

"You clearly weren't thinking at all! You didn't *drive* in your condition, did you?"

Audrey felt the prick of tears. "No...Eric drove me."

Mrs. Scott sighed. "I'm disappointed in you, Audrey. I expect more mature behavior from such an accomplished young lady."

Leo interrupted Audrey's sob. "Mom, it's not her fault."

He'd gathered himself off the couch and seemed to be assessing how best to hop over to her.

"Sit down, Leo," Mrs. Scott ordered. "You just got out of the hospital, for heaven's sake. This is between Audrey and me, and there will be consequences."

"You're not my mother!"

The words were out of her mouth before she knew it, and Audrey blinked up at Mrs. Scott, not sure what to expect in return.

Leo's mother exhaled. "You're right. I'm not. I'll call your mother tomorrow to discuss this situation. Right now I want you to go to your room and stay there till you leave for school. No talking to Leo, no TV, no phone. After school, come directly home, and we'll discuss this. Do you understand?"

Audrey sniffed. "Yes." She turned and headed to the stairs.

"Audrey! I need to talk to you."

"That will have to wait," his mother said.

Leo sighed. "Yes, ma'am."

A few hours later, Audrey made sure the house was silent before she tiptoed downstairs. She filled a glass at the kitchen sink, trying to moisten her cotton mouth.

"Is that you, Audrey Absolut?" whispered a voice in the dark.

Creeping into the family room, she found Leo's eyes in the moonlight.

"Or is it Absolut Audrey, like the ad?" he added.

She wanted to rush into his arms, but held back, remembering his cruel words. "So what'd you need to tell me?"

"Lo siento. Soy un idiota."

"Yes, you are." She inched closer.

"I said that awful thing about your dad...and after talking to him, I want to take it back. Will you please forgive me?"

Audrey charged forward and climbed into Leo's arms. He smoothed his hand in circles on her back, and she melted into him. Her head on his shoulder, she whispered, "Sometimes I worry my dad really *is* guilty."

"Don't say that. He needs you to stand by him."

"How was it? What'd he say to you?"

"It wasn't as bad as I thought it'd be, but I had to promise not to knock you up again." She pulled back from their hug to see him grin. "He performed a sexectomy."

"Oh God, Leo. I'm sorry you had to go through that."

His smile faded. "Well, I'm sorry my mom was so mean to you."

"She hates me now."

"No, she doesn't. She's just mad. And it could have been worse. The worst part of my father's punishments was missing all that swimming."

"Leo? Your dad won't come here, like he did that one night?"

"I don't know." He drew her head back to his shoulder and ran his fingers through her hair. "Just think. In seven months, we could've been parents."

"That's too wild to even consider." She sniffed. "I'm sorry I lost the baby."

"Shhh." He stroked her back. "It wasn't the right time for us. But it'll be different in the future, okay?"

Her eyelids drooped. "Audrey Absolut." She snorted, then shook her head. "I think Audrey Scott sounds much better."

Leo squeezed her tighter. "That'd make me the happiest guy on earth. But are you sure you want that angry woman upstairs to be your mother-in-law?"

46. You're Not Alone

The mattress sunk down next to her, and Audrey heard Mrs. Scott's voice. "Time to wake up." She felt Leo's mother tuck a strand of her hair behind her ear.

She groaned and rolled away.

"Your hair's so pretty, spilling over the pillow like that." Mrs. Scott sighed. "With two sons, I never got to buy dresses or tie up long hair in bows."

"And then Leo goes and shaves his head for swimming," Audrey murmured. When she heard his mother chuckle, she forced one eye open and felt a pounding headache set in. "What time is it?"

"Six." Mrs. Scott smoothed a hand over her hair. "How'd you sleep?"

"Not great."

"You look like one of the plebes I used to teach: tired and washed out."

Audrey groaned as she sat up. "Am I in trouble?"

Mrs. Scott frowned. "Yes. I'll speak to your mother later."

Audrey turned away, blushing furiously.

"So thankfully you didn't drive home last night. Where'd you leave your car?"

"Um, Alex's house?" Audrey massaged one temple.

"That's what I figured. I wanted to wake you early so you had enough time to retrieve it before school."

Audrey still felt fuzzy. "What do you mean, *retrieve* it?"

"You'll walk to Alex's house, drive your car home, then give me the keys."

"You're taking my car keys?"

"Yes."

"How will I get to school? How will I get home from swim practice?"

"Jason's taking Leo to school — maybe you can catch a ride. And I don't think swim practice is a good idea today."

Audrey felt her lip tremble.

"I know how important swimming is to you. But I'm concerned about you getting drunk, Audrey. I just want time to sort this out with you after school, after I get a chance to speak to your mother."

Sniffing, Audrey nodded.

Mrs. Scott tilted her head. "So, you spoke to Leo last night?"

Tears began welling up. "I'm sorry. I just needed to talk to him. He said something awful, and it really hurt my feelings…"

"I should've known better than to try to keep you two apart." Mrs. Scott scooped Audrey into a hug.

Surprised, Audrey cried harder. It felt so good, so comforting, to lean into her shoulder. She hadn't realized how much she'd missed her parents.

"There, there," Mrs. Scott murmured, patting her back. "You've had some really tough times, honey. Is that why you got drunk? Because you were upset about something Leo said?"

Audrey pulled back and gave a slight nod.

"That concerns me," Mrs. Scott said. "If you're upset, drinking's not a good idea. I want you to talk to your friends, or your parents, or even me when you're upset."

"I usually talk to Leo, but I didn't think he'd speak to me after he was such a jerk…"

"Do you know how much he loves you?" Leo's mom's crystal blue eyes were just as intense as his. "He told me you're the best thing that ever happened to him."

"He did?"

"He did. Now, I'm going to help him get ready for school, and I want you to go get your car."

"Okay."

Audrey yanked on clothes and trudged the two miles to Alex's house, her head throbbing more with each step.

When she pulled her purple car into the driveway, Audrey pressed a longing kiss onto the dashboard. Her father had made a point to buy a car in school colors. She had a feeling she wouldn't be driving her baby again anytime soon.

Another vehicle pulled up behind her. Audrey held her breath as she watched Jason and Cameron step out. She hadn't seen Cameron since her father's court martial.

Taking a deep breath, Audrey pushed open her car door and turned to face them.

"Hey, Audrey," Jason said. "I'm picking up Leo, but if you need to leave before us I'll move my car."

"That's okay. I won't be driving." She bit her lip. "Your mom's taking away my keys."

"Whoa." Jason stifled a laugh.

"Audrey?" Cameron smiled and stepped closer.

She was startled as Cameron embraced her.

"I'm sorry for everything you've gone through," she whispered.

Audrey felt tears coming yet again. Did Cameron know about the miscarriage? How could Bill Walsh's daughter want to hug Denny Rose's daughter?

Cameron pulled away, and Audrey stood frozen in place. She couldn't even cry, she was so confused.

"We'll give you a ride to school too," Jason said, ending the awkward silence. "C'mon, let's go get the cripple."

Audrey allowed herself to be guided by Jason's hold on her shoulder. Once inside, she climbed the stairs to collect her backpack.

Jason assisted his hopping brother to the car and placed Audrey's backpack next to the collapsible wheelchair in the trunk. Audrey joined Leo in the back seat.

"I figured I'd give Cam a ride too. She's student teaching today," Jason explained. He glanced at the backseat via the rear-view mirror. "So you were out late last night, huh, Audrey?"

She blushed, and Leo answered for her. "That's Audrey Absolut to you, Jase."

"You'll never let me forget this."

"Audrey Absolut—it's got a certain ring to it." Jason smiled. They stopped at a red light. "You're a drinker?"

She sighed. "That's only the second time I've had alcohol in my life."

Leo's eyebrows arched. "When was the first time?"

"My recruiting trip to Northwestern. It was fun…We should drink together sometime."

Jason cleared his throat. "I just celebrated my fifty-seventh day of sobriety."

"That's great, Jase," Leo said.

"But I'm still an alcoholic."

"What's your point?" Leo asked.

"My point's that you might want to think twice about getting wasted together. I thought I was just drinking with friends, blowing off steam, having fun, until suddenly it wasn't fun anymore. It was an addiction."

Audrey's eye-roll halted when she met Jason's gaze in the rear-view mirror. "I know you guys won't listen to me," he said. "I know you think I'm a party pooper, but isn't your dad an alcoholic, Audrey?"

She said nothing, so Jason forged on. "Well, alcoholism runs in families. It's just something to think about."

Audrey looked out the window, watching strip malls and palm trees pass as the city began stirring in the morning sunshine. She studied Cameron's profile, her long brown hair carefully brushed and perfectly in place. She hadn't said one word during the car ride.

"You must hate my family," Audrey murmured.

"What?" Leo and Jason asked in unison.

Cameron turned to look at her. "I don't. I don't hate your family, because I don't…I don't think your father's guilty."

"You don't?" Audrey asked, incredulous. "Why not?"

Cameron looked at Jason, who nodded as he pulled the car into the school parking lot. She took a deep breath and unbuckled her seatbelt, turning to face the backseat. "Can I tell you guys something and you promise to keep it secret?"

Audrey nodded.

"Your dad helped me out of a really bad spot once, Audrey. He was enormously kind to me. My dad found out about it, and that made them even better friends. I know your dad could never have hurt my dad."

Audrey absorbed this information. "He did something nice for you? I didn't realize you knew each other."

"Your dad was at meets a lot when I was the swim team manager," Cameron said. "But you're right. I didn't know your dad very well. I was desperate one night, and I turned to him for help. You see, I was…I was pregnant."

Audrey was speechless.

"I was the father," Jason said, turning to look at Leo. "And I'd just left town without a way for Cam to get in touch with me."

Cameron seemed very focused on trying not to cry.

"Did you miscarry too?" Audrey asked.

"No," Cameron said softly. "Your dad helped me pay for an abortion."

Jason reached across the seat to squeeze Cameron's hand.

"At first my dad was furious with your dad," Cameron continued, her voice shaking. "But he finally understood that your dad truly helped me. My dad said if you were ever in need of help, he hoped to be there just like your dad was there for me. But my dad couldn't help you when you needed it, Audrey. He wasn't here. That's not your fault, and I'm convinced it's not your dad's fault either."

Audrey nodded, overwhelmed.

"I hate to cut this short," Jason said, checking his watch. "But we gotta get you two inside before the first bell. Mom will be mad if you're late your first day back to school, Leo."

Audrey felt unsteady as she climbed out of the car. Jason unfolded the wheelchair and helped Leo into it. Audrey watched Leo steel himself before entering the school.

Jason squeezed his shoulder. "You're not alone in this, buddy."

Audrey now knew she wasn't alone either.

Gripping the wheelchair handles, Jason maneuvered through a sea of sleepy, very young-looking students. He wished he could shield Leo from their gaping stares and whispered conversations. But he didn't seem able to protect Leo from much of anything—never had been. Lost in thought, Jason rolled Leo down the hallway, barely aware of where he was going.

"You didn't rat me out," Jason finally said.

"Huh?" Leo looked up at his brother.

"That time I threw the basketball at you, when I was twelve. You didn't go home and tattle on me to Dad."

"I knew what he'd do to you."

"CS never put me in a wheelchair, though."

Leo shrugged. "If you'd stayed in town, it probably would've happened to you first."

They were almost to Leo's homeroom when they passed the assistant principal. Mr. Morrison reached out to shake Jason's hand.

"Good to see you, Jason." He looked down. "And Leo, we're glad to have you back."

"Thank you, sir."

"A lot of things are clicking into place since I heard what your father did to you. Your fight with Billy Ryan, his supposed retaliation, Jason telling me you'd be out of school for a while—I wish you boys had told me the truth."

Leo looked away.

"No wonder you moved so far away, Jason," Mr. Morrison said, shaking his head. "And no wonder you came back."

"Well, as you can see, I've done a *great* job protecting Leo."

Mr. Morrison sighed. "It's tough to protect yourselves from your own father. I'm wondering, should we expect a visit from him at school? I'd like to get security in place so we're ready."

"Anything's possible," Jason said, squeezing Leo's shoulder again. "But we heard from his CO he's to stay away or risk returning to jail. So far he hasn't been around. Uh, I gotta get to work, sir. I better get Leo to class."

"Can't you wheel yourself, Leo?" Mr. Morrison asked.

"Well, sir, my doctors don't want me using my sprained wrist for a while. Audrey's going to help me when we have the same classes."

"I see. Jason, go ahead. I'll take Leo where he needs to go."

"Thank you." Jason gave his brother a half-smile. "Catch ya later."

"Thanks, Jase, for everything."

As Mr. Morrison wheeled Leo into homeroom, the chatter of the students halted. Leaning down, he whispered, "I'll give Audrey a hall pass so she can take you to every class. I don't want you to be alone in this, Leo."

Leo nodded, looking up to find thirty sets of eyes trained on him. He'd never felt more alone.

47. A Different Kind of CS

April fourteenth, exactly one month after Jason's sentencing hearing, turned out to be a very busy day. He'd worked eight hours at the warehouse, met with his probation officer, and now headed to the after-school program for his community service.

As he drove, Jason mulled over his conversation with his PO. He'd been pleased with Jason's stellar AA attendance but was less impressed when Jason told him he'd do anything to protect his brother. "No vigilante justice," the PO had warned. "Call the authorities." Jason clenched his teeth all over again. Calling Child Protective Services all those years ago had only made things worse.

When he parked in the middle school parking lot, Jason found himself eager to see the kids. Community Service was a completely different kind of CS.

Inside, he approached the program director, Connie. She peered at him over her reading glasses.

"You're six minutes late."

"Yes, ma'am. I'll stay late to get in my three hours."

The crease in her forehead disappeared. "That's not necessary. The boys have been waiting for you on the court—pestering me about when 'Mr. Jason' would get here."

He grinned. "Better not leave 'em hanging then."

He trotted through the building to the dilapidated outdoor basketball court. He found a group of seventh graders taking turns shooting the one worn ball in their possession.

"Yo, Jason," one called, approaching him to exchange a choreographed handshake.

"That's Mr. Jason to you, my little man." Jason winked and peeled off his shirt. "C'mon, girls. Let's get started."

After some quick negotiating and calculations, the boys formed teams, and half of them also removed their shirts. Jason noticed the most talented player, Esteban, had made sure he joined the "shirts" and kept his gray long-sleeved top on, not even rolling up the sleeves despite the humidity.

Jason had a special fondness for Esteban, a quiet boy who seemed to grow taller between every visit. Esteban had a gift for the game, but he never talked trash. He just looked down when his peers jabbered and teased him.

Midway through the second game, Jason blocked Esteban, challenging him with tight defense. Pivoting to shoot one of his trademark fade-away jumpers, Esteban spun to his right just as Jason stepped to the left, and at their ensuing collision the boy howled in pain. It'd been solid contact, but Jason's internal alarm sounded when he heard the wounded cry, which was far out of proportion to the force of the impact.

After the game Jason pulled him aside as the other kids shuffled over to take a break at the side of the building. "Kind of hot out to be wearing a long-sleeve shirt," Jason said, wiping sweat off his face.

Esteban averted his eyes. "I'm not hot. It's only April."

"Lift up your shirt."

"No, man. It's cool." Esteban stepped backward.

"It sounded like you were injured when we collided during the game, and I want to see. Lift up your shirt."

Esteban froze, but he offered no resistance when Jason pulled up the shirt to find deep purple bruises lining his ribcage.

"I-I-I'm sorry." Esteban yanked his shirt back down.

"Your old man did that to you?" Jason asked, his voice barely a whisper.

"It was an accident."

Jason turned toward the building, relieved to find none of the other boys paying attention. "Hey, guys, go ahead inside without us. We're going to talk to Miss Connie for a second."

Jason guided Esteban to the school cafeteria.

"You don't have to tell her," Esteban said, his eyes pleading. "It was just an accident, I swear."

"You did nothing wrong, kid. I have to tell her. It'll be okay." He led Esteban to an empty office and pointed to the chair across from the desk. "Park it." Then he went to find Connie.

Jason shared his suspicion with her. Connie thanked him and asked him to wait outside while she spoke to Esteban. As Jason fidgeted in a chair outside the office, he remembered all the times he'd gotten in trouble as a student.

"You know, I wasn't pleased when they assigned a thief to be a mentor for this program," said Connie as she emerged from her office and closed the door behind her, securing Esteban inside. "But you did good, Jason. That boy is definitely being abused. I need to report this to Child Protective Services, and I was wondering if you'd like to make the call."

Jason sat silently, unable to think of what to say.

"It's okay to feel nervous the first time you make the call," Connie said. "I'll help you."

"I've called them before." He shook his head. "The first time, uh, well, it didn't go so well, ma'am."

Connie tilted her head, scrutinizing him. "Takes one to know one, huh?"

Jason winced. "Something like that."

"Come on." Connie led him to another office where he could make the call.

He did so, shaking the entire time.

"Go ahead and catch up with the other boys, Jason," Connie said when he was done. "I'll stay with Esteban. We'll do our best to help him, okay?"

"Yes, ma'am." Jason nodded, feeling a mixture of dread and optimism.

"Can I get you something to drink?" Lt. Meghan Monroe asked. "Water? Tea?"

From his perch in her office easy chair—nothing easy about his posture as he waited for his father to arrive for their supervised visit—Leo shook his head. "No, thank you, ma'am. Is that clock right?"

"Yes." The social worker studied him. "Somewhere you need to be?"

"No, ma'am. It's just my father's never late."

"Well, he didn't show at all for counseling last week. I paid him a home visit, but he refused to talk to me. Hopefully he'll make it this time."

Leo leaned back in the chair, silently disagreeing with her optimism. If CS wasn't early to the appointment, he wouldn't show at all. *She'll have to figure it out for herself.* The whole thing was stupid anyway.

At least he was out of the dumb wheelchair. It had been three weeks since his discharge from the hospital, and physically he was healing well. Emotionally things weren't quite so upbeat. During his last visit, Mr. Shale had informed him he seemed clinically depressed. *Big shock.* Mr. Shale suggested exercise as a possible help, since Leo flatly refused medication, but no one was talking about the pool. Instead Mr. Shale or Jason took leisurely walks with him through the neighborhood. That wasn't really exercise at all.

Per Matt's request, Leo had been helping out on deck with the team. From the get-go Matt called him SW for "Spleenless Wonder"—a nickname that was funny the first time and *way* old by the fortieth. Jealously, Leo had watched Audrey work her way back into swimming shape.

"So, if my father doesn't show up for counseling, what will happen?" Leo asked.

"It's a condition of his return to work," the lieutenant said. "He may be looking at a separation from the Navy."

Leo's stomach flipped. He wasn't surprised CS was AWOL from therapy, but it was shocking that he'd missed so much work. How was he surviving without the opportunity to boss people around all day?

After a few more minutes, the social worker finally sighed. "This is ridiculous. Are you up for a house call, Leo?"

"A house call, ma'am?"

"If Mohammed can't come to the mountain…" She grinned. "We'll go to him. Let's see what your father's up to."

His butt felt nailed to the chair.

Her grin vanished. "I won't let him hurt you."

His eyes narrowed.

"He's your father, Leo. You have to see him some time."

"I don't think you know what kind of man he is, Lieutenant."

"You might be surprised. I promise you won't get hurt. Let's go."

Not feeling like he had another option, Leo followed her to her car.

Leo's anxiety reached a peak as they stood on the front porch of his home. He flinched when Lt. Monroe pounded on the door.

"Commander! Please open up, sir!"

After a tense few moments, the front door creaked open, and Leo suddenly realized what the lieutenant had been trying to tell him. He barely recognized his father, who'd apparently ceased all efforts at personal hygiene. His hair frizzed out in an afro, and he sported an unkempt beard and moustache. He wore a stained sweatshirt and dirty jeans, and Leo wondered how long it'd been since he showered.

But the biggest change was his father's body language. Instead of his proud, rigid posture and penetrating gaze, he slouched and averted his eyes, which were gray and dull, just like his sweatshirt.

"You were supposed to be in my office thirty minutes ago, Commander," she said.

"Sorry." His voice was raspy, like he hadn't used it in some time. "I must've forgotten."

His father snuck a sidelong look at him, and Leo tried to hide his shock.

"May we come in, sir?" Lt. Monroe pressed. "You only have thirty minutes left of your time with Leo this week."

Clearing his throat, CS blocked their entrance. "It's, uh, kind of a mess."

"I'd like to see if you've made any progress toward the goals we discussed last week, sir." She shoved him out of the way and stepped into the foyer.

Leo couldn't believe CS allowed her to push him aside. When the lieutenant ordered him to come inside too, Leo held his breath as he brushed past his father to enter the house he hadn't seen for a month.

His father stared at him from just inside the door as the lieutenant bulldozed around the house. "How's your mother?" he finally asked.

"Fine, sir."

"Tell her…tell her I…I don't know what to tell her." He looked down. "I don't want her seeing me this way. I-I don't want you here."

"The lieutenant made me come. I don't want to be here either." He watched his father blanch at his words, and the shell of the man CS had become simultaneously flummoxed and saddened him. "What's wrong with you, Dad?"

"What's wrong with him," the lieutenant answered as she floated down the stairs, "is he's clinically depressed."

His father's face flushed.

"Your father's not taking good care of himself, Leo." Turning to him, she chided, "Commander, this home's even *more* of a pigsty. You haven't taken out the trash or cleaned the bloodstain in Leo's room. Have you been out of this house since I visited you last week?"

He hung his head. "No."

"I have to make a report to the Family Advocacy Board, and you're not helping your cause. Do you want to be dismissed from the Navy?"

"No!" he responded immediately.

"Then get to my office for our appointment next week. Meet with your doctor. Clean this pit up. If you don't follow through, I'll have no choice but to recommend a separation from the Navy."

Leo couldn't believe what he was witnessing. CS just stood there taking it.

"Your future's in your hands, Commander. Let's go, Leo."

"Yes ma'am." Leo followed the lieutenant out the door, sneaking a final glance at his father, who hadn't moved an inch and continued staring at the floor.

On their ride back to the base, the lieutenant tapped her fingernails on the wheel while Leo tried to make sense of the abrupt change from Cruel SOB to Crumpled Spirit.

"He's severely depressed," she said, speaking more to herself than to Leo. "I'm worried he'll kill himself, and there's not a thing I can do to stop it."

48. Saving Scott

Leo had tried out a fitness pool with an adjustable current once. The salesperson had been forced to crank it to the highest setting to prevent Leo from running into the wall. Today he just swam in the regular, non-propelled water of the high school pool, but Leo trudged along like he was swimming upstream, against the tide. This was day two back at swimming after a five-week hiatus. His surgeon, marveling at his fast recovery, had allowed him to return one week early.

"All right, ten one-hundreds pull," Matt told the group. Leo was still panting, having only just arrived at the wall, and Matt smirked. "Think you can keep up, SW?"

Leo shot his coach a dark stare. He was in survival mode for this practice, just trying to get through it. His stroke technique sucked, but he didn't even care. It didn't seem fair that it took forever to get fit but mere days to fall out of shape.

As Audrey strapped on hand paddles, she grinned at Leo. He'd been demoted to her lane, which was still the second fastest, but he was barely keeping up as the caboose.

"What does a spleen weigh, like a couple of pounds?" Audrey's eyes glinted with mischief. "You should be faster since you're pulling less weight now." Audrey just giggled as he glared.

"Yeah, Lenore," added Alex from the fast lane. "You should be leading this lane."

"Just give me a week, and I'll be back to kicking all your butts," Leo said, with more attitude than he actually felt. He choked down panic about how sluggish he was.

After practice Leo met Audrey in the hallway outside the locker rooms. They were both freshly showered but still wreathed with the scent of chlorine. Leo, for one, was thrilled to smell like a walking swimming pool again.

"Why are you wearing a tank top and shorts?" Audrey asked.

"Wanna join me for a run?"

"Ugh." Audrey looked like she'd eaten something sour. "I'm dead from practice. How can you even *think* about more exercise?"

"I'm dead too, but I have to get back in shape."

"Leo, don't overdo it."

He grinned. "I'll be fine. Will you tell my mom I'll be late for dinner?"

She nodded.

He snuck his hand around to the small of her back, drawing her close. "I'm glad we're back swimming together. I missed our post-workout kiss." He tucked a few strands of wet hair behind her ear, caressing her face.

Audrey gazed up at him.

Leo closed his eyes and inhaled deeply. "You smell like coconut."

"Mm-hmm."

He leaned in to brush his lips across hers, and Audrey surrendered in his arms. They shared tender, lingering kisses as his hands explored the finer points of her physique. He luxuriated in the warmth of her skin as her lithe body molded against his.

Fifteen minutes later, Leo jogged. His legs felt weighted with lead, but memories of their kiss kept him going the first two miles.

He allowed his mind to wander, feeling sweat stick his tank top to his skin, and found himself contemplating college. As far as the Navy knew, Leo was set to report for Plebe Summer at the end of June, just two months away. In turn he considered the mountain of debt he'd accrue if he attended FSU. He still hadn't made a decision.

As his breath quickened, Leo realized he was passing his neighbor's house. Just then his pink stucco home came into view, which brought him to a halt. He hadn't planned a particular running route, but it made sense that his feet took him on the familiar journey from school to home.

He bit his lip and surveyed his house, wondering if his father was inside. Their next appointment with the social worker lieutenant was supposed to be tomorrow. Had CS followed any of her instructions?

His throat tightened. He wanted to run from the house, the scene of shameful beatings and disappointment, but part of him felt drawn in. His father's brokenness called to him like a siren.

What if CS committed suicide and Leo could've done something to stop it? What if he was the only person who could help his father? Could he live with himself if he didn't?

Guilt overtook Leo as he realized his life would be much easier without CS in it. Yet he couldn't deny the nagging impulse to run to the house and check on him. Gripping his head with both hands, he agonized over what to do.

I should turn around and run back to Audrey's house. He could do it. He'd be crazy to approach his abusive father and willingly put himself in danger. But his body wouldn't turn around. Leo rested his sweaty hands on his hips and stared at his front door. Then be began to move again. He knew what he had to do.

His hand started knocking before he really intended to do so, but there was no response. What was taking so long? Had CS actually gone somewhere? Leo's hands trembled as he contemplated knocking again.

When at last his father opened the front door, Leo kept close watch on his expression. He saw what he thought was a glimpse of relief perforate his father's gloom, and for a moment he actually smiled. Leo knew he'd done the right thing.

His father looked worse than last week, if that was possible. He had dark circles under his eyes and his beard was even fuzzier and wild, his clothes grimier than before.

Leo swallowed. "I was just in the neighborhood, um, on a run." He felt like an idiot, trying to find words that wouldn't incite his father's anger. "Dad? Would you help me? Would you help me get back into shape?"

CS looked confused, and Leo smirked.

"Nothing increases my fitness like Commander Scott's boot camp."

His father's voice sounded strangely uncertain. "You want *me* to help you?"

"Yes, sir, um, maybe you could come with me on my run? You know, kind of like set the pace for me?"

His father's lips parted, and for a stunned moment Leo thought he might cry.

"I'll go change," he murmured and bolted upstairs, leaving Leo standing in the open doorway.

He stepped inside and shuffled through pizza boxes and old newspapers. The house was a disaster.

Leo heard bathroom pipes whine from upstairs as he entered the kitchen. Glancing at the piles of dirty dishes strewn about, he pulled a large plastic garbage bag from under the sink and shoveled in newspapers, soda cans, and food wrappers. He'd placed three full, tied-up bags next to the door by the time his father descended the stairs.

CS appeared completely transformed: all signs of facial hair vanished, his hair once again closely cropped, and his clean white T-shirt and dark blue shorts hugging his frame without one wrinkle.

Leo stood taller at the return of his military father, feeling the hairs on the back of his neck bristle.

CS's face darkened when he saw the bags, and Leo froze. Had he made a mistake?

"You didn't have to do that," his father said. "That's my mess to clean up, not yours."

"Yes, sir." Leo searched anxiously for the right words. "I was just standing around so I thought I'd make myself useful." He held his breath.

CS closed his eyes for a moment. "Let me start over. Thank you for cleaning up my mess, Leo." Their eyes met for a moment before CS attempted another smile, seeming to work facial muscles that had gone unused for weeks. "How about that run?"

Leo nodded and practically sprinted for the front door. They ventured into the approaching dusk, easing into a comfortable cadence. Expecting his father to struggle, Leo was surprised by his smooth stride, which urged him toward a respectable pace.

"This is great!" said CS as they headed toward the glow of the setting sun. "I sure love to run."

Leo couldn't even muster a response as the miles accumulated in the pool and on the street caught up to him. CS inched ahead for a while, then abruptly his energy seemed to crash as well. "We're both…faltering," CS said. "We'll finish with a sprint back home."

That's a good half-mile away. Leo cringed. He didn't think he had it in him. But he'd asked the master of fitness to help him, and this is what he got. What would his father do if he failed?

CS lengthened his stride, and Leo had no choice but to follow at a blistering pace. He could hear the harsh sounds of their labored breathing as he pushed himself to the absolute limit. He matched his father stride for stride, including a muscle-burning kick as they approached the driveway. Leo stumbled into the yard as the run finally completed.

Hand on hips, sweat dripping off his chin, Leo panted and watched his father do the same. Gradually his heart rate slowed, and he began to feel human again. He looked over to find his father stretching, and when their eyes met he grinned. After that short breather, CS looked like he could run another five miles.

"Think you can get fit in time for Plebe Summer?" he asked.

Leo took a deep breath. "I haven't decided on the Academy yet, sir." He watched his father's reaction.

Eyes flashing with anger, CS said nothing. "I guess that's your decision," he finally offered.

Leo's eyebrows flew up.

"But I think you'd make a big mistake turning down this opportunity."

"Why do you want me to go there so bad?" Leo asked, suddenly feeling bold.

CS snorted. "Why are you trying so hard to get back into shape? It's because you want this. You want to challenge yourself—you want to see what you're made of. I know this because you're just like me—well, sort of like me. You got the best parts of me: my fire and my drive. I've never seen somebody strive for excellence like you do. I've never seen somebody with so much to prove, and the Academy's *the* place to prove yourself. You can test yourself there like nowhere else."

Leo felt trapped by his father's unwavering gaze.

"I *survived* the Academy, but you could flourish there. I was a total ass who made all kinds of enemies, but *you* make people like you. I don't know how you do it. You must've inherited your mother's kindness and sense of justice. I don't know. You fight for people, and it'd be natural for you to fight for our country too."

CS cleared his throat. "You're a stronger person than me, Leo. You'd be perfect for the Navy, and the Navy would be perfect for you. Don't let my mistakes screw up your future."

Leo finally managed to break their gaze. His father's words had blown him away. He'd always wanted to please his dad, just make him proud for once, yet he'd always fallen short. Now CS was telling him he was the stronger one?

"You better head back to the Roses'," CS grunted. "You don't want to worry your mother. I'll see you tomorrow in that stupid lieutenant's office."

"Yes, sir."

Overwhelmed, he willed his feet to start moving again. Had his visit saved his father? Perhaps they were saving each other.

49. Mission Statement

Audrey skipped up to Leo in a post-practice outfit that mirrored his: a tank top and shorts. "No more studying!" she announced. "Just two days of class left—can you believe it's almost June? I'm actually up for joining you on your run today."

A bolt of panic shot through Leo. She hadn't wanted to run with him since the surgeon had cleared him over a month ago, and today would be a horrible day for her to start. "Um, I don't think so. I'm going at a fast pace today."

"Oh. Maybe we can both run on the track," Audrey said, undeterred. "That way if I can't keep up, you won't be miles ahead."

"No!"

Her eyes widened.

"I mean, I-I did a track workout yesterday, and I wanted to run the trail in the woods today." He checked his watch. "I gotta go."

He pivoted and never looked back, though he could feel her watching him go. He was nearly out the door when he realized he'd forgotten their post-workout kiss. But there was no turning back now.

Leo double-timed it once he was out of the building and came to stand at attention before Commanding Sadist on the spongy track.

"We're practicing frustration tolerance today," his father announced.

"Yes, sir."

The beginning of their biweekly Academy-preparation sessions typically involved Leo questioning why in the world he'd asked his father to help him, but the end was surprisingly exhilarating. Leo knew his father was right. He loved the thrill of testing himself, and CS was quite skilled at pushing him to the brink of physical and mental exhaustion.

Today he felt a little off his game, still worried about blowing off Audrey. And if his mother and brother found out he'd been meeting with his father, they'd go ballistic. His family had been worried enough when they'd heard Captain Payson had lifted his suspension, but once CS completed the mandated counseling, he'd had no choice. Technically this freed CS to see his family as well, but so far he hadn't visited the Rose house. This secret training was their only contact.

CS's voice was smooth and soft. "No matter what a superior throws your way, you're to show no emotion. Once you reveal even a tiny crack in your armor, your CO will go in for the kill. I want a look of ice no matter what I say. Understood?"

"Yes, sir." Leo arranged his face in what he imagined was a blank look.

"Good. Tell me the mission statement of the Naval Academy."

"Sir, the mission is to develop midshipmen morally—"

"Stop," CS said. "You paused too long. Drop and give me fifty."

"Aye, sir." Leo dropped to the track.

He'd barely finished five pushups before CS said, "Ten, hut!"

Leo hopped up and CS hissed in his ear. "Is there some sort of delay between hearing my orders and acting on them, Midshipman Scott?"

"No, sir."

"You dicking the dog just added ten more. Drop and give me sixty."

Leo fought to stay cool as he returned to the track.

CS again halted him and ordered him back up, chastising him for reacting too slowly and adding more pushups to the total. They played this little game until Leo had racked up one hundred pushups, which his father finally allowed him to complete without interruption.

Leo dragged himself back to standing, breathing heavily.

"Do you believe you were reacting too slowly, Midshipman Scott?"

Leo wasn't sure how to respond. "No, sir."

"Correct. Excellent, Leo." He nodded. "I was intentionally trying to throw you off, but you didn't take the bait." He shifted back into drill sergeant mode. "Now, tell me the mission statement of the Academy."

He still panted. "Sir, the mission is to develop midshipmen morally, mentally, and physically and, um, and to imbue them with the highest ideals of duty, honor, and loyalty—"

"What the hell?" CS stabbed his finger into Leo's chest. "I want you to know this inside and out. None of this hesitation crap will fly."

Then his father shoved him, and Leo stumbled backward, catching his fall by planting his hands behind him on the track. He winced and dragged himself back up.

"Let's try this again," CS barked. "Tell me the mission statement, word for word."

Leo began, but CS interrupted his stammer, ordering him to complete fifty pushups.

As Leo struggled to ignore the searing pain in his right wrist, his father leaned down by his ear. "That's the freaking worst pushup I've ever seen! Get your body weight evenly distributed to the right. Ten, hut!"

Leo returned to standing.

"Are you *trying* to piss me off?"

"No, sir." Leo felt the familiar tingle of terror climb up his throat. Any element of playfulness within the challenge evaporated when his father's eyes turned violet.

"What's wrong with you? How do you explain those lousy pushups?"

"No excuse, sir."

"Bull. You tell me what's going on."

Leo could barely breathe. He'd thought they'd come a long way these last six weeks, but now Leo knew he'd get hit no matter what he said. Once again he opted for honesty. "My wrist hurts. I apologize for my weakness, sir."

"Aw, the baby's wrist hurts?" CS turned away, hands on hips, and seemed to force some deep breaths. His voice had calmed a bit when he wheeled back around. "How'd you injure your wrist?"

"When I fell back, sir, I must have aggravated my wrist sprain."

"You sprained your wrist? When was that?" His father's fury now seemed to melt into curiosity.

Leo hesitated. "In March, sir. It was after we went to the restaurant…"

CS looked down. "It was me. I did that to you."

"It—it wasn't as bad as my ankle, sir, and—"

"You sprained your ankle too?"

"Y-Y-Yes, sir, but they both healed just fine…It sucked being in a wheelchair but it helped—"

"You were in a wheelchair?" CS looked horrified.

"I, uh, couldn't use crutches because of my wrist, sir…"

His father looked off in the distance. "I put you in a wheelchair. I put my son in a wheelchair."

Leo paused, unsure of what would happen next.

Abruptly CS pivoted and ran, disappearing toward the parking lot.

Leo stood, cradling his wrist and staggered by his father's response. Left to complete the workout on his own, he chewed his lip as he jogged around the track.

When Leo returned to the Roses', he found three accusing sets of eyes waiting for him.

"Audrey, please wait in your room while Jason and I talk to Leo," his mother said.

Audrey nodded and brushed past Leo, avoiding his questioning gaze.

Sensing he was in trouble, Leo instinctively stood at attention in the kitchen. His mother patted his arm. "Hey, relax. You're not a sailor yet. Have a seat."

When she grasped his hand to guide him to a chair, he yelped. She gasped and let go. "Did James hurt you again?"

As he sat at the kitchen table, Leo's eyes darted back and forth from his mother to his brother. "No, why would you say that?"

"Leo, the jig is up," she said, shaking her head. "Audrey told us she saw you and your father together at the track."

Leo closed his eyes.

"What'd he threaten you with to get you there?" Jason demanded.

"He didn't threaten me. I—I asked him to meet me."

"What?" Jason thundered. "What were you thinking?"

"I asked him to help me get ready for the Academy," Leo explained.

His mother seemed on the verge of tears. "He's helping you get ready? What, by beating you unconscious? Will you be ready for the Academy when you have a broken arm?" Her voice rose shrilly. "Will *that* help prepare you, Leo?"

Leo shook his head. "He *is* helping me. I fell on my wrist tonight, but it wasn't Dad's fault. I'll be fine, ma'am."

"I can't believe how stupid you are," Jason said.

"In ten days, when you turn eighteen, I can't stop you from seeing him, Leo. Though why you'd take that risk is incomprehensible to me. But until then, I forbid it."

"Why are you so mad, Mom?" Leo's stomach twisted in knots. "I didn't do anything wrong! I just spent time with my own dad!"

"In a normal family, it'd be fine to see your father. But we all know this family's far from normal." She studied him. "I'm guessing this wasn't the first time you met up with him."

Why did she have to ask that? "No, ma'am."

"How long has this been going on?"

"Since April."

"And you say you didn't do anything wrong?" she yelled. "You've kept this secret from us for over a month! You knew it was wrong, young man."

Leo looked away. "Yes, ma'am."

"For the next ten days I want you in this house unless you're at school or swim practice," she said quietly. "If you need to go for a run, Jason can accompany you."

"What about graduation parties?" Leo asked, gripping the table with his good hand.

"You can go only if you stay with Audrey the entire time."

"Great, so now Audrey's my freaking chaperone?"

She looked too angry to answer. She closed her eyes. "Go to your room," she finally hissed. "I'll call you when dinner's ready."

Leo balled his hands into fists. "Yes, ma'am."

A few minutes later, he heard a light knock on his bedroom door.

"Go away, Audrey!"

At first he felt satisfied as her soft footsteps faded down the hall, but almost immediately a deep longing swept over him. He wanted to hold her in his arms and forgive her for revealing his secret. But how could she go behind his back like that? Didn't she trust him? Why hadn't she even talked to him? He felt betrayed all over again.

He fell back on the bed, hugging a pillow, and his mind swirled with thoughts and images from the day. He simply hated having his parents upset with him. When his dad was mad, he usually felt pure fear. But his mom's anger was a different experience. He just felt horrible for letting her down.

How could he explain it to her? This need to be with his father despite the risk? *He* didn't understand the hungry yearning inside him, so how could he explain it to anyone else?

50. Skinny Dipping

The next day, Leo finished warm-up and looked over to see Matt wiping his forehead, sweating—even without the workout—in the late-May heat. "We'll keep building our aerobic base today," he informed them. "Four fifteen-hundreds."

Leo groaned along with his teammates. The four-mile set would take almost two hours to complete—the rest of practice. This was one of their last high-school practices together, yet Leo wouldn't allow himself to even look at Audrey. How could she have tattled and gotten him grounded?

He pushed off in a tight streamline to begin the first mile, taking smooth, easy strokes. By the third mile, he was actually enjoying the set. He felt himself drop deeper into a relaxing trance with each pull and kick.

Once the long set was over, he leaned back against the edge of the pool and ignored Audrey's stare. She finally pulled herself out and left Leo by himself.

"SW, come on over." Matt beckoned.

Leo approached nervously. Had he disappointed Matt somehow?

"What the heck's going on with you and Audrey?"

"Nothing, sir."

"I think I saw her crying during that set," Matt said softly. "One of those cries where you have to dump tears out of your goggles."

Leo sighed. "I'm mad at her. She went behind my back and told my mom something that got me in trouble."

"What'd she tell her?"

Leo squinted in the sun. "Audrey saw me with my dad. He's been training me for the Academy."

Matt whistled through his teeth. "And you think she should've kept that a secret? Get your head outta your butt. If *I* caught you with your father, I'd have your mom on the phone in seconds."

Leo lowered his head.

"I have less than one month as your coach. I don't want any time lost to bruises or broken bones. I don't think you can afford to lose any more organs, either," he added.

Leo looked up to find his coach smiling.

Matt cleared his throat. "I, uh, I'm going to miss you, Leo."

"I'll miss you too. You...you don't suck as a coach."

Matt laughed. "I'm glad to hear that. You don't suck as a swimmer either. Well, I better go...got a date tonight."

"I thought you said women sucked out your life force?"

"I did. I don't know what I'm thinking, but Jason set me up with this chick he knows, and I actually *like* her. She doesn't take any crap. Her taste in music does need some work, though."

Leo chuckled. "You need someone to broaden your horizons beyond the Dead, Matt. Good luck with that...you'll need it. Heck, *she'll* need it."

"No kidding. You and Audrey have been dating for what, almost three years? That's longer than any relationship I've had in my life, and you're half my age." Matt gave him a stern look. "Don't screw it up, Spleenless Wonder."

"Yes, sir." Leo headed for the locker room with a smile.

"Leo?" his mom called from inside the house.

"Nope, it's just me." Audrey walked into the family room to find Mrs. Scott cleaning up papers after her tutoring session. "Matt was still talking to Leo when I left practice."

"How was your day?" Mrs. Scott asked.

"Fine." Audrey played with a strand of wet hair.

"Fine, huh? You don't *sound* fine."

Audrey moved on to twirl the string on her shorts. "Leo's not speaking to me."

Mrs. Scott tapped the sofa cushion. "My son's an idiot sometimes. You did the right thing, telling me what you saw."

Audrey sat on the sofa, a safe distance from Leo's mother. Mrs. Scott patted her knee.

"Maybe Leo will come around when he hears I'm not grounding him any more."

"You're not?"

"I talked to Marcus Shale today and told him what happened. He said this probably isn't as much about Leo's dad as it is my fear of letting Leo go. It's time for him to make his own decisions." She sighed. "Marcus is right. I'm scared, but I need to let Leo go."

"But what if his dad hurts him?"

"The truth is if James wants to hurt Leo, he's going to do it. Keeping Leo in this house won't make a shred of a difference. I lived with my boys for years and was never able to stop him from hurting them."

Her eyes shone with sadness. "And I'm worried that keeping Leo away from his father will draw James to this house, where he could possibly hurt you too." She shuddered. "I just have to hope James has finally learned his lesson."

"Mrs. Scott? Why did Leo ask his dad for help?" Audrey asked after a moment.

"I won't pretend to understand their relationship, but I think Leo felt like he had to reach out to his father. He didn't have a choice."

"Yes, he did!"

"Audrey, your father's been convicted of murder, yet you continue to stand by him. You continue to see him and support him. Is this any different?"

Audrey felt anger flare within her, and it was all she could do to stay on the couch. But then she knew it was true. Even if there were incontrovertible evidence proving her father murdered another man, she'd never believe it. She needed her father and he needed her.

"Do you think my father's guilty?" Audrey asked softly.

"I honestly don't know. He never seemed like a murderer to me," she said. "Then again, James didn't seem like an abusive father when I met him. I'm realizing there's a lot I don't understand in this world. But I know your father loves you, and I think it's wonderful you stand by him."

The alarm clock showed a little after midnight, and Leo thought he'd waited long enough. Surely his mother was asleep by now, and he hoped Audrey wasn't. He crept down the hallway to her bedroom.

He'd been rehearsing a speech, and he was frustrated they hadn't had any time together tonight. Audrey'd gone to dinner with Elaine while he talked to his mother, and after that she'd kept her distance, even in the same house.

"Audrey?" he whispered.

At first she played dead but then rolled over to face him. He felt sick when he saw her tearstained cheeks and practically leaped onto her bed. "Oh, Audrey Scott." He gathered her in his arms. "I'm sorry I've been such a jerk. I could *never* stay mad at you."

She sobbed and clung to him like a life raft.

"I just wish you'd come to me first."

"Sorry." Audrey rolled away and turned on the lamp next to her bed, lighting the room's pink wallpaper and highlighting the shine of her eyes. She grasped his hands. "I was just so scared when I saw your dad yelling at you. I—I didn't know what to do."

Leo nodded. "I can't blame you for being scared of CS. I know what that's like."

"Then why, Leo? Why'd you go to him?"

"You didn't see him in April! He looked awful, Audrey. The social worker said he was going to kill himself. I couldn't just stand by and do nothing."

"So what if he killed himself? After what he did to you, he deserves to be dead."

"I probably should see it that way, but I don't. He's…my dad. He's my blood. As much as I hate him, I can't turn my back on him."

Audrey looked down. "Your mom told me we're the same. We both stand by our fathers despite them doing awful things."

Leo considered this for a moment. "Maybe. One big difference, though, is your father's probably innocent. My father's guilty as hell." He exhaled. "Our dads sure screw things up for us. I never want them to come between us again."

When Audrey looked up to smile at him, Leo had an idea. "Let's get out of here. *Vámanos.*"

"*¿Adónde vamos?*" she asked.

He rested his finger on her lips. "*Es un secreto.*" Hauling her off the bed, he pointed to her flip flops. "*Zapatos.*" He led her to his room where he slid on his own deck shoes and scooped up his car keys. They held hands and tiptoed past his mother's bedroom.

Audrey began giggling when the front door closed behind them, and once they'd cleared the block, Leo gunned the engine and cranked the radio.

"We're seniors!" Audrey screamed, the rushing wind stealing her words through the open car windows.

"No more stupid high school!" Leo shouted in turn. He reveled in the freedom of their joy ride, just the two of them. It felt for a moment like the speed and whipping wind could carry away their troubles.

"Tell me where we're going."

He grinned. "Patience, my little pet."

She watched carefully as he made a few turns. "I do believe you'll need to judge my routine from the water this time."

"I wanted to surprise you!" He sighed. "You're too smart for your own good, you know that? Maybe I should've been dating a blond *cabeza hueca* all this time."

"Maybe an airhead would better appreciate your stupid jokes."

Leo pouted.

He pulled into the empty school parking lot and cut the engine.

"What if someone catches us?" Audrey asked.

"Really, is there anything worse that could happen this year? Compared to my Oxy addiction, your alcohol binge, and our pregnancy, a little pool break-in's small potatoes."

Audrey laughed. "So true. Let's do this. I'm going to knock the judge's socks off with my routine tonight."

Leo looked down at his feet. "I'm not wearing any socks. But your routine might knock off some other items of clothing."

He entered the security code on the touchpad, relieved to find Matt hadn't changed it.

Darkness shrouded the pool, and he led Audrey to the diving well. They kicked off their sandals and stood with their toes curled over the edge. Leo felt strangely self-conscious. A light ocean breeze wafted across the surface, leaving small ripples in its wake. It was dead quiet.

"I've never gone skinny dipping before," Leo admitted.

"You *haven't?* It is the best feeling in the world." She grasped the bottom of his tank top and lifted it over his head. "It's a feeling of total weightlessness and freedom."

"Like going commando?" he asked.

"Um, yeah, I wouldn't know about that." Audrey traced her fingers over his chest. "I think I'll like skinny dipping with you a little better than with Elaine."

Leo cocked one brow. "Maybe we could call Elaine and invite her? A little three-way action?"

Audrey swiftly shoved him, plunging him into the pool with a resounding splash. She stood on the deck laughing as his head emerged from the depths. "You need to cool off, pervert."

Leo's eyes never left hers as he nonchalantly sculled closer to the wall. Quick as lightning, he launched himself out of the pool.

She shrieked and sprinted toward the fence, but he soon overtook her. He threw her over his shoulder as she squealed and squirmed. He headed straight back to the pool and leaped off the deck, crashing their bodies into the water together.

Audrey came up giggling. He kept himself afloat with an egg-beater kick, and she did the same. As she slicked her hair back from her face, her smile faded into a longing gaze. He watched her tongue sweep across her lower lip.

"Let's get these wet jammies off you, shall we?" Leo reached over to tug on Audrey's long nightshirt. She smiled invitingly and then submerged, allowing the thin material to slide up off her body. Leo whipped the waterlogged cotton to the pool deck.

They were even now: he clad in his boxers, she wearing only lacy panties. Kicking closer, he enveloped her and held his lips close, mesmerized by flecks of copper in her eyes.

He molded his mouth to hers and tasted a hint of her toothpaste. As he ran his fingers over her wet hair, he felt her chest press against his. Underwater kicks kept him afloat, and the effort accelerated his heart rate even beyond the excitement of touching her.

She grasped the elastic of his shorts and pushed them down his legs until he caught them with his foot. In turn, Leo skated his hands down her belly and hooked a finger around her panties as she wriggled free.

Unencumbered by sopping clothing and unburdened of family worries, Leo felt what Audrey had tried to describe: liberated and uninhibited. Catching his breath, he continued to kiss her, stroking her back as she caressed his stubbly hair.

"Argh!" he wailed, breaking away suddenly. "Do they make water-proof chastity belts? 'Cause you're gonna need one."

Audrey snickered. "I think the metal might rust."

"It's so *hard* to follow my promise to your dad!"

"No kidding," she breathed, glancing under the water. She swam closer to whisper in his ear. "There are many things my dad forgot to mention."

"Would you show me?"

She smiled at him and drew his face close, plying him with tender kisses as they submerged. Blinded by the chlorine and darkness, they relied only on their sense of touch to pleasure each other. There was a bout of giggles each time they surfaced.

As he tugged his wet boxers back on, Leo glanced at his shivering girlfriend. "I think I have a towel in the backseat." He wrapped his arm around her and led her to the car.

Audrey squeezed some water from her hair, tossing it behind her. "How'd I do, judge?"

"On a scale of one to ten, I give you an eleven," Leo said. He planted one last kiss on her lips. "I'm giving you a standing ovation as we speak."

51. Bon Voyage

Their fervent hug lasted longer than a cruise ship's pull away from the dock.

Audrey seemed to have trouble catching her breath. "I hate the Navy for taking you away," she cried.

Leo tried to memorize the feel of her in his arms and the sweet smell of her tousled hair as he felt his shoulder dampen with her tears. He couldn't believe he was doing this, willingly separating himself from her. Yet he refused to go into debt. Attending Florida State would bring a financial debt to his mother and an emotional debt to his father. He knew he couldn't look CS in the eye if he didn't follow through with his promise. The senator who'd recommended him wouldn't be too happy either.

As he held her, all the events from the past month flew through his mind: their exhilarating skinny dip, Audrey's class salutatorian speech at graduation, his birthday dinner—a relaxed gathering that had included his mother, Mr. Shale, Jason, Cameron, and Audrey, followed by cake at Audrey's house with Elaine and Alex, and grueling workouts with Audrey, who'd replaced his father as his fitness instructor.

Except for a phone call yesterday, his father had been noticeably absent through it all. Leo hadn't seen him since that night on the track. Though he'd sloughed off his mother's concern about the effect of his father's absence, inside it really hurt that CS had abandoned him.

Leo wiped away Audrey's tears. "I'll talk to you every chance I get. And you and my mom are visiting before you leave for school, right?"

"But that's six weeks away." She sniffed.

Jason cleared his throat. "Hey, buddy, we got a long drive ahead of us, and I need to be back Monday."

Leo looked over. "For your new job at Child Protective Services?"

"Yeah." Jason squeezed his arm to his chest, bulging his biceps. "I'm the muscle on the investigative team."

Leo turned back for one last look at Audrey before breaking away and approaching his mother. He gathered her into a hug. "I'm glad you're back, Mom."

She looked at him for a moment, then nodded, leaning into him. "Me too. Take care of yourself, Leo."

"I'll make you proud."

"I'm *already* proud. Just do your best."

Leo took a deep breath. Forcing aside his swirling emotions, he got into Jason's car. His brother instantly hopped in as well, as if to prevent Leo from stretching out the goodbye any further.

As they backed out the driveway, Leo locked eyes with Audrey, who stood next to his mother. He'd packed the framed picture she gave him away in his gym bag, but he held his other birthday gift from her: a tiny baby bracelet. Little white beads spelling "Scott" interspersed with pink and blue beads.

When he'd opened the box in her bedroom, he'd looked at her with shock. "This isn't your way of telling me you're pregnant again?"

She giggled. "No."

"Because I couldn't be the father this time." His eyes narrowed.

Audrey's grin faded. "This is a reminder of me, a reminder of us — what we shared this year."

He looked down. "But I don't want to remember the bad times."

"This isn't just about the past," she said. "It's about the future. I don't want to get all emo, but someday, Leo, I want to have a baby with you. When the time is right." She took the bracelet from his hands and cradled it. "This is my promise to you, for the future."

It was the best birthday gift he'd ever received.

Leo leaned back in the seat and looked out the window, jiggling his knee in the car. "So, is Cam mad you'll be gone this weekend?"

"Nope. She and her mom will be house-hunting the whole time. They say their house is too big...too many memories of her dad."

At a stoplight Leo turned to him. "Jase, can I ask you a question and you promise not to get angry?"

"That sounds like a giant setup." He looked over. "What is it?"

"I...I want to make one last stop before we head north. Maybe you could turn left at the next light?"

Looking ahead to the next street, Jason's face hardened. "No. I'm not taking you to see Constipated Stool-sample."

"Please, Jase? I promised him I'd say goodbye."

"You're talking to him again?" Jason's voice rose.

"You said you wouldn't get mad!"

"And *you* set me up." The light changed, and Jason edged the car forward. "Mom would be ticked off if she found out I took you to see Cat's Sandbox."

Leo couldn't help but laugh.

Jason also snorted as he turned left onto their old street. He pulled the car to the curb a half mile from their home and turned it off. He stared straight ahead with his hands squeezing the steering wheel. An air of indecisiveness filled the car.

"I know you think I'm stupid for wanting to see him," Leo said.

Jason sighed. "You're anything but stupid. I just don't understand why you're taking his side."

"I'm not taking anybody's side! Why do I have to choose Mom or Dad? Can't I have them both?"

Jason scratched his head. "I'm trying to wrap my mind around this, around why you want to see him — it's like we've got different dads. The second he threw me out four years ago, the second he gave up on me, I gave up on him. I promised myself I'd never let him hurt me again. But you...you haven't given up on him." Jason looked out the window. "I guess it's always been different for us. He actually gives a damn about you."

"I'm sorry Dad's like that." Leo looked at his hands in his lap.

Jason turned to face him. "I never blamed you for Dad loving you more."

"No, he doesn't —"

"He does, and you know it. Just accept it. I have. He hates me because I'm just like him."

"No, you're not! You — you care about people. You take care of me. You came back for me that night."

Jason sighed. "A lot of good that did. You conveniently forgot all the times I beat the crap out of you when we were kids."

"I'm sure I deserved it. I was an irritant."

"A what?" Jason lunged for Leo. "You *never* deserve to get hit!" He bunched Leo's shirt in his hand, clutching his collar. "You never deserve that, you hear me?"

Leo shied away from his brother's grip, and when Jason noticed his reaction, he immediately let go.

Jason sighed, looking down at his hands. "Case in point. The apple doesn't fall far from the tree."

"It does, Jase. You're nothing like Cast-iron Skillet."

Jason gave him a faint smile. "That's a new one." He started the car. "Let's get this over with. You don't leave my sight when you're with CS, okay?"

"Okay."

After pulling into their driveway, Jason joined Leo for the walk to the porch. Leo pressed the doorbell and the brothers waited.

"Awkward? Party of three?" Jason smirked.

Before Leo could come up with a retort, the front door opened wide.

Leo was surprised to see his father in uniform on a Saturday. "I've got to get to the base for a meeting." CS shot them a disapproving look. "You're late."

"You know what, this is ridiculous," Jason sneered. "I didn't have to bring Leo here."

CS's eyes darkened with anger.

"Jase…" Leo stepped between them, watching CS. "We have to get going too, Dad. I just wanted to say goodbye."

His father's face softened. "Come in for a second. I have something for you." He disappeared up the stairs.

Leo moved inside, but Jason hesitated a moment before crossing the threshold. Leo surveyed the spotless surroundings, shuddering when he saw his father's study to the right. He closed his eyes and tried to push away memories of beatings.

CS returned, carrying a navy blue, folded-leather document protector. He placed it in Leo's hands. "Open it."

Moments later Leo found himself staring at a diploma from the Naval Academy. Beautifully etched with gold writing, the letters *Ensign James Scott* gleamed in the hallway lighting.

"When things get bad, I want you to look at this," his father said. "There's a lighthouse when the seas get stormy. If *I* could make it through there, surely you can."

"I can't take this." Leo's hands quivered. "What if something happens to it?"

"Make sure nothing does," CS ordered.

Leo sighed. "Yes, sir."

Jason stirred next to him, and Leo prayed he'd keep his mouth shut.

"It figures your one magnanimous gift is your own freakin' diploma," Jason said.

Apparently not.

His father stared at Jason.

Leo stepped between them again. "It's okay, Dad. We'll be on our way."

He flinched when CS hugged him, smashing the diploma between them. But this time Leo hugged back.

"When you get to the Academy, you'll understand why I was so hard on you," his father said in his ear.

Leo stepped out of the hug, his heart pounding. "I, uh, I'll never understand that, sir."

He ducked out the door and ran to Jason's car, holding back tears as he clutched his father's diploma to his chest.

52. Sweet and Sour

Those brown eyes pierced his heart.

Leo heard voices downstairs — more plebe swimmers arriving to the lieutenant's home — and knew he should get down there to meet his new teammates. But it was so hard to return Audrey's senior photo to his duffel bag. The transition from Pensacola to Annapolis had jarred him, and he hadn't even made it inside the Academy walls yet. He already missed Jason, who'd just left to start the drive back to Florida.

He noticed a few other suitcases pushed to the side of the upstairs bedroom, and wondered how many swimmers would sleep in the house tonight before Induction Day began tomorrow. Lt. Winton, one of the company officers on the Yard, had been kind enough to allow the early-arriving swimmers to stay at his house. They weren't allowed in their dorm, Bancroft Hall, till I-Day.

A noise in the hallway drew Leo's attention. He looked up to catch a glimpse of someone entering the room, and he instinctively braced his shoulders and stared straight ahead, holding completely still.

"Yo, relax, *hombre.* I'm just your roomie."

Leo exhaled and examined the brown-skinned guy. Two aspects of his roommate immediately stood out: a friendly, toothy grin and a white sling over his shoulder, which held his left arm securely in place. His white tank top revealed bulging muscles as he let go of his bag to land with a thud at his feet.

Leo shook his hand. "I'm Leo Scott."

"Benito Dulce." He pumped Leo's arm. There was a fullness and innocence to Benito's face that made him seem younger than a college freshman.

"Wait a minute. How'd you know we'll be roommates? We're not supposed to find that out till tomorrow."

Benito winked. "Lt. Winton took me aside and told me to stash my bag up here, so I could meet my roommate. I think my stupid sling made him take pity on me." Pointing to his shoulder, Benito shrugged. "Torn rotator cuff. Just had surgery three weeks ago."

Leo nodded, wondering how the poor guy'd survive Plebe Summer with his shoulder in a sling. His ass would be in a sling, more like it.

A short, heavy-set woman trailed in the bedroom, breathing heavily from climbing the stairs.

"That's my mom." He turned to her. *"Es mi compañero de cuarto."* He looked blankly at Leo, clearly having forgotten his name.

"Leo Scott, *señora.*" Leo shook her leathery hand.

"Ah, hello." Her smile rippled crow's feet around her black eyes. "I don't speak English so good."

Leo nodded. *"Está bien, señora. Hablo un poco de español."*

"¿De verdad? You speak Spanish?" Benito's face lit up. "We'll get along great, *amigo.* I can feel it already." He repositioned his duffel against the wall, grimacing as he jerked his shoulder.

His mother paled. *"¡Ten cuidado!"*

Benito rolled his eyes. "Time to go, Mamá."

Mrs. Dulce patted Leo on the cheek. *"Tienes ojos de ángel,"* she said. *"Azul como el mar. Cuida a mi hijo, por favor."*

Leo grinned. *So my angelic eyes are blue like the sea!*

Benito stepped forward and urged her to the door, his cheeks aflame. *"Sí,* he'll take good care of me. Mamá, go talk to Lt. Winton downstairs—you can embarrass me even more."

When his mother left, Benito scanned the small bedroom. "Are we all supposed to sleep in here tonight? That's no privacy at all, *hombre.*"

"Better get used to zero privacy. I hear we have to keep our dorm door open most of the time. No privacy for us lowly plebes."

"Sweet. How am I supposed to get it on with the ladies? That's whack, yo."

Leo chuckled. "It's the military, yo. Are you ready for this, man?"

"I *was* ready." Benito collapsed on the twin bed. "Then my doctor told me I had to have surgery. Now I'm screwed."

"What happened to your shoulder?"

"Overuse injury."

Leo stared at Benito's bulk. "What events do you swim?"

Benito grinned. "You're probably wondering how a *gordo* like me doesn't drown, huh?"

"No...ahh..."

"I'm a flyer, but I've put on, like, twenty pounds since I had to stop swimming 'cause of my shoulder. I'm so out of shape, dude. It'll be ugly when I get back."

"I know exactly what that's like," Leo said, feeling instantly at ease. "I was out of the water for five weeks this spring."

"Why?"

Startled, Leo clamped his mouth shut. He hadn't planned on sharing anything involving his father. This was to be a fresh start, free of Calculating Schemer. "I had to get my appendix removed."

"That sucks, man." Benito's gaze glided down from his face and landed on the framed photograph in his hand. Rising from the bed, he peered over Leo's shoulder and whistled through his teeth. "Is this your lady? *¡Está buenísima!*"

Leo blushed. "That's Audrey."

Benito came around him gave him a knowing smirk. "Aw, dude, you're gonna miss her, huh?"

Leo's smile faded. "Yeah, big time." Leo sighed. "I already miss her."

"I didn't bring any pictures of my girl." Benito plopped back down on the bed. "We just broke up." He shrugged, doing his best to be nonchalant.

"What's her name?" Leo asked as he returned Audrey's photo to his bag.

"Lucia. She said she can't do the long-distance thing." He sighed. "I'll get her back though."

With a knock on the open door, a sandy-haired midshipman stuck his head in the room.

"Gentlemen, hello." He entered. "I'm Midshipman First Class Tom Sour, your squad leader in Second Company."

Leo snapped to attention. When Benito finally seemed to figure out he should follow suit, the midshipman was snickering. "Chill out, boys. We haven't started yet. You can begin all that tomorrow."

Leo sat on the edge of the small desk in the room. "How do we address you, sir?"

"You call me Midshipman Ensign Sour or Mr. Sour. I'll be one of the detailers overseeing your training for Plebe Summer. You can call midshipmen first class 'firsties' once the academic year begins." He eyed them. "Welcome to the team."

Benito grinned as Mr. Sour shook his hand. "I'm Benito—I swim the one and two fly."

When Mr. Sour shook his hand as well, Leo felt the strength in his grip. "Leo Scott. It's good to meet a senior on the team."

"Yeah, I'm one of the team captains. I'm a sprinter." Mr. Sour sized up Leo. "So what do you swim, Mr. Scott?"

"I'm a sprinter too."

"Really." Mr. Sour's voice dropped on the second syllable. "What're your best times?"

Leo swallowed, looked down, then met his eyes with a steely gaze. "Twenty-point-oh in the fifty and forty-four-nine in the hundred."

A brief yet noticeable iciness flickered across Mr. Sour's face.

Benito clapped Leo on the back. "You got skills, man!"

Mr. Sour pasted on a smile. "Sounds like our free relays just got a lot faster." He was suddenly all business. "You two ready for Induction Day tomorrow?"

"I hope, sir," Leo said.

"We'll soon find out. Report to Alumni Hall bright and early tomorrow." Mr. Sour chuckled, and he disappeared out the door and down the stairs.

Leo exhaled. "Figures our squad leader swims my events. He hates me already."

"What're you talking about?" Benito said. "He seemed really nice."

Leo studied his roommate. He was going to be in for a shock once Plebe Summer officially began. Leo sensed Dulce and Sour wouldn't be a palatable combination. He felt a flutter in his stomach, anticipating the start of his Navy career.

53. PT Redux

Leo heard a menacing howl in the recesses of his mind, followed by a guitar riff that built to an ear-splitting crescendo. Rolling over on his rack, he groaned.

"Leo!" Benito's voice cut through his unconsciousness, and he bolted upright. "Welcome to the Jungle" blasted in the dorm passageway.

The threatening hiss of Axl Rose halted then he heard a crisp female voice: "All Second Company plebes report to the p-way in sixty seconds, dressed in PT gear!"

Leo scrambled out of bed and flipped on the light. He flew over to his desk to wolf down a banana and tossed another to Benito, who caught it one-handed.

He grinned, pointing to his T-shirt and shorts as he shoved his feet into brand new white running shoes. "You were right, *amigo.*"

Leo had shared CS's advice to stuff down food at any opportunity and sleep in their PT clothes so they wouldn't be late. As they reported to their assigned spots in the passageway, Leo noticed they were the first plebes to arrive. Squad Leader Sour gave him a cool stare before returning to his conversation with a female detailer just about his height, and Leo recognized her as the company commander.

"You ready for this, Las Vegas?" Sour asked her.

"Whiskey, I've been ready for years," she said, then walked away toward another squad.

Whiskey Sour, Leo put together in his head. The Academy was rife with nicknames. But he had no idea why Tom had called her Las Vegas. And there was no time to figure it out as Mr. Sour started yelling at two plebes for being two seconds late then ordered the squad of ten to complete twenty pushups. Leo couldn't believe Benito was trying one-armed pushups.

Next came the chaos of rack races. Mr. Sour ordered them to sprint to their rooms and strip their sheets. Once they reported back to the passageway, they then had to scramble back inside and remake their racks. Leo was fast enough to tighten his sheets and help Benito with his rack the first two races, but when they arrived to the passageway too late the third round, Mr. Sour ordered the entire squad to sit against the wall for two minutes as punishment.

Leo's thighs burned, but he wasn't panting nearly as heavily as some of his cohort. Suddenly his squad was on their feet and hustling down the stairs to gather with the rest of the company outside.

Behind them loomed Bancroft Hall, the largest dormitory in the world. The building they'd just left housed four-thousand midshipmen in almost five miles of corridors. The dorm even had its own zip code.

The company commander surveyed them as they waited for all the squads to assemble. She looked to be almost six-foot, with freckles and brown hair cut in a bouncy bob. Three men flanked her. *Platoon commanders*, Leo reminded himself. He'd absorbed a lot of information during Induction Day.

After the company commander led them in a swift jog to the PT field, she addressed them. "Good morning." She surveyed the group. "Welcome to the Academy. As you may recall, I'm Midshipman Second Company Commander Viva Nevington. We'll meet in the p-way every morning at zero-five-hundred hours."

Leo wondered how he'd be on time considering the detailers had forbidden watches and alarm clocks. He wondered if the likes of Axl Rose would be his new alarm clock.

"Next we'll have at least ninety minutes of physical training," Nevington resumed. "This will be the hardest time of your life, so get ready for it."

As he listened to tiny groans and gasps, Leo felt a smile threaten to break through. *Here we go.* A thrilling energy coursed through him.

"Following our little workout this morning, we'll dress in our whiteworks for more training," Company Commander Nevington continued. "I'd like to introduce your platoon commanders and squad leaders who will oversee your conditioning. To my left…"

Leo felt his skin tingle as it did on the starting blocks. He couldn't wait to get this party started. But this was an endurance test ahead. *Chill out, amigo.* He was a sprinter, and making it through Plebe Summer would be more like a marathon. He needed to rein in his excitement if he wanted to last through the next six weeks.

"Mr. Sour's the leader for the Third Squad," Ms. Nevington announced. "We have a storied history in Second Company, and you plebes are privileged to be part of it. I know I'm honored to be your commander, and we're excited to have you on board. We'll begin with jumping jacks."

She had a platoon commander demonstrate the proper count for jumping jacks, and soon the company moved in unison. "One, two, three, ONE, one, two, three, TWO…"

The breathing was much louder by the time they reached fifty. Leo snuck a glance at Benito, who was moving his feet but keeping his arms by his side, trying to avoid jarring his shoulder. Sour snaked his way back toward them as a platoon commander demonstrated proper push-up technique. On cue, the company dropped to the grass.

Benito balanced himself on his right hand, and Sour's feet halted near his head. "Keep doing one-armed pushups, Midshipman Dulce," Sour ordered. "Spread your feet out wider."

Leo held his body motionless as Nevington called out instructions. Counting out fifty, Leo was shocked to hear the grunts of worn-out plebes as bodies hit the dirt. Hadn't his classmates taken the warnings seriously? They'd just be plain stupid to show up out of shape. His roommate's situation, on the other hand, wasn't due to a lack of planning.

Benito muscled through about ten one-armed pushups before he fell on his right side, exhausted. Sour screamed in his ear until Benito tried again, only to crumple to the ground. Seeming disgusted, Sour moved on to yell at another plebe for collapsing, and Benito stayed down, panting and sweating.

Meanwhile, Nevington told the plebes to hold the upright pushup position. Leo focused on his breathing as he held his arms locked straight at the elbows with his chin slightly raised. As the seconds ticked by, plebes fell to the ground, where their squad leaders advised them to stay. Leo trembled but held firm.

"Only ten plebes still up, Leo," whispered Benito. "Good job."

A violent tremor ripped through Leo's torso, burning his abdomen.

"Only four left," Benito urged. "You can do this. You're a badass swimmer—these *putas* don't have a prayer against you."

As ten more seconds passed, a trickle of sweat dripped off Leo's chin.

Benito's voice took on an edge of excitement. "It's down to you and one guy to your right! C'mon, Leo, just a little more. Only a few strokes to the wall, *amigo*. Bear down. You want it."

From within the throes of involuntary tremors, Leo noticed a pair of running shoes in front of him. His company commander? He clenched his teeth as salty sweat slid into his mouth.

"The other plebe just went down!" Benito hissed. "You won, Leo!"

Then Leo heard a female voice. "Well done. You can stop at any time, Midshipman."

Oh, how he wanted to just let go and fall to the ground, stop the tremors. But he wouldn't let himself. CS would've never let him off that easy. He hadn't passed out or vomited yet, so he still had something left.

She finally ended it. "Ten, hut!"

Leo wearily drew himself up, his muscles quivering.

"What's this plebe's name, Mr. Sour?" Ms. Nevington asked.

"Midshipman Scott," Sour replied.

The entire company went silent as his commander hovered at his left. Her voice dropped to the softest whisper. "Impressive start, Mr. Scott. Let's see how you finish."

His chest burst with pride, elated to be recognized by his CO so soon.

She then stepped over to Benito and ordered him on his feet as well. Benito didn't rise as quickly.

"Midshipman Dulce," Sour supplied, and Nevington nodded.

"Mr. Dulce, how could you show up to Plebe Summer in an arm sling?"

"I'll be out of the sling in a week, ma'am."

Fury cut through her voice. "There're only four answers a plebe should ever give: Yes, ma'am; No, ma'am; I'll find out, ma'am; or No excuse, ma'am!"

Benito sounded panicked. "No excuse, ma'am?"

Nevington turned to Sour. "Whiskey, why's he doing PT? Get him set up with marching tours in T-court."

Sour spoke softly, but Leo could hear what he said. "This MUFFIN's a swimmer. He can handle this." When she didn't budge, he sighed and nodded. "Let's go, Mr. Dulce."

As they departed, Nevington ordered everyone else on their feet. They endured more grueling exercises, pausing twice for water breaks, before a platoon commander took them on a run along the lengthy seawall.

Leo had a feeling he'd get to know the seawall quite well by the time he'd become an ensign. Eight-minute miles were a pedestrian pace for him, but other plebes began falling to the wayside after the first twenty minutes, where squad leaders screamed at them to move it.

Nevington surveyed the sweaty, shell-shocked company back at the PT field. "We obviously have some work to do before you *pathetic* losers are worthy of a Navy uniform. But we have to start somewhere, so go change into your whiteworks then report to the p-way for breakfast."

Plebes jostled Leo in their tight formation as they jogged inside Bancroft Hall. Soon he'd get some food. He was repulsed by his own smell, and his muscles were already shaky and sore, but he'd made it. He survived his first PT.

Fifteen minutes later, when Leo realized his roommate was the one plebe late to breakfast, he cursed under his breath. Benito hadn't arrived to the room by the time Mr. Sour had corralled them toward

King Hall, and it must have taken him a long time to change into his uniform with one arm. Everyone stood at attention around the dark wood tables, and Leo's stomach wasn't the only one growling.

"Midshipman Dulce!" Sour boomed when Benito finally slunk into the cafeteria. "Front and center."

"Yes, sir." Benito scurried over to his squad leader.

"What's today's breakfast menu, plebe?" Sour asked.

For a moment there was only silence.

"I'll find out, sir," Benito finally said.

"All midshipmen besides Mr. Dulce will give me ten pushups."

Leo hit the deck, squeezing in with prone bodies everywhere to carry out the punishment. When he popped back up, Whiskey had moved on to his next question. "What is professional knowledge, Mr. Dulce?"

"Sir, plebes will be able to summarize three newspaper articles, recite facts about the fleet, aircraft, weaponry, and the, uh, Marines, and recite the menu for each meal if asked by an upperclassman, sir."

"That is correct, Mr. Dulce. So why don't you know the breakfast menu?"

"No excuse, sir."

"Also correct. Give me another ten, plebes!"

Leo dropped, ignoring the protests of his classmates. *Poor Benito.* Leo made a mental note to memorize the lunch menu so this would never happen to him.

By the sixth round of pushups for Benito's failed menu guesses, Leo's sympathy began to wane.

Sour was relentless. "What's the breakfast menu today, Mr. Dulce?"

Benito looked around wildly. "Um, grits, sir?"

Sour burst out laughing. "Why on earth do you think we'd have grits?"

"It's a delicious southern dish, sir?"

"We're not in the south! Where are you from, Mr. Dulce?"

"New Jersey, sir."

"We were on the same side for the Civil War, idiot. Drop and give me ten, plebes!"

Finally Benito guessed scrambled eggs, sausage, and biscuits off the menu, which also included yogurt, bananas, oatmeal, and orange juice, and the famished plebes began shoveling down food.

After their huge breakfast, Second Company gathered again in the quad.

The hot sun bounced off the sea of white uniforms as the plebes repeatedly rehearsed proper saluting technique. Leo thought his long-sleeved tunic and round "Dixie cup" hat looked rather dorky compared to traditional whites worn by the upperclassmen. He knew Audrey would make fun of him when she visited in August—if he made it until then.

After they'd practiced saluting and standing at attention for longer than an invitational swim meet, their company commander explained the leadership structure of the Academy: the Superintendent was a three-star Vice Admiral and beneath him, the Commandant of Midshipman was Captain Sean Tracker. One of Captain Tracker's staff members served as the company officer for Second Company: Lt. Darnell Keaton.

That name sounded familiar to Leo, but he couldn't place it. Nevington told them they wouldn't interact with these officers unless they'd "screwed the pooch," so Leo determined never to meet them.

Sour reviewed the Honor Concept of the Brigade of Midshipmen. "Offenses like stealing, lying, and cheating can result in separation from the Navy," he told them. "Midshipmen are persons of integrity. They stand for that which is right."

"Midshipmen are persons of integrity," the plebes repeated in unison. "They stand for that which is right."

Following lunch, the plebes had four hours of instruction in small arms and first aid. Leo's heavy eyelids were much lighter once he held an M-16 rifle. The smooth, gleaming metal felt formidable in his hands, and it was frightening at first. The instructor informed the plebes they'd get to know their issued rifles very well as they spent time marching in formation with them.

Just when Leo teetered on collapse, Nevington dismissed the varsity athletes to meet with the athletic director while the remaining plebes practiced that marching with those rifles they'd just learned about.

The AD was a civilian who punctuated his speech with rousing shouts of "Go, Navy! Beat Army!" Most of them wouldn't be practicing their sports during Plebe Summer, they learned, but they'd have three hours a day during the school year for practice with their team.

"I'm won't lie to you," he said. "Varsity athletes have it tougher than other plebes. Division I student-athletes are often exhausted from the rigorous schedule, and you have all your military duties piled on top of that. You won't catch a break from memorizing professional knowledge, preparing your uniforms for inspection, shining your shoes, hitting the barbershop, or drilling in formation. It's not an option to miss class or practice. The only break you will get is eating evening meals with your teammates, who typically don't harass plebes as much."

After evening chow, the plebes' grueling day was finally complete. Leo and Benito sprawled on their racks after showering.

"Is nine too early for bed?" Benito moaned.

Leo chuckled. "That's twenty-one hundred to you, my man. Just think, once the school year starts we'll be in the middle of study hall this time of night."

"Ohhh..." Benito groaned and reached under his bed for something. He popped a pill then took a swig from his water bottle.

"What's that?" Leo asked.

"Percocet. I haven't taken any in a while, but my shoulder's killing me."

Leo suddenly felt hot. He rolled over to face the wall.

"You okay?" Benito asked.

"Yeah. I'm, uh, I'm just thinking about how all this will start over again tomorrow. It'll be a long six weeks."

"*Sí.* I guess we've been fully inducted into the Navy, *amigo.*"

Leo rolled back over and grinned. "*Bienvenido* to the jungle, baby."

54. Raison D'Être

From the driver's seat, Audrey glanced at Mrs. Scott.

"I'm glad you could join us for dinner," Leo's mom said. "I want to thank everyone for helping Leo get to the Academy. At times I wasn't sure he'd make it."

"I don't know how much help I was." Audrey sighed. "I didn't really want him to go."

"You're always a big help to my son. You're his *raison d'être.*"

"His *what?* I only speak Spanish, sorry."

"His reason for being."

Audrey blushed.

"I know you miss Leo, but financially he didn't have much choice. I'm hoping the Academy will work out for him."

"He seems to like it. His letters make those PT sessions sound almost fun."

"He *is* a bit warped, isn't he?"

They shared a grin as Audrey parked, but she winced when she noticed she hadn't left much room for Mrs. Scott to maneuver her canes out of the vehicle. Thankfully Leo's mother didn't comment.

Inside the restaurant, they found Mr. Shale and Matt already waiting for them. Mr. Shale held out a chair for Leo's mother, and Matt did the same for Audrey, who giggled.

"I got us a table for five, right?" Matt asked, returning to his seat.

Mrs. Scott nodded. "Yes. Jason and Cameron can't make it."

"Amy will be here once she finishes up at a crime scene," Matt said.

Mrs. Scott's face lit up. "You've been dating Detective Easton over a month, Matt! What's that, a new record for you? Tell us the juicy details."

Audrey leaned in eagerly.

Matt shot her a withering look. "It's going well, thank you."

"Sounds like Jason's quite the matchmaker," Mr. Shale said.

Mrs. Scott beamed. "My son has many hidden talents. Just think, Matt—Jason would've never met your girlfriend if he hadn't committed a crime. And then he got to know Amy even better because of James hurting Le—"

Mr. Shale broke the ensuing silence. "Jason sure knows how to turn a negative into a positive."

"Ah, Mary?" Matt asked. "What *is* James up to these days?"

She sighed. "He keeps calling me, wanting to talk. But I—" She glanced at Audrey and paused. "Audrey, honey, would you maybe take a walk outside for a bit?"

Audrey frowned.

"It's not that I don't trust you. I--—I want to talk about parent stuff without burdening you. You certainly have enough to worry about these days."

Audrey sighed as she rose from her chair, and Matt grasped her arm before she left. "While you're walking, how 'bout you figure out what you'd need to split to go under two minutes in the IM?"

Audrey strolled around the parking lot, miffed. In his emails, Leo had been asking her what was happening with his parents, and she'd have nothing to tell him again.

Following Matt's instructions, she calculated times for each fifty of the individual medley as she walked the perimeter of the lot. She kept her head down and was startled when suddenly a man blocked her path. She looked up and gasped as she found herself staring into cool hazel eyes.

CS's voice was smooth. "You look deep in thought."

"Yes, Commander. I-I'm working out some swimming times in my head."

"I'm sure you'll do great at FSU. Better than you did at the state meet, anyway."

Her cheeks flushed.

He winced and opened his mouth, then closed it. "How's Leo?" he finally asked.

"He's good. He, he likes it at the Academy."

"I knew he'd thrive there." He nodded. "But I wish he'd write me."

And I wish you'd go away.

"So, you're having dinner with Mary?"

"Yes, sir, Matt and Mr. Shale are here too."

His eyes narrowed. "Marcus Shale? What's *he* doing here?"

Audrey squirmed. "I, I don't know? Mrs. Scott wanted to thank people for helping Leo."

CS looked over Audrey's shoulder, and his jaw clenched.

"Evening, Commander."

Audrey turned to find Mr. Shale right behind her. "Audrey, we'd like you to rejoin us at the table now."

CS clutched her shoulder, and she wriggled beneath his firm hold.

"No need to rush out of here," he told her. "I want to talk to Mary."

"Mary's well aware that you wish to speak to her," said Mr. Shale. "I don't think now's the best time."

CS's hand brushed off of Audrey's shoulder as he stepped forward. "Stay away from my wife, Shale."

"You have no right to tell me what to do."

Audrey's heart fluttered. The air seemed to crackle with energy.

"When it comes to my wife, I have every right in the world." CS curled his hands into fists.

"How's everyone doing tonight?" A cheerful voice rang out behind them, and Detective Easton appeared. "Kind of hot to be standing around outside, don'cha think?"

When the detective's arm curled around her shoulders, Audrey finally exhaled. Detective Easton's friendly smile did nothing to mask her forceful presence.

CS inched away. "I don't want any trouble. I'm just here to see my wife."

"I see," Detective Easton said. "And did Mary invite you here, Commander?"

He looked away, visibly attempting to control his breathing. "No."

"Do you know the legal definition of stalking, sir?"

"No, ma'am."

"I suggest you go home and look it up. This is *not* the way to get on Mary's good side, showing up unannounced and harassing her dinner guests. It's not the way to get what you want. Can I count on you to leave now, sir?"

CS stuffed his hands in his pockets. "Will you tell Mary I need to speak to her?"

"I'll make you a deal," she said evenly. "If you leave now, I'll tell her that as soon as I see her."

"Fine." He walked away, and Audrey's shoulders slumped with relief.

When they returned to the table, Matt leaned over to kiss the detective on the cheek before they all sat down.

"So, you all ran into each other in the parking lot?" Mrs. Scott smiled warmly.

Mr. Shale's gaze shifted over to Audrey. "We ran into one other person as well."

Mrs. Scott paled. "James," she whispered.

When Mr. Shale nodded she turned to Audrey. "Are you okay?"

"I'm fine. The detective made him leave."

"The commander asked me to tell you he wants to speak to you," Detective Easton reported.

Audrey noticed Leo's mom's eyes dart over to Mr. Shale. "Do you think I should call him?" she asked. "Will that keep him away?"

Mr. Shale glanced up. "Uh…I can't answer that for you, Mary. That's for you to figure out."

"Why is she asking you what to do, Marcus?" Detective Easton asked.

Mrs. Scott answered for him. "He's a counselor. He gives good advice."

"That's not the only reason." Mr. Shale squirmed in his seat before taking a moment to compose himself. "I understand what it's like to grow up in an abusive home."

Mrs. Scott patted his arm.

"It's why I feel such a kinship with your sons, Mary," Mr. Shale told her.

Audrey trembled, still feeling CS's hand on her shoulder. She wished Leo could be here. She needed to feel *his* warm, strong arms around her. But she was also relieved to know he was miles away from CS. Leo was safe, no longer under his influence.

55. Screwing the Pooch

Leo whistled a happy tune as he strolled from the natatorium to his dorm room in Bancroft Hall, otherwise known as Mother B, he'd learned. When he realized he was whistling "YMCA," he smiled so wide he had to stop whistling. Las Vegas was a crazy company commander, and her choice of blaring wake-up music that morning had made PT slightly more tolerable. Her allowing him to squeeze in a swim during letter-writing time made the day even better.

Though he'd only had time to pound out five thousand meters in the ninety minutes she'd given him, it felt wonderful to be back in the water after two weeks of Plebe Summer. The pool had soothed his sore muscles and given him some hope that he could make it through the punishing mental and physical demands ahead.

He was relieved not to encounter any upperclassmen on his journey, thrilled to avoid the endless professional knowledge quizzes. As Leo entered his room, he caught Benito shoving something into a duffel bag, looking guilty as hell.

His roommate swiped at tears and appeared absolutely miserable — the lowest Leo had seen him.

"What's in the bag, buddy?"

Benito sniffed. "None of your business."

Leo bit his lip, eyeing Benito's shoulder. The sling was gone, but he still wasn't back to one hundred percent, and their detailers still harassed him for his injury.

"It *is* my business if you have something illegal in here. Detailers inspect our room all the time."

"You got nothing to worry about, Leo. They love you."

"I'm sorry it's been rough on you, but it'll get better once your shoulder's healed."

When Benito let out a miserable sigh and released his stranglehold on the duffel bag, Leo pounced and grabbed it.

"Hey!" Benito rushed after him.

Leo yanked open the bag and swiveled around. Benito closed his eyes, defeated. "What the hell are you doing with a gun?" Leo whispered.

Benito looked away, his shoulders hunched. "I just like to have it with me. It makes me feel safe. *Dámelo.*"

Reluctantly, Leo relinquished the bag. Benito tossed it under his rack and climbed onto the blanket. He hugged his knees to his chest.

Leo sat down on his own rack and waited for him to explain.

"I found out what MUFFIN means," Benito said.

"Really?" Leo feigned ignorance. He'd heard the meaning of the Navy slang days ago but hadn't had the heart to tell his roommate. Even his fellow plebes called him MUFFIN now.

"Most Useless Fat Eff in the Navy." Benito's head dipped. "I'll never get rid of that name. And I'm piling up punishments like there's no tomorrow."

Leo glanced at the dark space where the bag had disappeared under his rack. "You're not...you're, you're not gonna use that gun on anyone at the Academy, are you?"

Benito looked alarmed, then a slow smile gradually spread. "Relax, *amigo*. No need to call the MPs. I've thought about it, though." Looking off in the distance, he murmured, "I wouldn't mind taking a shot at Whiskey."

"Instead of a shot *of* whiskey?"

Benito managed a guffaw.

They were still laughing when Squad Leader Sour zipped into the room. "Inspection time, plebes!"

Leo and Benito clambered off their racks to stand at attention. Whiskey looked down at Benito's black socks. "Get some shoes on, MUFFIN!"

"Yes, sir!" Benito stuffed his feet into recently polished shoes and resumed his stance. After glancing at Leo's side of the room, Sour's gaze returned to Benito.

"What's the motto of the Academy, Midshipman Dulce?" He rifled through the contents of Benito's desk.

"Sir, the motto is *Ex Scientia Tridens*, meaning From Knowledge, Seapower."

Sour turned back to face him. "Too slow in your answer, MUFFIN. Both of you plank for a minute."

Leo narrowed his eyes as he dropped to the floor, holding his weight on elbows and toes. This was sheer cruelty, nothing more.

When Mr. Sour ordered them back up, Leo held his breath as Whiskey glanced down at the duffel bag.

"Your quarters are a *mess*, Mr. Dulce!" he hissed. He kicked the bag clear under the bed. "Since you're too freaking weak to do push-ups, I'll have your roommate pump out your share too. Midshipman Scott, drop and give me forty."

"Yes, sir."

Sour patrolled the room for contraband while Benito stood ramrod straight and Leo finished his punishment. Then Sour kneeled and pointed at a black mark on the linoleum floor. "Is that shoe polish, Mr. Dulce?"

Benito tried to see the stain without breaking attention. "I'll find out, sir."

"Damn straight you will." Sour rose and sidled up to Benito, grabbing him by the neck. "You'll find out right now." He pushed his head toward the floor, and Benito almost lost his balance. The section leader crouched next to him.

"Is that shoe polish?"

"I-I think so, sir!"

"That's not an answer!" he screamed. "Is that shoe polish, Mr. Dulce?"

"Yes, sir!"

"You don't have to be such a jerk, sir!" The words were out before Leo realized he'd thought them.

Whiskey glared at Leo, releasing his grip on Benito's neck and honing in on his next victim. Benito snatched a towel and wiped the mark off the floor before resuming his stance.

"Do you think *you* know how to train plebes, Mr. Scott?" Sour asked.

"No, sir." Dread prickled Leo's spine.

"Really? 'Cause it sounded like you were telling a firstie how to do his job. High knees for a minute. You too, MUFFIN."

The squad leader stalked over to Leo's desk as they jogged in place, high-stepping it. Up to this point detailers had ignored Audrey's picture, but now Sour seized the frame and threw open a desk drawer, tossing it inside. "That's another minute of high knees for displaying personal items, Midshipman Scott."

Leo closed his eyes.

Glancing in the open drawer, Sour tilted his head. "What do we have here?" He pulled out the diploma holder. There was only the sound of their labored breathing as he read the document.

Please don't hurt it, Leo prayed.

"Stop the high knees." Sour glared at him. "James is your father, then?"

"Yes, sir."

"A Navy brat. I should've known. Did your father swim too?"

"No, sir."

Tossing the diploma back into the drawer along with Audrey's framed photograph, he slammed it shut.

Leo jumped.

"What else do you have hiding over here, Mr. Scott?"

Unsure how to answer, Leo stood still as Whiskey hovered near his desk, looking into the built-in bookshelves. "When I was a plebe," he said, "I hid things I didn't want anyone to see in a special place."

Leo's eyes widened as Sour stepped onto his chair and then his desk. He reached his hand over the top of the built-in bookshelf to a ledge behind it. Extracting the baby bracelet, he appeared intrigued.

Leo's stomach clenched with fury.

Sour jumped down from the desk. "Scott," he read, staring at the beads. "Did your daddy send you here with your baby bracelet for good luck, Leah?"

Leo gritted his jaw. "No, sir." *If Sour so much as touched that bracelet...*

"I think somebody's close to being fried," he said. "You keep going at this pace, and you'll be restricted to the Yard for August break, with no visitors."

It was difficult now for Leo to maintain an impassive façade, and Whiskey seemed to sense him unraveling. He dangled the baby bracelet in his face.

"This contraband's illegal, Midshipman Scott, and should be destroyed." He tossed the bracelet on the floor. "Use that shiny black shoe of yours to crush it."

An image of Audrey swam through his mind. *Someday, Leo, I want to have a baby with you...when the time's right.*

"No, sir," Leo said, straightening his back.

"Are you disobeying an order, Mr. Scott?"

"Yes, sir."

Sour stepped even closer, grinning. Leo flinched at the crunch that accompanied the stomp of his shoe.

The next thing Leo was aware of was the smack of fist on flesh as his knuckles connected with Sour's jaw. The punch seemed to catch both of them off guard, and the squad leader reeled while Leo stood in a daze, gawking dumbly at his balled-up right fist. He looked on with horror as Whiskey regained his balance and wiped the corner of his mouth, leaving blood on the back of his hand.

Sour's face reddened with rage, and Leo steeled himself. He deserved it. A plebe simply did not hit a superior, and there'd be consequences.

As his superior stepped threateningly close, Leo braced himself. It was all he could do to keep his chin up.

"What were you thinking?" Sour screamed in his ear. "You *never* touch a detailer!" He prowled Leo's personal space. He'd just cocked his arm back when a firm voice called from the doorway.

"Whiskey!" Nevington entered the room. She looked down at little beads strewn on the floor and undoubtedly noticed the smear of blood on Sour's face. "What the *hell's* going on here?"

Sour took a step back. "This plebe just punched me!"

"He *what?* Midshipman Scott, did you just assault my squad leader?"

Leo's cheeks flamed. "Yes, ma'am."

She turned to Whiskey. "And you're going to solve the problem by punching him back, you boat goat?"

Sour paused, and Leo said, "I deserve to be punished, ma'am."

She spun to face him, eyes flaring. "Oh, you deserve a boatload of punishment right now, and you'll get it. But you're not taking Sour down with you."

She took a deep breath, and her gaze landed on Benito. "Clean this mess up, chow hound."

Benito kneeled to scoop up the damaged beads.

Nevington turned to Leo. "Lt. Keaton ordered me to report any significant disciplinary problems to her. I'd say this qualifies. Section Leader Sour, hold the deck while I accompany Midshipman Scott to her office."

He nodded.

"Grab your cover, Mr. Scott."

"Yes, ma'am." Still in a daze, Leo reached for his hat. His heart pounded as he walked out the door and followed her through the maze of Mother B. It appeared he'd royally screwed the pooch, and he wasn't looking forward to the aftermath.

They arrived at the anteroom of the company officers' offices, and Las Vegas paused. "You don't say a word unless one of us asks you a direct question. You got it, Mr. Scott?"

"Yes, ma'am."

She exhaled before knocking. "Here we go. Let's see what kind of mood the ice queen's in this afternoon."

"Enter!" called a crisp voice.

Nevington and Leo marched into the office, both turning to face Lt. Darnell Keaton exactly in unison.

She rose from her chair and returned their salutes. Despite his circumstances, she was one of the prettiest women Leo had ever seen. She'd pulled her ash blond hair back into a neat bun, and her blue eyes shone in the afternoon sunlight streaming through the window. She had full lips, and her tan uniform hugged her lean figure.

"Company Commander Viva Nevington and Midshipman Fourth Class Leo Scott requesting your assistance with a disciplinary matter, ma'am," Nevington said.

Leo trembled as his superior's eyes mowed him down. *You can do this.* Would this be his last day in uniform?

"What happened, Ms. Nevington?" Lt. Keaton asked.

"Midshipman Scott assaulted Squad Leader Sour, ma'am."

Her eyebrows shot up. "Assaulted?"

"He punched Mr. Sour in the face, ma'am."

Her eyes glinted with anger. "Is this the same Midshipman Scott I've been reading about in your reports, Ms. Nevington — the plebe acing every academic and physical fitness test you've thrown at him?"

"Yes, ma'am."

"The same plebe you've been bragging about?"

Nevington winced. "Yes, ma'am."

The lieutenant turned her frosty stare back to Leo. "Talk, Mr. Scott."

Leo had no idea what she wanted him to say. "No excuse, ma'am."

"We will *not* tolerate sailors punching their superiors, Mr. Scott. Tell me one reason not to give you your walking papers this minute."

"Ma'am, I-I love it here, and I want to stay. I don't know what came over me...It was a huge mistake, and I'm so sorry, ma'am. Please, please let me stay. I won't let you down again, ma'am."

She folded her arms across her chest. "What do you think about this, Ms. Nevington?"

"Midshipman Scott's done an excellent job, and Second Company would hate to lose him. However, striking a superior is an egregious offense, and I understand if you have to separate him. I guess I'd like to know why he lost his cool, ma'am."

"I don't care what led to the assault." The lieutenant's voice suddenly shook, and she reached for the corner of her desk.

Leo wanted to steady her elbow, but he didn't dare break his stance.

"There's *no* excuse for that kind of aggression." She stood stock still, seeming to forget to blink. A full minute passed, and Leo didn't know what to do.

Finally Nevington spoke up. "Lt. Keaton? Ma'am?"

The lieutenant sucked in a breath then shook her head, as if to clear it. "You said you wanted to stay at the Academy, Midshipman Scott," she said. "I'm not convinced of your intentions. You need to think long and hard if you truly want to be part of the Navy, and I'll give you the opportunity to do just that. Company Commander Nevington and her staff will oversee your punishment. You will march for twenty-four hours straight at T-court, beginning immediately. You'll also attend anger management counseling with one of our psychologists."

Turning to the company commander, the lieutenant asked, "Any questions?"

Nevington appeared taken aback. "I have one question, ma'am. Are we allowed to administer water during the punishment?"

"Of course, Ms. Nevington. No food, though. I want Mr. Scott to be hungry. I want him hungry to serve…hungry for training. I don't want a sailor who attacks the very man designated to train him."

"Yes, ma'am."

"It hasn't been a pleasure to make your acquaintance, Mr. Scott," she said. "Plebes do *not* want to get to know their company officers. It took you less than three weeks to find your way to my office, and it better be three years before I see you again. Is that clear?"

"Yes, ma'am."

"Dismissed."

They exchanged salutes, and the midshipmen exited.

Leo followed Nevington's verbal commands to the small arms storage unit, where he checked out his M-16. They then proceeded to T-court, the area right outside Bancroft. Leo held his rifle at an angle in front of him, shoulders back and eyes forward.

His company commander bit her lip. "Scott, what'd you do to piss her off? She seems to hate you."

Leo squinted in the afternoon sun. "Ma'am?"

"Short of separating you from the Navy, that's the worst punishment I've ever seen."

Wait, it was just marching, right? Twenty-four hours was a long time, but he thought he could make it. The mandated counseling actually sounded much worse.

"No matter how bad it gets, I want you to keep going," she said. "I meant what I said back there. I want you part of Second Company. Find the strength to get through this, okay?"

"Yes, ma'am." Beads of perspiration already dotted his forehead.

She glanced at her watch. "It's fourteen thirty-seven hours. You may begin."

Leo took his first step in a slow, measured cadence: the first step of thousands to come.

56. Million Blister March

Why in the world had he thought twenty-four hours of marching would be easy?

Sure, the first six hours had breezed by, his mind wandering through happy Audrey memories and interrupted by detailers offering him water every hour or so.

Knowing he'd be lucky to get a bathroom break, he'd carefully limited his intake. He was probably sweating off most of it anyway. He'd been hungry from the first moment of the march, and once evening chow had come and gone, the needy growls of his stomach echoed in his ears.

But around 2100, darkness settled into both T-court and Leo's spirit. It was deathly quiet as he made his way around the perimeter of the cement area. His arms ached from holding the rifle, and his heart ached with loneliness and self-reproach.

He hoped Audrey would forgive him for the destruction of her precious gift. Leo ground his teeth every time he replayed the sound of Whiskey's heel crushing their symbolized future together.

Knowing Audrey, she'd probably be more upset about his violence and subsequent punishment. Bracelets could be replaced — trust from his commanders could not. Audrey could buy him another gift, but she couldn't buy him an escape from the prison of the internalized CS. Leo now knew his father's aggression continued to haunt him, even though he was hundreds of miles away.

Around midnight, after ten hours of marching, blisters began to form. He'd only *thought* he was miserable before. His right foot was slightly longer than his left, so his right heel chafed on the back on his shoe, causing him to wince with every step. After he adjusted his gait, his left big toe soon smarted.

For a while, every step was sheer torture. Then around 0300 he supposed he'd bludgeoned the nerve endings sufficiently into submission, and his feet turned blessedly numb.

At 0500 T-court came alive with plebes gathering for PT. Leo dared not break his thousand-yard stare, but he was sure his Second Company *compadres* were getting a good look at him marching.

It seemed Las Vegas and two of her squad leaders were rotating shifts for watching him and giving him water, but so far he hadn't seen Whiskey. He dreaded their eventual meeting and was curious how MUFFIN was faring.

Leo plodded along, zoned out as the sun broke over the horizon. Second Company headed back from the PT field to begin the running portion of PT, and he could see the group jogging toward him. They passed him on the left.

He heard a familiar, urgent voice whisper *"¡Cóge!"* and looked over to see something whiz toward him. Leo caught the small plastic package and pocketed it as Benito winked at him, jogging past.

When Leo marched around the far corner of T-court, he reached into his pocket. He was elated to find a packet of energy gel. He squeezed the sweet goo down his throat.

The pounding high-noon sun illuminated the red cement in an undulating haze. His sweaty uniform clung to his body, and his march was almost a stumble at this point. Only two and one half more hours, but it seemed like a lifetime. *Just keep swimming.* He felt so exhausted he was close to tears.

"Keep marching," Company Commander Nevington said, suddenly falling into step next to him. "Don't look, but Lt. Keaton's watching you."

"Yes, ma'am." Leo tried to straighten his back and retract his aching shoulders. He grasped the water bottle she held out for him and took a swig.

"You don't look so good," she said.

Her brilliant white uniform was clean and neat, and she seemed rested and full of energy. Jealousy stabbed him in the eye.

"No, ma'am." Leo stuck to one of four acceptable responses for plebes.

"I thought you said you wanted to be here."

"Yes, ma'am."

"Remember that, then. Not much longer now."

"Yes, ma'am."

She broke off, and Leo trudged forward.

The longer this punishment lasted, the more the images of his father flooded Leo's mind. He remembered happier times, when CS had embraced him after record-setting swims. Though always slightly afraid and in awe of his father, in those moments, enveloped in his strong arms, Leo felt safety and acceptance like none other. Father and son would huddle together, carefully analyzing Leo's stroke rate and technique, while his mother looked on.

As the minutes ticked by, Leo also recalled the whippings and later the beatings. Because he strived so hard to please his father, he'd been physically punished probably fewer than fifteen times. But each of those frightening episodes was etched into his memory and branded into his flesh.

When finally the marching was over, Leo stood at attention on T-court, facing his company commander. They'd just returned from the small arms storage unit, where he'd handed over his rifle with a huge sigh of relief. He never wanted to see or hold the damn thing again. He'd hoped Las Vegas would let him go sleep, but there was no such luck. His shoulders drooped as she ordered him back outside.

"Have you learned your lesson, Midshipman Scott?" she asked, eyes stern.

"Yes, ma'am." He barely had the energy to speak.

"Good. I've been a big supporter of yours, but if you lay a hand on one of my staff again, I'll be the first to deep six your butt."

"Yes, ma'am."

She waited a beat. "I did a little research on you while you were marching."

Fear shot through him.

"I talked to Whiskey about your altercation," she continued. "Then I did some checking around. It seems your father, Commander James Scott, was disciplined for child abuse three months ago. Around that same time, you were admitted to the hospital for major surgery."

Startled, Leo willed himself to stay silent.

"You're wondering how I found this out, huh? You're not the only one with an overbearing Navy father, Mr. Scott. Captain Dr. Ray Nevington's stationed in Afghanistan right now, and he helped me do some investigative work. Your father's suspension's a matter of public record, but a physician also has access to Tri-Care insurance records. My father found the insurance claim from the Naval Hospital in your name."

The deep hopelessness and the knowledge that he'd ever escape his father's influence once again struck him. Now his company commander knew his disgraceful history.

Hot tears welled up. Lacking the energy to fight them, he felt them spill down his cheeks. "I'm sorry, ma'am," he said softly.

She seemed flummoxed.

Looking away, he said, "I deserved it."

"You deserved what?"

"The punishment. I, um —" He swallowed. "I got my girlfriend pregnant."

She gasped. "Was that bracelet for...for your baby? Are you a father?"

"No, ma'am." Leo sniffed. "My girlfriend miscarried."

The company commander seemed to struggle for something to say.

Tears cascaded down Leo's face. "The bracelet was a gift from my girlfriend. I put her through complete hell, and still she gave me a gift. It was a promise, for the future. Mr. Sour ordered me to destroy the bracelet, ma'am. I'm sorry...I'm sorry, but I couldn't. I couldn't follow his order, ma'am."

She stayed silent for some time. "That's an awful story, Mr. Scott. I'm not sure the average person would've reacted any different. I'm not sure the average person could turn the other cheek when he saw something so precious being destroyed. But a Navy sailor is *not* your average person."

She took a deep breath. "If you want to stay in the Navy, you'll need to control yourself much better than that. I don't care what you've learned in your family. The *Navy* is your family now, and you'll have to learn how to manage without lashing out. We'll train you, and Lt. Keaton believes you need counseling to help you learn as well. But this is on your shoulders now. It's up to you whether you'll embrace the training and counseling and become an officer worthy of the uniform."

Leo felt a fire light in his belly. He wanted to be self-disciplined. He wanted to be an officer. And he was determined not to let CS stand in his way. "I'll do everything I can to learn from the training and counseling, ma'am."

"Good. It won't be easy, but nothing worthy is ever easy. Lucky for you, it starts right now. Dr. Hansen has an opening at fifteen hundred. Let's go."

Leo gulped. "Yes, ma'am."

She directed him forward, and he once again felt shooting pains from his blistered feet. He'd just completed the Million Blister March.

Leo took a deep breath as they neared Bancroft, setting his jaw with determination. He'd already shed tears once today. That was enough.

As he worked through a mound of paperwork in the waiting room, Leo could feel tension radiate from his shoulder blades. His father's disparaging view of therapy, not to mention his own tendency toward privacy, made him skeptical of the whole process. He just wanted to get it over with.

After being escorted to the psychologist's office, Leo was even more uneasy when a blond woman resembling his mother greeted him.

She returned his salute then pointed to the sofa. "Let's dispense with the formalities. Have a seat, Leo."

"Yes, ma'am." He hobbled over and sank into the cushions.

"Welcome, Leo. I'm Lt. Commander Dr. Ina Hansen."

"Yes, ma'am." He liked how she called him by his first name. He hadn't heard it in a while.

"I'm a counseling psychologist, and I've been at the Academy for eight years now. Let's go over a few things before we get started." She referred to a paper inside the chart on her lap. "You signed this informed consent, and I'd like to highlight the information about confidentiality. What we discuss in here is private unless you're in immediate danger of harming yourself or others, or if minors or impaired persons are being abused. I also need to share your attendance, progress, and fitness for duty with your CO. Any questions so far?"

Leo's eyes glazed over. "No, ma'am."

"Are you paying attention, Leo? This is the only time I'll review this information."

He sat up straighter. "Yes, ma'am."

"What I'd like to do today is get to know you a little better, talk about what brought you in, get some background information about you." She glanced down at his intake paperwork and made a few notes. "Oh, joy—you're ordered to attend counseling." Her eyes met his. "Mandated referrals are soooo fun. Midshipmen just love to use their free time talkin' to me."

He decided to risk sarcasm. *"Free* time, ma'am?"

"Oh, right. No free time in plebe-land."

Leo was amazed to find himself smiling.

"Have you ever been in counseling before?"

Leo paused. No way he'd reveal his brief stint in drug rehab, but he didn't want to lie either. "Do I have to answer that, ma'am?"

She scribbled something.

"No, Leo. Let me tell you how it works. Although I'm your superior, I'd like you to drop the 'ma'am' as it'll get old for both of us real fast. Call me Ina. I need you to talk freely in here, and I need you to be truthful. This is probably the only place on the Yard where you won't get in trouble for voicing your opinion or not knowing the right answer."

Leo nodded. Maybe this wouldn't be so bad.

"Can you tell me why you're ordered to meet with me?"

He squirmed. "I punched my squad leader, ma'am."

"You punched a *firstie?* Then they sent you to counseling?"

"After a twenty-four hour march, yes, ma'am."

"Twenty-four hours?" She gaped. "In a row?"

"Yes, ma'am."

"When did this punishment end?"

"About thirty minutes ago."

"I'm impressed you're still functioning at this point. Now I get why you were limping." She rose to leave. "Stay seated."

Left alone, Leo's eyes traveled around the space, taking in the warm yellow paint, an overstuffed bookshelf, and a side table with a few toys and a candy bowl. Lust for her chocolates consumed him, but it would be too bold to take one, he was sure. Leo looked closer at the toys and snickered to see a little foam Eric Cartman. What was a lieutenant commander doing with a *South Park* toy?

Ina returned, and Leo's reflexes pulled him painfully to his feet.

"I *said* stay seated."

"Yes, ma'am."

She had a plastic container in her arms. When she kneeled and set it at his feet, soapy water splashed around inside.

Extracting a first aid kit from under the side table, Ina ordered, "Take off your shoes and socks."

Leo hesitated. "No, ma'am, you don't want to see this."

"Your feet are a valuable commodity as a plebe. If you can't walk or run, you're screwed. Shoes and socks off, now."

Leo sighed. Not only did she look a little like his mother, she could be a total nag too. He untied his shoelaces and removed his shoes before gingerly unrolling his socks. Caked-on blood stuck them to his skin. Once his feet were free, Leo stared at the bloody mess.

"Go ahead," Ina encouraged. "Give 'em a good soak."

He procrastinated, knowing pain awaited him.

She reached forward to help, but he blocked her. "No," he said. "I'll do it."

Leo gasped as the warm water stung his raw, exposed skin. His nose burned, but he fought off tears, and after a few minutes the tension drained from his shoulders as the water began to soothe.

"Who did this to you?" Ina asked. "I mean, who ordered the march?"

"Lt. Keaton ordered the Million Blister March, ma'am."

She grinned. "She's rather new here. She's the officer for Second Company?"

"Yes, ma'am."

"So, what made you attend the Academy?" She returned to her seat.

"My father."

Ina tilted her head. "I didn't ask who—I asked *what*. You had no choice in the matter?"

"Actually, I did have a choice. I missed out on a swimming scholarship at FSU, and it would've been expensive to go there, but I could've forced my family into major debt. I guess I kinda wanted to test myself here, to be honest."

"I'm a big fan of honesty, Leo. You're from Florida?"

He nodded.

"What part?"

Leo stared her down. If he told her he lived in Pensacola, she might know he came from a Navy family. She could probably find out anyway, but he felt overexposed as it was.

"I think I'm good here." He lifted his feet from the water and placed them on a towel she'd laid out.

Ina scribbled again in his chart, and he wondered what she was writing. Then she got out of her chair and kneeled down again, pulling some bandages from the first aid kit.

"That's okay, ma'am. I can do this."

"You're just like my sons—'I can do it myself!' We only have an hour, and judging by all those blisters, this job will take two of us."

Leo surrendered and allowed her to help him apply antibacterial cream and cover each blister with a bandage. Since he was spleenless, the cream was probably an especially good idea. He was touched a superior officer would help him like this.

"You have sons, ma'am?" he asked as they worked.

"Twin thirteen-year-olds."

Leo smiled, things clicking into place. "They like *South Park*, huh?"

She chuckled. "That's their favorite show. So, back to you, sounds like you're on the swim team here. What do you like about swimming?"

Fastening a Band-Aid to his toe, Leo pictured the high school pool. "So much. It's an individual sport. It's all on me—the victories, the defeats. I love how hard it is…Not everyone's willing to wake up before zero-five-hundred, and only the strongest can make it. It's also cool how soothing and refreshing the water is. It's like another world where you can't hear a thing; you're just alone in your thoughts. And to swim fast, you can't fight the water. You have to flow with it, feel it, surrender to it."

"You make me want to head to the pool right now, Leo!"

He blushed.

As they finished fixing his feet, she handed him some antibacterial hand gel. Leo heard a loud rumble.

"Was that your stomach?"

"Yes, ma'am."

"Tell me they gave you some food during the Million Blister March."

Leo lowered his head. "No, ma'am."

She stood up. "I swear," she muttered, opening a desk drawer. Ina dropped a nutrition bar into his hands.

"That's okay, ma'am. Evening chow's in only two hours." He tried to give the bar back.

"Leo, eat. Our sessions are important, and I want you to be focused. You can hardly concentrate if you haven't eaten all day."

He must have scarfed it down in seconds, and before he knew it she'd handed him another bar and a bottle of water. Her compassion almost made him cry.

After he finished his snack, Ina resumed her questions. "Have you ever gotten in trouble for fighting before, Leo?"

He swallowed. "Yes, ma'am...once in high school I punched a guy."

"What happened?"

Leo looked down. "I got suspended for a week."

"Wow. Your parents must've been pretty upset."

His eyes widened and his cheeks burned, but he didn't say a word.

Her voice was gentle. "Where'd you learn to hit, Leo?"

It was then he started crying.

In a daze, Leo stumbled toward his dorm room after therapy. Fortunately by the time his pathetic tears had started, there'd only been a few minutes left in the session. He'd been too upset to answer her questions, so Dr. Ina had just given him a little speech about the consequences of violence. How could he have let his guard down? It would never happen again.

Sleep. He needed sleep. He'd been awake about forty hours straight now, plus the marching, and he maintained a single focus on getting to bed as fast as possible. Unfortunately, Mr. Sour was waiting for him.

Leo wearily snapped to attention. When Whiskey stepped behind him to close the door, sealing them both inside, Leo's stomach dropped.

"How was that twenty-four-hour march?"

"Fine, sir." Leo noticed some swelling on Mr. Sour's lower lip and a bruise along his jaw. He felt the heat of his superior's glare and wondered what he was waiting for.

"What should I do with you now, Midshipman Scott?"

"I suppose you should teach me a lesson, sir."

"And how should I do that?"

Leo gulped, trying to be brave. "You should beat the living hell out of me, sir."

"I should. But Ms. Nevington warned me that if she sees one bruise on that pretty face of yours, she'll report me to the lieutenant."

"There are ways to hide bruises, sir."

"Aw, crap, Scott. You say something like that, and there's no way I can hit you. She told me about your dad, you know."

Leo's eyes closed. Would the entire freaking company find out his father put him in the hospital?

Sour bit his lip. "I, uh, also heard about the bracelet, and the, um, pregnancy. Don't worry—only Vegas and I know. I want to apologize for my behavior," he added, sounding well-rehearsed.

A firstie apologizing to a plebe? It was unheard of.

"Nevington told me I should apologize for destroying that baby bracelet. I thought no way. But then at practice Coach asked me where I got that bruise, and I had to tell him about you." Sour's mouth tightened. "Coach said I should *want* a teammate who's faster than me because that'll make me better. I thought about it, and I suppose he's right."

Pausing, Sour met his eyes. "I'm sorry, Midshipman Scott."

Leo had no idea what to do. He was supposed to receive punishment, not apologies. Then he remembered what Dr. Ina had encouraged him to say. "Permission to speak freely, sir?"

"Go ahead."

"I have something to say to you as well, sir. My psychologist, Dr. Hansen, she told me to ask you something." Leo cleared his throat. "How'd my punch affect you, sir?"

"Huh?"

"Um, how were you affected by my violence, sir?"

"I'm fine. I'm furious with you, and you better not try that crap again, but I'm okay now."

"She said that's how you'd respond, but I'm supposed to face the consequences of my violence. Dr. Hansen said I need empathy for the effects of my actions on others."

"She's some weird shrink, huh?"

"Yes, sir. Did it hurt, sir?"

Whiskey looked uneasy. "Well, yeah, it did hurt," he said after a moment. "My jaw's been aching since yesterday, and I couldn't sleep much last night. Vegas and Coach are questioning my leadership ability since I almost lost control and hit you back. And the other firsties are giving me crap for getting hit by a lowly plebe." His voice grew more incensed.

"I'm sorry, sir. I truly am," Leo said.

Sour continued to fume.

"You sure you don't want to hit me, sir?"

"It's tempting." He took a deep breath. "You do realize I'll to ride you the entire year for this, don't you, Scott?"

"Yes, sir."

"Good. Drop and give me fifty!"

Leo willed himself through fifty pushups, his body teetering on the brink of exhaustion. Finally Mr. Sour left him alone, and he curled up on his rack for forty-five minutes of sleep before evening chow.

57. The Ring

Jason rolled over and sprawled out on the pale green sheets of Cam's bed.

Her head rested on the crook of her arm, and she trailed her fingers across his chest. "I can tell you've been hitting the gym hard, babe," she cooed. "You're my hunk of man love."

Jason shivered and gave her a lazy smile. "Are you from Pearl Harbor, baby? 'Cause you're da bomb."

She groaned. "That was your pick-up line our senior year!"

"Worked then, works now."

"You need new material."

"All I know is *this*...was great." He gazed at her. "Way better than stealing a few minutes in the backseat of your car when we were seventeen." He stroked the hair softly framing her face.

"It *is* nice not to feel the seat divider pressing into my back. But I kind of miss the thrill of maybe getting caught."

"We still get that here. We're just lucky your mom's out of town tonight."

Cam tensed.

Feeling suddenly chilled despite the late-July heat, Jason pulled the sheet up and rested on his elbows. "You and your mom close on the new house soon. Why don't you help her move, then we'll get a place together?"

"Oh, not this again." Cam looked up at him. "Can't we just enjoy this moment?"

"You start teaching in a month, and like you said, your first year will be insane. With my night class, I'll be busy too. If we don't live together, we'll never see each other."

"Jase, we've been over this. My dad would've freaked if I lived with a guy before I'm engaged. My mom wouldn't be too psyched about it either."

"I'm not *some guy*. Besides, we're only twenty-two. That's way too young to get married."

"We're almost twenty-three. That's about how old our parents were when they married."

"Yeah, and look how great that turned out."

"Well, *my* parents had a wonderful marriage," Cam said.

"Didn't you say they were fighting that last year?"

She sighed. "Yeah. I don't know what happened, but my mom seemed angry with him all the time. I know she feels awful for some things she said before he died—things she can't take back now."

Silence hung between them.

"We'd be happier together than your parents are," she added.

He scowled. "How do you know, Cam? I love you, and you love me. But how do you know it would last?"

"I don't have my crystal ball with me, but you gotta have some faith! You need some faith in *us*. If anything happened, I'd fight for you…I don't want you to leave."

"Who said I'm leaving?" he said, more harshly than he meant.

Cam looked down. "I just spent the day shopping with Audrey. She should be all excited to go to school, but instead she's a mess. She misses Leo something awful, and barely gets to hear from him. I couldn't take that, Jase."

"Hey." He smoothed his thumb across her chin. "I'm not going anywhere. You saw that box at Marcus's apartment—that's my stuff from Seattle. I'm staying in Florida, okay? We don't need some silly ring to prove it."

Hurt crept across Cameron's face. "An engagement ring wouldn't be *silly* to me."

"I'm sorry, I didn't mean it that way." Jason pushed himself off of the bed. "I'm getting something to drink." He slid on his shorts.

He padded down the stairs, headed to the refrigerator, and grabbed a soda. He cringed thinking about his lame protests. Jason wanted nothing more than to marry Cam. He wanted to spend the rest of his life with her. But he didn't have nearly enough money to buy an engagement ring. Though he loved his job at Child Protective Services, the pay wasn't great, and he'd already taken out student loans for community college.

Noticing a photograph stuck to the refrigerator with a magnet, Jason studied a close-up of Mr. Walsh at the marina. His brown eyes gazed intently at the camera as he stood in his khaki uniform, arms wrapped around his wife and daughter. Their faces filled the frame, their bright smiles now locked forever in the past.

Would you approve of me as a son-in-law? Jason already knew the answer.

Who was he kidding? Lack of funds wasn't the only thing preventing him from popping the question. He wasn't worthy of Cam's love.

"At ease, gentlemen."

Roland Drake and James Scott obeyed Captain Payson's order. Roland sensed lingering tension between Scott and Payson, and wondered what his captain had in mind today. He took a deep breath, hoping to calm himself. For the last fourteen months, anytime a superior ordered him to report, anxiety immediately consumed him, and he prayed all over again that nobody had discovered his secret. He believed the only person who knew had been taken care of, but there was always a shadow of doubt.

Last June Roland had stood in his supervisor's office, just like he did today. At first he'd been excited that Lt. Commander Walsh wanted to see him. Perhaps a promotion? But as soon as he'd entered the office, he'd known Walsh was displeased.

"Where'd you get that ring?" he'd asked immediately.

"My Academy ring, sir?"

"Yes, Lt. Drake, your *Academy* ring. I was doing some fact checking for your promotion paperwork."

Roland's stomach had twisted.

"Turns out you never actually *graduated* from the Academy!"

"I can explain, sir! I-I just couldn't pass Engineering four sixty-two, but I made all the other requirements. I was so close!"

Walsh had been incredulous. "You were *close*? You lied on your resume! How has no one noticed this before?"

Roland's heart had hammered. "I don't know, sir. Nobody really checked it out, I guess. I didn't find out I failed the class again till right before graduation. I didn't know what to do, so I just showed up to my assignment at Norfolk and nobody said anything. I think they never filed the proper paperwork, sir."

Walsh had shaken his head, eyes flaring. "I return to my original question: Where did you get your Academy ring? They only give that to graduates."

Roland had closed his eyes. "On Ebay, sir."

For a moment he'd thought Walsh was going to laugh, but when he'd spoken there was no humor in his voice. "This won't turn out well for you, Lt. Drake. At best, you're looking at discharge. At worst, a court martial."

Roland had shook. "Please, sir, my wife's pregnant. I-I can't lose my job. We're having a baby girl...You have a daughter, sir. You know what it's like. Nobody discovered this for thirteen years. If you just deep six this information, I'm sure it'll never surface."

That's right, Roland reminded himself. *It will never surface.* Walsh hadn't ratted him out before his death a month later, and nobody else had ever figured it out. He tried to focus on what Captain Payson was saying.

"Commander Scott, you've been called to serve on the USS *Ronald Reagan*, which, as you know, is stationed in the Persian Gulf," the captain said. "Your transport to the bird farm leaves in four days—August sixth."

"Aye, sir," Scott answered. Roland could sense him stiffen.

"You tour on the *Reagan* will be three months," Payson added. "Lt. Commander Drake, you did an adequate job replacing Commander

Scott during his suspension. V-Four's safety ratings did take a dip, though, so I'd like to meet with you more frequently when you take over as air boss."

Roland nodded. "Yes, sir."

"You have four days to coordinate the transition of leadership, gentlemen. James, I want you to help Roland with the intricacies of running this unit. Nobody does it as well as you."

"Thank you, sir."

"Dismissed."

As Roland followed Scott into his office, he absentmindedly twisted the class ring. He'd had it engraved with his name. It might as well have been actually his. Scott's impending absence was the perfect opportunity to keep moving up the ladder, and as he prepared to begin the transition, Roland put a smile on his face.

James sat in the parking lot of a coffee shop, waiting for Jason to drop off Mary. His wife had finally relented and agreed to a meeting once he'd told her about his deployment.

Desperation washed over him. He was basically rudderless, with no direction since losing his family. Drowning in a sea of self-pity, James clasped his hands in his lap.

He watched a rusted compact car enter the parking lot and felt a catch in his throat when Mary got out, planting her canes and making her way toward the coffee shop with Jason trailing behind. God, she was beautiful. She was five years older than him, almost fifty, yet she'd hardly changed at all. He, on the other hand, had aged ten years in recent months.

As James approached them, his son visibly tensed. "You look good, Jason. You been working out?" he asked.

"Uh, yes, sir."

"And your mother tells me you have a new job."

Jason met his gaze.

"At Child Protective Services," James muttered, mustering a small smile.

Jason seemed relieved. "I'll be in the car, Mom."

"Thank you, Jase."

James held the door open, and Mary sank into the first big chair she encountered. He continued on to order lattes at the counter.

When he gave her the drink, Mary nodded her thanks. "You leave tomorrow?"

"Yes, at zero-six-hundred. How've you been, Mary?"

She sighed and twirled her wedding ring.

Is the ring merely a symbol now? he wondered. *Is there any love left?* Watching her struggle to answer, James turned to an easier question. "How are our sons?" Surely they could still connect as parents.

"Leo got in big trouble for punching his squad leader."

James's eyes widened, and she added with a hint of sarcasm, "Sound familiar?"

"Hey, I stuck to hitting plebes. I wasn't stupid enough to punch a firstie." Memories of their meeting at the Academy flooded him. The Yard was where their romance began...their family began.

"And Jason wants to marry Cameron, but he can't afford a ring," she continued. "I think they make a lovely couple."

"Sounds like you're moving on without me." Bitterness spiked his words.

"James—"

"Mary, listen to me. I want you back in our home. Audrey will be leaving soon, and it'd be ridiculous for you to continue living at Denny and JoAnne's. And I don't want our house sitting idle for three months while I'm away."

"This isn't about a house, James. It's about a marriage." Her eyes welled up, and she turned away.

His heart thudded.

"I don't know if I love you anymore," she rasped.

She was throwing him overboard. "Don't say that," he pleaded. "I can't lose you. You saved me, Mary...You're the only reason I graduated from the Academy. You're the only reason I get out of bed in the morning. Don't take my will to live."

She sat for a moment. "You're making this all about *you*."

Her eyes flared, then softened with pity, and James felt disgusted with himself.

Mary sighed and touched her wedding ring again. "I haven't made up my mind yet, and I can't be rushed simply because you're headed to the Gulf. There *is* one thing you can do for me, for our family, that'll make me promise not to initiate divorce — in the next few months at least."

"Tell me what it is, Mary. I'll do it."

She explained what she wanted and seemed surprised when he readily agreed.

After another moment, she gathered herself out of the chair.

James also stood. He placed his hands in his pockets and looked down. "Can I…can I hug you?"

She froze. After an eternity she nodded.

He folded her into an embrace, and Mary began to sob. He touched her soft hair, contemplating their past and their future. He was going off to war, and they seemed at war as well.

"Be careful, James." Tears distorted her voice.

58. Yes, Ma'am

Leo saw Audrey on T-court before she could see him, and she'd never looked prettier.

She'd pulled her thick auburn hair up high in a ponytail, and a sleeveless white shirt accentuated the soft curve of her breasts and hard definition of her arms. Eyelets and tiny sky blue flowers detailed the shirt, which she'd tucked into a navy blue miniskirt. Beaded sandals completed her cool summer ensemble. Already sweating in his whiteworks, Leo's body temperature rose further just looking at her.

Ignoring his mother and her companion, he ran toward his unsuspecting girlfriend. At the last second Audrey noticed him and gave him a dazzling smile. He scooped her up, twirling her around.

In that moment, Leo finally released the tension he'd been holding throughout Plebe Summer. It was now Audrey Summer, and the hairs on his body stood at attention as he held her tight.

"I missed you *so* much," Leo whispered into her ear, cradling the nape of her neck.

"I missed you even more than that!"

"Good to know you're still competitive." He smirked, holding her face next to his, cheek to cheek. Eventually Leo let go to greet his other visitors.

He grinned at his mother, but his smile faded as he noticed Mr. Shale standing next to her. Leo knew his father had been deployed to the Gulf, but he hadn't anticipated Mr. Shale taking his place. He hugged his mother then reached out to shake his hand. "Thanks for coming, sir."

"I hope it's okay I'm here," Mr. Shale said. "We didn't want Audrey driving thirteen hours all by herself."

"Yes, sir."

"Leo, you must be the handsomest plebe ever to wear that uniform," his mother said.

He dipped his head, then peeked at Audrey, studying her reaction. "Do you, uh, do you think my uniform looks dorky?"

"*Dorky?*" Sneaking a glance at his mother, she stammered, "Ah, no, um, you look, um, just fine."

He'd have to follow up on *that* when they were alone.

"This is a beautiful campus," Mr. Shale said. "How do you like it here?"

Seeing him reminded Leo again of the pain medication under Benito's bed. No matter how busy he was with studying, drilling, PT, or trips to sea on patrol craft, part of Leo's brain was constantly aware of the medication just sitting there, waiting. "It's the hardest thing I've ever done in my life," he said. "I go to bed each night completely exhausted, physically and mentally, having no idea if I'll make it through the next day. I love it."

His mother and Audrey looked at each other. "Yep, he's definitely warped." Audrey smirked.

"Hey! Are you guys ganging up on me?" Leo reached over to tickle Audrey, and she shrieked as his hands groped her midsection.

Pulling her close, Leo sobered. "I better not grow too attached to this place. I almost got kicked out of here already by my company officer."

"Who's Second Company's officer?" his mother asked.

"Lt. Darnell Keaton, ma'am."

"You're kidding me. She used to serve under your father in V-Four."

"She did?" Leo asked. "I didn't know that. She doesn't seem to like me much."

"Darnell's rather young," his mother mused. "I think she's only about twenty-six. I bet it's difficult for her here as a young, pretty officer. She probably has to act like a tough witch."

Leo shook his head. "That's *no* act, believe me."

They chuckled.

Glancing at her watch, his mother said, "There's an informational session for parents soon, and after that I want to show Marcus my old engineering stomping grounds in Rickover Hall. Why don't you take Audrey around the Yard, and we'll meet for noon chow?"

Leo loved that she was instantly at home at the Academy again. "Sounds good, Mom."

The group parted ways, and Leo draped his arm over Audrey's shoulders as he led her down the sidewalk. When they approached an officer, Leo let go of her and executed a sharp salute. She shook with suppressed laughter.

"What's so funny?"

"I'm loving Lieutenant Leo." Her eyes gleamed.

"That's Midshipman Scott to you, ma'am." He grinned. "And you better get used to it. I probably salute officers like twenty times a day. And there'll be a lot more middies to harass me once the Brigade returns in full force next week."

On their way to the chapel, Leo cursed under his breath as saw Mr. Sour approaching. The detailer halted, and Leo braced to attention.

"Introduce me to your guest, Midshipman Scott," Sour commanded.

"Yes, sir. Squad Leader Sour, I'd like to introduce you to Miss Audrey Rose."

Whiskey shook Audrey's hand. "You must be Mr. Scott's girl-friend — the one he talks about constantly."

"Yep, that's me. He better not be talking about any *other* girlfriend."

Leo said nothing, not allowed to be part of the conversation as a lowly plebe. Nevertheless, watching Audrey and Whiskey smile at each other, Leo felt grateful he'd given him another chance.

Mr. Sour looked down the sidewalk. "Time to harass another plebe now. Enjoy your stay, Audrey."

"Thanks."

As Whiskey walked away, Leo exhaled. "He doesn't like me very much."

"He'll come around. Everybody loves Leo."

"You obviously haven't met Lt. Keaton. C'mon, I'll show you the crypt of John Paul Jones."

"Oooh." She batted her eyes in mock anticipation.

"You only wish you went to the Academy too," he said, smirking.

"I *do* wish I could see you every day." She snaked her hand around his lean waist. "Especially in this uniform. Yummy."

He slung his arm back over her shoulders. "I'm so happy you're here."

"Want to see Herndon Monument?" Leo asked after their tour of the ornate chapel.

"How about your dorm room?" she countered, ogling his uniform.

He sighed. "No visitors allowed in Bancroft Hall. Sorry."

"Oh."

"But I can introduce you to my roommate. He's hanging out at our favorite spot by the water today."

"Isn't he with his family?"

Leo grasped her hand and they headed toward the Severn River. "He's restricted to the Yard with no visitors. He got fried."

"Fried?"

"It means he got in big trouble. He's in the system now, and they might kick him out if he keeps getting in trouble."

"That's awful."

"Yeah. Poor Benito. It would do him good to see his family."

As they neared a hidden cove, the sun glinted off the water, almost blinding Leo.

"Wow, how'd you find this place?" Audrey asked.

"Ah, CS told me about it," Leo stammered. "He used to come here...with my mom."

"Oh."

Once he stepped into the shade of an overhanging ridge, Leo's eyes adjusted, and he saw Benito. Leo recognized the midshipman manual *Reef Points* in his lap.

"Whatcha studying, buddy?"

Benito jumped to attention, his voice mocking. "Sir, the Honor Concept of the Brigade of Midshipmen is 'Midshipmen are persons of integrity; they stand for that which is right.' Brigade Honor Committees are composed of elected upperclass midshipmen, responsible for education and training in the Honor Concept—"

"Okay, okay," Leo interrupted, laughing. "Sorry I asked." He drew Audrey closer. "Benito, meet Audrey Rose."

"Hi, Benito." Audrey smiled shyly.

"Well, you're even prettier than your picture."

Audrey blushed.

"Es una langosta hermosa," Benito told Leo, admiring Audrey as she brushed past Benito to step inside their hideout.

"Thanks for calling me beautiful, but I'm not a lobster," Audrey replied, turning to face him. "Lobsters swim backward."

Benito bit his lip, startled.

When it clicked for Leo, his chest tightened. "Take that back," he said, crossing toward Benito.

"I'm sorry Leo. I didn't mean it."

"What's going on?" Audrey asked. "Why are you mad, Leo?"

"Tell her why you called her a lobster."

"No, just forget about it, *hombre*. It was stupid."

"Tell her!" Leo barked.

Audrey flinched.

Benito looked down. "We sometimes call girls lobsters." He sighed. "Because all the meat's in the tail."

After a moment of awkward silence, the lovely sound of Audrey's laughter filled the air. She shook her head. "Leo, chill out. I already know the Navy is testosterone city."

"Didn't that upset you, what he said?"

"I thought it was funny."

"I really am sorry," Benito insisted, looking miserable. "Restriction's making me *loco*, and that was a dumb thing to say." He scooped up his books and muttered, "I'll be in Mother B—give you two some privacy. Whiskey's probably hunting for a plebe to humiliate."

He slunk away.

Audrey laced her hand into Leo's, unfurling his fist. "You're scaring me again. I hate to see you so mad. It wasn't a big deal."

Leo covered his face with his hands. "I guess I'll have something to discuss in therapy this week," he said from behind his palms. He crouched to sit cross-legged on a tattered tarp and thumped his hands in his lap, looking down. "I'm sorry I scared you."

"Stop being so hard on yourself, Leo."

Without thinking he said, "Yes, ma'am."

Audrey giggled.

"Oooh, I like that." She snickered. "Call me ma'am again."

A mischievous smile surfaced. "I misbehaved, ma'am. I should be punished, ma'am."

"We can arrange that," Audrey countered. "On your feet, Midshipman Scott!"

Leo scrambled back to standing. Audrey prowled around him, sliding one finger across his chest. "You're so hot in that uniform, Mr. Scott. You're even fitter than the last time I saw you, which is hard to believe." Her finger slid up and caressed his face with the lightest touch. She gave a dramatic sigh. "My boy is becoming a man." She tossed her hair. "But how could you almost *golpear* Benito? Make love, not war."

"Yes, ma'am."

She leaned in close, her mouth inches from his ear, and he could smell the hint of sweetness in her perfume. "You're the hottest plebe I've ever seen. *Caliente*. Sizzling hot. You're forcing me to break all rules against fraternizing."

"I won't report you, ma'am."

"You better not report this, either," she added, and shoved him down on the tarp.

He smiled, surprised by her aggression.

"Remove your *camisa*, Mr. Scott."

"Yes, ma'am." He yanked off his tunic.

"Now lay back."

She climbed on to straddle him. The places where their skin touched grew warm. Audrey unbuttoned her shirt and tossed it aside, leaving only her lacy bra.

"Eyes forward, mister." She crawled up to hover over his face. Holding her lips tantalizingly close to his, she whispered, "Now kiss me."

Leo lifted his head and once their lips locked, the force of Audrey's longing pressed his head back to the tarp. Their legs tangled as he drew her body to his, making it hard to breathe. But he didn't care. She was his breath, his life.

Audrey lingered in their kiss as he kneaded the fine muscles of her back, stroking her silky skin.

"Keep...doing...that," she ordered, between kisses.

"Yes, ma'am."

His hands slowly traveled south, cupping her bottom as she rubbed against him, making him crazy with desire. Her mouth lowered to press soft kisses on the expanse of his chest, and he could feel his heartbeat skip.

"We have to make this last till Thanksgiving, ma'am."

She paused to look up at him with a smolder in her copper eyes. "Then you better make it good, sailor." The tarp transformed into their reunion cruise, and they christened its maiden voyage with tender caresses.

"I'm great at following orders," he whispered a while later, stroking her back.

"Then I order you to love me like this forever," she said. Her body had responded to his, sensuous and warm. "I order you to never let me go."

"Yes, ma'am." He closed his eyes, pressing her to his chest, reveling in their closeness. Obedient to a fault, he vowed to follow her wishes.

59. Hazing

Stationed on the deck plate in the middle of his dorm passageway, Leo shouted a rapid fire chow call on his designated day. "Sir, you now have seven minutes until Noon Meal Formation! Noon Meal Formation occurs outside. Firsties carry swords. The uniform is summer working blues."

Ms. Nevington stood about fifteen feet away, observing him with her arms crossed over her chest. Those upperclassmen not scurrying to their rooms congregated in the passageway around Leo.

"The menu for noon meal is roast beef and turkey sandwiches, coleslaw, crackers, bread, milk, and apple and rhubarb pie. The Officer of the Watch is Midshipman First Class Viva Nevington, Second Company Commander. The Midshipman Officer of the Watch is Midshipman First Class Tom Sour, Honor Officer."

The second class midshipmen, responsible for training plebes once the school year started, flitted around Leo like wasps over nectar. He eyed them warily as he spouted the meticulously rehearsed details. He was determined not to forget one word or pause one second. "The professional topic of the week is aircraft carriers," Leo continued. "The key events of the Yard today are: sixteen hundred men's soccer versus Maryland, nineteen hundred mass in the chapel, and twenty-one hundred glee club concert in Alumni Hall. You now have five minutes, sir!"

He began his fourth repetition, each time less intimidated by the predatory midshipmen, who had nothing on his father. CS had made him rehearse chow call on the track until he was hoarse. The number of midshipmen mulling about dwindled as the time ticked down. "Sir, you now have three minutes until Noon Meal Formation!"

As Leo continued, the last remaining youngsters turned away, looking dejected. Leo hadn't made one error. Ms. Nevington smiled at him before she departed.

"Sir, you now have two minutes until Noon Meal Formation!" Leo executed an about face and double-timed it to the stairs. When he came across an upperclassman, he yelled, "Go, Navy, sir!" as he navigated the labyrinth of Mother B.

Sliding into formation just as the music began playing, Leo sighed with relief.

"That was close, *estúpido*," Benito whispered. The roommates had mastered the art of speaking while barely moving their lips, so they often carried on entire conversations in formation.

Leo glanced at his roommate's neat black uniform. Benito had slimmed down considerably once he was able to resume physical training, and his muscular chest and shoulders now cut a strong yet trim profile. And their superiors had stopped picking on him.

"What, no Arabic?" Leo jabbed.

"You can't keep up with me, *hombre*." Benito's gift for languages had led him to major in Arabic, and he'd taught Leo a few words and phrases. "Wanna walk to practice together?"

"Can't," Leo whispered. "Got therapy today."

"Sucks."

"Yeah." Leo put on a big show of disliking the mandated counseling, but secretly he looked forward to meetings with Dr. Ina. It was kind of cool to talk about his life at the Yard, and for the most part he'd successfully staved off her attempts to delve into his family. "Hey, what's for dinner tonight? I forgot."

Benito ran down the menu while they marched, and Leo committed each item to memory. He couldn't imagine Audrey filling her mind with this meaningless drivel every day, though she surely faced her own set of challenges as a student-athlete at FSU. Though Leo loved the Academy, he did miss his girlfriend.

The tour bus pulled away from the curb and began the four-hour trip to the University of Alabama in Tuscaloosa. Audrey clasped her hands in her lap. This would be her first college swim meet.

In the seat across the row from Audrey was her roommate, Tatiana Goreva, a delicate freshman butterflier from Belarus. Tatiana put on a tough act, but Audrey knew she was miserably homesick. She'd cried practically every night in their room for the first few weeks, but she seemed determined to stick it out. Thankfully their coach had insisted Tatiana meet with the athletic department's psychologist. After just a few sessions, Tatiana already appeared to feel better.

"What are you swimming?" Audrey asked.

"The two hundred butterfly and the one hundred freestyle." Tatiana enunciated each word with care. "You swim the individual medley and breaststroke, yes?"

"Yep. Alabama's got a really good breaststroker, from what I hear."

"Do not worry," Tatiana assured her. "You will kick her ass."

Audrey grinned, amused by Tatiana's expanding vocabulary. As she reached for her Psychology 101 textbook, she saw one of the team captains whisper to her coach, then approach the front of the bus, grasping the seats for balance.

Morgan turned on the microphone and tossed her thick black hair to the side. "Okay, Lady 'Noles, time for some entertainment. Tatiana Goreva, come on down!"

Tatiana shot Audrey a worried look. But Audrey could only shrug. Tatiana made her way down the center aisle amidst claps and cheers. When she arrived at the front of the bus, Morgan slung her arm around her shoulders.

"We have a little tradition on this team called Seminole Idol. Each freshman sings for the whole team."

Audrey's eyes widened, and Tatiana's cheeks immediately matched her maroon team sweats.

"You'll listen to my iPod while you sing into the microphone," Morgan explained.

Audrey gripped the seat. This sounded awful.

Tatiana squirmed, and Morgan messed around with the dial on her iPod. Then she whispered in Tatiana's ear.

"But I don't know Katy Perry song!" Tatiana protested.

"That's okay." Morgan smiled as she unfolded a piece of paper. "Here are the lyrics." Morgan waited while Tatiana put on the headphones and adjusted the volume.

The team was already laughing by the time Morgan handed Tatiana the microphone and sat, surrendering the spotlight. Not only did Tatiana miss about half the first verse, she was horribly off-key. Some of the swimmers laughed so hard they snorted.

Though initially horrified, Audrey couldn't help but giggle at Tatiana's musical stylings.

Aware of her teammates' laughter, Tatiana cast aside her nervousness. She swayed her hips, licked her lips, and reached down to caress Morgan's hair. The swimmers howled.

Morgan yanked back the microphone. "Tatiana Goreva, everybody!"

Tatiana returned to the rear of the bus after thunderous applause.

Audrey rolled her eyes at the captain's next words: "Audrey Rose, come on down!"

Morgan had the song all cued up by the time Audrey arrived. When she heard the title she knew it instantly: a ballad about separated lovers. Audrey narrowed her eyes. "But that's a *slow* song!"

"You'll be fine—I overheard you in the locker room," Morgan said. "We want to hear those pipes, girl."

Audrey felt sick. She put on the headphones and was engulfed by violin, guitar, and drums. She stealthily decreased the volume so she could hear her own voice. Closing her eyes, she pictured Leo: his piercing blue eyes, smooth skin, long and fluid muscles, closely cropped black hair.

Audrey swayed to the music as she sang, aching for Leo. Her arm wrapped around her middle, pressing against the pain of his absence. She could almost smell him next to her.

When the song ended, Audrey opened her eyes, expecting to see her teammates laughing. Instead a few swimmers wiped their eyes. When she removed the headphones, the bus was silent.

"That was beautiful, Audrey," said Morgan, reclaiming the microphone. She winked. "I hope you get to see him soon."

Audrey nodded and returned to her seat.

"Okay, so showing up to the meet with all of us crying just won't do," Morgan announced. "The next song's a hyper dance number—just for you, Jacki! Get your butt up here."

Sinking into her seat, Audrey felt Tatiana's hand on hers for a reassuring tap. Her warm smile brought tears to Audrey's eyes. Tatiana was homesick, but Audrey was lovesick, and they comforted each other as best they could.

Once the five first-year swimmers had endured their hazing, the team settled into their seats to watch *Pride*, the true story of a swim coach who rebuilt a dilapidated swimming pool in inner-city Philadelphia and started the first all-Black swim team.

The moment the coach appeared onscreen, Audrey was riveted. Terrence Howard's beautiful hazel eyes reminded her of Leo's father, and thoughts of Leo and CS plagued her for the rest of the trip.

She pictured Leo at the Academy. *Are you where you want to be? Are you doing this for yourself, or for your father? Will you ever be free?*

Audrey sighed. She wished she knew the answers, but Leo himself probably didn't know.

60. Secrets

Leo snuck a glance at the pamphlets on the waiting room bookshelf: *Are You Depressed?...When It's Not Fun Anymore: Alcohol Poisoning...Dysfunctional Families 101.*

He quickly turned, worried the plebe in the chair across the room could read his mind as he looked at the pamphlets. He felt exposed—like his past problems, his secrets, were easy for others to see and judge. He was damaged goods.

He sighed with relief when Dr. Ina turned the corner. He returned her smile until he took in her crutches. Now she reminded him even more of his mother.

Rising and saluting, Leo pointed. "What happened, ma'am?"

"It's a long story." She shook her head.

He was supposed to tell her everything, but she barely shared any personal details. He followed her slow crutching down the hallway, and once they reached her office he tried to help her to her chair, but she shooed him away. He settled into her soft microfiber sofa and waited for the questions to begin.

"How was your weekend?"

"Good, ma'am. We had an intrasquad meet—plebes and second-class midshipmen against firsties and third-class midshipmen."

"How'd you swim?"

"Not great. I'm pretty tired." He grinned. "We won, though."

"Good for you. Is your roommate back swimming after his shoulder surgery?"

"Benito? Yeah, he's back in the water, but it'll take him a long time to get up to speed." Leo squirmed, glancing at her bandaged knee and the crutches resting on the arm of her chair. "Crutches suck, huh?"

"They do." Ina watched him closely. "You ever been on crutches?"

Thinking back to his hellish wheelchair experience, Leo refused to meet her eyes. "No, ma'am."

"Leo, when you mentioned Benito, you seemed to know what you were talking about—how long it takes to get back up to speed in swimming. Have you ever been injured?"

"Yes, ma'am." His eyes remained glued to the floor. Why couldn't they just discuss plebe life?

"What happened?"

Leo reached for a stress ball on her end table and squeezed it. His eyes darted around the room.

"That scar, for example." She pointed to his forehead. "How'd that happen?"

He decided to redirect the conversation. "My brother emailed me. He just got engaged."

"I see. He's your older brother, right?"

Leo nodded.

"You said your brother's girlfriend—now his fiancée—is the daughter of a man who was murdered?"

"Yeah, Cameron's dad was murdered about a year ago."

"And your girlfriend's father…" Ina squinted, appearing to concentrate. "He's in prison after he was convicted of that murder?"

"Yes, ma'am. Audrey's dad is in the brig."

Ina tilted her head to one side. "The brig? Audrey's father is in the military?"

Leo realized he'd revealed more than intended.

"That sounds potentially awkward, if I understand this correctly… Your girlfriend's father murdered your future sister-in-law's father?"

"It's *not* awkward. Cameron's fine with Audrey. They both were, um…They have something in common. And, uh, Cam doesn't think Audrey's dad is guilty."

Her brows knitted together. "Why does Cameron think that?"

Leo ran his hands over his stubbly hair. "Does this information go anywhere?"

"I can't see how this might relate to your fitness for duty, so probably not."

He bit his fingernail. "Audrey's dad helped Cam get an abortion. Both lieutenant commanders, both fathers, well, they were friends. Cam doesn't believe Audrey's dad could've ever killed her dad."

"Whoa. Cam thinks Audrey's father is wrongfully imprisoned? Do you think that too?"

"I don't know." Leo shrugged. "I can't believe Audrey's dad would be capable of murder."

"What do your parents think about you dating a girl whose father's in prison?"

He shrugged again.

Ina stroked her chin. "You said Audrey and Cameron have something in common?"

They were both pregnant and lost the baby. Leo looked down. He really liked Dr. Ina, and he didn't want her to know about his screw-ups. Maybe she'd hate him as much as his father seemed to. It was bad enough she knew about him punching two people. She'd want nothing to do with him if she knew he was a drug addict who got his girlfriend pregnant—if she knew his father had to beat him to rein him in.

"I fell," she said suddenly.

Leo looked up and met her eyes for the first time that session. "I was hiking with my family, and I fell. I slipped." She blushed. "My sons basically had to carry me down the mountain. *That* was quite an adventure. I'm waiting for the MRI results, but the ER doc thinks I tore my ACL."

"I'm sorry, ma'am."

"Thank you. It's a good thing I have a desk job." They were quiet a few moments. "What do Audrey and Cameron have in common?"

Leo sighed and looked at his hands, images swirling in his head: his father barging into his bedroom with fury flaring in his violet eyes...lying on the floor howling as he gripped his twisted ankle...

the sting of his father's shoe ripping into his side…fading in and out, seeing a deep coppery stain on the carpet.

"Leo, are you with me?"

He jumped. Confused, he blinked rapidly, rasping for air as he tried to get his bearings.

"Does that happen often?"

Leo couldn't seem to get enough air. "Does what happen, ma'am?"

"Did you relive something from the past? Or perhaps a voice was speaking to you just then?"

He smirked. "I'm not hearing voices, Dr. Hansen. I'm not that crazy."

"I don't think you're crazy at all, Leo. You looked frightened, and I think you were re-experiencing a past trauma." She grimaced as she adjusted the angle of her knee. "I asked you how often that happens, and I want you to answer me."

He tightened his jaw, overwhelmed by the psychologist's questions and in danger of losing his tenuous hold on self control. His heart thumped, and he willed her to stop asking.

"What were you remembering?" she pressed.

He felt a rush of adrenaline and a flash of heat in his face.

"Has that ever happened before, Leo?"

His fists clenched by his side.

"What're you hiding from me? Tell me. Let me help you."

Leo leaped off the sofa. "Shut *up!*"

Dr. Hansen shrunk back in her chair, shoulders stiff and eyes huge.

He towered over her, rage blurring his vision. "Shut the hell up!" he thundered. His arms trembled, and his chest heaved with each panted breath.

She slowly sat up, inch by inch, never taking her eyes off him. "Sit *down*, Midshipman Scott." Her voice was frosty.

Perplexed, he squinted at her. Then horror widened his eyes as he realized he'd lost control once again. His shoulders drooped, and he unclenched his fists. "Yes, ma'am." He sank into the sofa.

He felt the heat from his flushed cheeks as he grabbed his face in both hands. "I'm sorry, ma'am," he mumbled. "I'm sorry, I'm sorry."

At some point he became aware that his body was rocking and he'd curled into a ball. Tears tumbled down his face. "I'm sorry, I'm sorry."

When Dr. Ina finally spoke, her voice was gentle. "Someone hurt you."

He stopped rocking. He might as well tell her everything since he'd probably be kicked out of the Academy for sure now. A plebe just didn't get away with threatening a superior twice. "Yes, ma'am."

"Who was it, Leo?"

"My father," he whispered.

"He...beat you?"

"Yes, ma'am, but only when I was bad."

"How were you bad?" she asked.

He still couldn't look at her. "I did a lot of bad things. The worst was getting my girlfriend pregnant."

"I see. You said Cam and Audrey had something in common... Audrey had an abortion too?"

Leo looked up, expecting to see her enraged, but she looked at him with the same compassion she'd always shown.

He shook his head and felt tears again. "She miscarried."

"What'd your father do when he discovered the pregnancy?"

Leo looked away, his breath hitching. "He hurt my wrist, and my ankle got twisted too when I was trying to fight back—well, that was kind of more my fault, I guess. Then he kicked me, over and over, and...and, he whipped me. I passed out and had to go to the hospital."

"I want you to take some deep breaths now, like we practiced."

Leo nodded and tried to focus on his breathing.

Once he felt a little calmer, she questioned him again.

"What happened at the hospital?"

"There was internal bleeding, and they performed a splenectomy."

"Jesus." She blinked at him. "When was this, Leo?"

"March, ma'am."

"How long were you out of swimming?"

"Five weeks. Five miserable weeks. I was in a wheelchair."

Ina cleared her throat. "You didn't deserve that, Leo."

His eyes met hers.

"You did other bad things too?" she asked.

He sighed and felt even more ashamed, if that was possible. Tears slid down his cheeks. "I got hooked on Oxycontin. They did an intervention and got me into treatment. But my dad found out." Leo gave her a bitter smile as he pointed to the scar on his forehead. "That's when I got this."

"Where'd you get Oxycontin?"

"My mother...She's crippled, from a car accident. She takes them. She used to be in the Navy too, before her accident."

"I can't believe I'm hearing all this in our eighth session. So your father's in the Navy?"

His voice was low and dark. "Commander Scott. He's an air boss in Pensacola."

"I see. Are you still using Oxycontin, Leo?" When he shook his head she asked, "Are you using any other substances?"

"No, ma'am."

"How did you quit?"

"After my dad pulled me out of treatment, he made me pee in a cup every week. He said I didn't want to find out what would happen if I tested positive, and I believed him. He also made me attend the Academy. He told me I didn't know how to take care of myself and needed more structure."

"It seems to me you know how to take care of yourself quite well, actually. Have you been tempted to use again?"

Leo paused. "Not really."

"Leo, do you currently have access to pills?"

He hesitated again. "Benito has some Percocet under his bed, but I won't take any, I swear."

"I want you to bring those pills in to me."

"But they're not mine!"

"Tell your roommate it's against regulations to have unnecessary medications lying around, and you bring them to me. That's an order, Leo."

He closed his eyes and sighed. Now he'd have to tell Benito about his addiction. "Yes, ma'am."

"Did you go through withdrawal?"

"I had to go to detox."

"The more I find out about this, the more serious this sounds. So you were physically dependent on the Oxycontin, then." Ina frowned. "Depression can occur during withdrawal from that particular medication...Were you depressed?"

"I don't think so."

"Did you think about suicide?"

His head whipped up, and his cheeks burned red. His tears started anew, and he withdrew into himself, leaning forward with his head drooping between his shoulders. He squeezed his eyes shut. He'd promised himself never to tell anybody about that night — that awful night.

"It's okay, Leo. It's okay to tell me about it. Did you, uh, did you try to kill yourself?"

"I didn't do it," he sobbed. "I just took some p-p-pills into the woods, and I wanted to take them, but I couldn't."

"What stopped you?" she asked.

"Audrey." He looked up again, sniffed, and accepted tissues from her. "I had to say goodbye to her first. She kissed all my cuts and bruises." He remembered the feel of Audrey's soft lips on his forehead. "We made love. And then I didn't want to kill myself anymore."

"Do you think about hurting or killing yourself now?"

"No, ma'am. But when my dad finds out I've been kicked out of the Academy, he might kill me himself."

"Who says you're getting kicked out?" Ina's forehead creased.

"Of course you'll report me for threatening you, ma'am."

"No way." She shook her head. "You better not threaten me again, buster, but we're just getting started with therapy. You think I'll let you leave the Academy now? We can finally make some progress now that you've given me something to work with."

They'd have to talk about this stuff *again?* "Are you sure you don't want to separate me, ma'am?"

"You've already *been* separated, Leo. Separated from the chance to have a father who knows how to love you, separated from feeling worthy, separated from understanding this abuse isn't your fault...I don't want to separate you any further. I want to *join* you to good things in your life. I want you to understand yourself and like yourself better. I want you to see yourself as an intelligent, competent, caring, and sensitive young man. Why do you think Audrey loves you and stands by you? You have a lot to offer, and it'd be a shame if you let your father prevent you from realizing that potential."

Leo gawked. Why was she saying such kind things, especially after hearing all his shameful secrets? Did she say those things to everyone?

Ina smiled. "Now, our time's up. I want you back here next week, same time, same place. Good work today." When he didn't move, she gave a dismissive wave of her hand. "Goodbye, Leo. Scoot."

He sat still for three more seconds. "Thank you, ma'am." Rising, he plodded out of her office.

This was a different exhaustion than after his twenty-four-hour march, but exhaustion nonetheless. He'd never cried that much in his life. With a long exhale, he headed to practice. He'd have plenty to think about while he swam today.

61. Suspect

"Thanks for helping me pack," Cam said, smiling coyly up at Jason in the foyer of her house. She snuggled into his chest and kissed him. Then she angled back, rubbing her upper lip. "Ouchies."

Jason winked. "I don't shave on the weekends, toots. Remember?"

"I guess I'll get to know your quirks better now that we're engaged." She smiled at him again.

Drawing her hand to his lips, he planted a smooch right next to the glittery diamond on her finger.

"I *still* can't believe you proposed to me in the vice principal's office."

He laughed. "It was so great when Mr. Morrison called you down from your classroom. You looked terrified."

"Not funny!" She gave him a shove. *"You're* the one who got called to the principal's office all the time, not me. I thought I was in real trouble."

"Yeah, I guess I wanted a familiar environment so I'd be at ease for the proposal."

She snorted. But her smile faded when she turned to the closed door.

Jason nodded decisively. "Let's do it." He opened Mr. Walsh's study.

After standing untouched for almost fifteen months, the small den smelled musty and mysterious.

Jason surveyed the framed diplomas on the wall, the bookshelf full of novels and aviation manuals, the tidy desk. He came up behind Cam as she reached for the flip-a-page calendar on the desk. It still showed July third of the previous year. Mr. Walsh had written:

Barbecue at the Scotts 1800

Jason squeezed her shoulders and pressed a kiss into the nape of her neck. He left and returned with some empty boxes, banging them into the doorframe despite his best effort to be careful. "So your mom hasn't been in here since, since it happened, huh?"

"No." Cam replaced the calendar. "Well, I guess they had to retrieve some papers—life insurance documents and stuff—but I think my uncle did that."

"Why don't you let me pack up this room, Cam? You don't have to go through this."

"It's okay, I need to. My mom refuses to come in here, but I want his *family* to pack his stuff before we move. It's only right."

Jason nodded and tossed a book in a box.

Cam circled the desk and plunked onto the leather chair. She sighed as she rifled through desk drawers, piling office supplies to be boxed up together.

Jason had filled three boxes with books by the time Cam moved on to the computer. When she leaned over the side of the desk to unplug the printer, Jason snuck a peek at her curvy bottom.

She must have caught his eyes darting away when she plopped back into the chair. "Like the view, Mr. Scott?"

"Oh, *yeah*, sweetheart." He watched her wrap the power cord around the printer. "Hey, I just packed some unused paper in this box. Why don't I add the paper from the printer?"

"Sure." She handed him the stack of paper that had been queued up for printing.

When he took it, he noticed one of pages wasn't flush with the stack. He tapped the paper against the desk, but the unruly sheet wouldn't budge. He leafed through until he reached the offending piece and found blue ink covering the dog-eared page. "What's this?"

Cam looked up. "That looks like my dad's handwriting." She stood and snatched it from his grasp.

Her hands began to tremble as she read, and Jason flew to her side.

"It's a letter…a letter my dad wrote."

His brow furrowed as he read over her shoulder.

> My dear Darnell,
>
> Why the silence? Why the avoidance? I can't take this anymore. I know that day was awful, and I'll never forgive myself. I deserve your anger, your hatred, your punches, your slaps—anything but this gut-wrenching silence. Please, please tell me what you're thinking. Dare I ask you if it's over? Are _we_ over? It was real, Darnell. What we had was real. You know what I promised—just one more year and we can be together. I stand by my word. You can trust me.

The letter ended abruptly—no signature. He'd never had a chance to finish.

Jason said nothing, waiting for Cam.

She took a shaky breath. "He was having an affair." She gasped. "She was at our house! My mom made *dinner* for her!"

"Shh! You don't want your mom to hear."

"I don't care." Bitterness laced her voice. "My mom should know he cheated."

"Who's Darnell?"

"She worked for my father," she spat. "Lt. Darnell Keaton."

Jason blanched. "She's not at the Academy, is she?"

"I'm not sure," she said thoughtfully. "I heard she left the base, but I don't know where she went."

"She's Leo's CO! Mom told me." He clutched Cam's arm. "Darnell was having an affair with your dad? That's motive if I ever heard one."

Cam's mouth dropped open. "Are you saying Darnell killed my dad?"

"I don't know, but we gotta warn Leo. C'mon, let's go."

"You ever eat a grape leaf, *hombre?*" Benito whispered.

Standing at attention during a rifle drill, Leo took a quick sideways glance at his roommate. "Uh, nope."

"It's a staple in the Arab diet, according to my textbook," he said. "They put rice and crap inside and roll it all up."

"Fascinating. Sounds disgusting."

A section leader called out commands, and the company, one-hundred thirty members strong now that the fleet had reported for the school year, spun and shifted their rifles in unison. The infantry drilling went on for over an hour, and Leo derived deep satisfaction from the precise, choreographed movements. It was a thrilling synchrony of bodies moving together, command by command.

After the section leader dismissed them and the company dissipated in a scrambled chaos, Benito spoke to Leo again. "Hey, I think somebody's trying to get your attention over there."

"What're you talking about?" Leo looked toward the perimeter fence. Sure enough, two people waved their arms in wide overhead circles. Leo squinted. "Is that Jase?"

"Who?"

"He's my brother." His face was transformed by a brilliant smile. "I'm gonna see what he wants."

"Dude, you need to turn in your rifle and get back to our room," Benito warned.

"I'll make it," Leo called over his shoulder, already jogging toward the fence.

When he arrived, still wearing a silly grin, he noticed Jason's left hand grasping a set of binoculars and Cameron's left hand sporting some major bling. "Whoa, Jase, how'd you afford that rock?"

"CS gave me the money for the ring."

"*What?*"

Cameron nodded. "It surprised me too."

"I think Mom put him up to it. Anyway, you're damn near impossible to get a hold of," Jason said. "You didn't answer my emails, and you're not allowed to take phone calls? What if there's a family emergency?"

"You could go through my company officers."

"Yeah, well." Jason glanced at Cameron. "What I need to tell you can't go through them."

Intrigued, Leo stared through the fence. "Did you guys drive here?"

Cameron seemed to avoid looking at his rifle. "Yes, and we have to drive back soon so we're not late for work on Monday."

"Wow, that's a long road trip for a minute-long conversation. This has to be quick or I'm gonna get in trouble." Leo glanced over his shoulder at his fellow company members, now filing into Bancroft Hall. "What do you have to tell me?"

"Can't we meet somewhere later to talk?" Jason asked.

Leo shook his head. "Sorry, I'm stuck in my dorm room all night for evening study."

"On a Saturday night?"

"Welcome to the Navy." Leo grinned. "I can receive phone calls on Friday—can this wait till then?"

"No," Jason insisted. "Listen closely, Leo. I want you to get reassigned to another company."

"*What?* I can't do that!"

"You can and you will."

"What's this about, Jase?"

"We were packing up Cam's father's office, and, well, we found a letter he wrote to Darnell Keaton."

"The lieutenant?"

"Yeah, your company officer. It looks like they were having an affair."

Leo turned to Cameron. "Your dad and Lt. Keaton were having an affair?"

Cameron nodded and looked down.

"I'm sorry, Cam." Leo couldn't think of anything worse than a cheating father. "But what does this have to do with me?"

Jason took a deep breath. "I think your company officer murdered Cam's dad." Leo's eyes widened. "She fled Pensacola right after he died, Leo. It's got to be a scorned lover exacting revenge."

"Except my dad was pleading for Darnell to take *him* back," Cameron said.

Jason let out an exasperated sigh. "That letter could mean a hundred different things."

Leo watched them argue, absorbed in thought. "Wait a minute. So maybe we can free Audrey's dad if we can prove the lieutenant was the real murderer?"

"No, Leo." Jason stepped right up to the fence. "I don't want you anywhere near that lieutenant. She's bad news. That's why you have to get reassigned."

"You don't understand how things work here, Jase. I can't just change companies. What am I supposed to say — 'I request reassignment because my company officer's a suspected murderer'? No way! Second Company midshipmen are my friends, my family."

"*We're* your family!" Jason hollered. "I'm not sitting back and letting my kid brother hang around a killer — just to follow some stupid protocol."

"Have you told Mom about this?" Leo asked.

"No, we just found the letter early this morning and Patti, er, Mrs. Walsh doesn't even know. I had to beg Cam to tell you about it, but she agreed since she thinks you're in danger too."

Leo glanced back at the dorm. "Crap, I'm gonna be late. Jase, I gotta go. Sorry. I'll be careful. I promise. Thanks for visiting, and congrats on getting engaged."

"Leo!"

His brother's shout did nothing to break his swift stride.

Leo hustled to the small firearm storage unit in Bancroft Hall, and his stomach dropped when he found the metal gate locked. There'd be hell to pay if he didn't get his rifle logged and stored properly, and he couldn't exactly tote the weapon to his dorm room.

His heart hammered. Evening study time had already begun, and he had to get back to his room. Pronto. Scanning the empty hallway, he yanked open a storage closet and stashed the rifle, hiding it behind some mops and buckets.

Leo sprinted through the passageways, and finally made it to his wing. He slipped into his room and gasped when he discovered his company commander already there, dressing down his roommate.

Leo snapped to attention as Ms. Nevington halted her harassment mid-sentence. "Where've you been, Midshipman Scott? And don't try to tell me you were in the head—your roommate here already checked."

Leo winced. He'd involved Benito this. "I was talking to my brother by the fence, ma'am."

"No visitors permitted!" Her eyes flared.

"Yes, ma'am."

"Both of you drop and give me fifty."

"Yes, ma'am," the roommates responded in unison.

Once they finished, Nevington glared at Leo. "I hate to see what Lt. Keaton will do when she finds out you're in trouble again."

"Lt. Keaton, ma'am?" Leo's voice rose with alarm.

"After the assault incident, she ordered me to report your rule infractions directly to her."

"Please don't tell her, ma'am." He hated the telltale fear in his voice.

"You're not up for a twenty-four hour march again, Midshipman Scott?"

Leo paused to collect himself, willing his voice to stay steady. "I'll take any punishment you dole out, ma'am. Just please, let's not bother the company officer with this. It's Saturday night, ma'am."

Nevington sighed. "Tell me one good reason I shouldn't report you to her."

"What happens in Vegas stays in Vegas, ma'am?"

The strangling noise from Benito was probably his attempt to stifle a laugh.

Nevington glared at him. "Hilarious, Mr. Scott," she finally said. "I guess we'll give the lieutenant a reprieve from seeing your sorry butt in her office again. But I hope that little chat with your brother was worth it, because you just earned yourself five company tours after lunch this week."

"Yes, ma'am."

"Gentlemen, there's been far too much drama. It's only the middle of October. I want you to settle into plebe life and stop causing problems, got it?"

"Yes, ma'am."

"Carry on," Nevington instructed as she walked out, shaking her head.

Leo's shoulders slumped. He didn't exactly welcome the drama either.

"*Lo siento*, roomie."

"Just don't do it again, *gringo*." Benito grinned.

Leo settled at his desk and extracted a textbook from his backpack. *How was Lt. Keaton involved in the death of Lt. Commander Walsh?* He stared blankly at the page before him. He was determined to decipher this connection. He owed it to Audrey.

62. Rifling through the Past

Leo's mouth spread into a huge yawn as he tried to focus on his ocean topography textbook at his desk. Could this crap *be* any more boring? He struggled to clear his bleary eyes. If a firstie caught him snoozing during evening study, he'd get into even more trouble. Company tours would already cut into his study time.

Leo winced again as the thought of Ms. Nevington's disappointment in him. He hated the look of disapproval: tight jaw, downturned lips, annoyed eyes.

He'd dodged additional looks like that by hunting down the midshipman second-class in charge of stocking ammunition for the small firearm storage unit. Leo had heard the guy was saving up to buy an engagement ring, and thankfully $100 was enough to get his rifle back where it belonged.

Leo's heart raced all over again just thinking about the morning's subterfuge. He felt more awake with fear pumping through his veins, and Leo returned his attention to reading.

The room was quiet until Benito's frustrated sigh. He shook his head as he stared at his computer screen.

"What's wrong?" Leo asked.

After another long sigh, Benito said, "No good. Lucia went out with my cousin."

"Okay. But isn't she your ex?"

"My cousin's a snake. She deserves better."

"Sucks."

"Yeah." Benito tapped his laptop, as if unable to keep still. "I need to be there. Protect her from that *cabrón*. Thanksgiving can't come soon enough."

"A whole month." Leo imagined Audrey in her swimsuit, and his focus was totally shot. He returned his attention to his roommate. "At least your shoulder's holding up okay."

Benito nodded.

"But you're still slow as molasses," Leo added. "I thought you were a *good* swimmer."

He barely had time to duck as a pillow whizzed over his head. He chuckled as Benito cussed him out in seven different languages.

Leo approached, holding out the pillow as a peace offering.

Benito grabbed it and glared. "Ain't enough Percocet in the world for the beating I should give you."

Leo froze. He wheeled around and trudged back to his desk, remembering what Dr. Ina expected him to do.

He tried to read, but the words swam across the page. Abstract sea surface temperature readings and plate tectonics couldn't hold a candle to the thoughts bouncing around his brain.

Leo cleared his throat, his cheeks flushed before he even spoke a word. "So, I have therapy tomorrow."

Benito gave him a strange look. *"Sí?"*

"And, um, kind of an interesting topic came up in session last time." Leo kept his eyes focused on his desk. "You were just talking about Percocet, and well, you know, pain medication came up in my conversation with Dr. Ina too." Leo's head stayed down but his eyes peeked up. "Do you need those pills anymore?"

Benito shrugged. "Nah, I haven't taken any since July. They make me feel like crap. I was going to give them to my mom at Thanksgiving."

"Okay, good. Dr. Ina kind of ordered me to give them to her? Could I have them?"

Benito looked confused. "She wants my Percocet? What, she run out of hers? Is your shrink a junkie or something?"

Leo smiled. "Yeah, she probably could use some meds — she hurt her knee." He jangled his leg. "It's more like, well, it's more like… *I'm the junkie*," he finally said. He held his breath as he waited for his roommate's reaction.

Benito looked puzzled at first but then grinned. "Good one, Leo. You had me going there for a second. *Payaso.*"

"I'm not being a clown." Leo swallowed. "I was hooked on Oxycontin."

Benito's eyebrows shot up. "Oxy? *You?* That's some serious stuff."

"No kidding. Detox was a nightmare." Leo finally met Benito's eyes.

"Have you taken any of my pills?"

"No, I swear. I've…I've thought about it though. That's why when Dr. Ina forced it out of me, she made me promise to bring the pills to her."

"Dude, I'm sorry. I didn't mean to tempt you."

Leo shook his head vigorously. "No, this isn't your fault…How would you know? It's my fault. I don't want to think about those pills, but I can't help it. I'm so freaking weak sometimes I can't stand myself."

"*Weak?*" Benito gawked. "This from the guy who can do more pushups than anyone I know? This from the guy who's so smart he sets the curve in every class? This from the guy who put the smackdown on a very deserving firstie? I don't think so. You're super strong."

"You obviously don't know me very well."

"*¡Ay, Dios!* Thank God you're not perfect."

Leo looked up, startled.

"I mean, it sucks you were hooked on pills, but dude, it's hard living with Mr. Perfect all the time. Plebes refer to me as 'Scott's roommate,' and I hear about you all day long. I'm just saying it's nice to know you have problems too."

"Oh, Benito, I have a boatload of problems, believe me."

"Like what?"

Suddenly Ms. Nevington stormed into the room, springing the plebes to their feet.

She was in his face in an instant. "You think you have a boatload of problems? Just wait, Mr. Scott!"

Panic sent adrenaline coursing through him.

"Lt. Keaton's ordered both of us to her office immediately, and she sounded completely ticked off on the phone. Do you have *any* idea what this is about?"

"No, ma'am."

"Well, it's something bad if she's calling us in on a Sunday night." She exhaled. "We have to be there, like, five minutes ago. Let's move it."

"Yes, ma'am."

Leo grabbed his cover and preceded his superior out the door. He'd been through this drill before, with a painful, blistery outcome, and that was before he knew the lieutenant was capable of murder. He dreaded round two.

Firstie and plebe entered the ice queen's lair.

As they stood at attention, Leo felt ripples of hostility emanating off the company officer. She certainly seemed witchy enough to be a murderess.

Lt. Keaton sauntered around her desk, holding a piece of paper. "Company Commander Nevington, please look over this log and tell me what you see."

There was silence as Nevington read it. "This is a log from twenty October of this year, for the small firearm storage unit, ma'am."

As soon as the words escaped her mouth, Leo's stomach flipped with dread.

"That's obvious, Ms. Nevington. Tell me whose rifle wasn't logged in yesterday."

"Aye, ma'am." After scanning down the page, Nevington gave a little gasp and looked at him. "That would be Midshipman Scott's rifle, ma'am."

The lieutenant ripped the paper out of her hands and glided to her right, landing in front of Leo. She was much shorter than he, but clearly in charge.

Leo trembled.

"Captain Tracker ordered company officers to keep closer tabs on the weapon storage," she explained. "Hence I'm here on my one day off, reviewing the logs. Midshipman Scott, when I discovered the absent notation by your name, I had the officer of the watch check the weapon storage. Curiously your rifle's now back in place. What the *hell's* going on?"

Leo hesitated. He searched for an answer that wouldn't turn him into a snitch.

"Start talking now, Mr. Scott!"

"I-I-I was late to weapons storage, ma'am! It was locked, ma'am."

Her eyes blazed. "Why were you late?"

A truthful response was definitely unwarranted. He opted for silence, which apparently wasn't a wise choice either as she drew even closer. He could feel her hostility hovering between them.

Impending violence crackled in the air, and Leo recognized the threat in an instant. It had been quite a while since he'd been hit, and it almost felt comforting to await the beating. He'd broken a rule and needed to be punished. It was the natural order of things. However, this would be the first time he'd been hit by a woman.

The lieutenant's voice was shrill. "Do you think you're special, Mr. Scott? Do you think you're above the rules?"

"No, ma'am!"

"Bull. You think you can do whatever you want. You think you can hurt people and just get away with it!"

"N-N-No, ma'am." Who was *she* to tell him what he was thinking?

An image of Audrey's father sitting handcuffed in that awful brig flashed through his mind: Mr. Rose's sad eyes, Mrs. Rose's forced cheerfulness about leaving Audrey for months on end, Audrey's embarrassment about her father's imprisonment. Was this woman responsible for all that pain? Had Lt. Keaton murdered Lt. Commander Walsh, only to hide out at the Academy in the aftermath?

Keaton's breaths sounded ragged and shallow. "Scott, swear to God I'll separate your from the Navy unless you tell me right now how that rifle got back into storage!"

Leo's heart raced. This murderer would *not* force him to rat out his peers. "You don't want me here anyway, ma'am!"

"Mr. Scott!" Nevington reprimanded.

"You don't want me to expose your secrets!" Leo shouted. "It's all one giant setup to get rid of me!"

In a split second, the lieutenant delivered a walloping punch. The blow glanced off of his cheekbone and threw his head to the side with a stab of pain. Then Leo felt Las Vegas's hands on his elbows, steadying him to rejoin her at attention.

His rattled brain took a moment to come back online. If there'd been any doubt a woman of the lieutenant's stature possessed the physical force to strangle Mr. Walsh, it disappeared with that punch.

Keaton seemed stunned. Her lips parted and her eyes froze, unblinking, as she inched back. Leo felt a trickle of warmth on his cheek and noticed the Academy ring on her hand. She'd cut him.

Leo fought to keep his impassive façade as inside he stewed with strategies for exposing her. He was determined to make things right for Audrey.

Groping for her desk, the lieutenant sank onto it, staring right through them with glassy eyes.

Nevington finally spoke. "May we be dismissed, ma'am?"

Her head bobbed slowly. "Dismissed."

They saluted, pivoted, and exited.

A few feet down the passageway, Nevington ordered Leo to halt and glided around to face him. "What the heck was going on back there?"

"I don't know…I'll find out, ma'am?"

"Right." She exhaled. "You got that shiner from a wayward rifle butt during infantry drilling. You understand, Mr. Scott?"

"Yes, ma'am." His voice sounded hollow.

"You don't breathe a word of this to anyone while I figure it out."

"Yes, ma'am."

"So much for stopping the drama, Mr. Scott. Let's get back to our wing."

63. Tracking Down the Truth

Las Vegas took in the dark wood paneling and rich burgundy curtains of her quiet surroundings in the antechamber. She'd never visited the commandant's office before, and she hoped this would be her only time.

A lieutenant nodded to her from his desk, and Viva rose to enter. As she snapped to attention, her deep breath did nothing to quell her anxiety. She was quite possibly making a huge mistake, but Whiskey had agreed that she needed to come forward.

"Second Company Commander Viva Nevington reporting, sir."

Captain Sean Tracker rose and returned her salute.

Wow, he's got to be at least six-seven. Captain Tracker's sharp green eyes appeared to miss nothing.

"At ease, Ms. Nevington," he said. "I don't believe we've had the pleasure of meeting before?"

"No, sir." This was surreal.

"Well, I know you're one of our best volleyball players, but I don't know where you're from."

"Minnesota, sir."

"Really." He smiled. "We don't get many northerners in the Navy."

"It *is* the land of ten thousand lakes, sir."

Captain Tracker chuckled. "Oh yah, you betcha, Ms. Nevington."

She suppressed the urge to roll her eyes at his poor imitation of the northern accent, though she did appreciate his attempt at humor.

"How're you finding your duties as company commander?"

She paused. "It's been a mixed bag, sir. I'm quite honored to lead Second Company, but I often feel a bit overwhelmed—like I'm lost at sea, sir."

"I appreciate your honesty, Ms. Nevington." He winked. "I occasionally feel the same way as commandant. Now, what can I do for you today?"

"I've been deliberating all night whether to speak to you about this, sir, and I hope I'm not overstepping my bounds." She hesitated. "I need to report misconduct by my company officer, sir."

"Lt. Keaton?"

"Yes, sir."

"That's a serious allegation, Ms. Nevington."

"Yes, sir. That's one of two reasons I hesitated in reporting to you."

"And the other reason?"

"To be honest, making this report will get me in trouble, sir. I disobeyed an order, sir."

The commandant looked intrigued. "Go on."

"Yes, sir. Lt. Keaton called a plebe and me to her office last night, related to the log for the small firearm storage unit. The plebe hadn't turned in his rifle on time on Saturday, and the lieutenant was furious."

"Who is the plebe?"

"Midshipman Leo Scott, sir."

"Hmmm…" He appeared thoughtful for a moment. "What happened, Ms. Nevington?"

Viva bit her lower lip. "Lt. Keaton struck Mr. Scott, sir."

"She *struck* him?" His eyebrows traveled toward his hairline.

"Yes, sir. She…punched him in the face." Viva let that information sink in, then added, "The plebe was behaving disrespectfully and deserved to be punished, but I didn't think that was right, sir."

"And how do these events implicate you in misconduct, Ms. Nevington?"

"I'd discovered Mr. Scott was late returning to quarters on Saturday night, sir. I issued five company tours, but I should've known his rifle was late as well. Lt. Keaton had ordered me to report any disciplinary problems with Mr. Scott directly to her, and I disobeyed that order."

"Why is *that?*"

"No excuse, sir."

"I want to hear your reasoning, Ms. Nevington," he demanded.

"Mr. Scott assaulted one of my squad leaders in July, sir. I took him to see the lieutenant, and her punishment seemed harsh—a straight twenty-four-hour march. Lt. Keaton also ordered him to attend counseling. On Saturday, Mr. Scott begged me not to report his tardiness to our company officer, and foolishly I gave in, sir."

"I'm trying to figure out how the chain of command broke down like this when both you and Lt. Keaton seem like competent leaders." He stroked his chin. "This Mr. Scott sounds like an interesting character. Ms. Nevington, is it your duty to decide whether a superior's punishment is appropriate?"

"No, sir."

"What was the consequence of disobeying your company officer?"

"We never got to that, sir. I guess Lt. Keaton and I were both sort of stunned after she hit the plebe, and we just stood there until I asked her if we could be dismissed."

"How'd the plebe respond?"

"He seemed fine, sir…" She decided to forge ahead. "But just because he *looked* fine doesn't mean he *was* fine."

"What does *that* mean?"

"Sir, Mr. Scott has a history of being abused. His father, Commander Scott, beat him so badly last spring he had to have surgery. This makes the lieutenant's behavior even more egregious, in my opinion, sir."

"Ah. That's why I recognized his name." He rubbed his hand over his chin. "You did the right thing by coming forward, and I understand why you leap-frogged your company officer to make this report. I'll address this issue with Lt. Keaton. Is Mr. Scott still attending counseling?"

"Yes, sir."

"There'll be consequences for disobeying your company officer. She'll be in contact with you following my conversation with her."

"Yes, sir."

"But Midshipman Nevington, if Lt. Keaton attempts any sort of unfair retribution for your report today, I want to hear about it immediately. Do you understand?"

"Yes, sir."

He nodded. "Good luck against Army this weekend. You're dismissed."

Viva saluted and turned to rush down the passageway to her Monday morning class. *Would I love to be a fly on the wall for the commandant's meeting with the lieutenant...* Viva hoped she wouldn't regret making that report.

Ina had been shooting curious glances Leo's way since collecting him from the waiting room, but she hadn't asked him about his bruise. Yet. Now that they were in her office, she ordered him to sit as she crutched over to her desk and tried to yank open her drawer.

"Locked," she grumbled, reaching across her desk. Then she seemed to realize he was watching her. "I want you to look away for a minute, Leo."

"Yes, ma'am." He turned away and heard her fumble for something, followed by the sound of a lock turning and the drawer sliding open.

"Eyes forward," she ordered.

Leo watched from the corner of his eye as she stuck a chart between her teeth and crutched over to her chair, where she collapsed. She leaned her crutches against the armrest and opened the chart.

"So, last week we talked again about how your brother Jason got engaged to Cameron, whose father was murdered. Your girlfriend Audrey's father is in prison for the murder, but there's some doubt about his guilt."

She looked up from her notes, and he averted his eyes. *Would she go into the gory details?*

"And then you told me some things about your past."

Apparently not. He exhaled.

"How's your week been?" Her voice was gentle.

"Fine, ma'am."

"What happened to your face, Leo?"

"I collided with a wayward rifle butt during infantry drilling," Leo dutifully reported.

"You're a bad liar."

How did she know?

"Do I have to order you to tell me the truth? Is that the only way you'll answer my questions?"

"What do I do if I have conflicting orders, ma'am?" Leo asked, his voice uneasy.

"You were ordered to lie about how you got that bruise?"

"Yes, ma'am."

"By whom?"

"By my company commander, ma'am."

Ina inhaled sharply. "Did you assault a superior again, Leo?"

"No, ma'am." *More like a superior assaulted me.*

"Did you behave aggressively in any way?"

He ducked his head. "Yes, ma'am. I yelled. At a superior."

"You're getting good at that."

He cringed. Why not keep the embarrassment going? He reached into his backpack and removed a bottle of pills. The little white tablets rattled around as he handed it to her, looking at the floor. "As promised, ma'am."

"Thank you."

He reached down into his bag again to extract a folded piece of paper. He handed that over as well.

"What's this?"

"Benito thought it'd be a good idea. I guess he has an uncle who battled drug addiction or something."

Ina opened the paper and read aloud. "There should be twenty-one pills, ma'am. Signed, Benito Dulce." She seemed to stifle a smile. "Should I count them, Leo?"

"If you want." He shrugged. "I didn't take any."

One eyebrow arched. "Considering you lied to me five seconds ago, I think I *will* count the pills. Maybe someday I can take you at your word."

As Ina dumped the bottle's contents into her curved palm, Leo lowered his head and rubbed his hands over his shorn hair. He'd disappointed her. Again.

It wasn't supposed to be this way. He was supposed to join the Navy and turn his life around, becoming the best plebe the Academy had ever seen. Instead, he felt haunted by his past at every turn. Ina made periodic reports to Lt. Keaton about his progress in counseling, so he dared not mention his suspicions to her.

Apparently satisfied he hadn't taken any pills, Ina tossed the bottle toward a garbage can across the room. It fell short and rattled across the floor.

Eyeing her crutches, Leo popped up. "I'll get it, ma'am." He leaned down and dropped the bottle in the can.

"So how'd Benito react to your request for his pills?" Ina asked as he returned to his seat.

"Kind of strange, I guess. He said he was glad I wasn't so freaking perfect."

Ina chuckled. "What makes that strange?"

"Well, I'm *not* perfect—but I'm *supposed* to be. Benito made it sound like a good thing I screwed up."

"Who said you should be perfect?"

Leo hesitated, taken aback. "Everybody. Well, my father most of all, I guess."

"And striving to be perfect—how's that working for you?"

"*Working* for me, ma'am?"

"What are the upsides and downsides of trying to be perfect?"

"I guess it makes me work harder in school and swimming. Uh, the downsides? There aren't any I can see."

"Really? You seem to become quite angry when you fall short of perfection."

"Yeah, I pretty much hate myself when I screw up."

"It doesn't have to be that way, Leo."

He chewed on his fingernail. "Doesn't everybody hate themselves when they mess up?"

"Lord, no." She shook her head. "I'd be hating myself twenty-four seven if I got mad at my mistakes. I mess up all the time. Case in point: I just made a horrible throw to the garbage can. Now, if I was sitting here beating myself up for what crappy aim I have, I wouldn't be able to listen to you and enjoy our meeting. We're human, therefore we make mistakes. When we accept that, we tend to enjoy life a lot more."

Leo considered her words, but said nothing.

"Another downside of perfectionism is that it's hard to get close to people," she continued. "Benito told you he felt closer to you when he knew you weren't perfect. Nobody wants to be friends with a cold, robotic machine who never shows any vulnerability or weakness. You shared some of your screw-ups in here, and now I think I like you even more. It makes me want to fight for you."

"If it causes so many problems, why am I a perfectionist, then? Why can't I accept my mistakes?"

"Of course you're a perfectionist. What happened if you weren't perfect as a kid?"

"I was punished." His voice sounded pathetically small.

"You were *abused*," Ina corrected. "It was really smart for you to try to be perfect so your father wouldn't hit you. It was a survival strategy as a child, but it doesn't seem to be working so well as an adult. Many abuse survivors are perfectionists, thinking if only they can make their tormentors happy, they won't get hurt. But it doesn't work that way, because the abuse has nothing to do with you. It has everything to do with the abuser. You didn't have any control over the violence—only your father did."

"I *did* have control," Leo insisted, remembering the altercation in Audrey's kitchen. "When I fought back once, I made my dad stop."

"Ah." Ina nodded. "No wonder you hit your squad leader then… You think being violent is the only way to feel in control. You think violence is the solution to your problems."

Whoa. That did sound like him. "And it's not…?" he wondered aloud.

"What do *you* think, Leo?" Her eyes met his.

His heart thumped. What *did* he think? He had no idea! He felt unmoored, unanchored, drowned in doubt.

"I think…I think, um, I think I don't know what I think," he stammered.

"That's okay," she said. "I see that bruise on your face, and I know what *I* think. I want the violence to stop, Leo. No more bruises."

64. Florida Heat

Darnell Keaton waited for Captain Tracker to speak. "Have a seat, Lieutenant."

"Yes, sir." She positioned herself on one of the leather chairs facing his desk, crossed her legs, and folded her hands in her lap.

"Other than a few social functions, we haven't interacted much," he said. "Tell me about yourself, Lieutenant."

Okay, small talk. "What would you like to know, sir?"

"Well, for starters, how 'bout you tell me your career path up to this point."

"Yes, sir. I graduated from the Academy with a major in Aerospace Engineering, then I served on the USS *Normandy* for two years before heading to Naval Air Station Pensacola."

"What were your duties in Pensacola?" asked the commandant.

"I served in Air Department V-Four, assisting with safety and maintenance protocol of various aircraft, as well as teaching engineering to recruits, sir."

"Why'd you leave?"

Her heart raced. "It, um, it became too hot for me in Florida, sir."

He stared at her for a few moments. "That's right. You started with us in July of last year. It must've been hot."

"Sir, may I ask why you called me to your office?" She couldn't stop squirming.

He looked directly into her eyes. "I think you know, Lieutenant."

She felt a blush heat her face and broke eye contact. She'd been up most of the night mentally reviewing her altercation with the Scott plebe, desperate to figure out how to deal with the situation. Flooded with memories from Pensacola, she couldn't think straight. Her worries for the future made it impossible to focus on the present.

Of course she knew. The moment she'd picked up the phone that morning and heard the commandant's lieutenant's voice, she'd known. "This is about what happened last night, when I, um, struck the plebe, sir."

"Yes," Captain Tracker confirmed, the pleasantries of their initial exchange long gone. "How on earth did that happen, Lieutenant?"

"Sir, I lost control. There's really no excuse for my behavior, sir."

"There *is* no excuse, Lieutenant. I was hesitant to put someone so young in charge of a company when you first arrived to the Yard, but I have to say, until now you've done an admirable job. You have yourself a fine company commander, and your midshipmen's performance on academic and physical tests is near the top. However, you just opened yourself up to a boatload of trouble. Do you realize the plebe could sue you for assault?"

"Yes, sir." Her throat was so dry she could barely swallow.

"You ordered Mr. Scott to attend counseling. Is it helping him?"

"Dr. Hansen sent me a report a couple weeks ago. Mr. Scott's attending regularly, but progress is slow. Dr. Hansen was trying to build rapport with him. She said he's been a difficult client. But he hasn't had any further instances of violence to my knowledge, sir."

His voice rose. "Until last night, when he was the *target* of violence!"

Her frightened eyes never left her superior's. "Yes, sir."

"Given Mr. Scott's past, I'm even more disgusted by your behavior. Russell Payson, your former CO, contacted me about Leo Scott in June. Russell and I served together, and he asked a favor. He told me Leo's father, a commander, had been disciplined for putting him in the hospital."

Darnell's eyes widened.

"Russell felt awful that the abuse had been going on for years without his knowledge, and he told me he'd promised Leo the Navy would make it up to him. Captain Payson asked me to look after Leo by assigning him to your company. He thought you'd do a good job taking care of him."

Darnell covered her mouth. "I'm sorry, sir. I had no idea."

"Perhaps I should've shared this information with you sooner, but I never expected you to *hit* him, Lieutenant!"

"I made a huge mistake, sir."

"Yes, you did. Between your assault and your ordering him to march for twenty-four hours straight, I'm starting to wonder what you have against Leo Scott."

Darnell felt cold fear. She simply could not answer that question. Fighting for control, she felt herself slipping, overtaken by flashes of pain, flashes of shame. Swirling circles of hard hazel and soft brown swam haphazardly through her mind.

"Lieutenant?" She heard him ask. "Lieutenant?"

She shook her head to clear it. "Yes, sir?"

He looked at her with thinly veiled disdain. "I don't know what's going on with you, Lieutenant, but I'm concerned. I order you to attend counseling to regain control of yourself."

Darnell started to protest. "Sir——"

"Are you able to continue carrying out your duties, or do I need to suspend you?"

"I'll be okay, sir." Her voice shook. "This will never happen again."

"It better not. And I suppose it's rather obvious that Midshipman Nevington reported the incident to me. If I find out you retaliate against her unfairly, you'll regret it. And, if you don't make satisfactory progress in counseling, you'll find yourself right back in this office, and you'll be suspended. Am I making myself clear?"

"Yes, sir." A bead of sweat trickled down her back, and she steeled herself for what lay ahead. She would never allow some counselor to tap into her secrets. There was way too much to lose.

"Ugh, stupid heat wave," Audrey complained into the phone. "Wait—let me angle this fan better."

Leo heard her thump back down on her bed. "How hot is it?" He sat at his desk using a borrowed cell phone. It was one of those precious ten-minute windows of time when plebes were permitted to make calls, and he relished hearing his girlfriend's voice.

"Eighty-seven today, and it doesn't seem to be cooling down much tonight. I thought it wouldn't be a big deal when the AC broke since it's November, but it's like an oven in here."

"Yeah, without those ocean breezes, I bet Tallahassee can get pretty miserable. Here we've been in our winter blues for a week. I'll freak when we have our first snow."

"But you lived in Annapolis when you were a kid."

"That feels like forever ago," Leo mused. "I wasn't exactly going on ten-mile runs then either. PT should be interesting when it gets really cold."

"You must be in great shape."

He exhaled. "Well, my running's definitely improved, but my swimming sucks. You know how training has to be sport-specific to be effective."

"I know all about sport-specific training. Nancy believes in a *lot* of that. I remember telling my dad there's no way college practice would be tougher than Matt's workouts. Boy, was I wrong."

"How *is* your dad?"

Audrey sniffed. "He's in solitary, actually. Just when I thought things couldn't get worse. My mom hasn't been able to find out why yet, either. He probably broke some stupid rule."

The familiar guilt tickled Leo's heart. In his last email exchange with Jason they'd agreed not to say anything about the letter for fear of getting Audrey's hopes up. They still had no evidence to implicate Lt. Keaton. There was no way for Leo to get close to his company officer since every minute of the day was scheduled for him, and Jason and Cameron had no idea how to investigate her involvement. They'd scoured Cam's house but hadn't found anything else about the affair.

"I'm sorry, Audrey," Leo said.

"Let's talk about something else. How's therapy going?"

"*That* sounds like a really fun topic."

"I order you to tell me about your therapy, Mr. Scott."

"Yes, ma'am." He sighed. "Dr. Hansen wants me to tell her about the beatings."

"You have to talk about it?"

"When I'm ready. She said it'd help me to tell my story." His voice wavered, and he knew he sounded like an ill-tempered child. "But I don't wanna think about it."

"Do you trust her, Leo?"

"Yeah, she's a really cool lady. But I still hate being forced to go to her." Ina was highly skilled at extracting secrets, and he continued to worry he'd let his suspicions about the lieutenant slip out. Leo rubbed his cheek, touching the small groove left by her ring.

She *had* to be guilty as hell. Leo felt a stirring in his gut, a craving to expose her. He wondered what had happened after Nevington reported her. Las Vegas hadn't let him forget she'd been bagged with weekend restriction for her role in the mess. He owed her.

"I don't have much more time." He paused. "Are you still hot? Wait…of course you are."

She giggled.

"I have an idea to help you cool down."

"You do?"

"*Sí. Quítate la ropa.*"

"I can't take off my clothes. Tatiana could walk in any minute!"

"Oh, c'mon. She sees you in the shower all the time after practice." He harrumphed. "Lucky ho."

"Okay, hold on." The phone went silent. When she returned, she announced, "I'm wearing my pink bra and underwear."

Leo closed his eyes, letting his imagination go wild. "Good." He lowered his voice to barely above a whisper and glanced around the empty room, glad Benito was in the study lounge. "I want you to run your fingers through that gorgeous long hair, slowly, and tell me what it feels like."

"Soft," she replied.

"Now let your hand trail down your face," he urged. "Slowly… sensuously…trace the outline of your lips…let your fingers explore the tip of your tongue…now kiss the tips of your fingers…feel the moisture on your lips…"

Audrey moaned. "If this is supposed to cool me down, it's not working."

"Yeah, it's getting kind of hot in here too." He smirked. "Ready to keep going?"

"Oh, yes."

He closed his eyes and took a deep breath. "Slide your hand down that long, exquisite neck...your fingertips barely brushing over your hot skin...that touch in all the right places...your wet fingers landing on the curve of your breast...massaging—"

"Mr. Scott!" Whiskey yelled in Leo's ear.

Leo scrambled up, dropping the phone to the desk with a thud.

"Are you having phone sex in the *dorm?*" Sour hollered.

Leo felt a blush begin on his neck and spread upward, heating his face as he stood at attention. "Yes, sir?"

Sour gave him a hard look and shook his head. "Jesus Christ. End your call, plebe."

"Yes, sir." Leo picked up the phone as Sour walked away.

He cringed. "Did you hear that?"

Peals of Audrey's fabulous laughter met his ear. "You just got yelled at for having phone sex! That was so awesome!"

Leo narrowed his eyes. "I'm glad my mortification brings you such joy, Audrey."

She continued to giggle, gradually coaxing a low chuckle from him as well when he noticed Mr. Sour had left the room.

"I really do have to go, though," he added.

Audrey let out one of those long, satisfying sighs that follow a good laugh. "I'll see you *pronto*, Leo."

He smiled. *"No puedo esperar.* Till Thanksgiving, mi amor."

After ending the call, Leo strolled down the passageway to return the phone to its owner, an energized bounce to his step. If Benito had enjoyed learning Leo wasn't perfect before, he'd *love* the story of how Leo got busted having phone sex.

How freaking imperfect. And he didn't even care.

65. Case Notes

Leo chewed the inside of his mouth as he stared at Dr. Ina. They were once again at an impasse.

She'd been teaching him grounding skills to manage his flashbacks. Everything from deep breaths, which Leo had recognized from the way Coach Matt had taught him to calm down behind the blocks before races, to stranger approaches. Leo thought it was silly to repeat stuff like "Today is November fifth. I'm an adult. I'm safe. My dad isn't here" — particularly because that last statement was somewhat in doubt. CS was due back from the Gulf sometime in the next few days. As much as he hated to admit it, Leo did *not* feel safe.

Now that Ina had shored up his coping strategies, she urged him to dive in and revisit his childhood. But he'd remained firmly on the diving board, refusing to plunge into the swirling maelstrom of memories below.

However, today he finally relented. He chose the memory carefully. It was a time he hadn't personally been beaten, so he thought it would be easier to remember.

Ina sat back, her face neutral. "Just take your time. It's fine to take breaks."

"Yes, ma'am." Leo took a breath and willed himself to relax as he began to remember. "I was eleven, and Jase was, um, sixteen, I think. Mom was still in the hospital."

"How long had she been in the hospital?"

"Four months? Maybe five?"

Ina nodded.

Leo sat on his hands. "I came home from practice, and Dad was waiting for me. He was really mad."

"How'd you know he was mad?"

"His eyes. They, uh, they change colors. And they were almost purple. I know it sounds strange—you have to see them. Anyway, he was yelling at Jason. Well, my dad doesn't yell, really, but I could tell he was mad just from his voice. It gets, like, intimidating. There's an edge to it, you know?"

Leo paused. Suddenly he was right there walking through his front door again, stumbling onto CS interrogating Jason in the study. The hairs on the back of his neck bristled, and his stomach twisted, both then and now.

"What was your father mad about?" Ina asked.

"He got home from work, and the front door was unlocked. He'd already yelled at me once that week for forgetting to lock it—there'd been some break-ins in our neighborhood. I was the last to leave that morning, and, like an idiot, I forgot to lock the door."

"Eleven-year-olds do stuff like that all the time," said Ina. "Heck, I'm an adult, and I've forgotten to lock the door."

"Yeah, but you don't live with CS."

"You're right."

Leo took a deep breath. "He asked me if I left the door unlocked, and of course I had to admit it. Then his eyes…" Leo shifted. "His eyes got darker, and…" He tried to slow his breathing. "He, he reached for his belt. I knew I'd get it." He looked down. "CS told Jase to get out. But Jase, he didn't leave. He wouldn't leave."

Leo looked ahead, seeing it all unfold. "Jase said, 'Hit me instead. I should've reminded Leo to lock the door. Please, sir. Hit me.' I tried to stop him, but my dad wouldn't listen."

He could hear Jason's voice pleading over and over in his head, and he covered his ears to drown out the words.

"Your father beat your brother instead of you."

"Yes, ma'am. Right in front of me. CS m-m-made m-m-me stay and watch."

"Leo, I want you to look around and tell me what you see. What's on my desk?"

He blinked several times and saw cluttered piles of papers, surrounded by family photos. "It's kind of hard to see your desk, ma'am. It's kind of a mess."

"Yes, my desk is a disaster zone." She chuckled. "I don't suppose that'd fly in your father's house, huh?"

"No, ma'am." Leo's smile faded. "CS...he gave it to Jase really bad. And I didn't do one damn thing. I just stood there and watched it all happen."

He was surprised he wasn't crying. He'd certainly cried enough that day as he watched his father beat his brother, mocking him the whole time.

"Your brother wanted to protect you."

"It wasn't Jase's fault! *I'm* the one who left the door unlocked, not him. I'm the one who should've been whipped."

"Neither of you should've been beaten!"

Leo shook his head. "I'll never be able to repay Jase. I'll never be able to make it up to him."

"But Jason chose that himself. You didn't ask him to step in." She sighed. "It probably made him feel better. It's simply awful to stand by helplessly and watch your little brother get hurt."

Leo paused. He'd never thought of it that way before. "It wasn't right."

"No, it wasn't right. It wasn't right of your father to hit either of you. And it certainly wasn't right for him to force you to watch him hurt Jason. That alone is enough trauma to produce years of flashbacks...I'm starting to see where your overblown guilt complex comes from."

"My guilt complex?"

"You seem to feel overly responsible for the events around you. I bet you've tried to make it up to Jason, and I bet he knows how indebted you feel to him. I wouldn't be surprised if you've taken on blame for other things that aren't your responsibility."

Leo thought of how he'd told Mrs. Boyd he'd written Audrey's note in chemistry class. Had that been a whole year ago?

"So am I hopeless or what?" he asked. "You must talk to all your shrink friends about what a nutcase I am."

"Actually your flashbacks aren't as frequent or intense as they are with some," Ina said. "And no, you're not a nutcase. You're a kind, thoughtful young man trying to recover from some hurtful events in your past. You're doing a wonderful job."

Ten minutes later, Leo shut the office door behind him with a soft click. Closing his eyes, he tried to collect himself. He always felt bewildered and exhausted after a session with Dr. Ina. He couldn't believe he'd shared that with her. Yet she hadn't looked disgusted. She hadn't called him weak. He took a deep breath. He always tried to put his emotions behind him before he got to swim practice, but he was often quite distracted when he hit the water. Coach had even commented on his poor performance on Mondays.

Finally he felt steady enough to move, but he gasped as he saw what seemed to be Lt. Keaton in the waiting room as he passed. He peeked back around the corner and confirmed that it was indeed his company officer with her head buried in a magazine.

What was *she* doing there?

Hearing the steady approach of crutches down the hallway, Leo ducked inside a coat closet. As he closed the door he heard Dr. Ina's smooth voice.

"Are you ready, Lieutenant?"

He could barely make out the clipped response. "Yes, ma'am."

Dr. Ina crutched back down the hall, and Leo stood frozen in the darkness with a wool coat itching his face. Lt. Keaton saw Dr. Ina too? He rubbed his cheek for several moments, lost in thought. Suddenly he flinched and everything was clear. He knew exactly what he needed to do.

Leo was grateful his uniform was black. It was almost midnight, way past lights out, and he scurried down the desolate passageways of Mother B. He prayed no one would stop him.

This was an incredible risk, but now that he'd finally figured out a way to help Audrey, he had to do it. Her father's wrongful imprisonment had gone on way too long.

Leo approached the counseling offices and held his breath as he tried the door. According to his calculations, the cleaning crew should be inside, and he assumed they'd leave the doors unlocked while they worked. He exhaled as the doorknob turned easily in his hand.

He waited in the shadows as the whistling janitor ventured into an interior office, then returned to dump the contents of a garbage can into the larger trash bin in the hallway. As the janitor disappeared into each office, Leo inched down the hall toward Dr. Ina's. His heart hammered, but once the janitor exited Ina's office and headed to the next one, Leo slipped inside.

He crouched low behind her desk and was pleased to find he could see well enough with just the passageway lighting. His terror over getting caught nearly consumed him, but he used a few of Dr. Ina's grounding techniques to regain control. Leo dug around the surface of her desk, thinking of the day she'd had him look away as she did exactly the same thing. Eventually his hand found its way behind her computer monitor, and he grinned as he clasped a ring with two keys.

Easing one of the keys into the lock on the desk, Leo's heart sang as the drawer full of client charts slid out toward him. Everything had been so easy—almost too easy, and he stopped for a second to listen. He heard nothing but a faint whistling down the hallway, so he resumed his work and looked down at the alphabetically ordered charts.

He'd broken all kinds of regulations already, but he was about to breach therapist-client confidentiality, and after that there'd be no going back. He paused, his hand hovering over the charts. Audrey's big, mournful eyes filled his head. She hadn't been the carefree, joyful girl he'd met three years ago since her father's arrest, and she'd never be that person again as long as the injustice remained.

"Forgive me, Dr. Ina," he whispered.

Leo rifled through the charts, scarcely registering the names he passed until his fingers rested on *Keaton, Darnell*. He withdrew the thin chart and licked his lip as he opened the file.

After today's date, Dr. Ina had scrawled a note. Her neat handwriting filled the page on the right side of the chart. Leo lifted the page and underneath was a note from late October, which lay atop several more pages of notes and an intake report at the bottom of the stack. The left side of the chart contained some paperwork related to informed consent and HIPAA, which Leo promptly ignored. Turning his attention back to the case note with today's date, he began to read:

> 5 November, third session: Several minutes of silence between us to begin. DK finally admitted she barely slept at all this week and is desperate because it's hurting her work performance. She believes her insomnia was a factor in the assault of the plebe in mid-October. I referred her to Dr. Adams for anxiety meds, but also encouraged her to discuss her worries in therapy. DK asked if she could trust me, and I reviewed the parameters of confidentiality again. She's afraid of her current CO finding out about a reprimand from her previous CO. Told her if this past situation wasn't affecting her current fitness for duty, I wouldn't have to report it. DK then told me her former CO discovered an affair she'd had with a married coworker (which she mentioned in our second session).

Leo paused. CS was Lt. Keaton's CO. CS *knew* about the affair between Lt. Keaton and Lt. Commander Walsh? He continued reading:

> DK said her CO threatened to court martial them for fraternization, but then she stopped talking, appearing to dissociate once again. She wept for several minutes, then refused to continue the session. She reluctantly agreed to schedule for next week, when I hope we can get to the bottom of this trauma.

Leo flipped the page to read the case note for the second session, almost ripping it out of the chart:

29 October, second session: DK continues to seem
guarded and angry about her mandated counseling. She
did report the deep breathing was helpful, but wouldn't
answer questions about what prompted her to use it.
She appeared to dissociate during session, staring
blankly in space for several moments and tensing in
fear. Eventually she admitted today was particularly
difficult because it was the anniversary of the first
night she made love with her former boyfriend. She
said he was the kindest person she'd ever met and
"the love of (her) life." He reportedly doted on her
and promised he'd leave his wife once his daughter
finished college. They kept their relationship hidden
because he was her superior officer and married. DK
reported feeling immense guilt about the relationship.
The affair now seems to be over, but she wouldn't go
into further detail.

Leo scanned the intake report, noting the lieutenant's presenting
symptoms of insomnia, nightmares, being easily startled, increased
alcohol consumption, and feelings of irritation and numbness. Dr.
Ina had given her a preliminary diagnosis of post-traumatic stress
disorder, though she'd noted the precipitating trauma remained a
mystery as the client refused to discuss it. Leo tensed as he read:

When asked about her romantic life, DK shut down
completely, and I'm wondering if her past trauma
was related to this area. "Men are snakes," she
said. When pressed further, DK added that in her
experience men abused their power, and she was
determined not to do the same. Her assault of a plebe
on 21 October represented, to her, a complete abuse
of power and loss of control. She expressed deep
remorse.

Leo suddenly closed the chart, the papers slapping together with
finality. He sat back with a thud on the floor behind Dr. Ina's desk,
his jaw slack.

Working methodically, he returned the chart to the drawer. His
mind reviewed the evidence—the letter Jase and Cam had found,

Lt. Keaton's remorse for striking him, her mysterious trauma after CS discovered her affair, and her general opinion of men in power. Suddenly he felt sick. Her trauma was not such a mystery to him. He knew a man who abused his power.

"Audrey," he whispered as he rocked back and forth, a guttural moan escaping his lips. Tears spilled down his cheeks, and his stomach churned with bile and revulsion.

Leo wasn't sure how long he'd sat there, huddled on the floor next to a puddle of vomit, when suddenly the lights in Dr. Ina's office flipped on. Leo looked up, his vision blurry, unsure what was happening.

Then he heard her voice. "What the *hell* are you doing in my office?"

Leo flinched, turning his unfocused eyes toward her.

Ina came around the desk and inhaled sharply. "Did you read my files?"

He seemed to wake from his daze, and his face crumpled. "I'm sorry, I'm sorry," he cried, rocking back and forth again. "I'm so sorry, ma'am."

"Did you break in here? Did you read my files?"

"Yes ma'am." He nodded, scooting away from the mess on the floor.

"Why?" she shouted.

Leo couldn't remember how to put words together.

She became even more incensed at his refusal to answer.

The drone of the vacuum cleaner stopped, and the janitor, no longer whistling, poked his head into the office. "Everything okay, ma'am?"

Ina spun around, then turned back to stare at Leo. "Call the MPs," she said, smoothly and coldly. "We've had a break-in."

Leo nodded, accepting his fate. He wiped his nose.

"Don't move, Leo," she ordered.

"Yes, ma'am. Don't worry, I won't run." He stared straight ahead. "There's nowhere to run. I think my life might be over."

66. Arresting Developments

Leo did his best to avoid Dr. Ina's wounded eyes.

Each refusal to answer her questions pained him a little more. He felt cruel and ungrateful. Dr. Ina had done so much for him, and it killed him to hurt her this way. But he couldn't tell anyone. That way nobody could interfere with the plan he was piecing together — his plan to make things right. He'd put the real murderer behind bars, no matter what it took.

He actually felt relieved when the MPs showed up to arrest him.

"On your feet," one ordered.

"Yes, sir." Leo hopped up, stepping over the mess he'd made.

The other MP turned to Ina. "What happened here, ma'am?"

"I was dealing with a crisis in the infirmary, and I had to retrieve a chart from my office. When I arrived, I found Mr. Scott here — unauthorized."

Leo winced. *Mr. Scott?* She was all business now.

"Apparently he got in because the cleaning crew had unlocked the office. When I arrived my file drawer was unlocked and ajar, and when I asked him if he'd read my charts, he said yes."

The MP turned to Leo. "You read her charts?"

"Yes, sir."

"And is that your vomit on the floor, Mr. Scott?"

Leo grimaced. "Yes, sir."

"Why'd you do this? What made you throw up?"

Leo remained silent.

"Answer me now!" the MP threatened.

Leo still said nothing.

"It won't do any good. I've tried to get the story out of him already," Ina said.

"Ma'am, would you like us to call Annapolis PD?" the MP asked. "We can involve local authorities or we can handle this internally."

Ina paused. "What will happen to him, in both scenarios?"

The MP stroked his chin. "We'll return him to his quarters and post a guard outside while the commandant's apprised of the situation. Captain Tracker will likely order a Brigade Honor Committee investigation and hearing, which will determine his punishment. I'd say it doesn't look good for this one to stay in the Navy."

Leo couldn't believe it, but he felt relief at that news.

"If we call the local authorities, I'm not sure what'd happen," the MP continued. "They'd send some officers, who'd likely arrest him, and then it would go through the courts."

"Don't call Annapolis PD—I don't want them rifling through my charts," Ina said. "I want to find out what's going on with Mr. Scott first. I may involve local authorities later, but right now I want this handled internally."

"Yes, ma'am," the MP said.

"Ma'am, you can have the mess on the floor cleaned up, but we'd like you to avoid touching your desk for now, until tomorrow morning," added the other MP. "We'll set up a meeting in the commandant's office, and we'd like you to be there. We'll call you when we have the meeting time. Is that satisfactory to you, ma'am?"

"Yes, but I still need the chart for my client in the infirmary."

"Hmm…I guess we'll have to inspect the drawer now. Ma'am, I want you to slide your desk drawer open and take a look."

Ina complied.

"Does anything look out of place, ma'am?"

Leo held his breath. All he could see was Lt. Keaton's chart, shining like a beacon, but apparently Dr. Ina saw nothing.

"No, it looks fine."

"Try to remove the chart you need without disrupting the others, ma'am."

Ina lifted out a chart, hiding the name with her thumb, and nodded to the MP before closing the drawer. "One other caveat: I'm locking this office, and I forbid anyone from investigating the contents of my desk unless I'm present," she added. "There's confidential client information here."

"Understood, ma'am."

Leo listened quietly. It was almost like the officers and psychologist had forgotten about him.

But they hadn't. Nodding at him, the MP ordered, "Let's go, plebe."

Leo gulped and exited, flanked by the MPs, without meeting Dr. Ina's eyes. They marched him away from the therapy room, the place of secrets and hidden motivations. Now Leo possessed some of those secrets, and there was only one person he'd share them with — only one person he'd confront.

"You're *sure* this is her room?"

Leo glanced at the MP and nodded.

The officer again knocked on Ms. Nevington's door. After a moment came a faint "Just a minute!" from within.

The door swung open to reveal his tall, wiry company commander in a black T-shirt and shorts. Her hair sprang out in all directions, and her sleepy eyes widened upon seeing him.

"Midshipman Nevington, you're the commander for Second Company?"

"Yes, sir. Would you like to come inside to avoid waking the entire passageway?"

The MP shook his head. "This'll be quick. We need to advise you that Mr. Scott's being investigated for a crime and will be restricted to quarters for the near future. He's not to be out of his room other than trips to the head escorted by an MP."

Trapped at attention, Leo was unable to hang his head and avoid her disappointed glare.

"What'd he do?" she inquired.

"He broke into an office and read confidential information," the MP said. "We'll know more tomorrow—nothing will be sorted out at this late hour. We'll contact you after the commandant reviews the situation."

"You're telling me I'm not allowed to talk to a member of my own company until you allow it, sir?"

"That's precisely what I'm saying. Good night, Midshipman Nevington."

"Good night, sir." As she closed the door, she added, "The drama continues, Mr. Scott."

"Yes, ma'am." Leo closed his eyes.

When they reached his room, the MPs shoved him inside and closed the door behind him. Leo stumbled into the darkness and crashed into the garbage can.

"*¡Hijole!*" Benito bolted upright. "Are we late?"

Leo crossed the room to turn on the lights. "No, *idiota*, it's zero-one-hundred hours."

"What're you doing wearing a uniform at one a.m.?"

"Screwing up my life," he reported, collapsing on the bed.

"Well, can you turn off the stupid lights? We have to wake up in, like, four hours for PT."

"I'm not going to PT," Leo countered.

"What?" Benito looked confused. "What're you talking about, *hombre?*"

"There's an MP guarding the door, and I'm under arrest."

"Is this some sort of prank?"

"I wish. Listen, the less you know about this, the better. They'll interrogate me about what went down tonight, and when I don't tell them, they'll start asking you. Just go back to sleep."

"My roommate tells me he's under arrest, and he wants me just to fall *asleep?* I got your back, dude. You have to tell me what happened."

Leo stared at the ceiling. He was so tired and, to be honest, so terrified of what lay ahead. Feeling tears threaten again, he did what Benito had asked and went to turn off the lights.

Returning to his rack, he said softly, "You've been a good roommate to me, Ben. The best. You'll make an awesome naval officer."

Benito's voice rose. "Why does it sound like you're saying goodbye?"

"Please," Leo begged, feeling a lump in his throat. "Please don't ask me any more questions." His voice cracked. "I just can't talk about it right now. I'll explain things when I can, but I have to get some sleep. If you value our friendship, just let it go for now, okay?"

There was silence from the other side of the room, and Leo knew his roommate was trying to figure out his next move.

"I just want to help you," Benito finally said.

Leo's voice trembled. "I know. But you can help me by dropping it and going back to sleep. Please, *hombre.*"

This time Benito stayed quiet, but Leo knew he wasn't happy about it. Leo wasn't happy either.

The MPs had assembled a small work group in the commandant's office to discuss the future of Leo Scott.

Captain Tracker sat at the head of his conference table. Next to Ina was the MP not guarding Leo's room at the moment, and across the table were Viva Nevington and Tom Sour.

"So let's review the facts," the captain began. "Midshipman Sour, I'd like you to take notes."

"Yes, sir." Sour pulled a notebook from his backpack, and the commandant nodded to the MP.

"Sir, we were called to Counseling Services by a member of the cleaning crew at just past zero-hundred hours this morning. We arrived at Dr. Hansen's office to find her inside with Midshipman Scott, who was sitting on the floor behind her desk. He appeared distraught and had gotten sick on the floor. He admitted to us, and to her, that he'd broken into her desk and read confidential charts."

The commandant shook his head. "You found him in your office, Dr. Hansen?"

"Yes, sir. I was dealing with a crisis in the infirmary, and I needed to retrieve one of my charts."

He gave her a knowing look. "Dr. Adams apprised me of that situation. Sounds like you had a long night."

She glanced at the MP. "I think we've all had a long night, sir. I came to my office and Leo, uh, Mr. Scott, was on the floor. I started yelling at him, asking him what he was doing there. Then I saw my desk drawer unlocked and open, and he admitted to reading my charts."

"This makes no sense," Captain Tracker said. "Do you have any idea whose charts Mr. Scott would be after?"

"I thought about this all night, sir. Sometimes counseling clients worry about what their psychologists write about them, so he might've wanted to see his own chart. He hasn't been entirely forthcoming with me, and maybe he wanted to see if I'd figured out something about him. Or perhaps he was after another chart. He does know a couple of my other clients." She glanced nervously at the midshipmen.

"I'd like everyone to leave the room except for Dr. Hansen," the captain announced.

The midshipmen and MP immediately stood and headed for the antechamber.

"We're talking about Lt. Keaton?" he asked once they'd gone.

"Yes, sir, and I've also been seeing two other midshipmen in Second Company." Ina paused. "I noticed Lt. Keaton isn't here this morning?"

"I've chosen not to include her at this point. There's a strange dynamic between her and Mr. Scott, and I believe it's unwise to involve her. What do you think of that, Dr. Hansen?"

"It *is* odd that she's punished him quite severely on two occasions. But Darnell seems very remorseful for striking Leo, sir. I have a sense she wasn't entirely in control of herself when she did that."

"What do you mean?"

"Well…Her symptoms do seem to relate to her fitness for duty, so I can tell you Darnell appears to have a traumatic history. She's already dissociated twice in my presence, likely re-experiencing the trauma. She hasn't disclosed to me what happened to her. However, I believe she may have been dissociating when she hit Leo."

He nodded. "Well, then, it sounds like for the safety of both of them, let's keep her in the dark about this. I'm sure you're not too excited about telling Darnell her privacy may have been compromised."

"I've been considering how to handle the confidentiality issue, and I'll consult the state board today." Ina sighed. "This is my worst nightmare. Since I don't know whose charts were read, I think I'll delay disclosing the breach to clients for now, sir."

"Okay. Anything else we need to discuss before we bring the rest of the crew back in?"

Ina paused. "Leo seemed like such a good young man, sir." She looked down. "I feel so betrayed."

"I can imagine. This midshipman appears to be hiding many secrets. I'd like you to keep trying to get some information out of him."

"Yes, sir."

The captain called the rest of the group back in. "Okay, from what I'm hearing, we need to call an Honor Committee hearing ASAP. Given we have a breach of confidentiality involving therapy patients' rights, I want to move quickly on this to try to get to the bottom of things. Midshipman Sour, I'd like you to set up the hearing."

"Yes, sir."

Turning to Nevington and the MP, he instructed, "I want you two to interrogate Mr. Scott. If he's tight-lipped, see if his roommate can be useful. Dr. Hansen will also visit his quarters for questioning when her schedule allows. And there better not be any violence involved with the interrogation, or there'll be hell to pay."

"Understood, sir," Nevington said.

The commandant stood, followed by the others. He nodded to dismiss them. "Good luck. I'm afraid we might be too late to save this sailor, but at least let's minimize the damage."

67. Saving Audrey

His careful handwriting swam before his eyes, blurred by tears. They'd taken his laptop, forcing him to resort to snail mail.

Leo tried to get the wording right, but there was no suitable way to break it to Audrey. He was paralyzed by writer's block — or, actually, heart block. He cursed his weakness.

It was almost nine o'clock, and he knew they'd be coming for him soon. Benito had already slogged through PT, breakfast, and his first class by now, and Leo had done nothing but shower and stare at the unfinished letter. Studying for classes he'd likely never attend again seemed a pointless venture, and his concentration was hardly at its peak anyway.

He wasn't exactly sure of the how and why of Lt. Commander Walsh's murder, but he was relatively sure knew the who — he felt it in his gut. There was a reason Lt. Keaton hated men with the last name Scott.

Finally his company commander and an MP burst into the room, and Leo stuffed the pen and paper under his rack and sprang to attention.

"It sounds like you had a busy night, Midshipman Scott. Do you know why we're here this morning?"

"Yes, ma'am. You want to know why I broke into Dr. Hansen's office."

"Very perceptive. Let's hear it."

He said nothing.

She barely let five seconds of silence tick by before she ordered, "Drop and give me seventy-five."

He completed the pushups and snapped back up to attention, breathing hard and sweating.

"How can one plebe perform so brilliantly yet screw up so royally?" Nevington mused.

It was a good rhetorical question, and Leo kept his mouth shut.

Her next question was not so rhetorical. "Why'd you break curfew to go to Dr. Hansen's office?"

"No excuse, ma'am."

"Don't get cute with me, Mr. Scott. I want an answer to my question. Now."

Leo sighed. He hated to displease a superior. But he couldn't risk it. Zipping his lips was the only way.

"Get in the plank position," Nevington ordered.

"Yes, ma'am." Leo dropped and held his body parallel to the floor, his weight perched on his elbows and toes. It wasn't long before the trembling began. His body quivered as he supported the bulk of his weight with his core muscles.

She kneeled next to him. "You can stop at any time, Midshipman Scott. Just tell me whose chart you were after, and this will all be over. Otherwise we're in for a long day."

His only response was a grunt. More time elapsed, and the shuddering intensified.

"Why'd you break in to Dr. Hansen's office?"

Sweat poured down his neck. He wouldn't be able to hold himself up much longer.

Her voice sharpened. "You *will* talk to me before this is over!"

He finally collapsed.

"On your feet!"

Leo peeled his body off the floor, still trembling from the effort.

She put her face inches from his. "Are you ready to talk yet?"

"No, ma'am," he panted.

"Give me one hundred burpees then."

"Yes, ma'am."

Leo began the up-and-down exercise: squatting with his hands on the floor, kicking his feet back to a pushup position, returning to the squat position, and finally leaping up in an explosive jump before repeating the movement. Just the first ten had him breathing hard, and he still had ninety left. Perspiration ringed his collar, spreading and sticking his uniform to his chest.

He made his mind blank and heard only his steady, labored breathing.

Exercises completed, Leo stood at attention once again. His throat was parched.

"Why'd you break into the psychologist's office?" Las Vegas asked again.

"I can't tell you, ma'am!" Frustration crept into his raspy voice.

"Arms out," she ordered.

Leo lifted his arms to the side, parallel to the floor. It was easy at first, just like the twenty-four-hour march, but after a few minutes his shoulders burned and his mind screamed.

If he'd only come clean with Nevington or Dr. Ina, they'd probably fight to save him. But he couldn't think about self preservation, only about saving others. Audrey was one of several people on the line now, and her happiness was much more important than his.

His deltoids were on fire, and he willed his leaden arms to remain airborne. Nevington's face was mired in disappointment. The variations of PT torture were endless, and Leo knew she would not give up anytime soon. *Stay strong for Audrey*, he told himself, choking down a sob. *Save Audrey.*

According to the sunlight filtering into the room, it was almost noon by the time he saw Dr. Ina. She came to his dorm room as he was enduring the wall-sit exercise, his knees at a ninety-degree angle and his back against the wall, forming a human chair. Flames of pain blazed through his quadriceps, and sweat soaked his uniform. Nevington hovered over him, her now-hoarse voice not quite as intimidating as it had been at the beginning.

"On your feet!" she ordered, and both midshipmen stood at attention, saluting Ina.

Though he guessed Dr. Ina would likely ask him even more questions, he was happy to see her. Her interrogation couldn't be any worse than what he'd just withstood.

"At ease," Ina commanded. "Midshipman Nevington, I'd like to speak to you outside. MP, give some water to Midshipman Scott."

After gulping to his heart's content, Leo set down the water bottle and shifted back to attention when Ina returned.

"I let Viva head to Noon Meal Formation," she said. "Please bring some food for Midshipman Scott, then stand guard outside," she told the MP.

The MP nodded and left.

Ina pulled out Leo's desk chair and ordered "Have a seat," before crossing the room to sit at Benito's desk.

"You're not on crutches anymore, ma'am," Leo observed as he sat down.

Ina nodded. "Today's the first day my surgeon said I could go without them."

"How *is* your knee, ma'am?"

"My knee's healing well, Leo. How are *you* doing?"

"Fine, ma'am."

"Your company commander was tough on you?"

"No more than I expected, ma'am."

She leaned back in her chair. "So, I talked to the Maryland Psychology Licensing Board today. They're not pleased with your actions. They agreed I need to find out whose charts you read so I can inform my clients of the confidentiality breach. And you *will* tell me that information this afternoon."

A defiant glare was his only reply.

"I have clients out there living their lives, oblivious to the fact that some eighteen-year-old boy stole their private information. You're a psychotherapy client, Leo. How would *you* like that? How'd you like some stranger knowing your deepest secrets?"

Looking away, Leo realized the afternoon session would be a different kind of challenge. Emotional torture. Dr. Ina's guilt trip had arrived at its destination, landing squarely with a resonant thump.

Her voice rose. "Would you feel violated if some stranger stole your secrets without your permission? Would you be angry? Would you hesitate to trust again?"

He looked down. "Yes, ma'am."

"I would too, Leo. I'd be very disturbed. I'd feel even more violated if the person who stole my privacy refused to share why he did so." She waited a beat. "Of course, if you were just looking at your own chart, well, that'd be different."

Leo gulped. He felt awful. "I wasn't looking for my chart."

"Thank you for telling me that." Ina rewarded him with a warm smile. "I was just talking to Ms. Nevington. She told me the bruise you had a couple of weeks ago was from Lt. Keaton, not a wayward rifle."

He felt his cheeks burn. "I'm sorry, ma'am, but as I told you, my company commander ordered me to lie about that."

"Apology accepted. It's quite inappropriate for a superior to strike a subordinate. I wonder what happened to the lieutenant. Do you think she was reprimanded?"

Leo stared at his psychologist. He realized the game she was playing, trying to squeeze information from him. He took a deep breath to calm himself, then realized the irony of using the very skills she'd taught him to work against her. "I don't know, ma'am. What typically happens to an officer in that situation?"

"I would think the commandant would order her to attend anger-management counseling—just like your punishment for acting out in violence."

"I wouldn't know, ma'am," Leo said, mustering his best sweet smile.

With a knock, the MP returned carrying a sandwich and a soda. Leo devoured his food.

When he wiped his mouth at the end, Ina asked, "Have they allowed you to make any phone calls?"

"No, ma'am."

"Okay, then, it's time to call your parents and tell them what's happened."

Leo jumped. "After the awful stuff I told you about my dad, you'd force me to call him?" Two could play the guilt-trip game.

Ina cocked her head to one side. "You told me he was in the Gulf. I want you to call your mother."

"She, um, ma'am, she doesn't need to know about this, ma'am."

"Yes, she does, Leo. You might get separated. A mother deserves to know that about her son."

"I'm gonna wait until the hearing's over before I tell her anything."

"Leo Scott, you will call your mother right now," Dr. Ina ordered, sounding very much *like* his mother.

Leo sighed. "Yes, ma'am. I don't have a phone, though."

"I'm sure you can figure out where to get one, Leo."

He frowned. "Mr. Jones let me use his before. His quarters are down the p-way."

"Fine. Go call your mother."

He headed down the passageway to the plebe's room with the MP on his six.

Realizing it was just the MP following him — Dr. Ina wasn't going to monitor his call — Leo decided to get another painful conversation over with and opted to call Audrey instead.

He heard Audrey squeal when she answered. "How in the world are you calling me in the middle of the day?"

"Just got the chance to call, I guess. Wasn't sure if you'd be free?"

"I'm in between classes, sitting outside in the sun." Worry crept into her voice. "Um, Leo? Are you okay? You sound weird."

She knew him so well. He sighed. "I'm in a lot of trouble."

"Oh, no. What happened?"

"I can't talk about it, Audrey. I called because I have to tell you something."

Leo squeezed his eyes shut, his stomach swirling with dread. He hated what he had to do. If this worked, she'd want nothing to do with him ever again. If his plan didn't work, he'd want nothing to do with her—for her own sake. He'd never allow her to be tethered to a man in prison. He couldn't watch it happen again.

His reasons for what he was about to say were logical and sound. So why did his heart ache?

"What is it?" she prompted. "You know you can tell me anything, right?"

Swallowing tears, he choked, "I'm calling to break up with you. I-I, um, I don't love you anymore."

There was stunned silence on the other end of the phone, followed by a strangled cry. "Why, Leo? *Why?* How can you do this? You told me you loved me!"

He exhaled miserably and gripped the phone. *You can do this. You have to save her.* His jaw hardened with resolve. "I did love you, but not anymore. I can't do this long-distance thing. I don't want you to call or speak to me ever again."

Quickly he hung up, fighting the urge to vomit. He felt chills of self hatred bloom up his spine, his ragged breathing smothered by his hands cradling his face. He could only imagine the despair and confusion Audrey felt right now. *He* did that to her. But it was the only way.

Leo trudged back to his room with the MP. Slinking back into his chair, he faced Dr. Ina once again.

"How'd she take it?" Ina asked.

"Not well, ma'am. She...she cried."

"Did you tell your mother you weren't cooperating with us in the investigation?"

"Yes, ma'am."

"And did she encourage you to be more forthcoming?"

Leo shrugged. "She doesn't really care what I do."

Ina looked confused. "Really? Your mother doesn't care? I find that hard to believe." She stroked her chin. "What's her phone number? I'm going to call her."

"No, ma'am, you can't. I —"

"I want to call your mother."

"No!" he yelled.

"What do you have against me speaking to your mother? What are you hiding from me? Damn it, Leo! I'm trying to fight for you, and all you give me is one lie after another!"

He slumped in his chair. "I didn't call my mom," he finally said. "I called my girlfriend, ma'am."

"What'd you say to her?" She looked even more perplexed.

"I broke up with her," he confessed at a whisper.

"But you *love* her!" Ina protested. "You told me you wanted to marry her someday!"

"Where I'm going, she can't follow."

There was a loud knock, and Mr. Sour appeared. Leo leaped to his feet.

Sour glanced at Ina, who remained in her chair, her forehead wrinkled. "The Honor Committee's assembled, ma'am. Mr. Scott, you're to come with me."

All too eager to go, Leo snatched his cover off his desk and marched. He was one step closer to giving Audrey her father back.

68. Frayed Edges

Despite the warm sun on her back, Audrey shivered. Her tears had dried, leaving desperate tracks down her face, and she felt suspended in time, foggy and brutalized. The darkness enveloping her mind stood in sharp contrast to her bright surroundings on the campus quad.

She looked down at her phone. The screen flashed *Call Time* 1:26. One minute, twenty-six seconds was all the time it had taken to ruin her life. Eighty-six seconds and her *raison d'être* had ceased to exist. Leo had wrenched himself away without a moment's notice, without a hint of warning.

She'd been listening to a sad song by The Fray before Leo called, and the lyrics now played in an endless loop in her mind — a pathetic soundtrack to her devastation. What on earth had just happened?

Was he taking Oxycontin again? He hadn't sounded high on the phone, though it had taken quite a while for her to catch on before. Could he get pills at the Academy?

Was there another girl? Audrey felt sick. No, he wouldn't do that to her. Would he? Maybe he'd found a girl who shared his enthusiasm for the Navy. Maybe he wanted a girlfriend whose father wasn't in prison for murder.

Why? *Why?* Leo had sounded upset on the phone — almost like he was crying too. Had he truly wanted to break up? Had CS forced him into it?

With each thought, Audrey became increasingly panicked, increasingly riled. Her initial shock began to shift into hot rage.

How dare Leo do this to her? She was *devoted* to him, and he'd just slapped her in the face. How dare he shred their love without one shred of explanation?

She sat up tall. She'd show him. Oh, what he'd be missing.

Her defiance crumbled in a second. "I don't *want* to show him," she cried to no one in particular. "I don't want to prove how much he'll miss me. I miss him! I just want him back. Leo, Leo..."

Glancing at her phone again, Audrey began punching numbers.

After two calls failed to connect, Audrey praised God when Cameron answered.

"Audrey! How are you?"

Close to hyperventilating, Audrey couldn't even speak.

"What is it?" Cameron asked. "Are you okay?"

Audrey sniffled. "I'm s-s-sorry to bother you, C-C-Cam. It's just...Elaine and my mom didn't answer, and I d-d-didn't know who else to call."

"It's fine. I'm only grading homework. What's going on?"

"L-L-Leo broke up with me," Audrey wailed, her tears starting again.

"No! He couldn't have."

"He did. He just called me. He said...he said he didn't love me anymore!"

"Oh, Audrey. Sweetheart, I'm so sorry. I don't understand. Did he tell you why?"

"No, that's the worst part. He hung up right away." Audrey sobbed. "Eighty-six. Eighty-six."

"Audrey, honey, I can't understand you. What are you saying?" Cam asked, sounding frustrated.

Audrey took a deep breath. "Cam. Has Leo said anything to Jason? Is he seeing somebody else? Is anything wrong at the Academy?"

"Not that I heard. You know Leo hardly ever gets the chance to call. I'll call Jase and ask, okay? Just hold on tight. Leo loves you, and he'll come to his senses. I know it."

Audrey sniffed. God, she needed a drink. "Thanks, Cam. Call me as soon as you find anything out, okay?"

"Okay. Hang in there."

Audrey took a ragged breath and searched her backpack for some tissues. Maybe Leo's brother could make some sense out of this. She surely could not. She would never recover, not even in eighty-six years.

"It's simple, Midshipman Scott," Mr. Sour said.

Five upper-class midshipmen sat in a row of chairs behind the table: the Honor Committee.

"Unless you tell us of any mitigating circumstances related to the break-in at Counseling Services, we'll be forced to separate you from the Navy."

Leo stood at attention, barely holding on after the grueling interrogations and horrific phone call to Audrey. His precious Navy career was toast, but he was just numb. He refocused on the task ahead—the task that couldn't be completed from inside Academy walls.

Whiskey scrubbed his hand over his face. "Midshipman Scott, what's the Honor Concept?"

"Sir, midshipmen are persons of integrity; they stand for that which is right, sir."

"And how were you standing for that which is right, Mr. Scott?" he immediately countered. "How were you demonstrating integrity by stealing confidential information?"

Resignation slumped Leo's shoulders. He always failed. He'd tried to do right by Audrey, only to make her lose their baby then pretend not to love her anymore. He'd promised to never let her go, but he hadn't kept his word. His life had been full of attempts to make his father proud, yet he was once again screwing up.

Admittedly, his integrity was questionable. He had no business becoming a naval officer. "No excuse, sir."

"Do you believe you have honor, Mr. Scott?" Sour challenged.

Leo knew he was forever tainted. "No, sir."

The five midshipmen conferred for a few minutes while Leo maintained his stance of attention. He felt adrift, lost at sea.

The sound of Sour's voice broke through his trance. "Midshipman Scott, you're hereby separated from the Navy." He pointed to some documents. "Approach the table and sign these papers."

Leo signed several times, feeling increasingly repulsed each time he scribbled his poisoned last name. He was ruined.

"Midshipman Sour, take this PFC to his quarters to collect his belongings, then escort him off the Yard," said one of the committee members.

Sour nodded. "Let's go."

Leo marched to his room with Whiskey. He could barely feel his legs as they made their way through the labyrinth of Mother B.

Benito was absent, probably at swim practice. Sour looked on as Leo kneeled to pull a duffel bag from under his rack.

"Why'd the firstie call me a PFC, sir?" Leo asked as he stuffed in shoes and clothes.

Whiskey's voice was cold. "Private Effing Civilian."

Leo nodded with a half-smile. All the stupid acronyms and jokes of the Navy were now a thing of the past.

"Why are you doing this, Leo?" Sour asked.

He paused his packing, unable to look his squad leader in the eye. "I'm sorry for letting you down, sir. I didn't mean to. I, uh, I just don't belong here, I guess."

Leo stood and pulled Audrey's framed picture from his desk drawer, then gingerly set it inside his bag. He tossed in his father's diploma as well. His skin tingled. "Sir, may this PFC have privacy while he changes into civilian clothes?"

"Of course." Sour backed out of the room.

Leo stole a glance at Benito's rack, hesitating. Then he took a deep breath and reached under. His hand trembled as it grasped cold metal. Closing his eyes, Leo whispered, "I'm sorry, *hombre*," before placing the gleaming weapon and bullet cartridge in his bag.

Leo ripped off his uniform, still damp with sweat, and quickly changed into jeans and a T-shirt. The civilian clothing felt bizarrely loose. He looked around the room and felt sick as he surveyed the vestiges of his once-promising naval career.

He opened the door to find Whiskey waiting for him in the passageway. "Will you say goodbye to Midshipman Dulce for me, sir?"

"Will do. Where to, Leo?"

He'd considered calling Jason, but he couldn't risk his brother knowing his plan. According to Dr. Ina, he wasn't a good liar. "Sir, would you drive me to the airport?"

"Absolutely."

They marched down the passageway, side by side, while Leo memorized the sights and smells of the dorm he'd never see again. He steeled himself for the confrontation looming ahead. This time he would stand for that which is right.

69. Storm Warning

Leo held his breath as he handed over his duffel bag at the ticket counter.

He would never have attempted to get a weapon through security if not for an article he'd read and memorized at the Academy. The *Baltimore Sun* had reported on an assortment of recent undercover attempts to get weapons and explosive devices through airport x-ray machines, and they'd had an alarmingly high success rate.

After flashing a nervous smile at the agent taking his bag, Leo turned and headed to his gate. It was surreal to walk through the airport in civilian clothing once again, like he was taking a vacation from himself.

Swirling panic and dread consumed him, but he was on autopilot, resolutely determined to set things right. Maybe he had PTSD — feelings of distress and numbness sounded like something Dr. Ina would describe. She had taught him so much. And then he'd betrayed her. He wondered if guilt was another symptom.

He could hardly fathom what he was doing. For the first eighteen years of his life, the thought of breaking rules had terrified him. But Leo's world view had changed completely since he read Dr. Ina's notes.

When he entered the line for security, he noticed the bright smiles of a family ahead of him and heard them discussing their trip to Disney World. That's why people were *supposed* to go to Florida.

Leo wondered if the strangers around him could sense his criminal intent. He wasn't frolicking toward a vacation like they were. He was on a mission to make things right.

Ina exhaled when Leo's squad leader answered his cell phone. "Midshipman Sour."

"This is Lt. Commander Dr. Hansen, Midshipman Sour."

"Yes, ma'am?"

"Please tell me you still have Leo Scott with you." She held her breath.

"Um, no ma'am. I dropped him off at the airport a half hour ago."

"I need to talk to him!" She realized she'd just shouted and lowered her voice. "Why'd you kick him out of here so quickly?"

"I'm sorry, ma'am. I didn't know you needed to talk to him. After he signed his separation papers, they told me to escort him off the Yard."

"I didn't know he'd be gone so soon! I need to keep questioning him." She sighed. "Do you know where he was flying?"

"No, ma'am."

"Tom, how'd Leo seem to you after the hearing?"

"He was quiet, ma'am. He, uh, asked me to say goodbye to his roommate. He didn't say much in the car. He seemed kind of lost in thought, you know?"

"How was his mood?"

"His mood, ma'am?"

"Did he seem depressed? Down in the dumps?"

"Kind of, I guess. I mean, who wouldn't be? Ms. Nevington told me he begged her and the lieutenant to let him stay here before, and then he gets himself kicked out. It must've been pretty devastating for him, ma'am."

Ina clutched the phone. "Thank you, Tom. I need to think some things through, and I may contact you or Viva with some more questions later."

"Yes, ma'am."

Ina hung up. A good predictor of suicide was a prior attempt... Should she breach confidentiality and call Leo's mother without his permission?

Where was he headed? Home to Florida? How could they have let him leave before she had the chance to find out whose chart he'd read? What a freaking mess.

She sat back in her chair and rubbed her temples, feeling the pulse of a throbbing headache. Leo Scott sure had a way of complicating her life.

Mary heard the front door slam. "Mom?"

"In here, Jase!" she called. She looked up to realize how dark it had gotten—ominous clouds had gathered while she cleaned.

"Mom, what're you doing?" Jason scolded as he entered to find her wiping down the kitchen cabinets, perched on her canes. "You're going to fall!"

"I just wanted everything to be sparkling clean, before, before..." Her voice faded.

"Before what?"

"Before your father comes home."

"So, tonight or tomorrow the child abuser returns," Jason seethed. "Can't wait. Why kill yourself to clean the house just for his benefit? Don't do it, Mom."

"I want him to be in a good frame of mind. He'll be happy I've moved back home, but I'm worried what'll happen when I show him the divorce papers."

"You shouldn't be alone when you give him those. Let me be here."

"We've been over this, Jase. He'll feel less threatened if it's just me, and he's never hit *me* before. I don't think he'll start now."

Grunting, Jason swiped her dishrag and took over.

She watched her older son work. The muscles in his forearms reminded her of his father. Mary had agonized over the future of her marriage for the three months since James's deployment. But she couldn't deny the relief she'd felt in his absence, and her sons had also flourished. She knew her decision was the right one, no matter how painful.

Jason rinsed the dishrag and resumed wiping the cabinets. "There's a reason I came over. I want to tell you something. Leo broke up with Audrey."

"*What?*"

"I had the same reaction. Apparently Audrey called Cam, totally bawling her eyes out. She said Leo told her he didn't love her anymore and just hung up. What a tool."

"Are you sure? That's awful! Poor Audrey. I can only imagine what she's going through." Mary felt tears in her eyes. "I wish we could talk to Leo—find out what he's thinking."

"*I* wish we could tell him to get his head out of his butt. He better have a damn good reason."

The phone rang and Mary made her way over to answer it. "Hello?"

"Mrs. Scott?"

"Yes."

"This is Captain Sean Tracker, Commandant of Midshipmen, ma'am."

Mary's heart skipped a beat. "Yes, sir? Is Leo all right?"

"So you don't know."

"Know what, Captain?"

"Your son was dismissed from the Academy today, ma'am."

She was so stunned she barely heard his next words.

"You should've been called about this earlier, but somehow we had a communication breakdown because we were rushing Leo's Honor Committee hearing. I was about to leave for the day when Dr. Hansen asked me to call you."

"Dr. Hansen?" Mary blinked.

"Yes, ma'am, Leo was meeting with a psychologist, and she's concerned for his safety. She's right here with me. Dr. Hansen would like to speak with you, if that's all right."

"Yes, sir."

Jason had stopped cleaning and now stared at her.

"Mrs. Scott? This is Lt. Commander Dr. Ina Hansen. I'm sorry we didn't get the chance to talk before now, but I didn't have Leo's permission." Dr. Hansen paused. "I still don't, but I'm sufficiently concerned about your son that I'm breaking confidentiality to tell you this. Are you aware of any of the events of last evening?"

"No, doctor."

"Leo's been meeting with me since July for anger management issues. I'm very impressed with him. You have yourself a fine son, Mrs. Scott. My regard for Leo made what happened last night all the more shocking. He broke into my office and read my confidential files."

When Mary inhaled, Jason took a step closer.

"He wouldn't tell me whose chart he read, despite a full day of interrogation. I need to know, Mrs. Scott. But more importantly, I'm worried Leo's at risk for suicide right now. I know the Navy means a lot to him, and he may act rashly after being separated."

Mary tried to process this bewildering news. "What makes you think he's suicidal?"

"Well, his squad leader reported his mood was depressed on the way to the airport—"

"He went to the airport?"

"Yes, ma'am. And he broke up with his girlfriend, which makes me worried he's saying his goodbyes."

"Leo's brother just told me about the break-up. I can't believe it."

"And Leo has *contemplated* suicide before, even if he hasn't attempted it."

"*What?*" Mary held her breath.

"I'm sorry. I thought this might surprise you. Leo doesn't share information easily, does he? After his father beat him for his drug addiction, he took your pills out in the woods and considered taking all of them, but he stopped himself."

Mary could hardly stand. "Leo was doing so well at the Academy! How did things go wrong?"

"I don't know, Mrs. Scott. I'm just as confused as you are."

"Does this...does this have anything to do with Lt. Keaton?"

The phone line went completely silent. "What makes you ask that, Mrs. Scott?" Dr. Hansen asked after a beat.

"Darnell served under my husband in Pensacola," Mary explained. "It seemed like quite a coincidence when she became Leo's company officer, and I know Leo didn't like her at all."

Silence again. "Well, we're pursuing all leads at the moment. I just believed it my duty to report what's going on with Leo. I'm worried about what he might do. Let me give you my number so we can stay in touch."

Mary hung up the phone a few moments later and turned to Jason. This time she was the one to say, "Leo's in trouble." A wave of nausea passed through her. "We need to get to the airport. *Now.*"

Darnell entered her office and collapsed in a chair.

She'd slept maybe four hours the previous night, and the class of plebes she'd just finished teaching was as rambunctious as ever. Though it was only her second year at the Academy, she had already noticed a pattern of increasing energy in the plebes as they approached their first visit home for Thanksgiving. Darnell wished she could have some of their enthusiasm instead of feeling irritable and edgy all the time.

Her phone rang, and she cursed at the name of the caller. "Yes, ma'am?"

"Lt. Keaton, how are you this evening?" Dr. Hansen's cheerfulness sounded forced.

"Fine. I just finished teaching, ma'am."

"Yes. I'm sure it's been a long day, but I need to ask you to come to my office to discuss a few things."

"It *has* been a long day, ma'am. Could we just speak over the phone?"

"I'm afraid these are rather delicate matters. I'd like to meet in person."

Knowing the request could easily turn into an order, Darnell sighed. "Yes, ma'am. I'll come right over."

"Perfect. I'll meet you at the door to Counseling Services. Thank you, Darnell."

"Yes, ma'am."

Curiosity lifted her veil of fatigue, and fury began to gather as Darnell pulled herself back out of the chair and headed to Ina's office. If Ina had decided to disclose her affair to the commandant, everything would be ruined. She'd come to the Academy to *escape* fallout, not reopen old wounds.

A few minutes later, she could see Dr. Hansen waiting outside her office. *What is so freaking urgent?*

"Thanks for meeting with me, Darnell." Dr. Hansen gave her a warm smile and held open the door.

Darnell opted not to salute as a little sign of protest, but Hansen didn't even seem to notice, just turned down the hall to her office. Something had her completely preoccupied.

"Yes, ma'am," Darnell said. "I hope this won't take too long."

"Probably not."

Dr. Hansen's eyes darted around the office as they both sat. Darnell waited, hardly able to breathe.

"Darnell…In my discussions with Midshipman Scott, I learned his father's a commander in Pensacola."

Darnell felt physical pain at the sound of that man's name. She steeled herself for what was to come.

"Do you, uh, know Commander Scott by chance?"

Icy panic froze her in place. "Y-Y-Yes ma'am, he was my CO," she managed, feeling the room slip away.

"So Commander Scott was the one who discovered your affair?" Dr. Hansen added.

The room blurred completely as Darnell burst into tears.

70. Tropical Depression

Leo exhaled slowly when he saw his duffel bag emerge from the bowels of Pensacola Airport and begin its journey along the conveyer belt.

As it passed him, he yanked it up and kneeled to search it in one motion. He kept his eyes glued on his surroundings, scanning for any trouble.

When his hand brushed the metal of the gun, a bolt of hot fear jolted his heart. Punctuating his physical reaction was a clap of thunder followed by the steady rush of raindrops pounding the pavement outside. His plane had landed just before the thunderstorm arrived.

As he exited to passenger pick-up, Leo felt the familiar humidity envelop him. He was home. He flagged a taxi and quickly tucked his body inside, trying to avoid the rain. He gave the driver a familiar address and centered himself during the ride across town.

Soaking wet as he approached his house, Leo cursed his decision to have the taxi driver drop him off a block away.

A flash of lightning illuminated the night sky, and Leo froze on his neighbor's lawn, worried he'd be spotted. But there was only the sound of sheeting rain and the sight of his darkened house looming before him. He was so relieved his mother wasn't home.

Circling around to the back door, he dug in his bag and came up victorious with his house keys. After he slipped inside the laundry room, Leo toed the heel of one shoe and stepped out, setting his shoes to the side of the door and out of sight.

He glided down the hallway to his father's office. As he stepped from the hard tiled foyer to the soft carpet of the study, he willed himself forward into the corner behind an easy chair. Glancing around him in the dark, Leo decided this was the best hiding spot he could come up with and sank to the floor.

His muscles ached from the hellish interrogation. Rainwater dripped from his shorn hair, and he shivered. He quickly undressed, swapping his soaked clothes for a black T-shirt and jeans. He then extracted the handgun from the duffel, followed by the cartridge, which he jammed in place with a satisfying click. He had to remind himself to breathe. The dry clothing warmed him, yet he continued to shiver.

He'd camp out here until his father arrived. He grew increasingly uneasy as he realized he no idea how the confrontation would go down. Despite his best plans, there was no way to anticipate the wily Cobra Snake. Equally uncertain were his own future actions. Could he pull the trigger if he needed to?

Taking a deep breath, like Ina had taught him, Leo tried to find thoughts that would help him focus. Immediately he pictured Audrey, her brown eyes inches from his as she gently kissed his bruises, her soft lips soothing the cut on his forehead, the feel of her body when they'd made love…

"*Te amo*, Audrey," he whispered. "*Te amo. Te amo.*" Leo tried to bite back tears.

"Commander Scott called Bill and me into his office," Darnell said after her tears had subsided. Her voice was weary. "I was terrified something was up, but Bill told me to calm down…that it was probably just a routine assignment or something."

Darnell exhaled and wove her fingers together in her lap. "I just don't think I can talk about Bill, ma'am. It—it hurts too much."

"What's painful about discussing Bill?" Ina asked, doing her best to tread lightly.

"He's dead," Darnell answered.

"Dead?"

"Bill was murdered, ma'am." Darnell's tears began anew.

Ina paused for a moment, pushing puzzle pieces around in her head. "Wait a minute...Bill had a daughter. Is her name Cameron?"

Darnell nodded, but did not look up.

"And the man in military prison for the murder—is his daughter's name Audrey?"

Now Darnell met her eyes. "I think so. How'd you know that?"

"Leo Scott was dating Audrey. And his brother's engaged to Cameron."

Darnell stared at her. "What?"

"Darnell, were you ever a suspect in the murder?"

"No. Nobody knew about our affair except the commander."

Ina tilted her head. "Why did the commander keep your secret?"

Darnell broke away to stare off into space.

Ina had lost her again.

With each rumble of thunder and tick of his father's clock, Leo felt sicker. Then his stomach lurched at the sound of a car in the driveway. He tried to compose himself, but tensed all over again when he heard a key slide into the front doorknob.

"Mary?" his father called into the darkness, then flipped on the hallway light.

From his hiding spot, Leo watched him shake the water off his jacket. CS turned toward him and came into the study. When he stooped to turn on the desk lamp, Leo rose in the corner.

"Jesus!" His father inhaled sharply as he straightened. "You scared me!"

Leo said nothing, his hands behind his back.

"What're you doing here?" CS asked. "You should be in Annapolis."

"I got kicked out," Leo said flatly. "I was separated from the Navy."

CS took one menacing step forward before Leo stepped closer as well, raising the gun and aiming it squarely at his father's chest.

His father stopped in his tracks.

"Sit down," Leo ordered, sounding more authoritative than he felt. The weapon in his hand seemed to do something to his voice.

But his father didn't move.

"It was you," Leo sneered. "It was you. *You* murdered Mr. Walsh."

CS's eyes threatened to leap from their sockets. This time he did sit, staggering backward and collapsing into his desk chair, never taking his eyes off his son.

Leo noticed his fear, and couldn't deny how good it felt. But he braced for the fight he was sure would be coming.

He almost dropped the gun when CS said, "Finally. I've been waiting for this moment for over a year."

Oh my God, he did it. Audrey's sweet face floated before Leo's eyes once again. "Mr. Rose's been rotting in prison for a crime *you* committed!"

CS seemed to deflate. "How'd you find out?"

Leo laughed bitterly. "You wanted me to go to the Academy so bad. Well, my company officer was Lt. Darnell Keaton."

CS flinched.

"Jase and Cameron found out about Lt. Keaton's affair with Cam's dad, and we started to suspect her for Mr. Walsh's murder. But then I discovered you knew about their affair, and I realized the lieutenant was terrified of you. She hated me because I was your son. What'd you do to her, Dad?"

"I found out about the affair," he said simply. "You have to understand, Leo…Your mother wasn't giving me what I needed! Any red-blooded man would've needed some comfort in that situation. And Darnell, well, Darnell refused me. She was in *love* with Bill," he spat.

Leo shook his head. His father actually seemed to think he could justify his actions. "What'd you do to the lieutenant?" he demanded.

"I called them both into my office," his father began. "And I—I confronted them about the affair. I dismissed Bill—it's never the man's fault in that situation. I mean, have you seen how beautiful Darnell is? Of course I couldn't resist her…"

"Focus on your breathing, Darnell," Ina said. "A little slower, a little deeper."

Darnell nodded. She cowered in her chair like a frightened child.

"Commander Scott knew about your affair, but he didn't tell anyone?"

Darnell's voice quivered. "It was the worst day of my life. I worked so hard to become a lieutenant, and the commander threatened to tear it all down. He'd seen us kissing, apparently, and told us both our careers would be ruined. He was so hateful. He was angriest with me. He told me I was wrecking Bill's marriage...I was a whore..." She shuddered. "Those eyes...He—he dismissed Bill from his office. I didn't want him to go. I was so scared to be alone with the commander." She looked up, eyes wild.

"You're doing fine, Darnell."

"T-T-The commander told me our fate was up to me. If I'd try, try—" She closed her eyes for a moment. "If I'd try to *satisfy* him, to *please* him, maybe he'd ignore the affair. Maybe he wouldn't court martial us both." Darnell covered her mouth with a trembling hand.

Her rocking motion reminded Ina of Leo as he'd described how his father beat him. The commander had cut a wide swath of destruction.

"I didn't know what to do," Darnell cried. "I didn't want to destroy Bill's career. It was all my fault we were in this mess. So—so I let him." She clenched her teeth. "I let the commander take me. Right there in his office." Her breathing was ragged and shallow. Tears spilled down her cheeks. "I just laid there. I didn't say no."

Ina struggled to mask her disgust. "The commander raped you."

"No." Darnell shook her head. "I didn't fight him. I didn't say no."

"You did *not* consent, Darnell! He blackmailed you into having sex with him! What else were you to do?"

Darnell stopped her rocking for a moment and slowly raised her eyes. "I'm dirty," she muttered. "I'm a whore. It's a good thing Bill died, because I don't deserve him."

"She wanted it all along," CS said. "Darnell had refused me for years, but this situation finally gave her the opportunity. I knew she always wanted me."

Leo's stomach churned. "You raped her."

"That's what Bill said!" his father thundered. "I did no such thing! We—we made a deal, that's all. An even exchange: she'd submit to me, and I wouldn't prosecute them."

"But Mr. Walsh found out?" Leo asked.

CS swallowed. "The July fourth barbecue. It was so hot that night." He paused and looked straight ahead.

It seemed to Leo like his father had gone somewhere else.

"It'd been a week since I chewed them out for the affair, and when Bill and I started laughing about how drunk Denny was, it seemed to break the ice. I'm not sure why Denny got so hammered—maybe it was the pressure of the promotion he and Bill were gunning for. But JoAnne was sure ticked off at him."

CS sighed. "We were watching JoAnne and Patti try to wrestle a drink away from Denny when I put my foot in my mouth. I told Bill his wife was good looking, but nothing like Darnell—guy talk, you know. I was trying to pay him a compliment for bedding a girl like that."

Leo shuddered.

"That's when Bill looked at me like he'd figured something out. He accused me of rape. I told him he was crazy, and I explained how Darnell *agreed* to it, to save him. But he wouldn't back down. He said the captain would court martial me when he found out! Can you believe that? Then he grabbed Patti and hightailed it out of there before I had a chance to explain any further."

CS shook his head. "A little while later JoAnne asked me to help get Denny home. I knew I had to prevent Bill from destroying me, from destroying our family. I had to make things right."

"Darnell, did you murder Bill?"

Darnell blanched. "No! I loved him! Denny Rose murdered Bill."

"Why?" Ina asked. "What was his motive?"

"Denny and Bill were competing for a promotion. I was too horrified to attend the court martial, but I read in the papers that Denny was an alcoholic who'd hit his ex-wife, and that night, the night Bill died, well, Denny got blitzed. He claimed he couldn't remember what happened." Her mouth curled in a sneer. "Some excuse."

Ina's phone rang, and she ignored it. "How long was it between Commander Scott calling you into his office and the murder?"

"One week." She looked down. "I wouldn't talk to Bill. I couldn't after what happened to me. I guess I blamed him." Darnell began to cry again.

This is a traumatized, grieving woman, Ina thought. *Not a murderer covering her tracks.*

Darnell sniffed. "The last time I saw Bill I was so mean, so cold. He died before I could say I was sorry. He died before I could say goodbye."

The office phone rang again, and again Ina didn't answer. "Darnell, do you think the murder could have something to do with Commander Scott learning about your affair?"

She wiped her cheeks and shook her head. "Denny was convicted. He's guilty. Nobody thinks that."

"Leo Scott thinks that."

Darnell froze, her face flushing deep red.

"Last night Leo broke into my office," Ina explained. "I caught him after he'd read one or more of my charts. I think he was after yours, Lieutenant."

Darnell opened her mouth, but nothing came out.

"Leo told me he and Bill's daughter didn't believe Denny was guilty. I think Leo believed *you* might be the murderer. I think he had to read your chart to find out."

Darnell finally found her voice. "How the hell did he break in here? He read my *chart?*"

"He came in when the cleaning crew had the door unlocked, and somehow he found my desk key. I obviously wasn't careful enough with my records." Ina felt her face grow hot. "I'm so sorry. If you must take legal action against me, I can refer you to another psychologist. But I think you need to work through the aftermath of this sexual assault, Darnell."

This time when the irritating noise of the phone interrupted them, Ina picked up the receiver in a huff. "Yes?"

"This is Midshipman Sour, ma'am."

"What is it, Tom?"

"I'm sorry to bother you, ma'am, but I thought you'd want to hear this. Midshipman Dulce, uh, Leo's roommate, just confessed that he kept a gun in their room, and now it's missing."

"He had a gun?"

"Yes, ma'am. And he thinks Leo took it."

Ina froze. Leo Scott wasn't only a suicide risk. He was a homicide risk too.

Leo felt completely overwhelmed as his father continued spilling his story. It was as if he watched the scene from outside his body. He'd lowered the gun an inch, but still held it aimed at CS, who wouldn't stop unfurling this horrific tale.

"I helped Denny inside his house," CS said. "It was too tough to get him upstairs, so I tossed him on the sofa. He passed out pretty quick. JoAnne was totally embarrassed. She kept thanking me for helping them."

CS stared off into space. "I was terrified of losing my freedom, losing my family, if Bill said anything." He locked his eyes on Leo. "I did this for *you*, Leo! What kind of future would you have if your father was accused of rape?"

Leo looked away. *What kind of future do I have if my father is a murderer?*

"I came back here and waited," CS said. "You took Audrey home and went to bed. After about an hour, I drove to Bill's house. I don't know what I was thinking…I was going to talk to him, try to convince him not to tell anyone. I found him out back, sitting by himself having another drink.

"When I got closer, I couldn't believe it. Bill was crying! And right then I knew I'd never convince him to keep his mouth shut. That little bitch would try to save Darnell. He'd try to help her even if it destroyed his career. Well, I couldn't let him destroy mine."

Leo tightened his grip on the weapon, his stomach in knots. Here it came.

"Bill was drunk, and it was easier than I thought. I gripped his neck, and I…"

His father's voice faded, but after a few moments he said, "I strangled him."

Leo felt as if he were encased in lead, too heavy to move. Almost too heavy to think.

"Afterward I panicked." CS continued his relentless confession. "All I could think about was Denny lying on his sofa, passed out, and that Denny and Bill were vying for the same promotion. Heck, I taunted them about it every day, trying to shove a stick up their butts to motivate them. It was just too easy."

"How'd you get Audrey's dad to the woods behind the Walshes'?"

CS sighed. "I went to Denny's. The door was unlocked. I told him he needed to come with me, that he'd better follow my orders, and he did. He was still drunk. I got him into my car somehow and dragged him into the woods. It was hard, but we made it. I left him there and came home. I burned the gloves I wore and went to bed."

Finally. The horrific story was over. Leo repositioned the gun. "You're calling the cops to tell them exactly what you just told me."

His father smiled sadly. "No, Leo. I'm not doing that." He rose from his chair. "I spent too many years in juvie, in youth homes. I'm *not* going back to lockup."

Leo's heart thumped a terrified beat. *Te amo, Audrey.*

71. Eye of the Hurricane

Leo stood riveted by those stormy hazel eyes and was dismayed to feel the gun in his hand tremble. Leo hoped CS wouldn't notice.

"You think you can make me turn myself in," his father scoffed.

His deep, smooth voice sent chills through Leo.

"And what's your plan if I refuse?"

Leo's mouth felt dry. "If you won't turn yourself in, I'll be forced to shoot you."

"You'll never get away with it," CS said with a laugh. "Someone always finds out."

"*You're* the one always preaching responsibility!" Leo shouted. "I won't *lie* about what I've done. I won't hide. I'll spend the rest of my life in prison." His voice trembled. "My life's over, anyway."

Tightening his grip on the weapon, Leo's arm miraculously stopped shaking. "The way I see it, a Scott man belongs in prison. If you refuse to go, I will."

The smug look melted off his father's face. "Why are you doing this alone, Leo? Why didn't you tell your mother or Jason when you figured out what I'd done?"

"I wanted to, sir. But I'm trying to spare Mom and Jase. They still have a chance to be happy. If Mom knows you're a murderer, she'll feel even worse for not protecting us from you. She'll never recover from the guilt. If Cam finds out you murdered her dad, I can't see her staying with Jase, and he'll be crushed. I've already let Audrey go to save her from that."

"You broke up with Audrey?"

Leo nodded miserably.

His father looked confused. "If you kill me, how will you prevent anyone from discovering what I've done?"

"I'll make a deal with the prosecutor: a full confession only if they let Mr. Rose go free without naming Mr. Walsh's real murderer."

"You'd go to prison for the rest of your life?" He looked baffled. "You're sacrificing yourself…for me?"

For his mother, for Jason, for Cameron, even for Lt. Keaton, but Leo simply said, "Not for you. For Audrey."

"Why?"

"Because I love her."

"In my whole life, nobody's ever sacrificed himself for me," CS said, his voice trembling with tears. Leo watched him withdraw into himself, into his narcissistic wounds. Sensing an ache in his arm, he gave the gun a definitive shake. He dreaded what his father would do next.

CS took a deep breath, seeming to come to a decision. He stepped forward. "Give me the gun, Leo."

"No." When he took another step, Leo warned, "Don't come closer or I'll shoot."

CS inched forward. "Give me the gun."

Leo's breaths came in short rasps. "No, sir."

His father was coming for him, and now was the time to pull the trigger — now or never. CS would go Scott-free once again. He'd lie, manipulate, and threaten his way out of this unless Leo acted now.

Shoot him! he screamed inside his head. His father was almost on him now, and his finger tensed on the trigger, trapped in fear and indecision. Suddenly his father was right in front of him, and his hands enveloped his and slid the weapon away.

"You and I both know you'd never pull the trigger," CS said matter-of-factly. "You're not like me. You're not a killer."

Leo stood, panicked now that he'd been stripped of his one source of power. He braced himself for a beating.

But his father didn't hit him. He looked down at the gun, slowly running his fingers over the barrel, appearing deep in thought.

Leo's shoulders tensed. Would his father kill him or kill himself?

"You're not like me," CS repeated softly. "You have integrity... You do what's right. You're strong." His father stared at the gun. "I'm worthless," he whispered. "I don't deserve a son like you." He looked up and pleaded, "What do I do?"

Leo blinked rapidly, willing himself to speak. "It's all right, Dad. You—you turn yourself in. You can do it. You do it for your family, to set things straight."

His father returned to his desk chair and crumpled, holding the gun in his lap. Leo listened to the ticking clock and his stream of racing thoughts.

When his father shot his arm out toward his desk, Leo flinched. But CS just set the gun down. After a few moments, he picked up the phone.

Leo held his breath.

"Connect me with the police," he said.

During the ensuing wait, he looked up at Leo. Without unlocking his gaze, he told the police, "This is Commander James Scott at eleven thirty-seven Ridgeway. I want to turn myself in for the murder of Bill Walsh. Please send officers to my home."

Leo was bombarded with relief as CS hung up. The wave of emotion brought stinging tears as he stumbled backward into a chair.

"I wish my parents were here," his father said. "I'd be a different man if they'd survived that car crash. I miss my father, Leo."

"I miss my father too," Leo rasped, then forged ahead. The words tumbled out as his voice hitched with tears. "I wanted you to do the right thing for once. You always told me to do the right thing, but *you* never did—you never thought about anyone but yourself. You beat me when I needed a hug. You criticized me when I needed praise. I just wanted you to be proud of me. It was stupid...a stupid little-boy wish that will never come true."

"I've never been prouder of you," CS said in a voice Leo had never heard before. "I'm so proud to be your father…I'm sorry you can't be proud of me," he choked out before walling himself in with silence.

They gazed at each other through tears, waiting for the police to arrive.

A few minutes later Leo started when he heard the front door swing open. He'd heard no police sirens. But instead of men in uniform, Jason rushed in.

"Leo!" he shouted, looking relieved then desperate when he saw CS and the gun on the desk. "What's going on? We looked for you at the airport! You got kicked out of the Academy?" Jason's words came out in a breathless jumble, and he couldn't seem to decide where to focus his attention. "You're back from the Gulf?" he asked his father.

Mary appeared behind Jason at the tail end of his questions. Leaning on her canes, she narrowed her eyes at CS. "What's happening, James?"

His father looked straight at him. "Leo discovered something about me at the Academy." He paused. "I murdered Bill Walsh."

Leo nodded, watching his mother and brother recoil. He felt incredibly sad for his family. They'd never live this down. They'd never recover. But maybe the Roses and even the Walshes now had a fighting chance.

Jason shook his head. "No, it was Darnell Keaton!"

"What?" Mary asked.

"It was *not* Lt. Keaton," Leo said. "I broke in to my psychologist's office and read her chart. Then I just knew it was Dad."

"How?" Jason asked.

Leo turned to look at his father. "I guess part of me has always known. You acted so weird whenever I mentioned the Roses. And you treated Mr. Rose so nice in prison—that wasn't like you. You seemed sad and kind of guilty all the time, like you'd given up."

Leo turned to his mom. "Lt. Keaton hated me, Mom. She hated me because of my last name. Then I found out Dad had blackmailed her."

"What do you mean, blackmailed her?"

Leo looked at his father. "Dad forced the lieutenant, um, to have sex with him when he discovered she was having an affair with Mr. Walsh."

His mother covered her mouth.

"And then Mr. Walsh found out and threatened to tell Captain Payson. To stop him from talking, Dad killed him." Leo took a deep breath, struggling to get his last words out. "Then he framed Audrey's dad."

His mother leaned back against the wall as she sobbed, while Jason stood frozen.

"You destroyed us, James!" she shrieked. In a burst of fury she threw herself forward.

His father rose from his chair when he saw her coming. She pummeled his chest with her fists. He just took it, trying to steady her so she wouldn't fall.

"You murdered a man! You let Denny rot in prison!" she screamed through her sobs. "You cheated on me again! You're a predator! You ruined my life!"

Pain distorted his father's face.

Leo glanced at Jason, but his overwhelmed brother was useless. "He cheated on you *again?*" he asked.

His mother halted her assault.

"What do you mean *again*, Mom?"

She covered her face with her hands.

"Your mother's car accident," CS said. "It happened because she was very upset." He bit his lip. "She crashed her car after she found me with another woman."

Leo hadn't thought he couldn't hate CS any more. But hearing those words, knowing his father was to blame for his mother's disability, made him change his mind.

That confession seemed to knock Jason into action. He flew to their mother, replacing one cane in her hand and steadying her so she could walk out of the study. He never looked at CS.

"I'm sorry, Mom," he said when they reached the doorway. "I'm so sorry."

Finally the wail of police sirens began to compete with his mother's despair. Jason let go of her to answer the pounding on the door.

"Hello, Jason," said a familiar voice. "I heard the call on the radio and thought 'I *know* this family. Sounds like another Scott needs to turn himself in.'"

"Thanks for coming, Detective Easton." Jason opened the door wider, and the detective stepped in, followed by two uniformed officers.

Leo now stood next to his mother, and the detective nodded at them before scanning the area around CS. "Whose weapon is that?"

"It's mine, ma'am," Leo said. "I mean, it's my roommate's, but I was the one who brought it here."

She raised her eyebrows. "Is it loaded?"

"Yes, ma'am."

She slid on rubber gloves and placed the gun in an evidence bag she extracted from her pocket. Handing it to one of the officers, she asked, "Is anyone hurt here?"

The Scotts shook their heads.

"Seems this family's making a little progress, then."

She turned to CS, who peeled himself off the wall and stood at attention. "Commander Scott, I understand you want to turn yourself in for the murder of William Walsh. Is that correct, sir?"

"Yes, ma'am."

"Very well. I need to arrest you and take you in for questioning now. Do you have any weapons on you, sir?"

"No, ma'am."

Leo watched as the detective frisked him, secured him in handcuffs, and read him his Miranda rights. CS hung his head as she led him out of the study and handed him over to the officers.

Apparently the detective wasn't done yet. She returned to the study and sat on the edge of the desk, folding her arms across her chest. "Sit down, Mr. Scott."

Jason and Leo both looked at her expectantly.

"Leo, have a seat."

"Yes, ma'am."

She extracted a notepad. "Who does this gun belong to?"

"My roommate at the Naval Academy."

"I need a name."

"Benito Dulce." Leo spelled the name at her request. "He won't get in trouble for this, will he?"

The detective cocked one eyebrow. "Is Mr. Dulce aware that you have the gun?"

Leo shook his head.

"You took it without his permission?"

"Yes, ma'am."

"When?"

"This afternoon, ma'am." Leo sniffed.

She tilted her head. "How'd you get the weapon here?"

"Shut up, Leo." Jason inched forward. "Don't answer that."

She shot Jason a warning glance. "Not another word from you."

"How'd you get the weapon here?" she asked again.

Leo hesitated. He hated lying. His father's lies had wreaked havoc on his entire family. "I'd rather not answer that, ma'am."

She put away her notebook and crossed her arms again. "Do you know what I have to do now, Leo?"

He looked down. "You need to arrest me, ma'am."

"No!" Jason and his mother shouted.

"Please, Detective, he–he didn't fire the gun. This isn't his fault!"

"Jason, he's in possession of a gun illegally. I have to arrest him. You and your mother can come down to the station if you want, but he's definitely under arrest."

The detective ordered Leo up, and he barely felt fazed as she frisked him. If things had gone differently tonight, Leo knew he could've been arrested for murder. Weapons charges seemed minor. But his heart did pound when she slapped the cool metal handcuffs onto his wrists. Watching an arrest on TV was quite different than experiencing it himself.

Two hours later, Leo sat in an interrogation room, his head resting on his arms as he leaned over the table. When the door opened, he lifted his head.

"Dr. Ina!"

"Hello, Leo." She took a seat next to him.

"What're *you* doing here, ma'am?"

"I found out about the gun, and I was worried sick. I kept calling your house, but nobody answered. I didn't know what to do, but for some reason…I thought you'd probably go home." She shook her head. "So I took a flight down here. Crazy, I know." She started to reach for him, but stopped. "I'm so relieved you're okay."

He grasped her hand as he felt his eyes fill with tears. "My father's a murderer."

Ina squeezed his hand. "I know, Leo. And you're not."

72. Hugging Goodbye, Hugging Hello

Leo looked down at his lap. Suddenly he was overwhelmingly tired. He wished he were in a bed instead of in an interrogation room. "So, Lt. Keaton knows I read her chart?"

"Yes, I had to tell her," Dr. Ina said.

"Was she mad?"

"What do *you* think, Leo?"

He sighed. "Is she, um, is she okay? I feel awful for her." He fidgeted in his chair. "For what happened to her."

"She's one tough woman. Without breaking confidentiality—there's been quite enough of that already—let's just say I think she'll be all right."

"Do you promise?"

"No, because it's not up to me. It's up to Lt. Keaton to heal, just like it's up to you. Now that the truth's out about your father, I think you both have a good shot."

Despite himself he grinned. "No pun intended?"

Ina stared for a moment and shook her head. "You're awful," she said. "The only one I know who could turn gun charges into a joke."

There was a loud rap on the door and the detective and his mother entered.

"Would you like me to leave?" Ina asked.

Detective Easton shrugged. "I need to talk to you about some things, Leo, and it's fine with me if your mother and psychologist are here, but it's up to you."

"I want them here," Leo said immediately.

"Very well, let's all have a seat then." Detective Easton sat next to Leo, and his mother joined Ina on the other side of the table.

"I've been interrogating your father, Leo, and I want to verify some of his statements with you." The detective pulled out her notepad. "How long had you suspected that your father murdered William Walsh?"

"About twenty-four hours, ma'am, since twenty-three forty-five last night."

"That's when you broke into Dr. Hansen's office and read the chart for..." She consulted her notes. "Lt. Darnell Keaton?"

"Yes, ma'am." Leo gave Ina an apologetic look.

"I'm curious. How'd you know Lt. Keaton was meeting with Dr. Hansen?" the detective asked.

He blew out a breath. "I saw Lt. Keaton in the waiting room when I was leaving my session yesterday, and then I watched Dr. Hansen take her back to her office."

"I didn't see you," Ina said.

"I was hiding, um, in the coat closet." Noticing his mother's disappointment, he looked down.

"So what was in Lt. Keaton's chart that led you to suspect your father?" Detective Easton continued.

"A lot of things, ma'am. She told Dr. Hansen her CO found out about her affair with Mr. Walsh, and I knew her CO was my dad," he said. "That blew me away. My dad isn't exactly the forgiving type, and I wondered what he did with that information. And then the lieutenant started dissociating, and I knew something bad had gone down."

"Dissociating?" she asked.

Ina gave Leo an encouraging nod.

"It's like you zone out when you're flooded by traumatic memories, like you're reliving them," Leo said. "It happens to me sometimes. But Dr. Hansen taught me to take some deep breaths, and it's not so bad."

His mother reached across the table for his hand, holding it in hers with a sad smile. "I know what memories must flood you," she said softly.

After a pause, the detective forged on. "What else led you to suspect your father?"

"Well, Lt. Keaton told Dr. Ina she felt awful for hitting me, so that made me doubt she was the murderer." Leo let go of his mother's hand. "But really, I think I kind of knew all along it could've been my dad. I finally just accepted it, I guess." He sighed. "It made me sick."

"So what'd you do after you found out he was the murderer?"

"I decided I had to confront him." He looked down. "I promised myself if he wouldn't confess I'd—I'd kill him."

His mother gasped, but the detective didn't seem fazed. "You see, this is the part I had trouble believing when your father told it," Detective Easton said. "This is the part where you were a *complete* idiot."

Leo's eyebrows shot up.

"I should throw you in jail right now for such stupidity. How would committing murder help anything? How would getting yourself locked up make things better?" She gestured across the table. "How'd you think your mother would handle her son serving a life sentence?"

"I thought it'd help my mom," Leo said, massaging his temples. "And my brother, ma'am."

"*How?*"

"If I'd had to kill my dad, well, I was going to try to make a deal so Mr. Rose went free but nobody would know my dad was the murderer. That way Mom wouldn't feel guilty, and Cam wouldn't leave Jase."

The detective's forehead wrinkled, but she said nothing.

"Hey!" his mother shouted.

Leo jumped in his chair.

"You are *not* responsible for me choosing to marry your father. He gave me two beautiful sons, and I wouldn't trade that for the world."

Leo's eyes widened.

"And you're not responsible for me failing to leave your father when I should have. That's on me, Leo. You can't stop me from feeling guilty, because you don't have any control over that. I'd feel *much* guiltier if you were behind bars." She shook her head. "And I agree with Detective Easton. You were an idiot."

"Couldn't have said it better myself," Ina added and sat back in her chair.

Leo dared look into his mother's flaring eyes. "I'm sorry, ma'am."

"Maybe you're not a *total* idiot," Detective Easton chimed in. "I really can't believe what you did, Leo. You single-handedly coerced a murderer into confessing a crime almost eighteen months after he committed it. And this is a man who beat you mercilessly. I don't know how you got the courage to do that."

Leo was silent for a moment. "Audrey gave me the courage. I had to save her dad." He wanted to cry. Everyone was mad at him, and he just wanted to hug Audrey—smell her special coconut-chlorine scent. But he couldn't. She was lost to him forever.

"Leo, you did it. You're giving Audrey her father back." Ina said. "Of course she'll be upset at what your father did, but she loves you, and I'm sure she'll be grateful for all you've done."

"It doesn't matter, anyway." He rubbed his buzzed hair and looked at the floor. "I'll be stuck in prison on weapons charges."

The detective cleared her throat. "Actually, the charges have been dropped."

Leo's head snapped up.

"When your father found out you'd been arrested, he said he'd stop cooperating with the interrogation until you were released. He said one son with a police record was enough."

"So Leo's free to go?" his mother asked.

Detective Easton nodded and rose, tucking her notepad back inside her suit jacket. "But I may have some more questions for you, Mr. Scott. Don't leave town for a while."

"Yes, ma'am." Leo stood as well, his exhaustion dissipating. "Um, Detective? You're still dating my coach, Matt, right?"

She looked wary. "Yes?"

"Can you give me any dirt?" He grinned. "Like, any stuff I can give him crap about?"

"Well, he's a swimmer, so he's very flexible. And you know what they say about the benefits of flexibility." She knocked the heel of her hand into her forehead. "I forgot who I'm talking to—*you're* dating a swimmer, Leo. You know *all* about that!"

His cheeks flushed, and his mother looked decidedly uncomfortable.

"I'll meet you outside, Leo," she said, following the detective out of the room.

"Yes, ma'am." Leo turned to Ina, who offered a melancholy smile.

"I'll miss you, Leo. You made the Academy an interesting place."

"Yes ma'am," he said shyly. "I'll miss you too."

"So you'll be okay, then?" Ina asked.

"If you think I have a chance with Audrey, I'll definitely be okay."

"I meant what I said. I think she'll come around."

He looked into her kind eyes. "Thank you for helping me, ma'am."

"You're welcome. It was my pleasure." They stood together for an awkward moment. Leo wondered if it would be okay to give her a hug. Ina finally turned to the door and winced.

"Are you all right?" Leo asked.

"Oh, the old ACL's acting up again. It's been a long day, and I can't believe I'm saying this, but I miss my crutches."

"May I?" He gestured for her to lean on his shoulder.

Ina paused before leaning in. He wrapped his arm around her for support as they made their way out of the interrogation room. He got to hug her after all.

Leo thrashed about in his bed, exhausted yet fighting sleep. Jason had driven to Tallahassee to pick up Audrey and bring her to Pensacola. Since arriving home from the police station, he'd showered, eaten, and been tucked into bed, despite his protests of wanting to stay up and wait.

"I'll send her to you as soon as she gets here," his mother had promised as she sat on the side of his bed. "But, Leo, you've been through hell, and you need to rest." She cradled his face and kissed him on the cheek. "I don't know what I'd do if I lost you."

Questions about his father, his mother's accident, and their family's future had swirled through his mind, but Leo put them aside. They'd start figuring it all out tomorrow. "I love you, Mom."

An hour later, his brain was working overtime, caught in the past as he awaited the future. Memories of Audrey flooded him—the first time he'd caught a glimpse of her skinny dipping, their easy banter from the start. Then all the swim practices, pasta dinners, and study sessions they'd shared, cautiously disclosing deeper hopes and fears, though still keeping their ugliest parts hidden. But after Audrey's father had gone to prison and CS had beaten Leo for his drug addiction, there was no holding back. Then they knew each other completely, their vulnerabilities raw and exposed.

Leo had risked so much to get his father to confess, and now he prayed he hadn't lost Audrey in the process.

The door creaked, drawing him out of his reverie. And there she was.

She stood on the threshold of the dark room, the hallway lights creating a sleek silhouette. Leo sat up in bed and held his breath. Shadows veiled her face, and he strained to read her expression. They were motionless until Leo heard himself whimper, "Audrey."

A choking sob escaped her as she rushed to him, leaping into his arms as they covered each other with desperate kisses.

He felt her hot tears on his cheek as she pressed against him. He was in the best physical shape, but perhaps the worst emotional shape, of his life. Yet united with her, he could face anything, heal from anything.

Eventually, Audrey spoke. "Don't you dare do that again, Leo! Don't you dare make me fall in love with you, make me want to sacrifice *everything* for you, make me miss you so much it hurts — it aches — then leave. You promised never to let me go! You promised!"

"I'm so sorry." He held her tight, rocking her body with his. "I thought you'd hate me for what my dad did."

She pulled away. "Don't you remember? In the hospital I asked how you could still love me, and you said you'd never judge people by their father's actions. Do you think that only applies to you? Your father's a coldhearted murderer — I can't *believe* what he did to my dad, to my family. I'll never forgive him. But, Leo, you're not him! You're not responsible for what he did! It's *not* your fault."

Leo looked down. CS had polluted him. How could she not blame him too?

"You broke up with me because you thought I wouldn't forgive you for what your dad did? Well, now we know that isn't the case. And you broke up with me because you thought you might have to kill him?"

He recoiled. "How'd you know that?"

"Your mom told me. She called Jason on our drive back." Audrey gazed into his eyes. "You were going to pull the trigger?"

He let out a ragged sigh. "I thought I could do it...but in the end, I couldn't. I couldn't kill him. Because then I'd be like him. I don't want to be like him, Audrey," he pleaded.

"You're *not* like him! You are sweet and kind and wonderful and giving. *Te amo,* Leo." She brushed her lips against his, and he responded with hungry desire.

She broke away. "Oh, I'm still so mad! Don't you know I could never be happy without you? I *need* you! When you broke up with me, I thought about drinking myself into oblivion but I remembered how awful it was when you were hooked on Oxy. I didn't want to do that to you, or to me. We both deserve better." Her voice rose even higher. "And then I find out you contemplated murder? That's the stupidest plan I've ever heard!"

He looked away and bit his lip. "Why don't you hit me? Let your anger out. It'll make you feel better." *It would certainly make me feel better.*

"I would *never* hit you! I love you! Hitting doesn't equal love, Leo. Violence doesn't make anything better. After everything your father's done to you, haven't you learned that?"

Leo exhaled loudly. *Crap.* "You're right. Violence doesn't equal love." He clenched his teeth. "And it's disgusting I have to say this, but I am my father's son..." He took a deep breath. "In case you're worried, I promise never to hit you, Audrey. I love you."

"I know." She looked into his eyes. "I feel safer with you than anyone." She clung to him. "I just spent a long car ride with Jason. He's out of his mind worrying Cameron won't forgive him for what your dad did. But, Leo, I want you to know I don't hold this against you." She began sobbing. "How could I not want to be with you? You gave me my father back. You saved him, Leo. I've missed him so much."

Leo stroked her silky hair and relief swept over him. He'd exchanged his father for hers, and he'd do it again in a heartbeat.

Leo still hated his dark parts—the self-doubts, the inability to hide his tears, the sudden fury swirling within him like a dam about to break. But Audrey had returned, and he hoped her love would keep teaching him the right way.

He squeezed her tighter and vowed never to let her go.

And he knew he meant it this time.

73. Justice

Jason glanced at the alarm clock, glowing red in the dim light of early morning.

5:57.

His gaze swept down the swell of Cam's breasts, easily visible through her thin nightgown. They pressed lightly against coral-colored silk. He'd never seen anyone sleep so peacefully. In contrast to his own thrashing and twisting, Cam was quiet and still.

5:58.

He sighed. After depositing Audrey at his parents' house — check that, his mom's house — Jason had driven to the apartment and crawled into bed with his fiancée. He was still wearing yesterday's clothes. He hadn't had the heart to wake Cam and tell her what had happened. All she knew was he'd been searching for Leo, and part of him wished he'd never found his brother.

5:59.

Jason's throat felt tighter every minute. God, he wished he could get a drink. Just one drink would make this nightmare fade away. Well, maybe more than one.

He shook his head, hating his addiction, which still wooed him, trying to get him to believe he didn't deserve a good, sober life. He was the son of a murderer — how the heck did he deserve happiness? How was he good enough for the beautiful, intelligent, compassionate woman at his side? *Please don't let me lose Cam because of him.*

Finally the digits flipped to 6:00, and a jarring beep resounded. Cam groaned and blindly reached to the nightstand, her groping hand somehow locating the snooze button.

Jason tried to find his voice. "Hey, no snoozing this morning."

"You're here." Cam's lips curled into a dreamy smile as she rolled over and snuggled up to him. "Is Leo okay?"

"Yeah."

"Did you find out why he broke up with Audrey?"

"They're back together actually, I think."

Cam opened her eyes and chuckled. "They sound like some of my students. 'I love you forever.' Then the next day, 'Let's break up.' Then five minutes later, 'You're the love of my life.'"

"Leo and Audrey were never like that. Their love's deeper than most adults I know." He paused. "He thought he was saving her by breaking up."

"Saving her?" Cameron scooted up to rest her back against the headboard. Mussed brown hair framed her face.

"Cam, I have to tell you something. I don't want to, but I have to."

She looked alarmed. "What is it?"

"Leo's in Pensacola right now. He got kicked out of the Academy for snooping around, trying to prove Darnell Keaton's guilt."

"Did he find out anything?" She blinked repeatedly.

"He found out Darnell didn't murder your dad."

She seemed to stop breathing.

Jason looked down, breaking her expectant gaze, and let go of her hand. "It was CS," he whispered, daring to look back up. "My dad. My dad killed your dad."

She looked away and pulled back from him. "Wha—? Your? How? No. How do you know?"

"Leo confronted him, and he confessed." Jason felt sick. He ran his hands through his hair.

Her chest heaved as she stared at him, and he somehow managed to spill the terrible story. When he finished, Cameron's face contorted in anguish, and she let out a horrible cry.

Watching tears cascade down her face, Jason reached for her. When she flinched at his touch and backed away, he felt his stomach drop.

"My dad didn't have to die!" she cried. "It's *your* dad's fault! He stole him from me!"

"I'm sorry, Cam. I'm so sorry!" Jason pleaded. Unable to stop himself, he reached out to her again, and once more she rebuffed him, scooting to the edge of the bed.

Cam looked down at her engagement ring. "Your dad bought me this." She slid it off and held it away like she was dangling a poisonous spider. "This came from a murderer."

"No," Jason begged. "That's yours. *I* bought it, Cam. It's for you."

"Take it," she demanded, shoving it into his hand. Her voice was icy. "Take it and get out of here."

"No, no. Don't do this."

He tried to give her back the ring, but she held her hands in front of her face.

"Leave!" she screamed, collapsing into sobs. "Just go."

He clenched his teeth, fighting his own tears. He pushed himself off the bed and stuffed his feet into his shoes, filled with rage at the unfairness of it all.

"This is total crap!"

Her eyes widened.

"You said no matter what happened, you'd fight for us! You promised! You're full of it!"

Jason spun on his heel and stomped out of the apartment, slamming the door and running full-steam down two flights of stairs before collapsing in the front seat of his car. He held his head in both hands, feeling hot, angry tears seep through his fingers. He shook with fury and despair.

He'd get the biggest bottle of vodka ever made and down the whole thing at once, damn it.

Audrey's heart pounded a panicked beat as her eyes flashed open. At first she had no idea where she was, but then saw the Michael Phelps poster on Leo's wall and felt his body wrapped around hers like a blanket. He radiated heat, and she felt moisture at the nape of her neck.

She'd just dreamed his father had shot him, but no, he was safe. She exhaled a slow, steady breath.

Extricating herself, she eased off the bed. She hadn't woken him. The scar on his forehead had faded to just a faint line, and there was no physical evidence of this latest altercation with his father. He looked so peaceful. Audrey hoped he might soon find some waking peace.

As she padded down the stairwell, she heard a dish clank in the kitchen. "Mrs. Scott, is it okay if I take a shower?"

Turning the corner, she gasped to find her mother holding a coffee mug. Her mother barely had time to set it down before Audrey leaped into her arms. She whimpered as she clung to her mother.

"I'm waiting to hear from Captain Payson, but your dad may get out as soon as this afternoon," her mother breathed into her hair.

Audrey couldn't even form words.

"And the answer to your question is yes," Mrs. Scott added. "You may take a shower. There're clean towels in the closet. I assume Leo's still sleeping?"

"Yeah."

"All right, get going then," her mother said. "The second I hear your father's being released, I want to be there."

"Okay!" Audrey scrambled up to the bathroom. As she took off her maroon FSU T-shirt, she reminded herself to call Coach Nancy to explain her absence.

Stepping into the shower, she was enveloped by steam. As the hot water flowed down her body, she felt the shame of her father's imprisonment wash away. Audrey closed her eyes and exhaled deeply.

A draft of cool air hit her chest, and she opened her eyes, flinching when she saw Leo peer around the shower curtain. Audrey crossed her arms over her breasts.

"*Caliente.* Do you need company?" His eyes danced.

"Both our moms are downstairs!"

"I locked the door."

Audrey grinned. "I think you actually *enjoy* the possibility of getting caught. It makes you all excited or something."

He peeled off his pajamas and joined her. "Trust me, just being with you is exciting enough."

Audrey giggled.

The pulsating water cascaded down her back. Facing him, she fit neatly against his tall, muscular body. She grabbed a bar of lavender soap and lathered Leo's long arms, stroking and sliding over his muscles. He worked shampoo through her long hair, and she moaned with pleasure.

"The real thing's *so* much better than phone sex," she murmured.

Moving her hands down his ribcage, her fingers paused at the dip between his torso and thigh. There was a curve, a dimple, in the muscular space nearing his backside, and Audrey's hands lingered there before they moved behind him to draw him closer.

"This may require some flexibility," he said with a suggestive wink. "Fortunately, swimmers are very flexible."

Leo's mouth moved south, planting wet kisses on Audrey's chest and abdomen. She shivered as his hungry lips joined the misty water flowing down her body, creating a stimulation she felt all the way down to her toes.

Happy sighs punctuated the gurgling sound of warm water swirling around their feet as she contorted her body, and he responded in turn. She surrendered to him, reveling in wet skin and soft strokes. In the absence of a pool, this was the closest she could get to swimming with Leo.

Jason heard the chain on the other side of the door slide open before he fell backward as the door gave way. He glanced up to see Marcus peering down at him, looking confused.

"Well, *you're* not my morning paper," Marcus said.

Jason snorted as he righted himself.

"How long have you been here?" Marcus asked.

Jason slumped. "Dunno, couple of hours?"

"Why didn't you knock, you numbskull?"

He continued staring at his feet. "'Cause I didn't know if I wanted you to stop me."

Marcus inhaled and wrestled the bag from his grasp, tearing it open to reveal a large bottle of vodka with its seal still intact. "Get in here," Marcus ordered, leaving Jason sitting on the doorstep.

He heard the glug-glug-glug of the vodka disappearing down the sink as he slouched into the apartment. Jason hung his head, expecting a verbal lashing.

"You did good by making it here, Jase. That must've been an awful two hours, but you did the right thing. You've come so far with your sobriety…what made you buy this stuff?"

Jason dug into his pocket and removed the ring before tossing it over.

Marcus caught it and squinted at the diamond. "Is this *Cameron's?*"

He gave a hopeless nod. "She gave it back to me. It's over. She hates me now." He dropped to his knees with a thud and folded his hands over the back of his head, the story spilling out of him again.

Marcus kneeled next to Jason and listened. "So your mother's alone now," he said.

Emptiness consumed Jason. "We're all alone."

Leo and Audrey stood outside the Naval Air Station Pensacola Military Prison in the cool November breeze. She shivered as she eyed his short-sleeved polo. "Aren't you freezing?"

"It's, like, sixty degrees!" He grinned. "You're a wimp."

"Hmph."

"Are you sure I should be here?" Leo asked for about the tenth time.

"Yes! You're the reason we're having this amazing day."

He watched her eyes crinkle with anticipation and circled behind to wrap his arms around her. He couldn't be happier for Audrey and her parents, and he attempted to ignore the nagging twinge of sadness for his own family. Nuzzling his face into her hair, he planted a soft kiss on her neck.

Leo tensed as he saw Captain Payson approach. He fought the urge to salute and instead fidgeted until the captain shook his hand. "Hello, Leo. It's good to see you out of the hospital bed."

"Hello, sir."

"Audrey." He smiled warmly and shook her hand as well. "So, you're waiting for your dad's release?"

"Yes, Captain. Thank you for making it happen so quickly."

He looked pained. "Please don't thank me for anything, Audrey. We screwed up big time."

Audrey looked down, and Leo draped his arm around her shoulders.

"Is my dad in there, sir?" he asked.

A head shake. "James is still in a holding cell at the police station. It'll be a while before the paperwork's transferred over here for the court martial."

Leo nodded.

The captain studied him for a moment. "I spoke to Captain Tracker today."

Leo leaned forward at the commandant's name.

"Your psychologist briefed him about everything that went down last night. Though he's not pleased about the gun in your possession, he's willing to entertain the idea of you returning to the Academy, provided the Honor Committee reinstates you."

Leo's eyebrows shot up. "I—I never expected that, sir."

"It sounds like you had a rollercoaster ride at the Academy, Leo."

"Yes, sir."

"I feel partly responsible because I requested you be assigned to Lt. Keaton's company," he said. "Captain Tracker saw a lot of potential in you, and I think you should consider returning to Annapolis."

Leo felt Audrey tense next to him. "I'm sorry, sir, but I can't separate myself from Audrey again," he said. "I don't want to make the same mistake twice."

A brilliant smile lit up her face.

At that moment an MP walked out of the brig to hold the door open for an emerging couple. Mr. and Mrs. Rose strolled out with their arms wrapped around each other, both squinting in the sunlight.

"Daddy!" Audrey squealed, breaking away from Leo and sprinting to her father. She almost bowled him over as she leaped into his arms.

"Audrey girl," her father said tearfully. "I've missed you so much."

Leo dipped his head, trying to compose himself.

The three Roses continued their hugs and excited chatter for a few moments before looking up and seeming to realize there were others waiting for them. Mr. Rose approached his former boss and stood before him for a moment. Finally he shook his hand.

"I'd like you to stop by my office when you have the time, Denny," the captain said. "We have much to discuss. I hope to see you back in uniform one day soon."

"Yes, sir. Thank you for being here, Captain."

"Words are meaningless at this point, but I want you to know how sorry I am for all you and your family have been through," Payson said. "You've been very brave."

"We still have each other." Mr. Rose swallowed. "The Walshes aren't so fortunate."

"Very true. How're they taking the news?"

"I'm not sure," Mrs. Rose said. She glanced at Leo. "Do you know, Leo?"

"No, ma'am. Jason was going to tell Cameron, but I haven't heard anything."

"Well, I'll stop interrupting this family celebration," Captain Payson said. "I'll see you soon, Denny."

"Thank you, sir."

Mr. Rose then turned to Leo, and his heart thudded. Audrey reached for his hand and squeezed it.

"Your father's done horrible things, Leo. He's hurt many people." He paused for a moment. "But *you*, well, you've set me free. Captain Payson called me brave, but I think *you're* the brave one here."

Leo looked into his eyes, which sparkled with joy.

"I guess you redeemed yourself for knocking up my daughter." Mr. Rose's mouth set in a stern line. "And unless there's something I don't know about," he added, glancing at Audrey. "You've done a good job keeping your grimy paws off her since then."

Flames licked at Leo's cheeks as he remembered their recent shower. "And we didn't even need the chastity belt, sir."

"Come on." Mr. Rose shook his head and gestured to Audrey's car. "Let's see if I remember how to drive. We've got a stop to make before we head home."

74. Grave Matters

Cameron was all cried out.

Her eyelids drooped with fatigue, and she gazed down at the crumpled tissues littering her father's grave. With heaviness in her chest, she relived again her horrible day.

Her mother had exploded when Cam told her of her husband's affair, but shock froze her when she learned Jason's father was the murderer. She'd only had a few minutes to process the news before calls from the media began rolling in, seeking a reaction to James Scott's arrest and Denny Rose's release. Cameron had fled, overwhelmed by the intrusion.

She'd driven in an aimless loop for an hour, crying, before finding herself at her father's grave. She hadn't been to Shady Palms Cemetery since she'd learned of his affair. She'd been furious with her father, but now she needed his guidance.

Except for a cool breeze wafting through the trees, it was quiet.

"Why?" she pleaded. "Why'd you cheat on us? Weren't we good enough for you?"

She traced his name in the stone. "Will I ever look at Jason without thinking of what happened to you?" She choked back a sob. "Is it possible to love him and hate his father at the same time?"

Despite her anger, she knew death was too great a price to pay for infidelity. Her only comfort was that in the end, her father had been trying to do the right thing—trying to help a woman who'd been hurt by another man. His fatal mistake was underestimating that man.

"You didn't deserve to die, Dad." The breeze lifted her words, floating them away in sorrowful wisps across neighboring graves.

Denny pulled the car to a stop along the winding road. "I'll be back in just a few minutes," he said, surveying the ring of faces in the car.

"You want me to go with you?" Mrs. Rose asked.

"That's okay, honey. This is something I need to do alone." He brushed his hand along her cheek before leaning in to kiss her. He smiled at Leo and Audrey in the backseat. "I can't *believe* I'm free!"

He hopped out of the car and hiked up over the crest of a small hill.

He stopped in his tracks when he saw Cameron sitting near her father's headstone. Her lips were moving, but he couldn't hear a word. She looked utterly broken.

He hesitated. Should he leave? Maybe she needed help?

Cameron looked up, startled. "Mr. Rose?"

He noticed her swollen eyes as she stood. "I'm sorry, Cameron. Do you want me to leave? I don't mean to intrude."

"No, sir. It's okay if you don't mind my ridiculous crying. Um, what're you doing here?"

Denny slid his hands into his pockets. He nodded at Bill's gravestone. "I, uh, I never got a chance to say goodbye to my friend."

Cameron burst into tears again and propelled herself into his arms. He wrapped her in a paternal hug, patting her back as she sobbed.

"Do you miss him too?" she choked out.

"I do. I miss him every day." As they stepped out of their hug, Denny added, "Nobody could spin tales about catching huge fish like he could."

Denny returned Cameron's faint smile. "Wait a second—I hear congratulations are in order. You're engaged! Why isn't Jason with you?" he asked.

She cried harder.

"Oh, um, sorry, I didn't mean—" he stammered.

"It's okay." She pulled out another tissue. "I don't know what to do! Jason's father did this!" She gestured to the ground. "And it just hurts when I look at Jase now. All I see is his dad."

Denny shook his head. James's confession tied all three families intimately together now, and he wished one family's joy didn't have to mean the others' sadness.

"Cameron, what'd you tell me four years ago about why the abortion was so difficult?"

She sniffed. "That I loved Jase, and I didn't want to hurt our baby because it was part of him."

"Exactly. Do you still love Jason?"

She looked down. "Even more. He's such a good man, Mr. Rose. He's worked hard to become a better man, and I love him so much."

Denny nodded. "You know, our situations are kind of similar. Leo is James's son, and he's dating Audrey. But I didn't think twice about accepting him into our family. Because Leo's an incredible young man. I don't know Jason like I know Leo, but I trust your judgment about his character."

Cameron blinked up at him.

Denny sighed. "Did you ever think James's sons became good people not *despite* of James, but *because* of him? They know firsthand how important it is to treat others with kindness. They had to fight like crazy to survive. They had to seek love elsewhere—in Mary, and in you and Audrey. Your love's strong, Cameron. Maybe you could give Jason a chance?"

Cameron covered her face with her hands.

"I had a lot of time to think in prison," Denny said. "All I had was time. And I prayed to break free of my anger. I hoped I wouldn't be a bitter man. I promised myself I'd find the strength to forgive the murderer, if I ever learned who it was." Denny looked down. "I hate James for what he did, but I'll work like hell to forgive him one day. Life's too short to live in bitterness and regret."

Jason pulled up behind Audrey's car at the cemetery and watched Leo get out. He was out of his own car in an instant and grabbed his brother in a bear hug.

"So glad the gun charges got dropped," he whispered.

"Me too."

They exchanged slaps on the back. Feeling overwhelmed, Jason glanced up the hill. "Thanks for calling me, bro, but I don't know about this."

"You can't lose Cam to this, Jase. You just can't. We've lost too much because of Dad. You've got to fight for her."

Jason rubbed his hand through his hair. "What if she screams at me again? That look she gave me…I don't know if I can take it." He sighed. "I don't deserve her."

"What're you talking about? You deserve to be happy, Jase, and I know Cam is a big part of that." Leo waited until Jason looked at him. "I talked to my psychologist about you, you know."

"Uh-oh."

"She helped me see something. She said my family started a 'journey of healing' when you came back from Seattle," Leo explained, gauging Jason's response. "I know it's kind of cheesy, but she said when you got away from CS, you started healing yourself. You got into treatment, and you grew stronger. When you returned, you helped Mom and me a ton. If it wasn't for you, I'd probably still be hooked on pain pills. And look what Mom's done—she's so much stronger now. She's our mom again. She's there for us now. That's all on you, Jase."

Jason gave Leo a brooding stare.

"Even Dad—he's in a better place because of you too. He's where he belongs now. And he wouldn't have gotten there unless you and Cam found that letter."

"No, Leo, you did that. You put Cellie Scum behind bars."

"But I couldn't have done it without you." Leo glanced up the hill. "Cam just needs a little time to take it all in. I mean, I bet she's crazy with grief right now. I don't even know what to say to her. But *you* do. She needs you, Jase."

Jason sighed, feeling a slight surge of confidence from his brother's words. He put a hand on Leo's shoulder and nodded before heading up over the hill toward his fiancée.

Mr. Rose looked up and saw him approaching. He seemed to whisper something to Cameron, then walked away from her, clapping Jason on the shoulder as he passed.

Cameron stared at him, but he couldn't read her expression. He jammed his hands into his pockets, scared to get closer.

She opened her mouth then closed it.

"Cam —"

"I don't need to hear one word," she said, moving toward him. "Mr. Rose made me realize a few things. I love you. You're a good man, Jason Scott." When she flung herself into his arms, he gulped down relief.

"I'm so sorry, Jase. I love you. I love you."

He dropped his chin to her shoulder and smelled her flowery scent. The tension drained from his shoulders as her body melted into his.

"It's unfair to compare you to your father. You're nothing like him."

"You don't know how great that makes me feel."

Jason heard shuffling behind them and turned to find that the Roses and Leo had joined them. Leo gave him a goofy grin.

"Um, Jase, do you still have my ring?" Cam asked.

He beamed and dug into his pocket for the diamond. He moved to replace it on her finger when Mr. Rose interrupted.

"Hold on," he said. "Bill was my best friend. He can't be here to approve of this engagement, but he's here in spirit. I know he'd give his blessing."

Cameron glanced at his headstone and then back at Jason. "I think so too. My dad would be proud to have you as a son-in-law, Jase."

Jason gently slid on the ring and leaned in for a kiss.

Mr. Rose draped his arm across his wife's shoulders. "Can one of you drive Audrey and Leo home? I hate to cut this short, but JoAnne and I have a lot to catch up on." He squeezed his wife's shoulder and tilted his head to hers, their temples touching as they shared a smile.

"Oh, TMI, Dad," Audrey shrieked.

Mr. Rose laughed. "See you at home, Audrey," he called as he headed back over the hill. "But don't rush, okay?"

Audrey winced and shook her head. "It won't be safe for me to go home *ever again.*"

"That's all right," Leo said with a wink. "You can come home with me. It's been a long day. I think we both need another shower."

"We'll be the cleanest college freshmen around," Audrey said.

"Except I'm not a college freshman anymore." Leo sighed. "I have to figure out my life."

Audrey wove her fingers into his. "It's simple. You're getting an ROTC scholarship to Florida State. To swim with me."

"I *am?*"

"Of course, Mr. Scott."

A look of marvel bled into a wondrous smile as he squeezed her hand. "Yes, ma'am."

ACKNOWLEDGMENTS

Gratitude and blessings to:

Omnific Publishing Team Streamline, including Kathy Teel, Coreen Montanga, Emma Taylor, and Kayla Watson. Publisher Elizabeth Harper jumpstarted my writing career and Developmental Editor Jessica Royer Ocken has really helped me improve my writing!

Military and civilian personnel from the U.S. Naval Academy (like swim buddy Kris) for serving our country and sharing their expertise.

Ana Josefina Borge for help with my rusty Spanish (any errors are mine).

Coaches Jim Steen and Tim Morrison for their incredible mentorship.

Masters swimming friends Eric, Beth, and Joe, and all of the amazing individuals I've met through swimming for Anderson Barracudas, Turpin High School, and Kenyon College, particularly Gwynn and Maggie.

Janine, Cècile, Jacki (stay out of the SHU), Marilyn, Michelle, Maria, Shannon, Riem, Elke, Ashley, Aimee, Erin, Karina, Danni, Micci, Viva, Pamela, Jason, Sean, Emilie, Stine, Elise, Jamie, Suzanne, Michaela, Dee, Sara, Sandra, and Kristi for their support.

Lorne, Amy, and Ina for being there from the beginning of this crazy writing adventure.

Book Club #1: Colby, Jennifer, Sue, Janelle, Sally, Suki, Patty, Amy, Christy, Lisa.

Book Club #2: David, Joan, Jessica, Nan, Tom, Cindy, Crista, Beth.

Most of all, my family: Nancy, Roger, Jan, Laurie, Susan, Scott, John, Nicholas, Dylan, Henry.

ABOUT THE AUTHOR

People fascinate the psychologist/author (psycho author) known as Jennifer Lane. Her therapy clients talk to her all day long about their dreams and secrets, and her characters tell her their stories at night. Jen delights in peeling away the layers to scrutinize their psyches and emotions. But please rest assured, dear reader, she isn't psychoanalyzing you right now. She's already got too many voices in her head!

Stories of redemption interest Jen the most, especially the healing power of love and empathy. She is the author of the Conduct Series — romantic suspense for adult readers — and is currently at work on the third and final installment: *On Best Behavior*. *Streamline* is her first foray into writing for young adults, but she's found this sort of writing even more fun. A former college swimmer, Jen was able to put a lot of her own experiences into this book.

Whether writing or reading, Jen loves stories that make her laugh and cry. In her spare time she enjoys exercising, attending book club, and hanging out with her sisters and their families in Chicago.

check out these titles from
OMNIFIC PUBLISHING

← ··· →Contemporary Romance← ··· →

Boycotts & Barflies by Victoria Michaels

Passion Fish by Alison Oburia and Jessica McQuinn

Three Daves by Nicki Elson

Small Town Girl by Linda Cunningham

Stitches and Scars by Elizabeth A. Vincent

Trust in Advertising by Victoria Michaels

Take the Cake by Sandra Wright

Indivisible by Jessica McQuinn

Pieces of Us by Hannah Downing

Gabriel's Inferno by Sylvain Reynard

The Way That You Play It by BJ Thornton

Poughkeepsie by Debra Anastasia

The Redhead Series: The Unidentified Redhead and *The Redhead Revealed* by Alice Clayton

← ··· →Paranormal Romance← ··· →

The Light Series: Seers of Light and *Whisper of Light* by Jennifer DeLucy

The Hanaford Park Series: Eve of Samhain and *Pleasures Untold* by Lisa Sanchez

Immortal Awakening by KC Randall

Crushed Seraphim by Debra Anastasia

The Guardian's Wild Child by Feather Stone

Grave Refrain by Sarah M. Glover

→ Romantic Suspense ← →

Whirlwind by Robin DeJarnett
The CONduct Series: With Good Behavior and *Bad Behavior* by Jennifer Lane

→ Young Adult ← →

Shades of Atlantis and *Ember* by Carol Oates
Breaking Point by Jess Bowen
Life, Liberty, and Pursuit by Susan Kaye Quinn
Embrace by Cherie Colyer
Destiny's Fire by Trisha Wolfe
Streamline by Jennifer Lane

→ Anthologies ← →

A Valentine Anthology including short stories by Alice Clayton, Jennifer DeLucy, Nicki Elson, Jessica McQuinn, Victoria Michaels, and Alison Oburia

Summer Lovin' Anthology: Summer Breeze including short stories by Hannah Downing, Nicki Elson, Sarah M. Glover, Jennifer Lane, Killian McRae, Carol Oates, and Susan Kaye Quinn

Summer Lovin' Anthology: Heat Wave including short stories by Kasi Alexander, Debra Anastasia, Robin DeJarnett, Jessica McQuinn, Lisa Sanchez, and BJ Thornton

→ Alternative Romance ← →

Becoming sage by Kasi Alexander

CPSIA information can be obtained at www.ICGtesting.com
Printed in the USA
LVOW13s1024271013

358778LV00001B/87/P